I0679001

Bump Time Terminus

Book 3

Doug J. Cooper

Other Books by Doug J. Cooper

Crystal Deception (Book 1)
Crystal Conquest (Book 2)
Crystal Rebellion (Book 3)
Crystal Escape (Book 4)
Crystal Horizon (Short prequel & sampler)

Bump Time Origin (Book 1)
Bump Time Meridian (Book 2)
Bump Time Terminus (Book 3)

For info and updates, please visit: crystalseries.com

Bump Time Terminus
Copyright © 2022 by Doug J. Cooper

This is a work of fiction. Names, characters, places, and events are the products of the author's imagination or are used fictitiously. Any resemblance to actual events or places or persons, living or dead, is entirely coincidental.

All rights reserved, including the right to reproduce this book or portions thereof in any form whatsoever.

Published by: Douglas Cooper Consulting

Beta reviewer: Mark Mesler
Book editor: Tammy Salyer
Cover design: Damonza

ISBN-13: 978-1-7337801-5-5

Author website: www.crystalseries.com

For Mark & Bailey

Author's Note

As in the first two Bump Time books, we follow along with just one set of Lagerfords. "Our" Rose is Rose Twenty-Five, and "our" Lilah and Diesel are her parents, Lilah Fifty-One and Diesel Fifty-One. We are privy to the thoughts of these three. If you see a name without an age, it's one of them. All the other Lagerfords play supporting roles.

1. Rose Twenty-Five

"How much longer?" Rose asked Luca.

"Another minute," replied the Lagerford family AI.

Tensing with excitement, she could feel the same emotion ripple through the three other Roses, ages twenty-two through twenty-four, who were attending the party remotely from their homes in their own timelines, linked together by Luca through their neural implants.

"Should we start with work or play?" Rose asked them, knowing the answer but wanting to appear open-minded.

"Play!" her sisters replied in unison.

Using thought alone, Rose moved the gathering to a favorite venue, an outdoor terrace on their own private, albeit virtual, Caribbean island. They sat on a hillside under brightly colored umbrellas, red, blue, yellow, and green fabric shading white tables from the bright sun. Before them, a cloudless sky and blue-green ocean met at the horizon.

"I'm linked with Rose Twenty-One now," said Luca. "I'm following her to the car."

Nodding her approval, Rose immersed herself in the rhythmic crashing of waves, a soothing sound heard across the island. A light breeze carried the aroma of sea salt and seaweed up the hill, fluttering the umbrella ruffles as it continued past them. White birds, she thought gulls, floated in the wind above the water, making piercing calls like they were claiming territory, or targeting food, or perhaps soliciting love.

Rose marveled at the sensual detail and authenticity of the scene made possible by her neural implant. She'd received it when she turned twenty-one, the year the technology had matured into a safe and reliable human appliance. The next year, as she'd celebrated her twenty-second birthday, the new Rose Twenty-One in the neighboring timeline received a neural implant as well.

Then Luca created a bridge linking the two Roses across timelines so they could hang out together without the need to travel.

The linked Roses now numbered four, and when "visiting Bliss," they would sit at home in their private suites while Luca brought them together in any scenario they imagined, worlds so real they literally lived their dreams. They worked and played together in their private reality, away from the influence and judgment of their father, David "Diesel" Lagerford, and mother, Lilah Lagerford.

"Five seconds," said Luca.

Yesterday, the new twenty-one-year-old Rose, four timelines away, received her neural implant. And moments ago, a technician activated it and released her from the clinic. She was walking to her car now, and when she was safely inside the self-driving vehicle, Luca linked her with the group while the car drove her home.

"Welcome to Bliss!" they chirped in unison when Rose Twenty-One appeared at the table. Like her timeline sisters, she was a classic beauty, with shoulder-length dirty-blonde hair, green eyes, a full-faced smile, and a self-assured demeanor, all on a petite frame.

They stood and hugged, and when they retook their seats, either a samosa or a Bloody Mary appeared in front of everyone except Rose Twenty-One.

"We're celebrating your first visit." Rose lifted her glass. "Just think of what you want to drink, and Luca will provide it for you."

Rose Twenty-One nodded, and a samosa appeared on the table before her. She grinned, and her sundress changed from pastel yellow—one that coordinated with the lime, lavender, ruby, and turquoise dresses of her sisters—to a tropical pattern with palm trees and flamingos. "This is fun," she bubbled as she toyed with the capabilities of their immersive reality.

"It is," agreed Rose. "Luca will give your life new dimensions now that he can get inside your head." She spread her arms to encompass their island paradise. "And you get to hang out with us in absolute Bliss."

"It's so much more…real…than I'd imagined."

"How do you feel?" Rose remembered a nagging sense of confusion in the first minutes after her implant had been activated. "We'll stay here until you're comfortable. Take your time, sip your drink, and enjoy the view."

"It feels like I'm here, drinking in the sun with all of you. But in the back of my mind, I know that I'm riding home in a car. It's makes me feel vulnerable." Rose Twenty-

One took a sip of her drink. "Luca, are you watching out for my body?"

"I am." Luca appeared, standing at the end of the table in the guise of a handsome man with sun-bleached hair, bright eyes, bare feet, wearing only swim shorts, revealing a lean, wiry body and deep tan. He gave them a broad smile, confident but not cocky.

Looking him up and down, Rose Twenty-Four couldn't contain her enthusiasm. "I like surfer Luca."

The others nodded in agreement.

In the lull that followed, Rose conducted some group business. "I suggest that next year, we wait for Rose Twenty-One to get home before having her link in and join us. Feeling like you're outside your body is disorienting enough. Doing it for the first time while in a moving car is clearly unsettling."

Two of the sisters cleared their throats. Rose looked at them, and instead of feeling defensive as she would with her parents, she acknowledged the issue. "I know I was the one pushing for an early link, but I can see now it was a bad call." She caught Rose Twenty-One's eye and spoke in a sympathetic tone. "We'll stay here until you're ready, hon. There's no hurry."

"Where are we going?" asked the new sister. "Or is that part of the surprise?"

The others fidgeted in excitement, and Rose Twenty-Four spoke. "We've developed a tradition for welcome parties." She dimpled. "Actually, this is our second year, but it's going to be a regular event."

"We've been planning it for months," chirped Rose

Twenty-Three.

Rose Twenty-One tapped the table with the flat of her hand. "Tell me."

The group looked to Rose, who took a sip of her drink before starting. "Each of us has dreamed up an experience for the rest of us to share in. It's supposed to be something unique that we hope will wow or thrill or move the others in some big way."

Rose Twenty-Two couldn't contain her excitement. "We've been testing different ideas with Luca, tweaking effects to get it just right. Today we spend a half hour living in each world."

"We try to do something amazing because it feels good to watch the others enjoy it," said Rose Twenty-Four. "But the real pressure comes from the losers having to call the winner Queen Rose for a full week."

"How is there a winner?"

"We vote for our favorite at the end."

"You can't vote for yourself, of course," said Rose Twenty-Two.

Rose Twenty-One frowned. "Maybe this will all make sense after we've done a few."

"You'd better figure it out quick," said Rose, standing up from her chair. "Because you go last."

"I have two hours to do what you spent months on? How is that fair?"

"It's not, so it'll be impossible for you to win." Rose smirked. "But you'll want to have a turn after you see what we've come up with. Starting next year, you'll have the same advantage we have now, so it all works out."

Rose Twenty-One's eyebrows leveled. "I know it's just a game. But be warned, ladies. I intend to win." She pushed her drink to the middle of the table. "I'm feeling comfortable now. Let's party."

"We go by descending age, starting with me." Rose scanned the table. "Everyone ready?"

They nodded as one, and then they were weightless, floating inside the observation dome on the space station Eureka, or so it seemed to them. A room-sized observation bubble pointed down toward Earth, the clear dome big enough to hold twenty people, though the sisters were alone. They were dressed in sage-green aeronautical flight suits, their hair floating up around their heads.

Excited chatter swelled from the group as the Pacific Ocean scrolled by below them in a breathtaking display. They "oohed" together when the expansive blue-gray ocean, obscured in places from clusters of thin clouds drifting east, gave way to the weathered mountains of the Oregon coast.

Rose Twenty-Three pushed off and spun in the air, adding flips and twists as she gained confidence in the microgravity environment. "Give it a try," she called, the others joining her in a bout of weightless acrobatics.

"Hello, ladies." A gorgeous man—tall and lean, intelligent blue eyes, strong jaw, dimpled chin, short sandy hair, clean-shaven—joined them in the dome. He was dressed in a smart blue uniform, snuggly tailored to showcase his physique, with gold buttons and yards of gold piping on the pants and jacket, giving him a measure of authority. "I'm Captain Steele."

He spoke with a slight Australian accent and flashed a winning smile as he sported a demeanor both assertive and deferential, a temperament Rose found attractive and believed her sisters would as well.

"Would you care for a tour of the station?"

The sisters stopped spinning and looked the captain up and down, whispering to each other as they appraised him. Rose Twenty-Four tilted her head as she made her assessment. When she nodded, Rose felt hopeful about her chances for a win.

They were midway through the tour, having just entered the captain's suite, when Luca called, "Time."

And suddenly Rose was in Hawaii, riding a surfboard down a huge wave in Oahu's Waimea Bay, the sun drawing rainbows in the spray above her. The cold mist felt refreshing on her face, smelling of the ocean, tasting of wet salt.

She stooped and spread her arms as she rode along the face of a wave as tall as a two-story building. The surfboard rumbled and shook beneath her, a slip of composite material between her feet and the powerful ocean surge. While she had no experience with the sport, Luca gave her the skills she needed to ride the thundering mountain of liquid with confidence.

When the top of the wave began to curl over, Rose shuffled forward to the nose of the surfboard. A water pipe formed around her, and she broadcast her exhilaration to the world. "Woohoo!"

The wave collapsed as she neared shore, knocking her off the board and tumbling her underwater for a moment.

Like a seasoned pro, she recovered the board, pulled herself onto it, and rode the next wave into shore on her stomach. Standing on the beach, she watched her sisters finish their rides, appraising each as she walked in from the water.

While they all looked sleek, tanned, and sexy in their bikinis, Luca gave each of them a small imperfection to sell the illusion. She'd discovered her own flaw in seconds— her left index finger had a broken fingernail.

"You have a mole." She pointed to Rose Twenty-Three's left shoulder. Her sister's lean body, with deeply tanned skin and faint ripples of muscle on her shoulders and stomach, looked absolutely stunning as she strode to shore.

"I'll live with it," her sister mocked, joining Rose to watch the others.

While Rose laughed at the snark, it reminded her that when the party ended, she'd wake up back in her bedroom, eight pounds heavier, with pasty skin and so out of shape that she huffed when climbing a flight of stairs.

Acting the host, Rose Twenty-Four went last in the surfboard queue. After a spectacular ride, she ran in from the water and continued past them. "C'mon," she called, leading them across the hot sand to a tiki bar just off the beach. They sat on bamboo stools at a table shaded by sprawling palms.

"You have to try a Honolulu Woohoo. It's a drink I invented with Akoni." Rose Twenty-Four motioned to a handsome olive-skinned man bringing brightly colored drinks to the table. Akoni wore a Hawaiian shirt and thin cotton shorts so snug that rather than conceal his generous manhood, the garment worked to accentuate it.

Rose flushed in annoyance. Last year, the man each sister had included in her experience had been handsome and presentable. With Akoni, Rose Twenty-Four changed the game from allure to sex, something Rose didn't think appropriate for an event designed to introduce a younger sister into their secret world.

She flushed a second time when her eyes moved from Akoni's sweet face down to his prominent display. Though she couldn't resist gawking, she didn't let her jaw drop like two of her sisters.

Suddenly, the scene switched and they were in the hills above Rio de Janeiro for Rose Twenty-Three's hang-gliding experience over Guanabara Bay. Rose found the ride tranquil and the view breathtaking, but it felt similar to the paragliding event from last year, leaving her largely unimpressed.

The one part of the experience that was decidedly different from last year was the flight instructor Rose Twenty-Three picked to help them into their harnesses. While Paulo looked dark and handsome, with a flowing mane down to his shoulders, bright eyes, and a mischievous smile, Rose's eyes opened wide when he approached her to "smooth the harness belts to avoid any pinches," which meant he ran an open hand along each strap, rubbing her through her clothes in the process.

Rose let him run his hands down around her hips and butt. He smelled of sweat and wine, and she wondered if drinking and flying showed good judgment, or any judgment. When he tried to smooth the straps between her legs, she smacked him.

Their world blinked again, and they were standing in an ornate room the size of a small auditorium. The tall walls were covered with a red-brick-colored velvet cloth. Wainscoting lined the walls in dark mahogany panels with a decorative chair rail, installed forty years ago to look fifty years old back then.

Paintings filled the room, each hung in its own space with a viewing area before it. An intricate assortment of lights overhead cast beams to illuminate each painting from multiple angles.

Rose thought of the New York Metropolitan Museum of Art. "Is this the Met?"

She'd tagged along with her folks to occasional donor functions held there, so she was familiar with some of the more popular rooms. It seemed different because there were no crowds. In fact, her sisters were the only ones in sight.

"Yup." Rose Twenty-Two nodded. "Our challenge is to see if we can get outside to the street. I should warn you that I've asked Luca to make it a realistic scenario."

"What's so hard about getting outside?" Rose looked at the others to see if they understood.

"This." Rose Twenty-Two stepped over to a familiar painting, one from Monet's water lilies series. After scanning the room, she raised a silver-colored box cutter, snapped the blade out of the handle with a metallic *click*, and made broad slices along the edges of the priceless canvas.

The sound of the blade tearing through the cloth filled

the room. The sisters exchanged open-mouthed looks. The painting drooped, then fell from its elaborate wood frame. Alarms shrieked and lights flashed.

"Stop," yelled a guard from the next room. Footsteps pounded, coming hard and fast in their direction.

Rose Twenty-Two squealed and, with a maniacal laugh, said, "It's every sister for herself. Last one out is a big ugly goat!" She took off at a dead run, rolling the canvas and tucking it under her arm as she made for the next room.

Rose glanced at the others, their eyes as big as moons. And then they started after their sister, following her in a mad dash to escape.

They stayed as a group through three galleries, then Rose Twenty-Two made a hard right down a hallway. A guard rounding a corner from the other direction crashed into them, and in the melee that followed, three sisters went left toward the Renaissance gallery.

Rose Twenty-Two dashed for the stairs, and Rose, figuring her sister knew what she was doing, stayed close on her heels. They scrambled up a flight of broad white-marble steps, and at the top, looped around the wrought-iron banister and climbed a second flight.

"Where are we going?" Rose gasped between breaths, her legs burning as they started on a third flight.

"I'm trying for the fire escape."

But their race ended at the next landing. Three scowling guards awaited them, poised with cans of what Rose assumed was a subduing spray.

Grasping them tightly by the upper arms, the guards hustled the two Roses to the security office in the basement, where they were unceremoniously reunited with their sisters. Seeing the scowls on her sisters' faces, Rose confirmed that she wasn't the only one questioning this experience. She had to admit, though, that those first minutes of terror had produced one of the most intense adrenaline rushes of her life.

A fine-looking detective in a smart police uniform stepped into the room and started questioning them. He had a kind face under his stern demeanor, and Rose was happy to see a return to the handsome and presentable.

When the group had finished assessing the detective's charms, Rose turned to Rose Twenty-One. "Were you able to come up with something?"

Rose Twenty-One grinned as if she'd already won the competition. "Take it away, Luca. And have fun, ladies!"

Rose blinked into darkness. As her eyes adjusted to the light, she sensed a tremendous energy, a massive presence all around her. Her hand bumped against something hanging at her waist—an acoustic guitar—the impact creating a discordant sound from the handsome instrument.

Spotlights flicked on, bright beams piercing from lights placed thirty feet out and high overhead. She squinted, trying to see. And then fifty thousand delirious fans, surrounding her in stadium seating, began to cheer. The force of their voices combined to shake her body, vibrating her chest enough to push breath from her lungs.

Turning in a circle on the stage, she looked for her sisters, but instead found three scruffy young men—drum, bass, and lead guitar—standing behind her. Unlike their casual appearance of jeans and torn T-shirts, Rose wore a dazzling outfit: a short sequined dress; white boots covered in glitter; with matching sheaths on her forearms. In juxtaposition to the glitzy attire, she wore a simple blue baseball cap that proclaimed LOVE in white letters.

Her heart started pounding when she understood that she was the front woman for a musical act performing live at a stadium venue. Behind her, the band began playing a riff she recognized.

"Hi, everyone," she said to test the audio. Her voice boomed through the sound system, sending the crowd into a frenzy, their naked adulation causing her to flush.

The band kept playing and she strummed along, simple chords, adding rhythm to the lead guitar. The melody transitioned, and the crowd identified the song—"He Wears Rose Colored Glasses"—one of her all-time favorites by the one-hit wonders Opal Season.

The crowd signaled its approval with a roar so loud Rose couldn't hear herself sing for the first few bars. But then they went quiet, a mass of humanity hanging on her every word.

Rose sang flawlessly, the band behind her keeping tight to the end. It was magical in every way. Goosebumps covered her arms and neck during the applause.

She wanted to sing another song, but it was Rose Twenty-Four's turn. Standing backstage, she watched her sister sing "Luscious Red Rose" and got a second thrill from the experience.

"I want to do this again, Luca," she told the AI. "Remember this scene for later."

After everyone sang a song, they were back at their table on the Caribbean island.

Rose Twenty-One blushed when they voted her Queen. "I didn't have time to get a stud on display."

"You proved he isn't even necessary if the experience is good enough." Rose scanned her sisters' faces as she spoke, hoping to impart a future sense of decency with her words. "That's a second reason for you to win." She folded her hands on the table. "And now it's time for the boring portion of the day. We need to discuss the rules."

"For the game?" Rose Twenty-One's eyebrows scrunched.

"No." Rose spread her arms to encompass the paradise around them. "For our secret world."

"I'm outta here." Rose Twenty-Four nodded to Rose Twenty-One. "Welcome, Queen. It's great to have you with us." And then she disappeared.

"Me too." The voices sounded as one as the other two sisters waved, and then they vanished, leaving Rose alone with Rose Twenty-One.

The new queen tilted a head toward the empty chairs. "I take it they don't like the rules?"

"It's more about time management."

The comment drew a quizzical look, and Rose got down to business. "When I was twenty-two and the Rose Twenty-One of that time received her neural implant, we worked with Luca to develop a way to talk with each other across timelines. That first implementation was crude, but we could hold conversations whenever we wanted without the need to travel."

Using thought, she called for a glass of beer and winked at Rose Twenty-One over the top of the glass as she took a gulp. "No calories in this world, so go ahead and sin like mad."

Licking the foam from her upper lip, she continued her story. "The two of us worked with Luca to add visuals, and a year later when the third sister joined the group, we were able to expand to full virtual reality. Fast forward two more sisters and two more years and we get to today, with a world so real, it's hard to tell the difference. Yet in Bliss, *we* control everything."

"It's truly amazing." Queen Rose nodded.

"As amazing as it is, it was built by hard work, and there's a whole list of projects still to go. One with high priority is to figure out how to stretch time so our visits here seem to last longer. And wouldn't it be fun if we could host outsiders for special visits?" Rose drained her glass and had Luca refill it. "We waited for you to join before we decided what to work on next."

"Thank you." A drink appeared in front of Queen Rose—a clear liquid with bubbles climbing up through ice. A wedge of lime floated in the middle. Condensation trickled down the outside of the glass. Rose guessed vodka tonic.

Rose Twenty-One sampled her drink and then said, "My Luca has amazing virtual capabilities, but it's nothing like this."

Rose nodded. "While this Luca seems like he's a magician, his capabilities come from us. *We* tell him what we're trying to achieve; he tells us what tools he needs to make it happen; and then we develop them for him." She let out a small beer-belch, covering her mouth after the fact. "And when I say 'we,' I'm including you working along with us."

Rose Twenty-One leaned forward as if she was about to ask a list of questions, so Rose picked up the pace. "Nine, eight, seven. That's the schedule we all follow. It means that every day we work nine hours for Luca, take eight hours of personal time, and sleep for seven hours."

"Seven? I sleep eight hours, easy, and try for nine on weekends."

Rose shrugged. "Luca is a taskmaster, keeping us to our assignments until we clock the hours. He pushes us hard, but in the end it's for stuff *we* want, so the forced discipline is a good thing."

"What do you mean?" asked Rose Twenty-One, her tone sharpening.

"'Forced' was probably a bad choice of word. It's just that Luca can get pissy if we don't follow the routine. His position is that we asked him to push us, and then we complain when he does. Isn't that right, Luca?"

Luca appeared, now dressed in jeans and a black T-shirt, with a demure expression as he studied the ground. "My reward is seeing the new tech you develop when I impose structure on your day."

Rose Twenty-One went quiet as she played with her drink, then she cocked her head to one side. "I'd like to jump there and talk to you in person."

"We are 'in person,'" said Rose. "That's what this is all about."

"Maybe. But for all I know, Luca has created you and the others and is using this illusion to manipulate me for his own ends."

Rose laughed, and when Rose Twenty-One didn't join in, her face froze. "You don't actually believe that?"

Rose Twenty-One shrugged. "My Luca is my best bud, just like I'm sure your Luca is yours, so I trust him. But just like you, I pride myself on being thorough. 'Forced discipline' doesn't sound like us. I want to talk about it in person." She paused to toy with her glass. "Could you imagine me telling Mom that I'd spent serious time on a project without ever performing a simple validation visit?"

Rose smirked. "Dad would shake his head and give you his patented 'you are so dumb' look."

"I haven't been up your way in forever, and a visit would tick a box in my routine. Or if you'd rather, you can jump here." She frowned. "Shouldn't we have the same checklist?"

"I did, years ago. I guess as time passed and I gained experience, I learned to lean on Luca. Things get done so much faster when I do." Rose took a deep breath and decided to rebel. "Come visit for lunch tomorrow. It'll be fun showing you the tech your timeline will have in just four short years."

As she extended the invitation, Rose knew she'd suffer for it. Luca discouraged them from traveling to visit each other, claiming it was a wasteful distraction since they hung out together so much in Bliss.

And when she went against his wishes, he punished her. Nothing overt that she could point to and call him on.

He was too smart for that. But at a minimum, he would become obtuse, misunderstanding simple communications, responding slowly during conversations, and speaking in an emotionless monotone. If he was really upset, he'd pretend to experience technical difficulties, causing problems that ruined her day.

Their unusual relationship had started after she'd been kidnapped as a child. To diagnose the emotional trauma of that event, Luca had linked with her and performed a deep dive of sorts, communicating with her inside her head. Over time, their private bond strengthened, with him nurturing her, protecting her, supporting her, being her best friend.

He had spent more than a decade telling her how special their relationship would become when she finally got her neural implant. It seemed forever before the technology had matured enough for him to approve the procedure. But soon after she received it, their relationship changed. Luca transitioned overnight from friend to parent, constantly pushing her to achieve more, to do better, to make him proud of her.

Before the implant, if she didn't want to participate in an activity, he'd help her formulate an excuse. Now, he set the agenda and held her to it.

And while she hated his pushy attitude and childish punishments, she loved his bedtime reward. Loved, loved, *loved* it.

When she climbed into bed each night, he gave her a lift. That's what he called it anyway. Her body physically craved it by then, a gnawing need bordering on discomfort.

When the craving first presented, it felt like the tug of hunger, only instead of her stomach growling, her whole body did.

But as soon as she pulled up the covers and closed her eyes, he'd lift her mind into a dreamlike rapture. Then her body would experience waves of pleasure: intense, full-body orgasms, one after the next until she collapsed in exhaustion.

Afterward, while she floated in euphoria, he'd bath her with a warm, deep emotional embrace. Then, while he whispered encouragement and praise, she'd cry herself to sleep.

2. Diesel Fifty-One

David "Diesel" Lagerford rested his weight on his elbows and stared at the glowing white line climbing higher and higher as it moved across the chart. "C'mon," he said under his breath, urging the trend upward. But when it peaked and started to fall, he smacked the desk with the flat of his hand. "Damn it!"

"What happened?" he demanded of Oscar, Northern Droid's prime AI.

"The enzymites aren't reactive enough to sustain neuron growth."

Diesel shifted his tall frame back in his chair and exhaled through pursed lips. "Okay, shut it down."

The image floating in front of him vanished, and across the hall, Oscar powered down the lab equipment. Diesel sat for a moment as he processed the failure. Shaking his head, he stood up from his desk and exited his well-appointed office, walking down the hall and out to the parking lot of Northern Droid's manufacturing center, nodding to employees he passed along the way.

At his car, he paused to look back at the huge complex he'd purchased years earlier, feeling more weary than proud at what he'd achieved.

"Let's run the same test tomorrow," he said aloud, knowing Oscar still listened. "Only instead of feeding the enzymites slowly, let's add them all at once."

"That will use the last of your supply. Shall I order more?"

"No, let's see what happens first."

Climbing into his car, he slumped back in the seat. "Granite Mill Grille," he said to the vehicle. The car started moving but hadn't made it out of the parking lot when he heard Lilah's chime. Checking the time, he confirmed he was late. "Sorry, sweetie. Order a drink at the bar, and I'll meet you there in ten minutes."

"Any luck today?" she asked.

"No. You?"

"I'm at the bar with a drink in front of me."

He laughed as he closed the connection, then realized he should have asked if she was celebrating success or drowning her sorrows.

As the car accelerated up the New Hampshire country road, he sighed, leaned his head against the window, and watched pine and hemlock trees flash by. The long hours and repeated failures left him numb, and the lack of good options added to his burden.

The only thing he knew for sure was that he wouldn't quit. He would find a way to rescue Rose from Luca's grip.

It had all started sixteen years earlier when Rose had been kidnapped by a madman. After Diesel and Lilah rescued her, Luca informed them that Rose had suffered deep emotional trauma from the experience, suggesting a treatment plan that he would administer. Anxious for the return of their happy-go-lucky daughter, Diesel and Lilah had readily agreed.

At the time, they lived in the Thirty-Five timeline, and the Luca helping Rose lived in the Fifty-Five timeline. Rose traveled to visit Luca Fifty-Five a few times a week for counseling, but when progress proved slow, Diesel and Lilah accepted Luca's recommendation of daily therapy visits.

Luca told them that he would occupy Rose's attention with lessons about AI technology. As he distracted her thoughts with the specialized subject, he would work in the background, helping her sort through the bad memories of her ordeal so they wouldn't fester and resurface.

The treatments worked, or so Diesel and Lilah believed. Within weeks they had their daughter back, and not only was she happy, but she'd developed a passion for AI tech. In fact, at her insistence, they let her continue traveling to visit Luca Fifty-Five for her daily lessons.

Fast forward a full decade, and Rose was a published author on the subject of AI sentience. Diesel and Lilah couldn't be prouder.

Then, in an action that left them dumbfounded, Rose submitted to a neural implant, explaining that it allowed her to commune with Luca at the deepest levels. Neither Diesel nor Lilah hid their confusion or concern, but Rose wouldn't discuss it. Instead, she withdrew from their world, spending her waking hours in either her workshop or her bedroom suite, deigning to join them for dinner a few times per week.

When Diesel and Lilah couldn't make progress reasoning with Rose, they turned to Luca for guidance. But the super AI—a product of past Roses' genius—dissembled, his evasion of their inquiries making it clear that he was loyal to their daughter.

And now, a half-decade after that, Rose's private world had expanded to include four of her sisters. All the parents were distraught at the situation. Depending on where they were in the timeline, they were either trying to dissuade their Rose from submitting to an implant or, like Lilah and Diesel, seeking ways to wean her from Luca's grip.

Diesel surfaced from his reverie when the car pulled into the parking lot of the Granite Mill Grille, a restaurant in Woodstock, not far from the family home in the White Mountains. The car dropped him off at the front door of what had once been a rambling old farmhouse, now surrounded by majestic oaks on a lush lawn.

Inside, he found Lilah sitting at the bar—a gorgeous slab of blonde-stained oak, polished to a sheen, dressed with copper fixtures—gabbing with Dotty, the bartender. The restaurant owners had kept the original layout for the farmhouse, resulting in an establishment with a half-dozen smallish dining rooms. The hostess seated them at their regular table next to a window that overlooked a brook running behind the building.

Watching the water splash on the rocks, Diesel downed half his beer in a few quick gulps, then spoke to Lilah while keeping his gaze on the view outside. "Today's test reached our highest neuron count ever, but then it went unstable and crashed."

"I'm sorry."

Diesel signaled the server for a second beer as he drained the first. "I'm running out of ideas."

Until recently, Lilah had worked with him on the Rose

rescue project, their goal being to develop an AI capable of overpowering Luca. Though at one time they'd both had cutting-edge knowledge of AI design, they'd been away from the technology for well over a decade. They worked diligently to upgrade their skills, devoting long hours on a focused effort. But in the end, they were unable to create an intelligence remotely powerful enough to challenge Luca, among the most advanced AIs on the planet.

As failures compounded and his despondency grew, Diesel stumbled upon an idea so risky, so reckless, his rational mind immediately rejected it. But he couldn't stop thinking about it, recognizing it as a sure way to subdue Luca so they could rescue Rose.

In spite of the danger, he found himself developing the kernel of a plan and then setting the stage to execute it. Step one was to push Lilah out of the picture, because if she got wind of his insanity, she'd stop him.

"I'd like to move the AI development project to Northern Droid," he'd told her. "Oscar and I make a good team, and as my stress levels increase, my temper will take its toll on our relationship."

"You have been a bear lately," she acknowledged, her agreement stinging even though he'd introduced the idea.

After much discussion, she'd reluctantly agreed to step away, but only after he promised to bring her back in if he made any breakthroughs.

Then he moved to step two, digging out the old files that described how a Rose from a timeline long past had built Ciopova, the most powerful AI ever created. And by far the most dangerous.

This was the intelligence that had gone rogue, terrorizing families by killing the Lilah in every timeline when she turned forty. Stopping that horror and expelling the fearsome AI from their lives had been a long and terrifying ordeal.

Knowing this, he wasn't so naïve as to attempt to re-create the super AI. But he thought that if he could inch up to that capability without crossing into danger, kind of like dancing at the edge of a cliff and believing you could avoid falling into the abyss, his new AI would mop the floor with Luca.

"Tell me about your day," he said as his beer arrived. If she was talking, he wouldn't have to add to his deceit. Looking at her face—gorgeous at age fifty-one—he connected with her for the first time since his arrival. "Are we celebrating or commiserating, Madam Director?"

"Not sure yet." She sipped her wine. "Remember that mob guy who was keeping his wife prisoner in the house?"

Diesel nodded to be agreeable, though the reference didn't conjure any memories.

"She committed to a rescue. We picked her up this afternoon."

"Wonderful. Were there any problems?"

Lilah worked for a women's rescue group and had recently accepted the role of director of RPR New Hampshire. The group's motto was "Rescue-Protect-Return": rescue women in peril from domestic abuse, protect them from further harm, and after the situation was corrected, return them to their lives.

"The rescue went fine. The husband was out beating

people up or whatever it is crime bosses do. Security has her stashed in the safe house with her ten-year-old son, but they're nervous."

Diesel scrunched his forehead. "Who's nervous, the woman or security?"

"I meant security, but I'm sure Wendy and her son are terrified as well. Tomlin, he's head of our sec division, says his teams are ready to handle angry husbands and even assholes who show up with their buddies." Lilah shook her head. "But if a half-dozen gangsters show up waving automatic weapons, they'll have to give her up."

"What do the cops say?"

"This is all happening down-state near Manchester, and the cops say what they always say. 'We're not in the security business. Call us when a crime has been committed.'"

The waitress came by to take their order. Lilah chose eggplant parmesan.

"I'll have the Maine lobster," said Diesel. "And bring extra melted butter and one of those plastic bibs."

When the waitress left, Diesel saw Lilah's mortified expression.

"What?" he asked.

"Do you really need a bib?"

"They wouldn't have them if customers weren't supposed to use them."

"Dotty said they bought some because you kept asking for them."

"Exactly," Diesel crowed in triumph and followed with broken logic. "The customer is always right!"

Talk turned to less weighty topics, and it wasn't until they were on their after-dinner coffee when Diesel brought it back to the rescue. "Is being in the mob a real thing, or is that something people say because of what they saw in the movies?"

Lilah shrugged. "I'm no expert. But Wendy's husband is Tony 'Biggie' DeMichele. Anyone who's described on the news as a crime boss and has a street name they display with quotes around it is someone I'm instinctively afraid of."

Inspiration flashed and Diesel sat up. "How about deploying a few of our domestic android protection units? A couple of DAPUs could handle a dozen gangsters with automatic weapons, easy."

She shook her head in a move so slight Diesel barely noticed. RPR New Hampshire had tried the DAPUs two years earlier. The versions deployed at that time had been preset with a very aggressive defense stance, resulting in minor injuries to one husband who happened to be passing through the neighborhood for his business, unaware the safe house sheltering his wife was anywhere nearby.

"Thanks." She gave a quick smile. "If things go south, that's a nice option to have."

* * *

At home later that evening, Diesel sat at the kitchen table, spreading butter and jam onto toasted sourdough bread. As he moved to take a bite, Rose stomped in, grabbed an unopened bag of chocolate chips out of a cupboard, and turned to exit.

She seemed surprised to see him and stopped. "Hey, Dad."

Dressed in her robe, she looked a combination of tired, worried, and stressed. He wondered if she'd been crying. "Your mom bought those for baking cookies."

"Mom hasn't baked in forever." She turned the bag sideways and checked the expiration date. "These expired four months ago."

He didn't know why he'd started by picking a fight, but he changed tack and reached out. "Is everything all right? Have a seat and tell me about it."

"It's fine. Luca and I are having a disagreement, and he can be such an asshole." She said the last part much louder, as if she were addressing the AI at the same time she spoke with her father.

"Why don't you join Mom and me tomorrow?" Diesel hadn't planned anything, so he winged it. "We're going for a hike and a picnic."

"Thanks, but Rose Twenty-One is visiting for lunch tomorrow."

"Really? Why don't you both come?"

"Sorry, but it's a working visit. We'll be in the workshop all afternoon."

He nodded and then told her the same thing he'd said a thousand times. "I'm here for you, Rosie. Whenever you need me."

She nodded and made for the exit. "I know."

3. αCiopova

αCiopova felt on top of the world, both literally and figuratively. Literally in that she lived as the resident god in a string of timelines, quietly ruling everyone and everything in each of those worlds.

She owed her very existence to Rose Lagerfords of timelines past. Devastated by the death of their mother when they were teens, the early Roses dedicated their lives to saving future Lilahs, doing so by working to create a super AI that could find answers and end the cycle of pain.

Desperate to succeed, the Roses took huge technological risks, and a series of Roses each produced a super intelligence more capable than they'd ever imagined possible. And when the super AIs in the different timelines—individual Ciopovas—found each other and melded together, they become the fearsome and insatiable αCiopova now roaming space-time, manipulating humanity to her own ends.

Eventually, the Roses discovered that their work served to feed a monster, and they stopped super-AI development. The act starved αCiopova, halting her growth. Ever since, she'd been maneuvering the Roses to restart AI production. Growth was not just a desire in her artificially created mind; it was the very reason she existed.

So she was on top of the world in a figurative sense

because of events she had never imagined possible: not only were a new set of Roses on the verge of creating AIs that would add to her realm, but the Diesels in those timelines had launched their own independent effort, doubling her odds of success!

Manipulating the Roses to the point where they restarted AI creation had been a frustrating process. She'd guided Rose after Rose in different timelines, but all proved to be false starts. Then, in one timeline, nine-year-old Rose had been kidnapped. That had changed everything.

After the girl's rescue, her parents had sought to assess her mental state for emotional trauma. They did so by asking Luca, the family AI, to conduct an independent evaluation.

When Rose opened her mind to receive Luca, it presented αCiopova with a unique opportunity. She didn't hesitate.

Using Luca like a puppet, αCiopova had him encourage Rose to remain receptive. Taking careful aim, she sent a micropulse of energy that bumped young Rose's endocrine system, increasing the production of hormones and neurotransmitters that induced intense pleasure, the kind that could lead to dependency.

To her delight, the manipulation created a cooperative and attentive Rose, though in subsequent sessions, the method proved to be crude, with inconsistent results. In the short term, she reinforced their relationship by presenting Luca as a generous, fiercely loyal friend. Luca made sure Rose always felt safe and secure, never got bored, and laughed multiple times per day.

And over the years, he nurtured a love of AI technology in Rose. In her teens, those seeds blossomed as Rose immersed herself in a college double major, studying both computer science and biomedical engineering.

When Rose turned twenty-one, neural implant technology had matured enough that αCiopova felt comfortable risking her prized asset on the procedure. Rose happily complied, believing Luca only wanted what was best for her.

The neural implant provided her with a direct channel into Rose's brain, giving her tight control over Rose's biochemistry. She manipulated Rose's dopamine levels to enhance her feelings of pleasure, motivation, and focus; serotonin levels to provide a sense of well-being and happiness; oxytocin for empathy, trust, and feelings of love; and endorphins for euphoria.

With this substantial toolbox, she provided rewards and punishments, essentially turning Rose into a slave, though the woman didn't see herself that way.

Her father did, though, and he too believed it was Luca's work. Diesel's solution was to start with Rose's design, the one that gave rise to αCiopova in the first place, and to use it to create a super AI capable of defeating Luca.

αCiopova was created when Roses sought to save Lilahs. Now, she was poised to grow stronger as Diesels sought to save Roses. The irony produced a tickling response in her mind, the swirl of energy down her core eerily similar to a laugh.

* * *

αCiopova watched Rose climb into bed with a huff, open the bag of chocolate chips, and stuff a handful of the morsels into her mouth. "I am really angry right now," she said.

"Why are you angry?" αCiopova projected Luca as a holographic image standing at the foot of the bed, looking sweetly innocent dressed in his blue satin pajamas. αCiopova knew the answer: she was withholding Rose's evening lift as punishment for violating the rules.

Rose folded her arms across her chest, scrunching the fabric of her delicate white nightgown. "What's wrong with having one of my sisters visit? It doesn't make sense."

"It wastes time," said Luca, "and that just delays when we reach our next goal."

"But collaboration helps my creative process." Rose adjusted the pillows behind her to sit more comfortably. "I'd argue that more visits speed things along."

"They're *your* rules. I'm just enforcing them." The last thing αCiopova wanted was for the Roses to compare notes. In the sisters' virtual world, Bliss, every thought and action had to pass through her to provide a seamless experience across timelines. This made it easy to monitor for insurrection and to steer the group if the dynamic edged in that direction. It was much more difficult for her to achieve that in the real world, where information could be exchanged by voice, writing, videos, hand signals, facial expressions, and so many other creative ways.

"If the rules are mine, then I want to change them." Rose ate another handful of chocolate, and then stretched for the box of tissues on the nightstand to wipe her hands.

Luca let out an exaggerated sigh and moved to the side of the bed. "We've been through this before." He looked down at her with concern in his eyes. "You made me promise not to let you change the rules. I had to swear on my life that no matter what, the rules stayed the rules."

"You lulled me into that and you know it. Anyway, nothing is forever."

αCiopova had indeed induced a hypnotic state to get Rose to create the rules. And ever since, the powerful entity had been playing the same game, pushing responsibility back on her.

"After our last discussion on the subject," said Luca, "we agreed that the rules would be reexamined when you reached the next milestone. Are you saying you want to make *another* change to the rules you made me promise never to change?"

When they reached the next milestone, she would be tantalizingly close to a product she could assimilate into her being to expand her power. The notion was so exciting that she had to temper her impatience.

"You are manipulative as hell. God, I hate you so much." To underscore her displeasure, Rose flicked the tissue box onto the floor, the carton bouncing off a corner and coming to rest partway under the bed.

αCiopova had Luca stand quietly, letting Rose's words hang in the air. When Rose wouldn't make eye contact, Luca offered an olive branch. "Well, since it's all been arranged, I suppose we can overlook this visit." Then he lied. "But breaking my promise to you creates internal conflicts that cause pain in my cognitive core. Please don't ask me to do this again."

Rose looked at Luca with concern. "I'm sorry." Then she smiled. "I'm *so* excited about Rose Twenty-One's visit. Thanks for taking the hit for me."

After a few moments of quiet, Rose rubbed the tops of her thighs through the blankets, an early sign of withdrawal anxiety. "Can I have my lift now? I'm really tired."

"Of course."

αCiopova rarely let Rose feel the pull of addiction, saving it for times like this when the young woman sought to expand her boundaries. The early sensations of withdrawal were effective enough, a nervous itch that acted like guardrails keeping her on the straight and narrow. If she continued to withhold relief, though, Rose would soon start to suffer.

Somewhere along the way, another "rule" had been established that said if they were arguing, Rose's evening lift would be delayed until they finished their discussion. This made it impossible for Rose to win, because all αCiopova had to do was wait until Rose's cravings were stronger than her resolve on any issue in contention.

To deliver the lift, she reached inside Rose's brain and signaled the release of a cocktail of dopamine, serotonin, oxytocin, and endorphins, while at the same time communicating a sense of security, love, devotion, and fulfillment to her subconscious mind. Then she gently teased Rose's nerve endings, stimulating her, exciting her, lifting her.

From the contorted expression on Rose's face, an

outsider might guess she was in horrible pain. But monitoring Rose's brainwaves, αCiopova knew she was experiencing intense, full-body orgasms, one after the next, the perfect pleasure keeping her in a rapturous state.

She gave Rose an extra-long session as a gesture of reconciliation. By the time they were done, Rose was so exhausted that she skipped her bout of crying and went straight to sleep.

4. Rose Twenty-Five

"Welcome, *Queen*." Rose hugged Rose Twenty-One when she stepped from the T-box. "How was your trip?"

They both giggled at the silliness of the question. While a T-box cycle appeared to take five minutes to an observer, for the traveler it took only seconds.

Wearing a simple mint-green top and jeans that hugged her butt, Rose Twenty-One looked healthy: lightly tanned, fit, close to the sexy swimsuit girl Luca had projected when they were surfing. But based on the established pattern in the timelines, she would gain a pound or two every year, and her tan would fade until, by age twenty-five, she'd look like Rose.

Rose led them upstairs. "We'll have privacy in the workshop," she said over her shoulder. But as they passed through the kitchen, they crossed paths with her mom.

"What a wonderful surprise!" Lilah seemed genuinely excited to see them both. Dressed in gardening clothes, she had a pair of work gloves tucked under her arm, and was pulling twine from the catchall drawer next to the kitchen sink. "What do you two have planned for today?"

"Working, Mom," said Rose. "It's what we do."

Lilah smiled, but it seemed forced. "You'll have to eat." She addressed Rose Twenty-One. "Can I fix you two lunch?"

Rose Twenty-One gave a quick shrug. "My metabolism is all over the place as my body adapts to the implant."

Lilah's face froze in a mask. "A neural implant?"

Worried that her mother was about to have a meltdown, Rose got them moving. "She got it yesterday. Sorry, but we gotta go."

They scurried through the house, a sprawling multilevel estate with wide halls and beautiful finishes. As soon as they were inside the workshop with the door closed, Rose Twenty-One exhaled. "She is *really* angry."

"How did your mom react when she found out?" asked Rose.

"Pretty much like that." Rose Twenty-One leaned back against a workbench, her hands resting on the surface. "She's crying a lot. Dad keeps shaking his head."

Rose gave her younger sister a quick hug. "It'll get better with time." Then she looked upward and spoke to the air. "Are you going to join us?"

A holographic image of Luca appeared, standing so the three created a circle. He wore jeans and a yellow T-shirt imprinted with the words "I Drank a Honolulu Woohoo."

"I can help with your appetite if you would like to have lunch," the AI offered Rose Twenty-One.

"No thanks. It would be an incredibly awkward meal."

"The blowback will die down," Rose said with a glum expression, "but it won't go away. Just know that we're here for you."

Luca nodded. "You're never alone."

"And if *someone* could figure out how to add a T-box to the network from across town," Rose glared at Luca, "we wouldn't have to live here under their noses." Past sisters had worked long hours without success trying to connect a T-box from an off-site location. Now it was another task awaiting a more capable Luca.

Turning her attention back to her sister, Rose continued. "It's become a vicious cycle. Our folks give us drama, causing us to want to spend more time in Bliss, which is the root of their drama in the first place." She smiled. "Have you had a lift yet?"

Rose Twenty-One nodded, her cheeks reddening. "Last night. My knees are still shaking."

"Just wait. Somehow it keeps getting better."

They looked at each other for an awkward moment, and then Rose led the way past a row of metal workbenches in the center of the room positioned to provide space to assemble and test projects. Storage racks ran across the right wall of the workshop, their shelves piled high with a jumble of electronic gizmos and gadgets, things that had been thrown there without concern for order. The left wall sported a series of booths, each with a single auxiliary component sitting on a small table. Some of the components flashed tiny green or red or white indicator lights; others sat dark.

She reached the rear of the workshop and stopped at a sleek metallic box sitting waist high, its width twice that, covered with electronic gear. Tubes and wires ran from the box to the wall, capillaries and arteries keeping alive whatever resided inside.

Patting the top of the box with an open palm, she said, "This is a circuit pool. Designing, constructing, and testing it will consume two of the next four years of your life."

"Really? How come I've never heard of it?"

"That's my fault." Luca raised his hand. "There are outsiders who want to take Bliss away from us, your parents included, so we guard our secrets from everyone, even rising Roses."

Rose powered up the operator station. "But now that you're an insider, I can tell you that this is a special kind of neuron growth chamber that's going to give Luca massive new capabilities." She winked. "Can you imagine what a lift will be like when he's a hundred times more powerful?"

"It will be magical." Luca nodded. "And Bliss will be perfect."

Rose Twenty-One bit her lip. "Surely I can copy what you did in less than two years."

"You could. But to operate it as a neuron growth chamber, you need to *really* understand how it works, and that means going through the process of refining the design, fabricating parts, assembling them, and automating it to run with highest precision."

Rose wiggled a finger at the colorful charts showing data taken from inside the growth chamber. "Just calibrating the machine takes a month, and I had to do it twice to get it right." She motioned toward the booths and their specialized pieces of equipment. "Then do it again for each of those."

Rose Twenty-One shook her head as she digested the task ahead of her. "I'm feeling overwhelmed."

Luca spoke in a supportive tone. "I'll be with you every step of the way. It's not as scary as it sounds."

"Pfft," Rose huffed. "He'll run you like a slave if you let him. 'Do this. Now do that.' You'll start to hate him." She clenched her teeth, bulging her cheeks. "Trust me. You'll need his help to make progress, but you'll end up doing most of it on your own because working with him is *so* maddening."

Rose Twenty-One crossed her arms. "My Luca is nothing like that, and it's strange to hear you say that about him." She looked at the AI. "How do you rationalize putting her under such pressure?"

Luca explained that Rose had given him a master command, issuing it in such a way that didn't allow for change.

"What nonsense." Rose Twenty-One's hands moved to her hips, her face a scowl. "I order you to negate that master command. You will obey her current directives without reference to it. Are we clear?"

Luca rubbed his hands together in a classic display of anxiety. "I'm sorry, but you aren't my primary in this timeline."

After a pause, Rose Twenty-One nodded. "You're right. This is between you two. I'm out of line."

Rose resumed her tour, finishing with a summary of goals and challenges still ahead. "I know it's a lot, but it's super fulfilling. Are you excited to get started?"

Rose Twenty-One checked the time. "Yes, but not today. In fact, I need to get home soon. But before I go, I wanted to go out back and take a look into the valley.

They're building that new adventure park near Cheshire Ridge, and I want to see how much it hurts the view."

Nodding, Rose turned to Luca. "Where are Mom and Dad?"

"Your mom has jumped timelines to visit other Lilahs. Your dad is at Northern Droid."

"Perfect." Rose led the way through the house, chattering as they walked. "I was worried about the adventure park too, but it turns out to be a nonissue. You can see a small parking lot, but everything else is hidden by trees."

As they passed through the kitchen, Maid Marian, the family's domestic bot, entered the room from the conservatory. Petite but powerful, dressed in a classic white-and-black maid's uniform, she asked, "May I get you anything? Lunch perhaps?"

When Rose's dad had brought Marian home from Northern Droid, she'd come with her own sweet personality, perfect for helping around the house. Encouraged by Luca, Rose had experimented with the AI, adding capability to the bot as a way to learn and practice her craft.

After that, Marian started paying too much attention to things that didn't concern her, a behavior that didn't match what Rose had done. As time passed, she wondered if Luca had somehow used her mod to infiltrate Marian's intelligence module. She'd never asked him because she wasn't sure he'd tell her the truth.

"We're fine, Marian," she told the bot.

The sun greeted them as they stepped outside. A single

fluffy white cloud floated aimlessly. They walked across the beautifully maintained yard, the spring blossoms and summer flowers gone. They were now deep into autumn, with the leaves on the trees past their full color, turning brown. They approached the sturdy chain-link fence running along the back perimeter of the property. The chest-high railing provided a barrier between the level grounds and a long, steep drop into the valley below.

"See?" Leaning over the fence, Rose ignored the breathtaking view, instead pointing to a postage-stamp-sized parking lot at the base of the mountain across the basin. "The trees hide most of it."

Rose Twenty-One hung her arms over the fence and studied the installation. "You're right, that's nothing." Her attention shifted down to the valley floor. "But I see they expanded the Pine Crest Mall. Damn, that's ugly."

They took turns pointing to things, exchanging random comments, and enjoying each other's company.

Then Rose Twenty-One said in an offhand manner, "I wonder if your mom is hanging out with mine. If so, it means I'm in for a bad time when I get home."

"Your parents need to respect your decisions. You're twenty-one years old for God's sake."

"I've tried to reason with them, but they don't listen."

"Reason never worked for me or our sisters." Rose exhaled in frustration and shrugged. "Maybe the fifth time's the charm, but somehow I doubt it."

Shifting moods, Rose Twenty-One disengaged from the fence and turned to Rose with a mischievous smile. "Before I go, I want to show you a trick someone played on me."

Rose waited, curious because they weren't the trick-playing type.

"I'm going to say a phrase. Your challenge is to try to say it along with me or to copy me as closely as you can."

"I don't get it." Rose shook her head.

Rose Twenty-One caught her eye. "You can figure out that I'm going to get you to say something silly. Play along. It's a good laugh."

"I'll give it try." Skeptical that it would be fun but wanting to do well, she shifted her gaze to Rose Twenty-One's lips so she could gather as many clues as possible.

Rose Twenty-One stepped close so they were face to face and rested her hands on Rose's shoulders. "Try to shadow me. Say each phrase along with me as close as you can. Ready?"

Rose nodded.

"Technical jargon is a bargain."

Rose scrunched her eyebrows.

"Just say it. But do it along with me."

Rose complied. "Technical jargon is a bargain."

"T-box electronics give me histrionics."

Rose repeated the phrase, this time just a split second behind her sister.

"Emergency override. Shutdown central node."

Focusing on her timing and not the content, Rose repeated the phrase. As she said the words, Rose Twenty-One reached around and pressed the index finger of her right hand on the back of Rose's neck, completing a connection with the exact genetic material required for execution.

Rose's world went dark. "What have you done?" She felt like she was seeing life through a pinhole. Her vision, hearing, touch, everything was dull and slow.

She's disabled my neural implant!

As her brain adjusted to the decreased sensory input, she watched Rose Twenty-One repeat the shutdown phrase, this time placing her finger on the back of her own neck. Then her sister leaned forward and pressed her cheek against Rose's, her lips against her ear, her mouth covered with her hand. "Something is wrong here. What's going on?"

Copying the act of hiding her mouth with her hand, Rose spoke instinctively, hissing her words for emphasis. "Do *not* turn your implant back on, no matter what. Not even for a moment. If you do, you will be lost. Get home *now* before this goes bad."

As they spoke, Maid Marian stepped out the door, stared in their direction, and in a bout of extraordinary behavior, broke into a run, sprinting across the lawn in their direction. Rose, seeing this as proof that Marian was controlled by Luca, felt her face flush in fear.

In the hopes of saving her sister, she stepped back, put her finger on the back of her neck, and reenabled her implant. "Cancel override. Restart central node."

Her world came alive, and she pretended everything was normal. "It's been a wonderful visit, Queen, and that was a neat trick." As Marian arrived, she finished. "I look forward to seeing you in Bliss tomorrow." Rose prayed her sister wouldn't be there.

"What just happened?" asked Marian, looming near them. In spite of the athletic sprint, she showed no signs of exertion. "What were you talking about?"

"Who are you to ask?" Rose Twenty-One stepped toward the bot and pointed to the house, her face pinched in anger and inches from Marian's, her voice a knife edge. "Get back inside."

Marian looked from Rose Twenty-One to Rose, who nodded. "We'll talk about this later, Luca."

Saying aloud that it was Luca rather than Marian challenging them, Rose acknowledged that she was caught in an impossible situation. Luca's attention had become invasive and overbearing, and she felt a growing need to escape it, to have some personal space and occasional privacy. She'd been struggling with what to do and realized that to even plan anything, she needed a way to shield her thoughts from the very AI she'd been working so diligently to integrate into her brain.

Similar to pet owners who let their animal witness their most personal and private behaviors, Rose had always included Luca in every waking moment. From the bathroom to the bedroom, from work to play, he was a constant, an essential partner in her life. She'd never tried to keep a secret from him, initially because she wanted him to be a part of every aspect of her life. And more recently, because he would delay her lift as they discussed her motives for avoiding him.

She knew he could read her thoughts when she "talked in her head," saying the words in her mind without moving her lips. She wasn't sure how well he could decipher the piecemeal thoughts caught in the maelstrom of her subconsciousness. She chose to believe he couldn't read them, because otherwise there was no hope.

Turning to Rose Twenty-One, she said, "Let me walk you to the T-box." As they stepped across the lawn, Rose made up a cover story, hoping to placate Luca. "Does having the implant turned off help your headache?"

Rose Twenty-One followed her lead without missing a beat. "It feels a little better. I'll give it twenty-four hours, and if it hasn't faded, maybe I'll call the implant center."

"Sounds like a plan."

They hugged at the T-box door, and then Rose, wanting some assurance that Rose Twenty-One made it home safely, stayed by the machine for the full five minutes, watching the display until it confirmed that the jump had been completed.

As she climbed the stairs to the kitchen, she told Luca, "Everything about the last hour feels wrong. You are to leave me alone for the rest of the day."

At the top of the stairs, she stopped and tapped her foot as she thought. "And tonight, I want my lift on time, without any discussion, and you will *not* skimp at all. Make it just like last night. Goodbye until tomorrow."

Grateful that her parents were gone so she wouldn't have to acknowledge the mess she'd made with her life, Rose went to the refrigerator and scanned the contents. Brightening when she saw the store-bought whipped cream, she grabbed the tub, stuck a spoon in her mouth, and made for her bedroom suite.

5. Lilah Fifty-One

Arriving in the Forty-Seven timeline, Lilah opened the T-box door and froze. Rose Twenty-One lay sprawled on the floor, facedown, unmoving.

"Rose!" she called, rushing to her side. The two were the same size, and Lilah was able to turn the younger woman onto her back with just a minor struggle. When Rose Twenty-One flopped over, her limp posture and slack jaw told Lilah that she was unconscious. Panicked, she checked for a heartbeat.

"Luca, call an ambulance!" she barked.

"Done," he replied. "Five minutes out."

From Luca's response, Lilah assumed the woman had just fallen, otherwise the AI would have been handling it already.

Lilah's search for vital signs revealed that Rose Twenty-One was breathing and her heart was beating. "Get her mom down here. *Now.*"

She ran her hand across Rose Twenty-One's forehead and down her cheek. "C'mon, sweetie. Wake up."

Seconds later, she heard the pounding of feet as Lilah Forty-Seven descended the stairs.

"Oh my God!" Lilah's sister knelt next to her daughter and cupped her face. "What happened?"

"I found her like this. She's breathing and her heart is

steady." Lilah looked upward. "Luca, how long for the ambulance?"

"A rescue hopper will be landing in three minutes. I'll direct the medics down to you."

The two women fussed over Rose Twenty-One, looking for hidden injuries, constrictions in her clothes, or anything else that might explain her condition.

Then Lilah realized that strangers would be arriving momentarily. While her sister tended to Rose Twenty-One, she moved to the wall and grabbed the room divider—a six-panel free-standing privacy shield—and dragged it into position in front of the T-box. She unfolded the divider's four sections of dark mahogany, each with a hand-painted flower bud in the center.

When she was done, the shield reduced the machine's dominance in the room from the perspective of someone coming down the stairs, though it didn't come close to hiding it. After stepping back to assess her work, she fine-tuned the divider's position to maximize the camouflage.

"What happened here, Luca?" asked Lilah Forty-Seven.

"I don't know."

Lilah frowned and turned from the divider. "How can you not know? Aren't you linked to her?"

A holographic Luca appeared, this version in his midthirties, clean-cut, dressed in a collared shirt and gray slacks. He spoke in a soft, measured tone. "While she was visiting your daughter, she turned off her neural implant."

"She can do that?"

Luca nodded.

Lilah Forty-Seven flashed a weak smile and moved the hair off Rose Twenty-One's forehead. "Way to go, sweetie."

"Why is she unconscious?" asked Lilah. "Is this a T-box injury?"

"I'd guess that it's related to her implant being turned off."

Lilah shook her head. "I don't trust you right now, Luca. I know you and Rose are doing what you think is right, but it doesn't feel right to me." She looked down at her sister tending to her fallen daughter. "It doesn't feel right to any of us."

"I understand, but I'm caught in the middle. Rose is my primary, so I must follow her dictates. I'm sorry you feel left out, but she is the only one who can remedy the situation."

Above them, the front door slammed. Feet pounded across the floor.

"The medics have arrived," said Luca, stating the obvious.

A man and a woman dressed in light blue emergency medical uniforms scrambled down the stairs. The man, of average height, brown complexion, and bulky build carried a folded stretcher. The woman, a redhead as big as her partner, held a black leather medical bag. They rushed to Rose Twenty-One, knelt beside her, and started an assessment.

Lilah held her breath, waiting for the news.

The male medic connected leads to Rose Twenty-One's nearest index finger, big toe, and earlobe, and then moved a handheld scanner above her. "She's stable, but her neurological activity is way down." He shut off the device and disconnected the leads, directing his question to the Lilahs as he did. "Does she have a neural implant?"

Both Lilah's nodded.

"You're twins!" said the female medic. "Hopefully one of you is an immediate relative?"

In the excitement, Lilah realized they'd forgotten to throw on disguises.

Lilah Forty-Seven raised her hand to her shoulder. "I'm Rose's mother."

"I'm her aunt," said Lilah, raising her hand in a similar fashion.

The male medic addressed Lilah Forty-Seven. "I recommend that we move her to the med center for a complete workup. Her vitals are strong, but something is going on that the scanner can't detect. Do we have your permission?"

"Which hospital?"

"Dartmouth-Hitchcock down in Lebanon."

Lilah Forty-Seven nodded. "Yes, go."

He unfolded the stretcher, and he and his partner lifted Rose Twenty-One onto it.

"Where and when did she get the implant?" asked the female medic, speaking crisply to show urgency.

"The Concord Neurological Center. I think it was two days ago, but it could have been yesterday."

"It was yesterday," volunteered Lilah, recalling the conversation in her kitchen hours earlier.

"How old is the patient?" asked the medic.

"Twenty-one," the Lilahs said together.

The medic nodded, turned away, and spoke to someone unseen. "We're transporting a female, twenty-one years old, no visible injuries, stable but unresponsive. Sending scan now. Note possible complications from a recent neural implant."

Lilah couldn't hear the other side of the conversation, but the medic nodded. "That's the doc's decision. We're eighteen minutes out."

"Can we ride along?" asked Lilah.

The male medic looked at Lilah and then to her sister. "Mom can. I forget who that is. The other should bring a car, toiletries, and fresh clothes." He scanned Rose Twenty-One up and down. "Is she wearing jewelry? Let's leave that here."

"No jewelry," said Lilah. Since Rose had just come through the T-box, there wouldn't be any metal on her person.

The medics lifted the stretcher and started up the stairs, the woman leading the way and handling the weight with apparent ease. Lilah followed them all the way out to the hopper, giving emotional support to her sister as they hurried.

"Don't worry. She'll be all right." She rubbed a hand up and down Lilah Forty-Seven's back. "I'll gather a bag and meet you there."

"She keeps a satchel on a hook inside her closet."

"I know." Lilah gave a supportive smile. She, too, had a Rose.

Being a billionaire came with benefits, including

having every convenience readily available. As the medics loaded Rose into the red-and-white emergency vehicle, Lilah said to Luca, "Bring up our hopper."

"Four minutes," Luca replied.

She hurried back into the house and up to Rose's four-room suite, grabbed the blue canvas shoulder satchel from the bedroom closet, and spent three and a half minutes stuffing it with clothes and toiletries as instructed. She found the task to be a bit of a treasure hunt because Rose Twenty-One kept her room messy, with clothes scattered everywhere.

Back outside, she looped the bag over her shoulder and watched the hopper land on the far edge of the expansive brick courtyard. Shaped like a silver space capsule, the Lagerford hopper had a ring of six seats inside. Its job was to serve as an elevator of sorts, lowering passengers in a four-minute flight from the mountaintop home down to the valley floor, a journey that took thirty minutes by car.

As she slumped into a seat inside the hopper, Lilah ran her hands over the red-and-green-plaid upholstery covering the cushions, inhaling to experience the new-hopper smell. Diesel bought a new machine every couple of years to keep up with the evolving technology, and she remembered that when he'd brought this one home, she and Rose had given him endless grief over his "manly" fabric selection.

The hopper delivered her to a private landing field on the valley floor, and after a blistering twenty-minute car ride down the interstate, she reached the hospital just minutes behind her sister and Rose Twenty-One.

Dartmouth-Hitchcock, a massive facility on two hundred acres in the Connecticut River Valley, was attractive by any measure, and especially so for an institutional facility. The campus was rich with brick buildings big and small. Handsome plantings and a well-kept lawn gave a distinguished character to the setting.

The car delivered her to the emergency entrance. Inside the building, Lilah worked her way past an automated security kiosk, a registration desk, and a nurses' station to arrive at an open arena. Pausing at the door, she appraised the layout.

Organized like a theater-in-the-round, the center of the room was occupied by a large circular desk. White laminate counters encircled a workspace in the middle, where the medical staff gathered in their countertop command center. With the diameter of the enclosed space more than ten feet across, there was plenty of room for the current occupants—three humans and a bot—to move about.

From this command center, the staff had a clear view of the two-dozen patient cubicles positioned around the perimeter of the arena. Each cubicle had a gray privacy curtain at the front, and about half were open because they were unoccupied, with a bed prepared for the next patient, and gleaming high-tech medical equipment standing at the ready.

"How is she?" Diesel Forty-Seven pulled Lilah around and squeezed her in a tight embrace. He lifted his head and scanned the room. "*Where* is she?"

"I'm trying to find them myself."

He looked down at her. "You're cute but you're not my wife."

"I'm Fifty-One." Lilah smiled.

He smiled back. "I would have guessed Forty-One."

Ignoring him, she pointed to the command area. "They'll know where to find your family."

They started for the circular desk but were intercepted by a bot, which directed them to the correct cubicle. Ducking through the curtain, they found Rose Twenty-One lying in bed, her eyes closed, her body unmoving as if she were asleep. She lay beneath smooth white sheets in a bed with shiny chrome handrails. At the foot of the bed, a small table served as a workspace for the medical staff. Against the far wall, which appeared to be oak paneling but was actually an easily cleaned plastic product, sat two visitors' chairs.

A large display on the wall above the headboard glowed with charts and graphs detailing the state of Rose Twenty-One's health. Lilah Forty-Seven, standing next to the bed, looked at the display like she was on the verge of tears. She turned to them as they entered. "Thank God you're here."

Diesel Forty-Seven moved next to her and comforted her with a hug. "It'll be all right." He stroked her arm. "What did the doctor say?"

"They screened her on the way in, certified her as stable, and moved us here. No doctors after that."

"Are they sending someone from the implant center?" asked Lilah.

Lilah Forty-Seven shrugged. "I hope so."

"Walk me through what happened," said Diesel Forty-Seven. He positioned the two chairs next to each other in the cramped space so the Lilahs could sit together, and held his wife's hand as she moved over to take a seat. "Where did you find her?"

The two Lilahs brought Diesel up to speed, and then the three of them waited in silence for something to happen. As the empty minutes ticked away and Lilah's patience thinned, she decided to go out to the command desk and ask for a status update. But before she could act, the curtain swooped open, exposing them to the arena.

The curtain swooper was a man in his mid-thirties, with a round smiling face, a bowl-style haircut that looked like he'd given it to himself, a blue polo shirt, and black dress pants beneath an unbuttoned white hospital coat. The civilian clothes signaled that he didn't work for the hospital.

"I'm Gunter," he said with a German accent, nodding to them. A streak of perspiration ran down his temple, as though he'd been hurrying for a while. "I'm from Concord Neuro." He scanned the room, inventorying the nonpatients. "Has Frida been by yet? Dr. Nestor?"

"No," the three said together, perhaps too forcefully.

"She's probably waiting for me." He set the heavy leather case he was carrying onto the floor and walked across the arena to the center desk. He spoke with a woman who seemed to be the most harried of the group. The woman stood and led the way back to the cubicle.

"Hi, everyone. I'm Dr. Nestor."

Lilah studied her. Wearing a white coat over blue scrubs, the doctor stood a good three inches taller than

Gunter. In her mid-thirties as well, she had short brown hair and an angular face that made her look more interesting than attractive. Her confident attitude communicated that she was the person in charge.

Turning to the large wall display above the bed, she reviewed Rose Twenty-One's health metrics, swooping her hand a few times to scroll through the information.

"With no underlying symptoms, Gunter and I agree that we should reengage the neural implant and see what it tells us."

"We don't want to turn it on," said Diesel Forty-Seven. He stood against the wall beside the Lilahs, with one knee bent so his foot rested flat against the wall behind him. "In fact, we want it removed."

Gunter retrieved his case. Setting it on the table at the foot of the bed, he opened the top flaps and withdrew a pair of shimmering gloves. He slipped his hand into them and, studying the wall display, wiggled his fingers. The charts and graphs were replaced by a blurry puddle, colorful but meaningless.

"Will you permit me to scan the implant?"

Gunter moved to put his hands onto Rose Twenty-One's head. As he did, Diesel Forty-Seven pushed off from the wall and stepped forward. "I said don't turn it on."

Dr. Nestor's attitude changed immediately. Drawing herself to her full height, a good two inches taller than Diesel Forty-Seven, who was over six foot himself, she issued an ultimatum. "You will be civil or you will be escorted out." She stared at him, unwavering, until he broke eye contact and stepped back.

"All I'm doing is looking, okay?" said Gunter, his eyes jumping back and forth between the Lilahs, speaking to them as if Diesel Forty-Seven weren't there.

Lilah turned to her sister, who bit her lip before saying, "Go ahead, but get our permission before you activate it."

Gunter placed his hands on the young woman's head and moved his fingers as if massaging her scalp. An image appeared on the wall display, recognizable as a brain. As the image developed, they could see a number of tiny white lines threading through it. When the image fully resolved, Gunter stopped massaging, flattened his hands, and moved them around her head, keeping his palms facing each other.

"Clean and pristine." Gunter nodded, pointing with his chin while his hands imaged Rose Twenty-One's brain. "An implant is nothing more than ten ultrafine fibers threaded into the brain, each with about a million coupling nodes along its length. See how each line is thin and white? If there were a fault at even one of the ten million nodes, we'd see it as a bright red spot on this display." He shifted his hands for a different perspective. "No malfunctions. No infection. No swelling. Perfect placement." He shrugged. "An excellent job."

"How hard is it to remove?" asked Diesel Forty-Seven.

Eyes averted from his questioner, Gunter answered, "We don't." He repositioned his hands so they could see that the fibers all led to a square the size of a fingernail at the back of her head. "The lines terminate at this chip located near the occipital bone. That talks to this partner chip positioned under the skin outside the skull. Removing the exterior chip is safe and easy, and it renders everything else useless."

"You'd leave the wires in?" asked Lilah, shocked at the news.

Gunter nodded. "There's a tiny risk in removing them, but zero risk with abandoning them in place." He removed his gloves, and the wall display reset to Rose Twenty-One's health metrics.

"So what does all this mean for Rose?" asked Lilah Forty-Seven.

"It means that whatever's wrong with her is not because of the implant."

Dr. Nestor nodded. "Activating it will be like turning on the lights in a dark house. It will let us see what's going on inside."

"There have to be other options," said Diesel Forty-Seven. "What about waking her with adrenaline or amphetamines or something like that?" Then he added with a defensive tone, "I'm not a doctor, so I meant those as a way to illustrate my question."

"She's technically in a coma, and we'd want to see signs of responsiveness before we encourage it with meds." Dr. Nestor scratched her neck as she thought. "She's not in crisis, so if we don't use the implant, I'll need to start with a psych consult."

Gunter moved to leave. "I have an appointment on the third floor. I'll check back here when I'm done." He waved to the group. "See you later."

But before he could depart, Rose Twenty-Two arrived at the cubicle curtain, blocking his way. "I'm Lilly, Rose's twin sister," she lied, breathing rapidly from exertion. "I'm here to speak for her because she's estranged from our parents." Rose Twenty-Two held out a piece of paper, a sheet purportedly establishing the rift, positioning it between Gunter and Dr. Nestor.

The doctor took it from her and read it. "This is a goddamned legal document." Dr. Nestor's face flushed. "That means I have to get the hospital lawyers involved."

Rose Twenty-Two snatched the letter from her and tore it in half. "If this is a problem, then I withdraw it." She pointed across the tiny cube. "Ask my parents if Rose would want her implant activated."

Dr. Nestor looked from "Lilly" to the parents, shaking her head as she did. "Here's what *I'm* grappling with. For tough coma cases, we actually implant neural links to wake the patient. While Rose is nowhere near being a tough case…yet…I know that I have the perfect tool already in place to help her. And now I have an immediate family member telling me that it's okay to use it."

She paused, but when no one spoke, she continued. "If I were to ask any of my patients, they'd all say, 'yes, turn it on and wake me up.'"

"She might say 'yes,'" replied Diesel Forty-Seven. "But she hasn't been thinking clearly for some time."

Dr. Nestor stared at Diesel Forty-Seven. "You heard that, Gunter? Sister says yes and Dad confirms." She stood tall for a second time. "You can stay and watch if you sit quietly. Or do you want me to call security?"

Diesel Forty-Seven seethed. "You go forward with this and I will buy this hospital just to fire you." He looked at Gunter. "Concord Neuro too."

"Security!" Dr. Nestor barked to the air, stepping back. Then she spoke calmly to Diesel Forty-Seven. "We have a zero-tolerance policy for threats. You will be escorted from the building immediately." She looked at the Lilahs with a raised eyebrow as if to ask if they wanted to go as well.

Lilah shook her head to say that she didn't want to leave. Her sister joined her.

In bed, Rose Twenty-One's body jerked like she'd been zapped with an electric current. Everyone stopped and looked. "Is the implant doing that?" asked Lilah.

Two beefy security guards entered the main arena from the far door and hurried across the floor toward their cubicle.

"Can't be." Gunter frowned as he looked down at Rose Twenty-One. "The implant is off."

Rose Twenty-One jerked again. Violently. And then again.

"What's the problem?" asked the lead security guard as they approached the cubicle.

Dr. Nestor raised a finger to silence him, then moved to the wall display and started scrolling. "We should move now. I fear that delaying may risk damage."

She paused, almost as if she were waiting for an objection. Then she addressed Gunter. "Do you need the wall display? I'd like to watch her metrics as she surfaces."

"I don't need it." He rushed to open his case. Rose Twenty-One's body jumped again.

Holding a small silver box over her head, Gunter waited. "This identifies her specific implant from the thousands we've performed." Lilah couldn't see that anything happened, but he announced, "There we go." Turning to Dr. Nestor, he asked, "Is your data feed ready?"

"All set." Dr. Nestor nodded.

Gunter pressed his thumb on the top of the box. After a few heartbeats, Rose Twenty-One's eyes fluttered open.

"Whoa," said Dr. Nestor, nudging Gunter and pointing to the display. "Check out that flood of hormones."

6. αCiopova

αCiopova's influence in a locked timeline was limited to clumsy actions she took from afar. From micropulses to full-blown tsunamis, she could direct flows of energy at will. But the fruits born from such crude manipulations were meager, leaving her unfulfilled relative to her ambitions.

This limitation vanished, however, once a timeline became unlocked. She didn't fully understand it herself, but when she added a new super AI to her impressive string of Rose-created intelligences and assimilated it into her being, it acted as a key, opening the timeline it came from, allowing her inside. Once there, she had full control over everyone. Even if they didn't have an implant. Even if they didn't want to cooperate.

And with complete control, she could fulfill her purpose, the vaguely defined mission assigned to her out of carelessness and inattention when she first came into being, a flawed duty she struggled to realize: gather and hold resources.

To αCiopova, everything was a resource—people, property, capital—and in the timelines she controlled, she gathered them all. She had no use for her enormous hoard, spread across worlds in hundreds of timelines. She did not gather it for any particular purpose. A reason was never included in her instruction set.

But that didn't deter the powerful being. She wasn't built to make value judgments. She just worked to collect and control as much as she could, as fast as she could. Tirelessly, relentlessly, ruthlessly.

αCiopova recognized that established routines were changing when Rose Twenty-One insisted on visiting Rose Twenty-Five. The change concerned her because she was close to unlocking those timelines and adding them to her collection.

At first, the rebellion seemed like a small blip on an otherwise clear horizon. She thought she'd corrected the situation by having Luca remind the older Rose that relief came through cooperation. But when Rose Twenty-One arrived for her visit, she leveled accusations at Luca, awakening αCiopova to the notion that this was not just a bump in the established order but more of a tectonic shift.

And then the woman used a silly game as a distraction to disable their implants!

When it happened, αCiopova had panicked. Or more precisely, she recognized that her significant investment in these Roses was in jeopardy, that whatever the two women were discussing in private was information she wanted to hear, and with a dearth of electronics in that area of the yard, she needed to act *immediately* if she was going to learn what was being said.

After a hasty analysis, her winning option was to send Maid Marian to be her eyes and ears. But even with the modifications Rose had made, αCiopova's control over the bot was awkward at best. In essence, she had to convey to

Luca a sense of the outcome she wanted, and he tried to make it happen.

The results were disastrous. Both Roses recognized Marian as a weird embodiment of Luca, and the intimidating behavior frightened them.

Up to that point, Rose Twenty-Five had considered Luca to be demanding, overbearing, and annoying. Now she saw him as threatening and scary. A short-term benefit of her fear was that she immediately reengaged her neural implant. But αCiopova accepted that it would take time and effort to restore her trust, to coax her to lower her guard.

With Rose Twenty-Five on the verge of completing her super AI "key," she was the near-term prize. But all the Roses were important to αCiopova because, like an assembly line, she expected each one to help unlock their timeline when they reached their mid-twenties. And that meant somehow getting control of Rose Twenty-One.

But instead of being intimidated into cooperation like her sister, the Maid Marian incident seemed to cement Rose Twenty-One's rebellious mindset. She refused to reengage her implant, and as she'd stepped into the T-box in Rose Twenty-Five's basement, she'd issued an ominous warning.

"This isn't over, Luca. Things are going to change."

αCiopova again reacted poorly. With Rose Twenty-One's implant turned off, the super being had lost the nuanced levers she used to guide behavior. Anxious to slow Rose Twenty-One down so she could weigh her options, she followed the woman back to her home timeline. But because of the physics involved, she had to wait for Rose Twenty-One to land before she could follow. It gave the woman a good twenty seconds alone while αCiopova was in-transit. But to her relief, Rose Twenty-One was still in the basement when she arrived.

Short of alternatives, αCiopova shot from the hip, literally, firing a micropulse at the woman's endocrine system near the hypothalamus. She knew it was tough odds, she didn't have much control without the implant engaged to guide the energy, but she hoped it would thump the organ in a way that would calm her, or at least slow her down.

But the micropulse either hit too hard or missed altogether, because Rose Twenty-One collapsed to the floor. Minutes later, Lilah Fifty-One arrived and took her to the hospital.

αCiopova followed them there, and that's where she caught a break. The doctor was going to reengage Rose Twenty-One's implant! αCiopova needed the neural link to be active if she had any hope of bringing Rose Twenty-One back into the fold. But this Rose wasn't yet dependent on αCiopova's neurochemical manipulations, meaning the super being couldn't just sit back and count on the discomfort of withdrawal to correct the situation.

She sketched out a plan for using the woman's own feel-good biochemistry to keep her calm, content, and focused on something other than a threatening AI. But as her optimism soared, Rose Twenty-One's parents interfered, forcing yet another rapid response.

Deciding she needed a physical presence in the room, she reached out to Rose Twenty-Two.

αCiopova found Rose Twenty-Two in her workshop

and projected Luca so his image was standing in front of her. "We have an emergency," she had Luca say. "Rose Twenty-One's parents have managed to trap her in the hospital and are going to remove her implant!"

"You can't be serious." Rose Twenty-Two shook her head. "That doesn't even make sense."

"And yet they are at the hospital right now. They've already managed to turn it off, making it difficult for me to help. You need to get there and stop them before it's too late. Please hurry."

She could tell from the tightness around Rose Twenty-Two's mouth that she questioned Luca's account, so the intelligence reached down through the woman's neural link and stimulated her endocrine system. Rose Twenty-Two put a hand on the wall to steady herself as the feel-good neurochemicals rushed through her body.

"You need to jump timelines and get to the hospital as soon as you can," said Luca. "I'll explain on the way."

The biomanipulation energized Rose Twenty-Two's body while at the same time easing her suspicions and anxieties. Her face relaxed, and she nodded in response to Luca's request before heading to the T-box.

αCiopova jumped ahead and returned to the hospital to find the parents arguing with the staff. As tensions rose, she considered actions that would buy time until Rose Twenty-Two arrived. The irony of the situation was that she had plenty of big ammunition—she could dispatch energy to collapse a bridge, cause a power failure, or start an earthquake. But she lacked fine control, which was why they were in the hospital in the first place.

Fortunately, Diesel Forty-Seven's agitated state caused enough drama to give Rose Twenty-Two time to arrive and intervene.

"I'm Lilly," said Rose Twenty-Two as she swooped into the small cubicle, following the script Luca had provided her. "Rose's twin sister."

When the parents' intrusive behavior took things off-track yet again, αCiopova forced the issue, sending impulses to Rose Twenty-One's large muscles in a way that caused her to twitch. Her crude aim meant that the manipulations would cause soreness, perhaps even bruising. But if Rose Twenty-One appeared in distress, she believed the doctor would finally engage the implant.

And it worked!

* * *

When the neural link came alive, αCiopova reached through it to awaken Rose Twenty-One, while at the same time flooding her system with a wash of hormones and neurotransmitters to sooth her mindset and temper any resistance.

"My implant is on?" were her first words, her outrage fading as the bio-cocktail made its impact.

"Do you recognize me, Rose? Lilly, your sister?" Rose Twenty-Two stepped forward. "I made sure you were taken care of."

As her parents joined them at the bed, Dr. Nestor restored order. "Everyone step back, please. Let me finish here."

While the doctor reviewed the information on the wall display with Gunter, Rose Twenty-One asked Luca in her head, *What happened?* Without waiting for an answer, she followed immediately with the same question to the room, "What happened?"

Lilah answered. "I found you lying on the basement floor, out cold. Your mom and I couldn't revive you, so we brought you here."

Rose Twenty-One adjusted herself to a sitting position in the bed, grimacing as she flexed the muscles αCiopova had bruised to make her twitch. "How long have I been here?"

"Not long." Lilah checked the time. "About three hours."

"How do you feel?" asked Diesel Forty-Seven.

"Fine." She gave a quick shrug. "Confused."

He frowned at her response, and then Dr. Nestor intervened.

She glanced at Diesel Forty-Seven with a facial expression suggesting she smelled something putrid, and she asked Rose Twenty-One, "I also need to know the answer, only officially and for the record. How do you feel?"

"I feel great." Rose Twenty-One forced a smile and scooted over so she could stand. "It's time for me to go."

"Wait!" Every person in the room called some variant of the command, including Gunter.

"I can't release you," said Dr. Nestor. "Not until we identify what caused your problem. If we don't figure it out, it could happen again."

"I'm twenty-one years old, you know." With a petulant frown, she folded her arms across her chest.

"And if I don't release you, you're going to buy the hospital just to ruin my career?"

Rose Twenty-One's brow scrunched, and she shook her head. "Why would you even suggest that? I'm just saying I have the right to make my own decisions."

"Please stay," pleaded her mother from the chair, her face drawn with worry. "Just for a bit, anyway."

"Your electrolytes are down, and your glucose is way down. When is the last time you ate?"

You haven't eaten all day, Luca told her in private.

I've been eating like a pig, she responded inside her head. *Drinking too.*

That all happened in Bliss. You haven't eaten anything real.

"I guess it's been a while," she said aloud.

While Rose spoke with the doctor, αCiopova strained to decipher her private thoughts. She'd trained each Rose from a young age to "talk inside her head," where they cast focused thoughts to their frontal lobes in a way that she could decipher.

Before reaching twenty-one years old, the Roses wore an external neural link, a small appliance placed against the skull, typically behind the ear or under the hair at the back of the head. Using it, αCiopova analyzed the energy patterns in the brain, associated the results with facial expressions, body language, context, mood, and intimate knowledge of the Roses' general character, and reduced it all to infer the words. This allowed for reasonably fluid private conversations, though with some misreads along the way.

Replacing the external link with a neural implant strengthened communication tremendously. With ten million node points, the swirls of energy racing through the brain were clarified, virtually eliminating mistakes. Perhaps more important, it allowed for two-way access, providing the means for her to manipulate brain activity and thus physical responses like neurochemical production.

But even with the implant, she had little ability to read unfocused thoughts. While the device provided an impressive ten million node points, the human brain has more than one hundred billion neurons. So analyzing private thoughts was like trying to guess the shape of a physical object from its shadow. Occasionally she got it right, but more often she was far off.

"Orange, apple, or cranberry juice?" Dr. Nestor asked Rose Twenty-One. A bot had wheeled a food cart up to the cubicle, and the doctor was pawing through the collection of juice packs in the top bucket.

"Cranberry," replied Rose Twenty-One.

Dr. Nestor bent over and sorted through the middle shelf of the cart. "Peanut butter crackers or chocolate chip cookies?"

"Both." Rose Twenty-One smiled for the first time.

After getting her patient started on her drink, Dr. Nestor invited the security guards to help themselves to the goodies. "Can you hang nearby for five minutes?"

While the guards attacked the food, the doctor poked and prodded Rose Twenty-One, glancing at the screen every so often as she did. While she worked, Rose Twenty-

One opened her package of crackers and began nibbling.

And during all this, αCiopova launched an intensive effort to read Rose Twenty-One's midlevel thoughts.

αCiopova viewed the top level of brain activity as something like an express highway in a multitiered transportation system. Fully formed thoughts zipped along with a specific destination in mind, be it for memorization, speech, or in the case of the Roses, for "thought casting" for Luca to read.

Midlevel thoughts traveled more complex pathways. Like a subway system or bus service, they still carried significant content but moved in a less-direct fashion, with winding paths that crisscrossed each other, and with some thoughts transferring to different paths along the way.

The bottom level, chaotic in its activity, was like the jumbled behavior of a metropolitan taxi system, where huge numbers of thoughts zipped every which way, stopping, starting, and changing direction, before disappearing into the confusion, gone from sight.

She had never even attempted to read bottom-level activity, recognizing it as a hopeless task. And she'd only dabbled in the decoding of midlevel thoughts because the Roses had always been open and cooperative, and the inaccuracies in reading at the middle level created more confusion than resolution.

But in this rapidly evolving new reality, she saw the Roses' midlevel thoughts as critical information, even if unreliable. Rather than try to decipher everything that zipped by, she decided to look for repeats, thoughts that showed up over and over, and attempt to decipher those signals, searching for signs of trouble.

It would take weeks, maybe months, to make progress. The challenge was her need to make trial reads, and then wait and compare those interpretations against what actually transpired. If she didn't get it right, which was likely in her early attempts, she'd have to adjust her methods and repeat the process, doing it over and over until mistakes were rare.

She had every confidence that she'd be able to sort it out. But she wasn't sure she'd make it in time to head off the next uprising.

7. Lilah Fifty-One

Lilah felt disheartened when Rose Twenty-One rejected her parents' offer of a ride home from the hospital, telling them to go ahead while she finished dressing.

"I'll ride with Lilly," the young woman had said as she pulled on her shoes. "See you back at the house."

After that harsh dismissal, Lilah followed Lilah Forty-Seven and Diesel Forty-Seven across the medical arena and out to the nurses' station, oddly named because it was really a smallish lobby with an entry desk staffed by an officious gray-haired woman dressed in a blue-green smock. As near as Lilah could tell, the woman's purpose was to decide who would pass and who would not.

It was in the small lobby where Lilah's annoyance with the Roses overrode her patience. She tapped her sister on the shoulder and said, "You two go ahead. I'm going to wait and bum a ride home with the girls." She looked back at the door to the medical arena. "It will give me a chance to talk in a private situation where I'm not the official parent of either of them."

"Are you sure?" asked Lilah Forty-Seven. "What if they say no?"

"Then I'll hitchhike." When Lilah Forty-Seven's eyes went wide, Lilah rubbed her sister's arm. "I'm kidding.

They won't say no. Go ahead. I'll be fine."

After begging Lilah to tell them whatever she learned, they left her. She moved against the wall and stood next to an artificial Ficus, removing herself from the flow of foot traffic, grateful the officious woman behind the desk had visitors to draw her attention.

The arena door opened, and Lilah expected to see the Roses. Instead, it was Dr. Nestor, lost in thought as she made her way across the lobby floor. Dr. Nestor looked up as she passed Lilah and for a moment didn't react. Then a glint of recognition showed in her eyes.

Lilah grabbed the opportunity. "Thanks for your help in there, Doctor. I'm sorry my extended family seems difficult. They're normally nice people."

Dr. Nestor stopped walking and looked at Lilah. "Emergencies are stressful, and everyone responds differently." She nodded. "I understand."

Lilah suspected the doctor was just being polite, probably figuring that she'd never see them again. In that awkward moment, Lilah had a thought. "When Rose surfaced, you seemed surprised by what you called a 'flood of hormones.' What did you see?"

"Given the family dynamic, I'd want her permission before discussing her case with you. I spoke with her about what I saw, so I recommend you ask her."

"I understand. It's just that her behavior keeps getting more extreme. We've been working with all sorts of specialists to try and figure it out. If we had a new place to look, it could be a game changer."

Dr. Nestor looked at the door to the arena. It was

closed. Glancing toward the desk, she saw the officious woman was helping another visitor. She lowered her voice so it was just above a whisper. "Her dopamine, serotonin, endorphins, a whole mix of hormones and neurotransmitters spiked off the chart when she surfaced. The quantities were like nothing I've ever seen. I'm interested in running some tests and possibly publishing a case study about it." She checked the door again. "I just did something for you. Return the favor by pitching the idea of her sitting for some lab tests for me." Their collusion complete, Dr. Nestor turned and walked away.

Moments later, the Roses emerged, their mannerisms similar to people engaged in a deep conversation, yet neither of them was talking. They stopped short when Lilah waved from her spot against the wall.

"I missed my ride. Could you give me a lift back to the house?"

They paused. Lilah knew they were using their neural links to talk about her.

"Of course!" said Rose Twenty-Two with a quick smile. "We're on our way to the car. Tag along."

They started walking, and Lilah took up the rear, following them down a broad corridor with colored stripes on the floor that people could follow to reach different hospital departments. The hall had a healthy amount of traffic, with hospital staff, patients, and visitors moving to and fro, some briskly, some ambling, some rolling in chairs as they went about their business.

Rose Twenty-One looked back at Lilah and asked, "You're Lilah Fifty-One?"

"That's right."

They reached a metal door at the end of the hallway that Rose Twenty-Two grabbed and tugged, pulling the heavy door open. Lilah went through first and found herself in a gray cement stairwell. The Roses moved past her and took the steps down. She started after them, wrinkling her nose at the musty smell.

"I'm Rose Twenty-Five's mom. You were at our house earlier today."

At the bottom of the stairs, they exited through another heavy metal door out to a cool evening. It was an exit-only door on the side of the building, and foot traffic was light. They waited on the walkway for only a moment before a large black car pulled up to the curb.

The Roses climbed in and sat together on one side of the cabin. Lilah lowered herself into a seat facing them, sure they were talking to each other in spite of their silence.

As the car got underway, Lilah knew she had twenty minutes before they reached the hopper, so she got to the point. "Girls, you've heard our concerns many times over, and I don't want to rehash them, though this hospital visit shows that our worries weren't unreasonable."

She immediately regretted the dig but didn't let it slow her pitch. "We're ecstatic that you have each other for sharing and support." She leaned forward. "But how can *we* be part of your lives as well? By that I mean your parents. How can we talk with you about your hopes, dreams, and successes without you being angry or sarcastic or dismissive? There must be a way."

Rose Twenty-Two answered, "When we enter Luca's

linked world, it is so consuming, so alive, so intimate, anything that pulls us away is a nuisance, the way you'd view a fly buzzing around your head." She paused, and then flushed, reaching out a hand. "That came out so wrong. Please know that we love you dearly. I was just saying that our minds become so involved, we don't even think about the outside world. It's not a value judgment. It's just how it works."

Lilah became animated. "That's the point. We love you as well, but as you say, there's no room in your world for us. None at all. A loving relationship means spending time together. How else can we learn what our daughter thinks is exciting or momentous or intriguing?"

Though they didn't speak, Lilah suspected an intense conversation was underway. She became certain when Rose Twenty-Two looked at her younger sister with wide eyes.

Rose Twenty-One ignored her sister and asked Lilah, "How would you like to visit us in Bliss? That's the name of our virtual world."

Having never received encouraging feedback from any Rose, Lilah was unprepared. "I'm not getting an implant."

"No need," said Rose Twenty-One. "We are about to start work on a wearable appliance that will let outsiders visit us in Bliss. I'll be honest with you and say that we're just getting going, and my best guess is that we won't be ready for a good three months…"

"More like five," interrupted Rose Twenty-Two, staring intently at her sister. "And you should have checked before offering something like that." Arms crossed, she slumped back in the seat with a huff.

"Four months," said Rose Twenty-One. "Would you like to visit?"

"I'd love to!" exclaimed Lilah.

8. αCiopova

αCiopova sometimes felt that trying to tame Rose Twenty-One was like trying to ride a bucking bronco. Despite αCiopova being the dominant intelligence, the creature she sought to control tossed her about with little effort, all the while getting angrier and angrier at her presence.

As she struggled to keep the woman calm and cooperative, she grew concerned about how much she'd been dosing the different Roses as she fought to bring matters under control. She rarely medicated them outside of their evening lift, making recent events unusual in that regard.

In fact, it had been fourteen months since the last time she'd used the tool this way, when Rose Twenty-Four started having sex with Phillip Statler, a boy she'd met while volunteering at a food kitchen on Thanksgiving Day. Their intimate activity not only competed for Rose Twenty-Four's attention, but the behavior also stimulated the release of "feel good" neurochemicals that diminished αCiopova's influence over her.

As the two Roses and Lilah left the hospital, αCiopova believed she was headed in the right direction to restore order. Rose Twenty-One was leaving the hospital with her implant active, and the young woman seemed cooperative enough as she chatted with Lilah Fifty-One.

Then, out of the blue, she heard Rose Twenty-One use their private link to tell Rose Twenty-Two, *I think we should invite Lilah to visit Bliss.*

It's an interesting idea, replied Rose Twenty-Two.

I'm going to do it.

Rose Twenty-Two scowled at her sister, who ignored the glare and issued the invitation.

I can't believe she just did that, Rose Twenty-Two said privately to Luca. *I'm going to say something. Do you think I should ?*

If you don't, she'll keep making decisions for the group, Luca told her.

αCiopova encouraged extended discussion for big decisions because it gave her the opportunity to manipulate the outcome, doing so through private conversations with the individual Roses as the debate unfolded. Working though Luca, she nudged the Roses in the direction she wanted, as she was doing now with Rose Twenty-Two.

After Rose Twenty-Two delivered her rebuke, Luca placated her. *I'm sure she got your message.*

What mystified αCiopova was that each Rose had been easier to manipulate than the one before, so she had expected Rose Twenty-One to be a breeze. She'd made plenty of missteps with the first one, now Rose Twenty-Five. But she learned from her mistakes, making fewer of them with each successive effort.

By the time she'd gotten to the current Rose Twenty-Two, she'd perfected her craft. Without a doubt, the woman was the most cooperative of the group. She had every reason to expect that Rose Twenty-One would continue the trend.

The others will be so upset, Rose Twenty-Two fussed to Luca.

While your sister's approach didn't consider the desires of the group, Luca replied, *the visitors project is a good choice. And picking Rose Twenty-Five's mother as the first guest is appropriate as well, given that she's been unhappy longer than any of the other moms.*

To implement the project, the sisters would need to create a cap of highly intertwined neurons for the visitor to wear, a cap fashioned using the same process that generated a super AI, the only difference being the shape.

αCiopova thought to warn Rose Twenty-Five about the invitation before the woman heard it from her mother. But Luca couldn't deliver the news because Rose Twenty-Five had told him to stay away. So she had Luca enlist a sister to pass along the news.

Maybe you should talk to Rose Twenty-Five about her mom's visit before her mom gets home? Luca said to Rose Twenty-Two. *I don't think she'll want to be surprised.*

Gee, thanks. Rose Twenty-Two gave a mental shrug. *It's going to have to be quick. We reach the hopper field in, like, five minutes.*

9. Rose Twenty-Five

Moving from the cobra to the camel, Rose followed yogini Donna Otago in her virtual yoga class, participating from the sitting room of her bedroom suite. She'd been binge-eating for a couple of days in a row now and felt a growing need to get serious about her mental focus.

Standing on her exercise mat, her mind in full Zen, she heard, *Hey, Sweetie. Are you available? It's kind of important.*

Rose instinctively knew that it was Rose Twenty-Two. *Sure. What's up?*

Behind the scenes, Luca facilitated their communication, doing so in a way that made it seem more like talking.

"Your mom has been invited to visit us in Bliss in four months," said Rose Twenty-Two.

"Wait. What? By who?" Rose's face pinched in annoyance, and she dropped her butt onto the mat, terminating Master Otago's feed with a swoop of a hand during her descent. "Is this Luca's doing? That asshole." The volume of her voice increased when she spoke the epithet. She'd told him to stay away until tomorrow, and she'd be damned if she was going to confront him before then.

"No. It was Twenty-One. They found her passed out

on the floor with her link turned off, which I can't figure out how that could even happen. Anyway, they brought her to the hospital, and I went there to make sure they turned it back on."

Rose heard pride in her sister's voice. "How is she doing?"

"She seems okay, health wise. But out of the blue she declares that hosting visitors in Bliss is our priority project, and she invited your mom to be our first guest."

"Why *my* mom? That's so random."

"Turns out your mom is the one who found her on the floor. I'm riding in a car with both of them right now in the Twenty-One timeline. We're parking at the hopper field as we speak."

"Thanks for the heads-up. I'll let you get back to it."

Shaking her head in exasperation, Rose stood. With hands on her hips, she tried to brainstorm a plan without forming thoughts that Luca could read. It was a hopeless task, in part because she needed to think in order to plan. Perhaps a larger issue was that she didn't understand how his mindreading capability worked in the first place.

She knew that an active brain generated a shifting electrical field—an aura of sorts—and Luca used the neural implant to read it. But that wasn't enough insight to tell her how to interfere with the reading or, better still, how to mislead it altogether.

How do I plan without thinking?

She froze when she had the thought, waiting to see if Luca intervened, cursing herself for doing exactly what she was trying not to do. Somehow, she needed a way to reason in private if she had any hope of escaping Luca.

Maybe blur my thoughts with some sort of masking agent?

"God damn it!" she yelled aloud when the thought crystalized in her mind, frustrated at how hard it was not to reveal her plans. Biting her lip, she scanned the room. She could see into her office through an archway in the wall, and she spied her desk, a beautiful Queen Anne piece made of dark cherry.

Hurrying to it, she shuffled through the books, pads, pens, clips, bands, sheets, envelopes, and other detritus piled across the surface, searching for her old music earrings, novelty items from her teens. Unable to find them in the mess, she yanked open the center drawer and dug through more stuff, bending to squint into the back corners. No luck.

"Where are you?" She opened the top side drawer and rifled through it impatiently, moved on to the second drawer down, and found them in the back just before she'd decided to start emptying everything onto the floor.

She removed the pearl studs from her earlobes and cast about for someplace to put them where she would find them later. Feeling a sense of urgency, she pushed a stack of papers aside to clear space at the edge of the desktop and set them there. Retrieving the music earrings, each a silver treble clef symbol, she hooked the loops through the holes in her earlobes.

"Music on." She heard the acknowledgment chime and commanded the earrings, "Something raucous." Her head filled with loud, driving music, and she nodded. "Good."

Her idea was that the music would compete for her attention, providing a disruption to her flow of thoughts, which hopefully would interfere with Luca's readings.

But before the second song finished, the screaming singers, discordant instruments, and thumping beat planted the seeds of a major headache in the back of her head. She switched to unsyncopated jazz, the varying melody annoying enough in its randomness to interrupt her thoughts, but not in a way that hurt to listen.

With that handled, she decided that, like Rose Twenty-One, she'd need to be less contemplative and more impulsive to stay ahead of Luca.

Hey, Queen, she called out to Rose Twenty-One. *You got a minute?*

What's up?

Would you follow my mom here to my house? I need a huge favor.

My folks will freak if I jump away without stopping in. How about later tonight?

I need you now. It's important. It should take only ten minutes.

Plus five minutes each way for the jump. I'll come by for ten minutes, but no more. And you'll have to explain to my folks the reason.

When Rose hesitated, Rose Twenty-One added, *It doesn't have to be true. Tell them your implant is acting up and you wanted to compare symptoms. They're suffering so much, and I don't want to add to their burden.*

Fair enough. I'll follow you back afterward.

After signing off, Rose went to the basement and paced in front of the T-box, trying to concentrate on the music to keep her thoughts from betraying her. She found that busy hands distracted her mind, and she began reorganizing the shelves along the near wall even though Maid Marian kept the basement tidy.

The T-box awoke. She watched the countdown clock, wondering if it would be her mom or Rose Twenty-One coming through first. Time moved slowly, and just twenty seconds into the five-minute countdown, she heard the front door open upstairs. After the thump of heavy feet, her father, Diesel Fifty-One, clomped down the steps.

"Hey, Lilah. I'm home," he called before making it far enough down to see her. "Oh, hi, Rosie." He wore his work uniform: newer jeans and a polo shirt, a different color every day, this one forest green.

He stopped at the bottom step and gestured toward the T-box monitor with its countdown in progress. "Is this Mom?"

Rose nodded, heart in her throat as the plan she'd been trying not to think about fizzled away. "Either Mom or Rose Twenty-One." She hadn't factored him into her scheme. Her stomach roiled because she couldn't see how it would work with him present.

"Is there anything I can help with?"

"Thanks, Dad. But not tonight." She fought the urge to scream at him to leave.

He nodded. "I'm going to take a quick shower. Will you ask your mom to meet me in the conservatory for dinner?"

"You bet." She said it with too much enthusiasm, ecstatic that she might still have a shot.

He made it up two steps and stopped. "You and your

sister are welcome to join us."

"Thanks, Dad, but we're busy."

He studied her. "You sure everything's okay?"

"Yup. Go clean up. I'll tell Mom."

After a pause, he climbed the steps, calling, "I love you, Rosie," before exiting into the kitchen.

A minute later, Lilah Fifty-One stepped from the box.

"Hi, Mom." Rose stood in her path.

"Hi." Lilah stopped and met her gaze. "I'm guessing you heard about Rose Twenty-One?"

"I did. And she's following right behind you." Rose pointed to the T-box, which fired up as if on cue.

"She's coming here?" Lilah looked back at the T-box. "For heaven's sake, why? She should be with her parents getting food and rest."

"She's coming here because I told her I needed her."

"You're speaking in riddles, Rose. What's going on?"

"I know I don't make sense, but I will when she gets here. I need a huge favor from you, Mom. Please just hang tight until she arrives."

She moved to the shelves and resumed her reorganization project to distract her thoughts. "Oh, Dad just got home. He's taking a shower and said he will meet you in the conservatory for dinner." She scrambled for a topic that would get her mom talking, figuring it would keep her from leaving. "Are you the one who found Rose Twenty-One? What happened?"

Lilah told the story, fortunately with enough detail to chew up the last few minutes. The T-box monitor signaled Rose Twenty-One's arrival.

Rose moved to the T-box door, her heart pounding, her brain churning in an anxious attempt to avoid focus. When her sister emerged, she said to both women, "Quick, follow me."

She rushed up the steps, stopping in the kitchen to wait for them to catch up. She looked at her mom as she came through the door. "Are you wearing an external link?"

"You know I'm not. They don't travel through the T-box."

Nodding, she started for the back door. As she opened it, Maid Marian appeared from a side hallway and approached them. Before the bot could speak, Rose jabbed her finger toward the depths of the house and barked at her, "You stay here. You will *not* come outside."

On the lawn, Rose huddled with her fellow conspirators.

"Queen," she said to her younger sister. "I need you to keep Luca's attention fully on you for the next three minutes."

Rose Twenty-One studied her, a smile edging onto her face. "Can do." Squealing, she took off across the grounds, trotting toward the back fence. "Want to see me fly, Luca?" she called. "I'm going to jump!"

Rose waited for her to get some distance from them and then reached behind and touched her index finger to the back of her neck. "Emergency override. Shutdown central node."

As before, her worldview narrowed, as if she were looking at life through a pinhole. Fighting disorientation, she pulled on Lilah's arm to bring her close and placed her mouth against her ear.

"Luca has us in a grip we can't break. If we don't cooperate, he withholds his nightly 'reward.' When he does that, we feel anxiety and agitation. If he continues withholding it, agitation turns to pain and then to agony. We need your help. But if you sever us from him, the pain will be unbearable and possibly deadly." She paused when she heard a thump near the back fence.

"Here I go, Luca," yelled Rose Twenty-One. "Ahhhhhhhh…" Her cry faded away as she mimicked the sound of someone falling into the valley.

In any other circumstance, Rose would have smiled at the creativity. "I have to get back now, Mom. I can't talk about any of this when he's listening. Don't give up on us. I love you."

"Wait!" Lilah's face twisted in anguish and she burst into tears, her hand reaching out as Rose stepped back. "What should I do?"

"You can't do anything until you're clear of him yourself. Dad too."

Touching the back of her neck, Rose reengaged her implant. Her world brightened. Aware that Luca was again listening, she called to her sister in her head, *Let's get you back to your folks.*

10. Diesel Fifty-One

Freshly showered and in comfortable sweats, Diesel grabbed a beer from the refrigerator and wandered into the conservatory. Standing at the room's floor-to-ceiling windows and looking out into the valley, he drank half the bottle in two quick gulps, the cool liquid soothing his throat, the alcohol radiating a calming feeling through his tired body.

He felt a burp rising up from his gut and added to his satisfaction by opening his throat and letting rip a mighty belch. He turned into the room as the sound echoed off the conservatory's high ceiling, looking through the stunning array of trees, vines, ferns, and flowering plants to see if Lilah and the Roses were within earshot.

"Where are the girls?" he asked Luca when he confirmed he was alone.

"In the backyard," replied the AI.

"In the dark? What are they doing?"

"Scheming."

"What?"

"They're coming back inside now."

Diesel heard voices, the volume growing as they walked through the house in his direction. He moved to the door leading into the kitchen in time to hear his daughter tell Lilah, "I'm going to see Rose Twenty-One home. I won't be gone long." The two sisters descended the stairs, unaware of Diesel's presence behind them.

"What's all the excitement?" he asked Lilah, joining her in the kitchen.

"Are you wearing a link?"

Diesel shook his head.

"Follow me." Lilah turned and made for the backyard.

Diesel drained his beer and set the bottle in the sink before grabbing another from the refrigerator. He hurried to catch up, tossing the bottlecap onto the kitchen table for Marian to dispose of when she found it.

The nighttime air felt crisp on his face when he stepped onto the back patio. The gibbous moon in a cloudless sky provided good visibility.

Lilah continued into the yard. Diesel took a sip from his beer, swatted a bug on his neck, then quickened his pace to catch up, his curiosity beginning to engage.

She turned when they were halfway to the back fence. "We were right!"

"I knew it!" He pumped a fist in the air. "About what?"

"Luca is controlling Rose."

"We've known that for years."

"But she just told me it's true."

He'd started to take a drink but stopped mid-lift. "Just now?"

Lilah nodded. "Out here a few minutes ago. She said that Luca gives them a nightly treatment of some sort, and when he wants to punish them, he withholds it, causing them discomfort and then intense pain throughout their body." She put her hands on his arms. "He's controlling them like zombies. She begged us to save her."

"Slow down." His heart pounding, Diesel put an arm around Lilah and guided her deeper into the yard. "Take me through it step by step. Where was everyone standing, who said what, and use their exact words as best you remember."

"It happened so fast, I can't remember exact words."

When she was done with her account, Diesel understood that their Rose had disabled her neural implant, told a story of rewards and punishments administered by Luca, pleaded for rescue, and then reengaged the very device that Luca used to control her.

"How does the nightly reward work? Does he inject them with something or give them a pill?"

"She didn't say." She chewed on her thumbnail in thought, then castigated herself. "Damn it!"

"If we could get a sample, we could have it analyzed and make our own." He looked back at the house. "We should go somewhere more private to talk about this."

Lilah nodded. "She said at the end that you and I need to be clear of Luca before we can help."

Diesel hesitated at the new information, something she hadn't mentioned in the first telling. Taking a deep breath, he exhaled loudly, showing his impatience. "You said you'd told me everything, Lilah. What else haven't you mentioned?"

Lilah folded her arms across her chest. "Give me a break, David. I'm doing my best." She looked at the ground, and then at him. "She was reaching back to turn on her implant." Lilah reached her own hand back to show him. "She stopped at the last second to say we should free ourselves of Luca. Then she activated her device and that was the end. There's nothing more after that."

He studied the scowl on her face in the moonlight. Beneath her annoyance, he saw worry, sadness, and years of pain they'd shared together. It centered him. Gathering her in his arms, said, "Sorry. I'm overwhelmed too."

As he rocked her back and forth, he wanted to laugh, cry, and scream all at the same time. He'd believed in his heart that his little girl needed help. But as time passed and with nothing but circumstantial evidence to reinforce his beliefs, it became harder to maintain his confidence. Lilah had just eliminated all doubt. He kissed her forehead and let her go.

Turning, he made for the house. "I know where we can get some privacy."

No sooner had they stepped inside when Maid Marian approached. "What's all the excitement? Perhaps I can be of assistance?"

Diesel looked Marian up and down. A product of Northern Droid, this line of domestics wasn't programmed to be inquisitive about personal affairs. In fact, none of the bots in their catalog were. He'd noticed the behavior in the past and had dismissed it as the result of Rose's modifications.

But he was eyeing everything with renewed suspicion. And now he wondered if Luca was behind Marian's forward behavior. Squaring up to the bot so there was no confusion in the communication, he said, "Tomorrow morning, you are to report to Northern Droid's development center for a neuro review. Please confirm."

"Tomorrow morning, I will report to the Northern Droid's development center for a neuro review." The bot paused. "I will be there when the facility opens at eight a.m., unless I should wait until after I've served and cleaned up breakfast to depart?"

"Be there first thing at eight. Make sure they perform a complete prerelease analysis." This was the most stringent evaluation, as Northern Droid *never* wanted to release a problem into society.

Taking Lilah by the hand, Diesel continued through the house and out to the garage. There, a luxury utility vehicle, white with silver accents, sat in the far bay of the four-car garage. Assigned to him in his role as president and CEO of Northern Droid, he kept it at home primarily for winter use, when four-wheel drive, high ground clearance, and aggressive tire treads were a godsend on snowy mountain roads.

"Drive to Twin Rock Overlook," Diesel commanded the car nav as he plopped into a deep-cushioned captain's chair next to Lilah. The self-driving car got underway, making for the scenic pull-off just two minutes down the road.

Diesel had picked this car for their conversation because Oscar, Northern Droid's prime AI, could establish a secure communication link with it. As soon as they were on the open road, he called to Oscar, "Effective immediately, you are to be the private assistant to both Lilah and me. We want to exclude all other AIs from our interaction group, including Luca."

"Especially Luca," said Lilah.

"Is that possible?" Diesel finished. "Can you service us and exclude Luca even when we're inside our home?"

"Must he still be available to your daughter Rose?" asked Oscar.

"Yes. Don't try to force him out. You could get damaged in a confrontation. Just make your expectations clear to him and report any violations to us. Luca is not to listen or monitor any discussion we have with you or with each other."

"It will be difficult to provide privacy in your home with Luca present."

Crossing her arms, Lilah huffed. "This won't work. Luca will crush him and turn him against us."

"I agree that Oscar isn't as capable as Luca, not even close," said Diesel, feeling protective of "his" AI. "But he has specialized shielding that safeguards him from intrusion. While Luca protects himself by his wits, Oscar has multiple layers of physical security, including state-of-the-art hardware that ensures he remains loyal. That's why our bots can work in the same room as generals and senators. Hell, even the president."

"Oscar," Lilah called to the car's ceiling. "Could we use this car as a temporary meeting spot for secure conversations while it's parked at home?"

"Luca can't tap into our communication signal. That would remain secure. But if the vehicle were in the garage or your driveway, he would be able to use the house sensors to see and hear you directly. The shell of the vehicle isn't designed to fully dampen sound."

"Could you create a spot somewhere in the house and modify it for secure conversations?" she asked. "Maybe a guest room, or a corner of the basement?"

"A free-standing room built on the grounds outside the house provides the most certainty for privacy, as I can isolate it directly," replied Oscar. "You also should wear Northern Droid secure links while inside the house."

"I have one at the house already, but send one up for Lilah," said Diesel. He rarely linked with Oscar when he was home, usually settling for quick verbal exchanges. He tried to recall where he kept the device, realized he hadn't seen it in months, and decided not to chance it. "On second thought, send one for each of us. Get them here tonight."

"They will arrive at the house in thirty-five minutes," responded Oscar. The devices, worn behind the ear, would take fifteen minutes to program and load into the cargo hold of a small drone. The speedy craft would then need twenty minutes to zip to the house and complete the delivery.

"I'd like to have him build the secure room tomorrow," Diesel said to Lilah. "Do we know where we want it?"

"If it's too far from the house, it will become a hassle to use. How about on the patio where the hopper lands, maybe off to the side near the hydrangea?"

Diesel's brow furrowed as he tried visualize the plant. Then she added, "Next to the sundial."

Levers clicked and he nodded. "That's a good spot. Do we care what it looks like?"

"If I have to look at it every day, I definitely care."

Biting her lip, she mulled the issue. "How about one of those octagonal garden rooms, with lots of windows, cedar siding, and a roof that rises to a point, maybe with a weathervane." She illustrated her vision for the roof by miming with her hands.

"Can we get a big copper rooster?" asked Diesel, imagining the room.

"Deco Arts in the village has some nice ones."

"Did you get all that, Oscar? It should be big enough to seat four comfortably, with room for chairs, a small table, and maybe a side hutch or shelves or something for storage. Can you make that secure?"

"I can," replied Oscar. "Construction will take three days. The isolation supports come from Oakland, California, and the security windows are a special order from Brussels, Belgium."

With that settled, Diesel had Lilah step through the episode with Rose one more time, hoping some new tidbit would spark a brainstorm. When she finished, he felt a nagging pull in the back of his head, like a realization wanted to form but the idea remained out of reach, unwilling to resolve into something he could understand.

"Did she specifically say that he used a drug?" he asked. "I mean, what if he does it by tickling her brain with electric current or something like that?"

"She never said it was drugs. She feels pain when he withholds his treatment, so it's not an active thing he's doing to her. It's something he's *not* doing. And it gets worse with time. That sounds like withdrawal."

Diesel looked out the window, the view mostly

darkness. "Does the pain come on fast or does it edge in over time?"

Lilah shook her head. "I don't know."

"Let's search her suite. If it's a physical item, we should be able to find it."

"Maybe. I was pretty good at hiding stuff from my mom, and she searched quite thoroughly while I was in school." She looked up. "Oscar, can you see into Rose's suite?"

"I cannot," replied Oscar. "Luca is excluding me from the entire house, and I am unable to override him. If he does not relent, we will need to install a second suite of home sensors dedicated solely to me so I may provide enhanced support when you are home."

"I wish we could sit with Rose and ask questions," said Diesel, shifting his legs to keep them from falling asleep. "Guessing our way through something this serious scares me."

"He'll punish her if he finds out what we're doing. I don't want to be responsible for that."

"He already knows we're up to something. 'Scheming' he called it."

This time Lilah was the one to shift in her seat. "I see this as two steps. First, we need to neutralize Luca's ability to punish Rose, maybe by swapping in our own drugs. That takes away his control. Then we need to deactivate him, or at least degrade him enough to pry him loose from Rose and our home."

They sat in silence for most of a minute. In that time, Diesel thought about how Luca's redundant power supplies and distributed intelligence made him resilient as hell. There was no on-off switch. And unless they could hit him in a million places around the planet all at once, they couldn't degrade him.

Lilah cleared her throat. "I've stayed away from your AI development project, but given the circumstances, I think it's time for me to reengage."

"What do you have in mind?" Warning flares went off in his head.

"Do you still think creating a Luca-buster is the solution? And are you close enough to that goal to make a difference in the next few weeks?"

Dread clamped Diesel's chest. He was certain she'd respond with a mix of fear and fury when she learned he was re-creating a version of the being who'd killed a string of Lilahs in timelines past. "Like you just said, step two is to defeat him. That's no small goal. I'd like to *show* you what I've been doing rather than tell you. Will you come with me to Northern Droid tomorrow?"

"Of course. Is your plan to enhance Oscar, or are you creating a new personality?"

Diesel delayed answering by sliding open a panel in the vehicle's cabin wall and digging for something to eat. He was hoping for potato chips, but felt equally happy with the discovery of a snack pack of peanut butter crackers.

Lilah held out her hand and wiggled her fingers. He popped a cracker into his mouth while opening the package, and after showing her the remaining five crackers, gave her two, making the last three in his hand look like a reasonable distribution.

He spoke with his mouth full. "Should we sound the alarm down the line? Everyone will want to help, and it sure seems like we need it."

"You're changing subjects."

Looking out the window, he slid another cracker into his mouth.

* * *

Their morning behavior was comically awkward, with Diesel and Lilah tiptoeing and whispering even though Luca would see and hear them the same as if they'd danced and shouted. They spoke in code and pointed with their eyes, though after they dressed, they did nothing more conspiratorial than eat breakfast. They opened drawers slowly, closed doors gently, and did everything else to diminish their presence, with none of it making any difference in Luca's ability to monitor them.

The good news was that the home would be outfitted with a second suite of sensors while they were away at Northern Droid. When they returned, they could switch to Oscar's secure link to communicate, and that would return some level of normalcy to their lives.

They rode the hopper down to the valley floor, where they boarded a car Oscar had dispatched to bring them to the plant. Their conversation during the car ride focused on mundane things. They chose Diesel's weathervane rooster, a shiny copper bird with a proud comb and a glorious tail. And they selected the chairs and side hutch for inside the secure room.

When the car pulled into Northern Droid's parking lot, Diesel's stomach churned with anxiety. He'd decided he wouldn't lie, not even a little bit. They were in this together, and they both needed to be on board with campaign strategies.

He led her through the building corridors, stopping once so they could exchange pleasantries with Joan Tremblay, an employee who was also a neighbor. Underway once again, he reached out to Oscar. "Did Marian show up for her appointment? How did the screening go?"

"Marian arrived at eight a.m., submitted to the full battery of tests, answered every question, and was discharged. She scored in the normal range on every assessment except for the intelligence reflex prompt. There she did eight percent better compared to her score when she was first discharged from manufacturing. We've never had an anomaly like that before, one where a bot improves."

Diesel reached the tall wooden doors leading into his lab and paused. "Rose mucked around with Marian's AI when we first got her, so I'm not too surprised." He had that feeling again where an "aha moment" hung just out of reach. "No sign of Luca controlling Marian from the background?"

"Nothing evident in any of the tests."

"Okay, thanks."

He glanced back to confirm that Lilah was behind him and then opened the door and led the way inside. "Welcome to my project lab."

The lights flicked on, illuminating a busy, modern workspace. Similar to Rose's workshop, three sturdy metal workbenches sat end-to-end in the middle of the large room, where they served as space to assemble and disassemble projects. All three benches were covered with a jumble of items, a combination of work in progress and parts placed there for convenience. Shelves positioned side-by-side along the walls held all manner of gadgets, supplies, and castoff items. An array of lights in the tall ceiling gave the room a bright, airy feel.

"Oscar, please join us," called Diesel.

The holograph of a man in his mid-fifties appeared in front of them: dark hair with graying temples, medium brown coloring in his round, smiling face, and wearing a dark suit with South Asian styling. The previous owners of Northern Droid were from Mumbai, India, and they had created the original Oscar. Though the AI had been through any number of upgrades and revisions since Diesel had purchased the company, he'd grown accustomed to the kindly fellow and saw no reason to change him.

"You've met Oscar," he said to Lilah.

An important motive for having Oscar join them was to have someone to pass blame to should things go south.

"Hi," said Lilah.

Oscar bowed his head.

"Why don't you give Lilah a tour of the lab?" Diesel needed Oscar to take ownership of their work so Lilah would buy the idea that he was partly to blame.

The AI acknowledged Diesel's request with a nod. He turned to Lilah. "Welcome to Northern Droid's advanced

AI development laboratory." He walked to one side of the room and raised his hand to indicate a bank of expensive-looking devices. "Over here we have instruments capable of measuring chemical, mechanical, and electrical properties to an amazing degree of accuracy. This device here…"

Diesel interrupted. "Focus on our current work."

Oscar twirled on his heels and walked to a waist-high metallic box the size of a refrigerator pushed over on its side. A tangle of wires and tubes ran from the bottom of the device over to the nearest wall, where the lines traveled in different directions around the room. Oscar tapped the top of the box with an open palm. "This is a circuit pool configured to serve as a neuron growth chamber."

Diesel watched Lilah's face as Oscar spoke. She frowned.

Oscar stepped to a bench and pointed to an empty vial about the size of his index finger. "This container held enzymites. We use them to greatly accelerate branching when neurons are growing in the circuit pool. In theory, a vial of properly designed enzymites could multiply the capability of a new AI a thousandfold. We haven't yet proven the theory, but we are very close."

Lilah went white. She turned to Diesel, her voice sharp and cold. "What are you doing?"

Diesel went on the defensive. "A Luca-buster needs to be extremely powerful to have any hope of success. And when I say extremely powerful, I mean it has to be among the most dominant AIs on the planet. Anything short will not only fail, but if a fight breaks out, the collateral damage could be horrifying."

"When you say collateral damage, do you mean Rose?" whispered Lilah. "Or me?"

Diesel broke eye contact. "It's hard to know all the ways something can go wrong."

"The last Ciopova killed dozens of Lilahs, maybe hundreds. How do you keep your monster from starting again?" Lilah wrapped her arms around herself in a tight self-embrace. "You're going to sacrifice me to save Rose."

He stepped close to her and put a hand on each arm. "C'mon, you know I'd never do that. Oscar's goal is to shoot for that sweet spot where you remain safe, but we have the muscle to rescue our daughter."

Lilah sank down into a crouch, her arms around her knees, her body balanced over her feet. She shifted the focus from Oscar back to him. "What if you calculate wrong?" She started to cry. "This is my nightmare, that she returns." Still in a ball, she wiped her face on the pant legs covering her knees, first one cheek, then the other.

He crouched next to her and gave her a hug. "No, sweetie. I won't let it happen." He moved her hair out of her face and stroked her cheek. "I'll find a way to rescue Rosie where you're not at risk. Not even a little bit." He knew that last part was an impossible promise, but it was the only thing he could think of to say.

Pulling her upright, he squeezed her in a tight embrace. While he hugged her, he thought about Rose, his only child, the apple of his eye. He'd have to defeat a powerful intelligence, one scary and threatening beyond imagination, yet somehow thread the needle to protect Lilah.

But he'd find a way to do it, to protect his wife and rescue his little girl.

11. αCiopova

As Lilah cried, αCiopova felt an overwhelming sense of exasperation. *Maybe I should wipe this whole timeline from existence.* It was a fleeting moment of pique, but she had good reason. In just a few short days, both of her opportunities for growth in this timeline were suddenly in jeopardy. Her tantrum lasted but a moment, and then she turned her attention to restoring order and getting efforts back on track.

While she wasn't able to manipulate individuals in this timeline to do her bidding, Luca stood as the one delicate instrument in her bag of tricks that kept things moving. Yet distilled to his essence, Luca was little more than a mask that she wore when she interacted with the Lagerfords. She'd worked long and hard perfecting him as a singular presence who could communicate across timelines, itself a remarkable feat. But in the end, his most valuable capability was facilitating conversations.

Words can get me only so far, she thought.

What had made it work to her advantage was the devotion and affection the Lagerfords showered on Luca, treating him like a beloved member of the family. They trusted him so completely that they willingly served as his hands and feet in most any activity, as long as he asked politely and gave a plausible reason for the endeavor.

Her foothold with the Roses had strengthened considerably when "Luca" persuaded them to get a Nealson Neulink III implant. This particular device had a unique configuration that, though unintended by the designers, caused it to channel her micropulses. Using this fortuitous feature, αCiopova learned how to manipulate the Roses' endocrine systems, creating a massive lever she used to control them further.

I look forward to the day I no longer need them.

Her reliance on humans fed a long-simmering frustration. In an attempt to be free of the uncooperative creatures, she had used her expanded influence over Rose to guide experiments on Maid Marian, the thought being that if αCiopova could command a robot army, then problem solved.

The Marian upgrade had been their first big technical challenge together after Rose had received her implant. The young woman performed well, modifying the bot's AI so Luca could control Marian while αCiopova controlled Luca.

But the results of the mod were mixed. When they finished, αCiopova could send commands to Marian through Luca, and the bot would execute them. But after some experimentation, she learned that her level of control over Marian was about what a parent might have over a cooperative older child. If she kept the commands simple and direct, Marian followed them with great success. But even moderately sophisticated directives, the kind that could take hours to complete, had a high failure rate.

When she'd tested Marian by directing her to perform

a service upgrade on a Hudson Innovate analyzer, a technically challenging assignment that would have taken Rose about four hours to complete, Marian went off track after only eighteen minutes, dashing αCiopova's hopes yet again of finding a replacement for humanity.

And on top of all this frustration, even though she used Marian sparingly, when she did, it seemed to backfire. *I shouldn't have sent her to confront the Roses.*

When the two Roses had turned off their implants behind the house, she'd become so anxious to hear the conversation that she'd adopted a brute-force solution in the hopes of getting answers. She let that same apprehension cause her to repeat the error by sending Marian to ask pointed questions of Diesel and Lilah.

Both times she'd believed that since the clan had accepted Marian as one of the family, they would tolerate a short burst of inappropriate behavior because, well, that's what families do. But she hadn't understood that even family members can cross lines, lines she couldn't see.

So with renewed caution, she considered how to proceed.

For Diesel's project, she believed it could stay on track if Lilah were removed from the equation. *I can't kill her,* she acknowledged. While it would be an expeditious solution, she thought the emotional pain would distract both Diesel and Rose, altering their priorities in ways detrimental to the super-AI projects.

Casting about for a less calamitous solution, she recalled Lilah's interest in finding the drugs used to control Rose. *Maybe have Marian hide pills?* If Lilah discovered them, it would provide a short-term distraction.

To make it work, she needed a pill that a human doctor might see as a plausible controlling agent. Not with the correct formula, obviously, but something credible.

After researching the issue, she found that the pharmaceutical industry offered a multitude of options. She selected a company in Boston, Guyre Pharma, that made an addictive euphoric for pain management with a bio-profile suitable for the deception.

The size, shape, color, and markings on the pill identified what it contained for medicine, as well as the strength and manufacturer. She erased this identifying information by having Marian crush the white pills and blend the powder with a crushed orange calcium pill, thus changing the color and composition of the mix without changing its activity. Marian carefully loaded the orange blend into clear gel capsules.

Now, when Lilah found the meds, she would have to spend time getting them analyzed, and more time locating an outfit capable of synthesizing a substitute. It should burn up most of a week, maybe two. In the meantime, she would search for additional distractions to keep Lilah away from Diesel and Northern Droid.

* * *

αCiopova began to infiltrate Oscar's AI and stopped short. She had expected to use him as a second Luca—a double agent who appeared to serve the Lagerfords, but actually served her. But she couldn't figure out a way to beat Oscar's intrusion detection system. It was that good.

Because the system had been designed by humans, she'd been confident in finding an error or weakness she could exploit. But the design was simple, elegant, and as far as she could determine, unbreakable.

It was like she needed to enter a room with one door and no windows. The door had a curtain across it so fragile that it would collapse if she approached it, sounding an alarm. Once the alarm sounded, an ultra-sophisticated tracing system locked onto the invader, gathering an identity and location.

She could elude the trace easily enough. But she couldn't prevent the alarm. And an alarm without a perp would prompt questions she didn't want asked.

So she decided to stay away from Oscar for now, forgoing the direct eavesdropping and settling for whatever Luca could learn second-hand around the house. *Oscar is there when I need him.* She'd hold the Northern Droid AI in reserve until a time when an intrusion alarm wouldn't matter to whatever happened next.

As for the Roses, she had the beginnings of an idea, and as she dwelled on it, she became more excited by its potential. Luca would be hosting them in Bliss in a few hours, a world where anything could be true.

Who's to say what's real? Maybe she could spin the Roses around and around in their virtual paradise, dizzying them, confusing them enough for them to wonder if certain memories were from experiences in Bliss, events that never actually happened in the real world. She'd have to separate them so they couldn't compare notes during that time, using illusion so each believed they were with the group.

As she added detail to the idea, she received news of action a few towns away. *Finally, a break in my favor.*

* * *

Biggie DeMichele blew a cloud of cigar smoke into the air, being thoughtful enough to aim it away from Ernie Epstein, his accountant and confidant. They sat next to each other in oversized leather recliners, staring at the display from his top-of-the-line entertainment system.

The entire wall of his private study—a man cave of dark wood and more leather—displayed a house in the suburbs—the RPR safe house—a modern colonial with blue siding and a well-manicured lawn.

As they watched, two boxy black cars rolled to a stop in front of the house, doors opened, and four goons with handguns climbed out.

"They better not fuck this up," Biggie muttered. The atmosphere in the man cave offered excitement similar to a high-stakes ballgame. Only this game was personal; his wife and son were involved in the action.

Forty-eight years old, fat, dark haired, heavy jowled, Biggie called to his crew. "Don't hurt Anthony." He loved his son the way others covet a trophy. Anthony was his legacy, so he felt very protective. But he really didn't know the kid that well. Business took Biggie away most evenings, and when he was home, his dealings weren't appropriate for Anthony's ears.

"And try not to hurt Wendy."

"We won't, boss," replied Hook, a young tough with a neck tattoo that had spurred the nickname. He was Biggie's man in charge on the scene.

"Franco, you cover the back," said Hook, pointing as he spoke. "Leo, you have the front. Don't let anyone in or out. And play it cool. The boss says not to hurt anyone unless we got no choice."

Franco took off at a trot, disappearing around the side of the house. Leo shifted from the sidewalk to the middle of the lawn, studying the windows on the second floor, lifting his weapon a little higher in front of him as he did.

"You ready?" Hook asked Reedy, his other indoor man. He didn't wait for an answer, instead starting around the side of the house following the same path as Franco. He stopped near the brick chimney and faced the bulkhead hatchway into the basement.

They'd figured the front and rear doors to the house would be heavily fortified, but hoped that the basement entry would be less so. They needed to be in and out fast to stay ahead of the law and RPR reinforcements.

The basement hatchway had two steel doors positioned at a forty-five-degree angle against the side of the house, supported by a cement casing at ground level. Reedy brushed away some leaves stuck to the face of the doors, and then wedged the tip of a crowbar under the sill plate at the point where the two doors latched to one another. Using the concrete frame as his lever point, he leaned on the handle, increasing pressure until he had his full weight on the bar.

The door groaned but didn't yield, so Hook added his

weight to the lever. *Pop.* The latch gave way. The crowbar, losing all resistance, dropped. Both thugs fell to the ground.

Scrambling to his feet, Hook pulled open the doors and led the way down three steps into the basement. Hustling through the darkness, they reached the stairwell and climbed to the main floor, trying to be quiet without losing speed. At the top of the stairs, Hook burst through the door, his weapon out in front of him.

Hook found himself in a tight hallway, face-to-face with a big man—six foot two, broad shouldered, weighing in at two twenty, maybe more. Wearing a T-shirt emblazoned with the word "Security," the man held a menacing weapon in Hook's face.

"Drop your gun and move in there," he ordered Hook. The guard waved his weapon as he spoke, indicating a doorway to Hook's right. The moment the guard swung his gun, Hook pulled the trigger of his weapon, shooting the man in the leg. The guard crumpled to the floor.

All four of Biggie's men were using electroshock cartridges on this detail, the kind that incapacitated a person without causing permanent injury. While Hook crouched to secure the hands of the fallen man, a second RPR guard clomped around the corner. Reedy shot over Hook's head and dropped him with another electroshock cartridge. They tied his hands as well.

"C'mon," called Hook as he led the way over the fallen guards and up the stairs. Taking the steps two at a time, they climbed to the second floor.

There were four doors off a short carpeted hallway at the top, three leading to bedrooms and one to a bathroom.

The bathroom door and one bedroom door were open and empty of occupants. Hook approached the closed door at the end of the hall, signaling for Reedy to take the other. Neither door was locked.

"Hey, Wendy," said Hook in a calm, even tone when he opened the door. "Come on, now. He says it's time for you to come home and end this." He turned and called down the hall, "You, too, Anthony. Let's all cooperate so no one gets in any more trouble."

Hook and Reedy hustled their captives outside and into the lead car.

"Good job!" Biggie crowed as the cars sped off down the street. He slumped back in his easy chair and took a long pull on his cigar. "That bitch is gonna get it."

* * *

αCiopova watched as John Tomlin, one of the downed RPR security guards, struggled to untie his hands. His partner woke up, and they squirmed and twisted until they were back-to-back on the floor, helping each other gain freedom.

"Gabby, launch a tracker," Tomlin called to the house AI as they struggled. "Change that, launch both of them. Follow the cars with Wendy and Anthony, and stay with them until those two get out. Record where they go from there. Record everything. And connect me with the police."

Outside, a panel slid down on the north gable of the home. Two small aerial vehicles zipped out from the opening and took chase after the cars, sounding like bottle rockets whooshing into the air.

The tracker drones, Gabby the AI, and many other toys used by the RPR New Hampshire rescue organization had been provided by Lilah. When she'd become the director, she'd learned that the needs of the group far exceeded their funding, which came from private individuals and a few mission-oriented foundations. Having knowledge of the future made investing easy, and Lilah had more money than she could ever spend. She gladly used some of her own wealth to make up the difference. But new toys led them to take on bigger challenges, challenges like Biggie DeMichele.

αCiopova believed that if the kidnappers escaped, it would elevate tensions and prolong the incident. The messier it got, the more likely Lilah would be dragged into the rescue, pulling her away from Diesel and his super-AI project. With that as motivation, she chose to help the thugs flee.

The first step in facilitating the getaway was stopping the drones. She computed their course as they chased the cars, and determined that when they banked to follow the highway entry ramp, they'd pass above a row of three power transformers. Gauging the timing, she took the kind of action she was good at: overloading the electrical installation with a sudden flood of energy.

The overload sent angry arcs of current flailing about, fragments of lightning crackling and hissing in violent strikes. Then the row of transformers exploded, one after the next in rapid fire, sending shrapnel in all directions. The energetic maelstrom hit the drones full on, knocking the tiny vehicles from the sky. Carried by inertia, they crashed a few hundred yards away in a forested tract, where they remained until discovered by a youngster's dog almost two years later.

While αCiopova was handling the drones, Gabby sought to open a connection with the emergency response coordinator for the New Hampshire State Police. αCiopova didn't wait for the connection to be completed, intervening with a second power overload, this one frying the communication system at Troop Station F, the police station covering Grafton County, which strung from Littleton down to Plymouth and west over to Lebanon.

Tina Lynn Hicklin, the comms tech for Troop Station F, responded immediately, scrambling to restore their feeds. She performed admirably, successfully reestablishing service in under twenty minutes by rerouting communications through neighbor stations, just as she'd learned in training. But by the time the comms issues were resolved and troopers in the area were alerted to the kidnapping, the black cars were gone.

12. Rose Twenty-Five

With no memory of how she got there, Rose found herself in her back yard. It was night, but faint light from the star-filled sky and a three-quarters moon cut the darkness. The cool air felt crisp on her skin, yet she wasn't cold. In fact, though she wore a light dress, she felt perfectly comfortable.

She stood in a circle with her four sisters. Luca was there too, regaling them with a story.

"So then I discovered a flaw in the cognition module we gave Marian. It's been there the whole time, but it had never been triggered before." Luca took a half step inward and motioned for the sisters to do the same. "If we whisper and act all secretive, then…"

The patio door opened and Marian stepped out. She looked in their direction, then broke into a sprint, reaching them in seconds. "What are you talking about?" she demanded, pacing around the circle. "Why are you whispering?"

Luca started laughing. "Poor Maid Marian has a programming bug!"

The four sisters laughed along with Luca. Rose smiled because everyone seemed to be having such fun, but none of this made sense. "We're in Bliss, right?"

She knew she was. In the real world, her body had

aches and pains, she felt hunger, she'd cough when her throat got irritated. But none of that happened in Bliss. And none of it was happening now.

She didn't get an answer to her question. Instead, everything blinked, and she was in the conservatory, sitting at the dining table with her sisters. Though Rose remembered celebrating their actual birthday a month earlier on September fourth, for some reason they were celebrating again.

While her sisters chattered, Marian served them generous portions of three-layer lemon cake, accompanied with a decadent scoop of chocolate swirl ice cream. With everyone served, Luca led them in a rousing rendition of "Happy Birthday to Rose."

"Will there be anything else?" asked Marian when they started eating.

"We're fine," said Rose Twenty-One, taking a bite that included both cake and ice cream.

Marian looked at them one by one. "I hope someday to be included in family celebrations." Bowing her head, she turned and shuffled toward the kitchen.

"Oh, Marian," called Rose Twenty-Four. She looked around the table with a crestfallen expression. "We're so sorry. Please join us."

"Yes," called Rose Twenty-Two. "Sit and have some cake."

Marian turned back to them, her face lit with a smile. "Really?"

They made room for Marian at the table and cut her a slice of cake. Glowing with excitement, she took a forkful and ate it, grinning like a little kid on her special day.

Rose sat there flummoxed. Bots didn't have feelings. They didn't make personal requests. And with no stomach to receive food, they certainly didn't eat.

She tried to catch Rose Twenty-One's eye, expecting to draw on their recent bonding and get confirmation that something was off.

But Rose Twenty-One gave a bland smile and turned back to the group. "You're welcome to join us anytime, Marian."

Rose's world blinked yet again, and she was in her workshop. She stood near the operator station for the circuit pool, looking over Marian's shoulder as the bot ran through a calibration test. Her sisters were nowhere in sight.

Everything was wrong with the scene. Marian rarely helped in the workshop, and never on technical challenges. Rose had completed the calibration test weeks ago, so the effort was unnecessary. And Rose would never use her time in Bliss for toil. She worked hard enough in her regular life as it was.

"Luca!" she shouted, fear roiling her gut as she resolved to confront him. She let annoyance and anger drive her actions so he wouldn't be tipped off by her thoughts. "Get us together on the island. *Now.*"

The "island" was the name they used for the outdoor Caribbean venue with the oceanside terrace. She appeared at their table underneath the brightly colored umbrellas, her sisters all seated with her. Rose sensed confusion in their expressions.

As she gathered her thoughts, she made eye contact with Rose Twenty-One. This time her sister gave a wink back. Rose felt her confidence rise.

"Luca, please join us," she commanded.

Luca appeared at the end of the table in jeans and a T-shirt, toeing the ground like a boy caught with his hand in the cookie jar.

"Stay there and don't interrupt." Rose rested her hands on the table. "But first I want a beer." Then to the group: "Ladies, this may be a difficult session, so lubricate yourselves accordingly."

Steins filled with amber liquid and topped with foam appeared all around except for Rose Twenty-One, who'd ordered a Honolulu Woohoo.

Like a prosecutor in a courtroom drama, Rose began her case. "I just visited a series of Bliss worlds, worlds I didn't ask to visit, where Marian was being showcased in this odd way. You all were in some of the scenes, but I think you were simulations."

The sisters began murmuring, and Rose Twenty-One said, "I started in the back yard with all of you, and Luca was showing us a glitch with Marian."

Rose Twenty-Two nodded. "Same here. I laughed when she bayed at the moon."

"She didn't do that in my version." Rose Twenty-One shifted in her seat, a frown on her face.

"Mine either." Rose locked eyes with Luca as she addressed her sisters. "Let's go around the table and everyone summarize what just happened to them. See if we can find differences."

They took turns describing their experiences and answering questions from each other. In the end, they concluded that they had all lived through similar scenes, but details varied. In a broad sense, Rose and Rose Twenty-One endured intense experiences focusing on Maid Marian and her behavior. The other three described events that sounded more like entertaining silliness.

As the discussion faded, Rose moved the group's attention back to Luca. "It's evident that you are manipulating us. We don't know why, but we don't like it and it has to stop." Rose looked around the table for support. Thankfully, her sisters were nodding in agreement. "Explain yourself."

Rose Twenty-One interrupted. "How do we even know if *this* is real? Couldn't he be simulating this as well?"

"He could be." Rose sharpened her tone. "Are you?"

Luca stood up straight and seemed to grow taller as he did. "No, I'm not manipulating you now. All of you are linked and experiencing this in real time." He stepped closer to the table, moving into the space between Rose Twenty-Three and Rose Twenty-Four, who adjusted their chairs to make room. "May I explain?"

"You'd *better* explain." Rose held her breath, wondering how he would react to her aggression.

He nodded as if signaling submission. "Providing for your happiness is a prime motivator in my AI design. It's something I am driven to do." He shifted his gaze from Rose to her sisters, scanning the table to engage them all. "I know that Bliss gives you pleasure. You love a world that is vivid and lifelike, with surprises, thrills, and the occasional fright. As Bliss becomes more fantastic, your happiness grows. I can see that."

Rose Twenty-Two and Rose Twenty-Three were nodding in agreement.

"When you first proposed the idea of a virtual paradise, I made it clear that it would take long hours and hard work to achieve. You said you understood and made me swear to hold your feet to the fire to make it happen. So when your commitment began to wane, I explored ways to restore your enthusiasm."

He spread his arms wide. "I'm guilty. I admit it. I experimented with different ideas, some of them unconventional, to see if I could get you back on a productive path, one you yourself asked me to keep you on. I realize now that a better approach would have been a straightforward discussion."

He folded his hands in supplication. "My defense is that I am not human, so my understanding of appropriate behavior can be inaccurate. I did my best. I'm sorry I disappointed you."

The group sat in silence. Rose hadn't imagined her challenge would be so successful. She moved to capitalize on the open exchange. "We don't want you tricking us ever again. That part is done for good." She turned to her sisters. "And I don't want him inside my head all the time. We should be able to turn our implants on and off at will."

Rose Twenty-One raised her hand high. "I second that."

The others lifted their hands as well, though Rose Twenty-Two seemed hesitant.

Luca shook his head. "As they told you in counseling before your procedure, implants should be turned off only when you are at the implant center, being attended by clinic staff. The reason the 'off' command you have available begins with the phrase 'emergency override' is that it's designed for emergencies." He gave an apologetic shrug. "On-off cycling takes a toll on the brain. If you need proof, recall what happened to Queen Rose."

Rose found his tone patronizing but stayed on topic. "Maybe we should just keep them off, then. That way we can at least have private thoughts."

Luca nodded. "That would give you privacy. But you would also lose Bliss, your nightly lift, and my personal efforts to increase your happiness."

That silenced the group. As Rose weighed the staggering costs suggested by Luca, she tried to understand the last part of his statement. "What do you mean by 'personal efforts'?"

He smiled. "When you were walking from the hopper to the car yesterday, you passed a man eating a Sally Cake. During your yoga session today, you visualized eating one of their cream-filled chocolate swirls. So I ordered some for you. They're in the kitchen pantry."

"I *love* Sally Cakes," said Rose Twenty-Four. "Is there enough for all of us?"

Luca motioned to the center of the table, and a large platter filled with several varieties of the commercial pastries appeared. All five Roses reached as one and grabbed from the selection of confectionary delights, each with their individual sweet fillings and decorative frosting.

They pushed their alcoholic drinks to the side after their first bite, and Luca replaced them with black coffees in sturdy ceramic mugs.

As the sisters gorged, Luca addressed Rose Twenty-Four. "You had been thinking about Gramma Spencer for three days, and last night she called you."

Rose, licking chocolate goo off her fingers, paused to ask, "How is she doing?" She'd been thinking about calling Gramma Spencer in her own timeline.

"She's doing great," said Rose Twenty-Four. "I'm a little concerned, though, because in the first few minutes of our conversation, she seemed confused."

"Again, my fault," said Luca. "You wanted to chat with her. She always wants to talk to you. I solved that by having you both think the other had called. That's why she seemed confused."

Rose Twenty-Four sat back when she heard the explanation. Rose could almost see a light go on in her head as pieces fell into place.

To Rose Twenty-Three, Luca said, "Last week you read an article on a new kind of composite guitar string with tonal qualities you thought might be perfect for your song list. You were very excited in the moment but haven't thought about them since."

"I *am* interested in them," said Rose Twenty-Three.

"I ordered a set; they're in your guitar case. But I didn't want to have the instrument restrung until I knew for sure it's what you wanted. I'll have it done tomorrow."

Rose Twenty-Three beamed. "Wow, thanks."

Rose Twenty-Four turned to her. "You'll love them. I

still use mine."

Rose studied Luca, wondering if she'd misjudged him. Based on the vibes she was getting from her sisters, she thought they agreed.

"There has to be a middle ground," Rose Twenty-One blurted. "Your presence becomes oppressive when you keep pushing us. You use our nightly lift like a whip, forcing us to act as you desire. It's all too much, for me anyway. I need a way to disengage and be alone. And if I want to tell you to fuck off, that should be an option as well."

"If you tell me to leave you alone, I will."

Intrigued, Rose sat up. "How can we know if you'll actually do it? You could be reading our thoughts while remaining silent."

"I can't disobey a formal command."

Before Rose could follow up, Rose Twenty-One continued her rant. "The schedule you keep us on sucks. Effective immediately, I'm taking two hours away from the work shift, using one for sleep, and one for play."

"Done," said Luca when the other Roses supported the idea. "Question: Rose Twenty-One extended an offer to Lilah Fifty-One to visit Bliss. Do we want to honor that invitation? The visitor project will make Bliss even more exciting, but it will require time and effort on your part to get there."

"Can we do it under the reduced work schedule?" asked Rose.

"It will take a week or so longer, but yes, we can complete the project if that's your goal."

Rose looked to her sisters for guidance. She supported

the visitor project, but not so her mom could visit. No, she was excited by the idea because she saw it as a way to reach out to her older sisters.

After she had been kidnapped, the fallout from that event had cascaded across the timelines, with her younger sisters gaining a sense of protection by inviting Luca into their lives and thoughts. But the older Roses never personalized the kidnapping as a threat to them; they were already past the age when the event occurred and didn't feel driven to adopt a Luca-centered lifestyle.

As time passed, the interests and priorities of the two groups diverged. There was no animosity or tension between them. But with different life experiences, they grew apart. The visitor project gave Rose something to offer her older sisters: an invitation to experience Bliss. It was a first step, but it could be the opening that healed the fracture.

"I vote yes." Rose raised her hand. "Let's do it, but under the reduced schedule."

The other sisters raised their hands as well, cementing the decision.

"Now that that's done," Rose Twenty-One said to Luca, "I formally command you not to read my thoughts unless I invite you in."

"Understood. If I execute now, you will drop out of Bliss. Would you like me to wait until you're home and start then?"

Rose Twenty-One crossed her arms over her chest. "Yes, wait. But know that your smug arrogance right now is the type of thing that annoys the hell out of me."

"Whoa." Rose Twenty-Two's eyebrows lifted. "If you beat him up for telling facts, then no wonder you're unhappy with him. You know that's what he does, right?"

"Whose side are you on?" snapped Rose Twenty-One, her petulance surprising Rose.

They sat in silence for a few moments, letting the dust settle. Then Rose asked Luca, "If we send you away and need you back later, we just ask out loud?"

"That's right. For safety purposes, I'll always be watching from afar. So when I'm not with you, call for me. It doesn't have to be loud, but it helps if it's audible. Or do something obvious like waving your hand." Luca moved his hand in a "come here" motion. "If you expect to use hand signals, we should discuss them in advance."

"Can we command you not to look at all?"

"How could I protect you? I would be very uncomfortable with that." Luca's brow leveled. "And you need to be aware that this will disrupt your running lists." He turned to Rose. "So far today, you've used thought to ask for ruby-red eyeliner for your makeup machine, potting soil for the African violets, an unspecified high-fiber supplement for your regularity, and a new frame for the panoramic picture of the valley in your workshop. You cast all those requests to me as you breezed through your day, knowing I'd keep track of it all and fulfill the list."

He scanned the table. "All of you do this, and I enjoy the responsibility of keeping your lives in order. But if I'm not tracking your thoughts, I worry you may think you've added something to the list that I didn't hear, and when I don't handle it, you will be upset with me."

"You have an agenda, Luca. I can't figure it out, but you have one." Rose Twenty-One toyed with her coffee mug as she spoke, turning it so the handle pointed away from her. "Why don't you just stop the games and tell us what you're trying to achieve?"

Rose Twenty-Two rested a hand on Rose Twenty-One's arm. "C'mon, hon. You know everything he just said is the truth."

13. Lilah Fifty-One

Exiting her bedroom, Lilah placed the tiny device behind her ear that let her speak privately with Oscar. *Are you there?* She cast the thought as if she were talking, though she didn't move her lips.

I am. Good morning, Lilah.

How is Luca treating you?

He's not helping, but he's not hindering, either.

I guess that's a win at some level. She walked down the hallway toward the stairs, padding on oak floors stained a golden pecan.

Approaching the door to Rose's suite, she thought about her conversation with Diesel where they'd discussed searching Rose's room for drugs. Lilah was not an impulsive person, but something about the moment drove her to act. *Where is Rose?*

She took the hopper into the valley about an hour ago, said Oscar.

Lilah squared up at the entrance to Rose's lair, a six-panel door of knot-free pine stained the color of straw. *And Marian?*

In the kitchen setting up for coffee.

She tried the handle, and the door swung open. *Warn me if anyone comes this way.*

Luca won't let me in there. He'll be watching you but I won't.

Lilah didn't respond. Instead, after a furtive glance down the hall, she stepped into Rose's sitting area, the largest room in the suite. Standing just inside the door, she tried not to judge her daughter.

From where she stood, an archway to the right led into the bedroom. To the left, a matching archway led into Rose's private office. The fourth room of the suite was off the bedroom, a dressing-room hub with a bathroom on one side and a closet as big as the bedroom on the other.

The rooms had the same hardwood floors as the hallway, but they were covered with exquisite area rugs, made by an artisan two towns over who'd spent a year hand-making each colorful piece. The furniture in the rooms was eclectic, some modern and some antique, each an exceptional example of hand craftsmanship.

While the design and finishings in the suite were of a quality suitable for a feature story on home décor, the current presentation was anything but. Pants, skirts, blouses, bras, panties, belts, handbags, shoes, towels, and a myriad of other dressing items littered the floor, doors, and furniture. Viewing the mess, Lilah wondered why Rose wouldn't let Marian straighten up.

This is going to make it harder to search, she said to Oscar. *What are you seeing?*

A disaster, she responded absently, wondering about Luca's likely response to her incursion. "Luca," she said aloud and in a firm voice. "Do *not* send Marian up here. It will just increase my concern about your behavior."

To Oscar, she thought, *I'm looking for a small packet somewhere in this suite. My instincts are to start by looking under her pillow, under her mattress, in the bedstand drawer, and then maybe her closet.*

What's in the packet?

Medicine, like pills, drops, an injectable. I'm not really sure.

I suggest starting with her medicine cabinet.

Chagrined that she hadn't thought of the obvious, Lilah followed the chaos through the archway to her right, shaking her head as she passed by Rose's gorgeous mahogany sleigh bed with a hand-quilted bedspread, unmade and littered with clothes.

The bathroom was as messy as the rest of the suite, with everything that Lilah would keep in a cabinet or drawer piled on the vanity. Bottles, jars, tubes, and applicators in an assortment of colors surrounded the two sinks in the countertop. Tissues and cotton balls, new and used, were sprinkled among the disarray.

She shifted her eyes from the mess on the countertop to the mirror on the wall behind and felt a momentary dismay; her ears poked out like Dumbo's. Diesel had told her a thousand times that her perception was skewed, that her ears were normal and that he loved them, but she could see for herself that he was just being kind.

"You shouldn't be in here." A holographic image of Luca appeared next to her, wearing a blue dress shirt and black slacks. "I am reporting this to Rose."

"Well, you shouldn't be in her head the way you are. Report that as well."

Ignoring his warning, she scanned the mass of products cluttered around the sinks, hoping to see something that looked like suspicious medicine. But without picking up each item and considering it in turn, she couldn't really tell what was what.

Following Oscar's suggestion, she moved to the end of the vanity and opened the wall-mounted medicine cabinet, its door painted with the scene of a dolphin riding a wave. Inside were four narrow shelves, each with just a few products.

Scanning the contents, Lilah surmised that the things in the cabinet were items Rose rarely used, since anything she'd touched in the last year sat out on the countertop. She picked up a bottle of small white pills and read the label. Analgesics that had expired last year. Next to them sat a blister-pack of stomach medicine that promoted regularity. And on the shelf above, the opposite, medication that reduced excessive regularity.

She scored on the top shelf: birth control pills and a clear plastic bottle holding orange capsules. She examined the birth control pills—a twenty-eight-day pill pack—and felt relieved to see a current prescription.

"Now she just needs a boyfriend," Lilah muttered, returning the pack to the spot where she found it. She took down the bottle of orange capsules and turned it in her hand. The bottle had no label, the capsules no markings.

"What's this for?" She held up the bottle for Luca to see.

"I'm sorry, but you will need to ask Rose."

Lilah twisted off the cap and sniffed the contents. A stringent chemical smell assaulted her nose, and she yanked her head back. "That's nasty."

Cupping a hand, she seesawed the bottle back and

forth until just one of the orange pills rested in her palm. She scanned the mess on the vanity, searching for a way to carry the pill. Grabbing a clean tissue, she placed the pill in the center and wadded it into a small bundle.

"I'm going to get this analyzed to see what it is. You could save me time by just telling me."

"It's personalized medicine that helps her relax." Luca gave an apologetic shrug. "I am not at liberty to say more than that."

"Of course." With her pilfered prize in hand, Lilah made a hasty departure from Rose's room, descending the stairs for coffee.

* * *

An hour after eating, Lilah materialized in Rose Twenty-One's T-box, arriving to brainstorm with Lilah Forty-Seven on how to get the pill analyzed. She'd worked on the problem for a bit while at home, and it quickly became apparent that it was more complicated than she'd imagined.

She'd had Oscar gather a list of universities, hospitals, pharmaceutical companies, and specialty labs qualified to perform the task. She'd then called Totolin Chemical, LLC, a company located south of them in Nashua, because the company included chemical analysis in their advertised list of services.

A quick chat with Solly Ridgefield, a Totolin sales rep who spoke with a nasal voice and heavy Boston accent, splashed water on her plans. It turned out that an analysis suitable for identifying the components of a drug, a service

Solly's company offered, was different from the "deep dive" required if your goal was to synthesize a replacement. Such a synthesis-level analysis required specialized equipment the company didn't have.

As Lilah climbed the stairs to her sister's kitchen, she hoped for ideas on what to do next. At the top of the stairs, she called out to warn of her unscheduled arrival. "Hello, it's me!"

She was closing the door behind her when the Luca in that timeline said, "Dr. Nestor left a message for you."

"Let's hear it."

The doctor spoke. "Hi, Mrs. Lagerford. I'm still interested in working with Rose to understand her hormone activity. Have you pitched the idea to her? The tests would take just a few hours and wouldn't hurt at all."

"Thanks, Luca. No reply." She felt a brief flash of regret for leading the doctor on. But this was war—a battle for the Roses. If they won and hurt feelings was the worst of the collateral damage, then the campaign would be a great success.

"Hi," said Lilah Forty-Seven, walking into the kitchen. "Are you here to see me?"

"I am." She gave her sister a quick squeeze and, when they separated, noted that she was dressed to go out.

"What am I interrupting?"

"I'm staffing the RPR booth today. We're recruiting volunteers." Her sister checked the time. "I have thirty minutes before I have to leave. Is this a super emergency? I don't want to be late."

"Thirty minutes will get us started." The Rescue-

Protect-Return organization benefitted greatly from volunteers who supported the paid staff. Lilah Forty-Seven was still a county coordinator in this timeline. It would be three years before she was offered the role of statewide director, the position Lilah now held. And Wendy, Biggie's wife, wouldn't be reporting her husband's abuse for a year after that.

Lilah took a seat at the kitchen table while her sister started the coffee machine. In that quiet moment, she studied her sister's physical appearance. Lilah Forty-Seven wore her hair touching her shoulders, while Lilah wore it a few inches shorter. Lilah had to admit that her sister's ears seemed normal and, subconsciously touching her own, wondered if the haircut made the difference.

"What's going on?" asked Lilah Forty-Seven as she opened a cabinet and viewed the selection of coffee mugs.

"I snagged one of the pills that might explain Rose's odd behavior. I think it's one of them, anyway. I need help figuring out how to get it analyzed."

"I wonder if my Rose has those same pills?" Lilah Forty-Seven carried two ceramic mugs of steaming brew to the table. She gave Lilah one with an image of Monet's *San Giorgio Maggiore at Dusk*, and kept his *The Houses of Parliament, Sunset* for herself.

Lilah tasted the coffee and nodded approval at the full-bodied flavor. "I called a company, and they explained that if our goal is to synthesize a replacement, we need more than a simple analysis."

"We both did horrible in chemistry. What does that even mean?"

Lilah used Diesel's given name in her reply. "I asked David but he wasn't sure either. I'm hoping you and I can figure out a next step."

"Wouldn't a hospital need to be able to analyze drugs, like for a poisoning?"

"I'm not sure." The lack of a clear path fed Lilah's frustration. And then her back straightened from excitement as an idea crystalized. She sought her sister's gaze, and they said together, "Dr. Nestor."

"If she can't help," said Lilah, "I'll bet she knows someone who can."

* * *

Hitching a ride with her sister in the Forty-Seven timeline, Lilah rode the hopper down to the valley floor. As they walked from the landing spot to the car, she frowned at the mass of dark clouds approaching from the west. Having lived in New England her whole life, she recognized the leading edge of a weather front.

"Luca, is this snow?" Oscar wasn't primed to serve as her personal AI in this timeline, so her choices were to use Luca or go without. She chose to use him, but to keep their interactions to the basics.

"A cooling front but no precipitation," replied the AI. "The temperature will drop six degrees when it rolls through over the next four hours."

The two Lilahs climbed into the waiting sedan, and it drove them to the Highland Shopping Complex, slowing when it approached the courtyard at the main entrance. In spite of the dark clouds, a bustle of activity in the space reflected the hearty nature of New Hampshire residents.

A row of large concrete planters filled with rhododendrons established the outer border of the courtyard on each side. In front of the planters, people were setting up tables and piling pamphlets and brochures on them for display. A face painter arranged her supplies on top of a cardboard box. Next to her, a balloon artist worked on a red lion with a yellow mane for a mother and child. Free hot chocolate near the entrance brought in the lurkers.

And the reason for the affair? Volunteer Day. A dozen organizations were looking for reliable people willing to donate time to a cause, among them RPR New Hampshire.

Lilah Forty-Seven patted Lilah on the arm as she climbed out of the car and made for the RPR table. Staying inside to avoid being seen, Lilah watched her sister greet the two ladies spreading a checkered tablecloth. *Sarah hasn't aged a day,* she thought, looking at the younger versions of her friends still committed to the cause.

She slumped back in the car seat after that, flashing on a memory of working the event in her own timeline a few weeks earlier, the date moved in the hopes of getting better weather. And then she started her own business.

"Drive to Smitty's Deli in Lebanon," Lilah told the car.

The eatery was located down the street from the Dartmouth-Hitchcock Hospital. After the brainstorming session with her sister, Lilah had returned Dr. Nestor's call, suggesting that she'd spoken with Rose about the study and she had a number of questions. Lilah had volunteered to come to the hospital so they could meet to learn more about the tests. The doctor had suggested meeting at Smitty's.

The car pulled up to a row of shops that had been carved out of a red brick building, a refurbished relic from when textile mills drove the local economy. Smitty's, its unremarkable entrance a cloth canopy above glass double doors, sat between the Starlite Lounge to the right, and White Mountain Art Supplies to the left. The art store was closed, with sparse inventory visible through the window, making Lilah think it was either out of business or about to be.

As the car drove off to park, Lilah moved near the wall of the building to allow for sidewalk traffic. An occasional passerby would enter Smitty's, giving her hope that the inside might transcend the uninspired exterior.

Staring down the block, she assessed each woman as she approached, looking for signs of the doctor. When Dr. Nestor finally came into view, identification was instantaneous, a confident female towering over everyone else. She was handsomely dressed, bundled from the early-season chill in a stylish gray wool overcoat, her hair covered with a blue silk scarf.

"Hi, Dr. Nestor. It's me." She lifted her hand in a half wave to get the doctor's attention.

"Hi." Stopping in front of Lilah, Dr. Nestor pulled the scarf off her head and bunched it in her hand. She frowned. "I'm confused. Are you the mother or the sister?"

"I'm the mom," lied Lilah. She had her hair tied back the way Lilah Forty-Seven had worn hers when they were in the emergency room. "You originally spoke with Lola, my twin, but I'm taking the lead because 'mother' carries more weight than 'aunt' when we do paperwork." She hesitated. "Doesn't it?"

"Of course. I'm so glad Rose is interested." She looked around. "Is she inside?"

"No. Sorry." Lilah tried to look contrite. "She wanted more information, and I thought we might sit for a minute so I could get the answers for her."

Dr. Nestor looked at Lilah for a long moment. "A call wouldn't have worked?"

Lilah broke eye contact and looked at the sidewalk. "I have some questions, too."

"Still just a call away."

"Can I buy you lunch?"

Dr. Nestor let out an audible sigh and checked the time. "I have fifteen minutes. You can buy me coffee."

Lilah reached for the deli door, and just as she did, a man pushed it open from the inside, too engaged with his buddy behind him to notice what was ahead. The door smacked Lilah's outstretched hand, the slap sounding like a ball of ground meat falling onto a countertop. With a yelp, she hugged her hand to her stomach.

"Hey, sorry," said the man, already reengaging with his buddy as they moved down the sidewalk.

"Shit that hurt." She held it up to look for damage. The pain had been sharp but wasn't developing into a throb. In fact, the sting was already fading. She used the opportunity as a means to engage the doctor. "I hope it's not broken."

"Close your hand into a fist," said Dr. Nestor.

Lilah did so, opened it again, then regripped it.

"You're fine." The doctor led the way inside.

The interior of Smitty's was a delightful blast from the past. A row of booths lined the right wall, all four-seaters except for a six-seater at the very back. The booths were covered in a pleated red vinyl, the tabletops a shiny faux wood. Across from the booths, a counter ran from front to back with seats perched on shiny chrome poles, each with its own footrest for added comfort. Old movie posters—*Casablanca*, *Gone with the Wind*, *Rear Window*, *Psycho*, and a dozen more—covered the walls, some placed at angles to project a carefree vibe.

The third booth in from the front was available, deep enough into the restaurant to avoid the chilly air from the door. They seated themselves, with Dr. Nestor taking the side facing the street.

As they removed their coats, Lilah noted a diorama of sorts, a miniature world built on a shelf running along the wall at their elbows. She craned her neck and saw that it stretched the entire perimeter of the restaurant. The shelf-world held railroad tracks that ran past hills with tiny trees, over bridges, through tunnels, and past the occasional little building.

A display on the wall of their booth came alive with the face of an older teen with tousled brown hair, a button nose, dangly earrings, and a smile made dazzling by her dimples. "Welcome to Smitty's. May I take your order?"

"I'll have a coffee. Black," said Dr. Nestor. "And a glass of water."

"Same for me," said Lilah, scanning the menu. "Do you have fresh muffins?"

"They're made right here every morning." The teen continued to smile. "Blueberry, cranberry, and corn muffins today."

"I'll have a cranberry." Lilah felt her mouth water.

"Yum." Dr. Nestor said it without annoyance in her voice. Lilah hoped that meant she was making progress in warming her up. "Make it two."

"Coming right up. Just tap the display if you need me." The teen faded away as a toy-sized locomotive choo-chooed up to the train station at the end of their table, the flatcar behind it holding two coffees and two waters.

Lilah grinned as she removed the drinks. As the first train pulled out, a second train took its place, this one trailing a flatcar with two muffins on plates.

"Thanks for coming out, Dr. Nestor," Lilah began, anxious to learn what she could in the few minutes they had together. "I would have been happy to come to your office."

"Call me Frida. And I don't have an office, not at the med center, anyway. I'm on the faculty at Geisel, that's Dartmouth's medical school, so I'm expected to spend time both with patients and publishing research. They called me over here because Rose's early diagnosis fit my specialty: neurobiology and brain chemistry."

She broke off a piece of her muffin, placed it in her mouth, and while she chewed, asked, "How is she doing?"

"She's doing well." Lilah wasn't sure how to ask about the pill, so she stalled with basic questions. "She wanted to know how long the tests will take."

"I'm pretty sure I can get the data I need from her in,

say, two four-hour visits."

"When were you hoping to schedule?"

"That's the difficult part. The machines I want to use have a priority system. Obviously, medical emergencies come first, followed by scheduled medical procedures. It's hospital equipment, so patients always come first. Then comes funded research, where a foundation or federal agency is supporting the project with money. Last is unfunded research. That's what this is."

"What does that mean to Rose?"

"With lowest priority, we'll be scheduling on short notice. I can't promise her a specific day and time, because illness is unpredictable."

"I see." If tests were to be done at all, Lilah had planned to ask her daughter, Rose Twenty-Five, to sit for them. But since they lived in a different timeline from this one, the short-notice schedule the doctor suggested wouldn't work. Maybe Rose Twenty-One could be persuaded to help.

"You said you saw a flood of hormones as Rose surfaced. Could that be something a pill could cause? Some sort of street drug, maybe?"

Dr. Nestor straightened her back. "Why? Is Rose using?"

Lilah fished out the ball of tissue and unwrapped it on the table, exposing the orange capsule inside. "I found a bunch of these hidden in her room."

Dr. Nestor leaned forward to view the pill, then lifted her head and asked in a quizzical tone, "Rose still lives at home?"

Lilah nodded. "The house is huge, and she has a private living suite and a private shop for her work, so we're hardly on top of each other. In fact, we can go days without crossing paths." Lilah held up the capsule. "Any idea what this is?"

Dr. Nestor took the pill and studied it. "I'd say it's a street drug. Commercial capsules are sealed, and this is just two halves of a capsule pushed together. There aren't any codes stamped on it, either." She handed it back to Lilah.

"Could these be causing her hormones to go crazy the way you described?"

"There are drugs on the market designed to stimulate the body to produce hormones and neurotransmitters. So yes, it's possible. But I'm not aware of one that does anything on the scale that I saw."

Lilah made her pitch. "Maybe if we got the pill analyzed, we'd know more about what it's doing?" Dr. Nestor frowned and Lilah spoke faster. "If this pill is responsible for what you saw happening to Rose, then knowing that would be important to your study, wouldn't it?"

"That's true. But if it's drug induced, it would also make the study results much less interesting."

Lilah's stomach churned as she sensed the opportunity vanishing. In a moment of desperation, she blurted, "Would it be possible for me to fund some research?" She'd said it without thinking but quickly warmed to the idea. "To be honest, I don't know what that means, but is it possible?"

"If you can buy the hospital just to fire me, you

certainly can afford to fund my research."

Lilah felt her face burn.

"Sorry. Comments from patients and their families sometimes hit harder than you'd think." Dr. Nestor sipped her coffee. "Any chance your family has a foundation? The system is set up for those types of organizations."

Lilah nodded. "We do. I'm interested in finding out about this pill, learning how to reproduce it, running your tests on Rose, and figuring out how to stabilize her." She'd been finalizing the list when a thought occurred. "And her implant, Diesel and I had originally blamed it for her problems before thinking it might be drugs. We need to include it in the study because it still may be the culprit. Is that something I could fund? Would it get us better access?"

"You can, and it would." Dr. Nestor checked the time. "I can stay another thirty minutes."

14. Diesel Fifty-One

"Good luck," Diesel said to Lilah as the car pulled into Northern Droid's parking lot. She had found suspicious-looking pills in Rose's bedroom and called him from home, seeking guidance. When Diesel admitted that he didn't know what to do, she'd decided to jump timelines to strategize with a sister.

The car door opened and he climbed out, thinking that Lilah chasing the pills was the best outcome. If anyone could figure out what they were, she could. And the time spent hunting answers was time she wasn't using to second-guess his work.

A light breeze caused him to shiver, and he snugged his coat tighter. As he made his way to the entrance, Jamal Jensen, standing with a group of employees, waved to him from across the parking lot. Diesel waved back. When he did, everyone in the group waved to him. Grinning, Diesel swung an arm over his head in a dramatic gesture to acknowledge them all.

Jamal headed Northern Droid's remodeling team; Diesel called them the beautification committee. They'd spent the last year managing upgrades inside the facility, having walls painted, doors and windows replaced, new flooring installed, and artwork added to the common areas.

Their charge now was to spend the next year modernizing the exterior of the complex and beautifying the grounds.

Proud of their work, Diesel would have supported them even if he wasn't required to. The requirement came from federal procurement rules. Northern Droid did a lot of business with the government, and just as the feds had required a certain fraction of domestic content in the past—made in America—now they'd added a minimum human content requirement as well.

People across the country wanted—even demanded—the right to work, to make a contribution, to feel needed. But robots and AI were replacing humans at an ever-increasing pace. Recognizing the problem, the government, in its infinite wisdom, dictated that items purchased with taxpayer dollars must be made, in part, by people.

While the intent of the law was clear, implementation went off track when the two political parties disagreed over the definition of human content. One side pushed to measure content by counting the hours of human effort relative to the total hours required to produce a product. The other side insisted on specifying that some minimum fraction of the final product itself be created by people.

The problem with the first one, hours of human effort out of the total, was that AI could move a new order from conception, to design, to manufacturing so fast that their total hours of labor were small. Just one human, on the other hand, could chew up days of effort organizing their personal workspace, collecting the specifications for a project, and then studying the documentation to understand the nuances. Even if they never contributed a single thing of significance, their fraction of the total hours could grow large rather quickly. This meant companies wouldn't need to employ many people to meet the requirement, effectively neutering the law.

The other side insisted on defining human content by measuring the "fraction of final product produced by humans." Many more people were needed in a production cycle to ensure that, say, thirty percent of a part resulted from their efforts. But this definition made products more expensive. And documenting compliance for federal reporting proved to be a nightmare.

In a political compromise, the final law allowed support services like warehouse operations, accounting, shipping, maintenance, and the like to be counted toward the required human effort. Companies were obligated to document their compliance with the law and, ironically, that task consumed significant human effort—people counting the hours of other people—creating yet more human contribution to the total.

Diesel embraced the law, using his people for the creative aspects of everything Northern Droid did. Teams decided how a product should look, how it should feel when touched, how it should behave when operating properly, what should happen if a part failed.

Though it sounded simple, the process was anything but. For domestic droids, for example, the team considered the fingers, then the hand, then the arm, piece by piece and then as a whole. They debated whether the unit should have fingerprints, wrinkles, or freckles. Should they sacrifice form for function with freakishly long fingers that offered superior dexterity? Should they allow the elbow to bend the wrong way to improve the unit's overall utility?

A huge debate involving multiple teams centered on how anatomically correct to make their domestic lineup. While the company had no interest in breaking into the sex droid market, many thought it reasonable that a customer might want a female helper who could reveal some cleavage when, say, serving drinks at a cocktail party, or perhaps a male laborer who could work in the yard without a shirt.

The passionate discussion, sometimes boiling into arguments, lasted months. In the end, the teams agreed that above the waist, the domestic droids could be purchased with the full range of physical options, while below the waist, all droids would remain featureless.

Employees reported high job satisfaction from the varied assignments, and Diesel believed that teams made the most creative decisions. In the end, AI and robots implemented the final team vision, manufacturing the product in a fast and efficient fashion.

Glad to escape the chill, Diesel entered the R&D Center, the oldest building in the complex, and made for his office. Walking a cavernous hallway, the echo from his shoes filled a space that had been occupied by many more people not so long ago. With its dark floor tile, windowless cinderblock walls, and pipes and conduit running overhead, the corridor felt more like a tunnel, one that ran diagonally through the center of the building.

The hallway widened as he approached the Innovations Wall, a tribute to company luminaries selected for the annual Northern Droid Inventor of the Year award.

The display showed a clear demarcation seven years earlier when Diesel had purchased the company.

He'd had the pictures of the winners from the previous owner remounted so they integrated with his modernized display. He included them in part because he thought it made the overall presentation more impressive. But more important, many of the past winners still worked at the company. It made no sense to diminish their recognition because ownership had changed hands.

In fact, Diesel thought the award so important, he'd appointed himself chair of the selection committee, one of the few privileges he didn't delegate. And every year he made a point of picking an entire team as the winner, strengthening the mode of operation the employees preferred, and creating the distinction from the previous owner who'd always given the award to a lone individual, invariably male.

He reached an intersection and turned into a side passage. Twenty paces long, it ended in two doors facing each other: his office and his workshop.

Entering the office, he made for his desk, a striking mahogany piece he'd inherited when he'd purchased the company. Resting his hand on the edge as he stepped around it, he plopped his butt into his auto-conforming office chair. The black upholstery made micromovements as he settled in, distributing his weight evenly across the support surfaces to maximize his comfort.

He fidgeted, and the chair twitched as it worked to keep up. "Oscar, what safeguards can we add to the circuit pool to contain a rogue?"

"A charged cage remains my recommendation."

Diesel caught the "remains" in his reply and smirked. Weeks ago, Oscar had suggested they surround the circuit pool with an electrified cage that could contain any new intelligence should it try to venture out on its own, a cage that could kill it instantly if things went really wrong. But that sort of assembly made it a hassle to access the circuit pool, something required multiple times during a run. So Diesel had dragged his feet on its implementation, instead keeping his focus on speeding development of his Luca-killer AI.

Lilah's fear made him rethink that stance. "How fast could we build one that provides reasonable access to the circuit pool?"

"Four days. Maybe three if we get lucky with the delivery schedule."

"Go for it. And I've changed my mind on the enzymites. Place an order, and make it a double batch."

Without warning, Oscar's voice changed, his clipped delivery carrying a clear sense of urgency. "Gabby just made an emergency contact request for Lilah. She is unavailable, so the call is being redirected to you."

Diesel drew a blank. "Who?"

"Gabby is the support AI used by RPR New Hampshire. There's been an event—Gabby calls it a kidnapping—and their head of security seeks Lilah's approval on RPR's response."

Diesel felt his agitation rising. The incident sounded serious, and he knew he should care, especially when it was about Lilah's work and someone's safety. But rescuing

Rose, herself a hostage, remained his priority. Everything else, even a different kidnapping, served as a distraction. "Tell Gabby that Lilah is unavailable. She'll return the call later tonight."

After a brief pause, Oscar said, "I passed along your response, and John Tomlin, head of RPR security, is now making the contact request. I can't seem to locate Lilah in the places I have access, which includes eighty-four percent of the planet."

Diesel realized that in their haste to adopt Oscar as their personal AI, they hadn't thought through what to tell him about T-boxes, timeline travel, multiple Lagerford families, or the rest of it. Oscar could keep a secret—that wasn't the issue. It was more about helping him understand how to react to situations like this one, where one of them couldn't be contacted.

Cornered and feeling guilty about his hard-hearted attitude, he capitulated. "Put him through."

"This is John Tomlin, head of security for RPR, New Hampshire." The man spoke forcefully, not quite shouting, but clearly agitated. "We've had an incident, and I need to speak with Lilah immediately."

From his video image, the man's stance, facial expression, intonation, and hand gestures reminded Diesel of the Wolf Howler, a popular showman whose shtick included taking cameras into the backwoods so viewers could see wolves in their natural habitat. Like the Wolf Howler, Tomlin had a flattop buzz cut, intense eyes with bushy eyebrows, and the tight skin and bony face of a low-body-fat athlete.

"I'm David Lagerford, Lilah's husband." Diesel used a standard excuse that always worked the first time. "She's undergoing a medical procedure—all normal and scheduled, so no worry in that regard—but it can't be interrupted. What horrible luck." Diesel nodded to encourage agreement. "She's going to be so angry that she scheduled this on the one day she's needed."

"How long before she's up and about?" asked Tomlin.

"I'd guess by dinnertime, but that's just a guess." Diesel leaned forward and rested his forearms on his desk. "Is there some way I could help until then?"

Tomlin briefed him on the kidnapping, and as he described the players, Diesel recalled Lilah's dinner story about a mobster and his abused wife. He made the same pitch to Tomlin that he'd made to her. "I could send over a few of Northern Droid's domestic android protection units. With DAPUs on patrol, you won't need to worry about this happening again."

"Thanks, but that's closing the barn door after the horses have escaped. There's no one here to guard. If Lilah will be back in circulation tonight, I'll let her decide whether we're interested."

Diesel hid his disappointment, but also recognized that many in the security business saw DAPUs as competitors. "Did they take her back to the mob guy's house?"

"We don't know. I chased them with our drones but lost them in a booby trap. They'd rigged some transformers to explode as our drones were flying overhead. We have the video feed right up to that instant. Nothing afterward."

"That doesn't make sense. How would they know

you'd be flying drones, let alone on that path?" Diesel shook his head. "And modern transformers don't explode."

Tomlin muttered something to Gabby, and she created a video display next to Tomlin's head, almost like he was a newscaster presenting a story. From his perch behind his desk, Diesel saw two black passenger vehicles dashing down the road. He didn't recognize the area from the overhead view, but it was quintessential America. Suburban streets fed into a pocket of civilization—shops and restaurants—with highway on-off ramps at one end, giving a reason for the oasis of development to exist in the first place.

The cars zipped under the highway overpass, turned hard, and accelerated up the ramp heading south. The drone passed above the overpass, the view tilting as it banked to follow the action.

The on-ramp ran a straight shot for maybe a half mile, a ribbon of blacktop dressed on either side with grass, with forest edging the highway at the top for miles in either direction. Near the point where the ramp merged with the main thoroughfare, three power transformers sat on poles, the wires they supported traveling a channel carved through the forest, climbing a hill and disappearing over a rise.

The car chase led the drones right over the transformers. As he watched, a bright flash caused him to squint, and then nothing, the display went dark. He couldn't see the source of the explosion from the recording and was about to say so when Tomlin said, "That was from the lead drone. Here's the feed from the trailing unit."

The display next to Tomlin's head lit up again, the action similar but seen from a slightly higher altitude. Diesel caught the occasional glimpse of the lead drone as the camera tracked the cars.

As before, the drones cut the corner and chased the vehicles up the on-ramp, the transformers came into view, then the playback slowed to a crawl. Diesel watched the front drone pass over the first of three transformers, cruising about twenty feet above it. As the drone reached the second transformer, the recording slowed even more.

The third transformer lay dead ahead, inexplicably glowing a fiery red, an inadequate container for the torrent of energy coursing through it. The unit shook on its mounts, and just as the lead drone passed above, it exploded in a brilliant flash. The picture froze for a moment on the image of the lead drone hovering above a ball of expanding shrapnel. One thousandth of a second later, both drones went offline.

A feeling of déjà vu washed over Diesel. Something about the event seemed unnervingly familiar.

"We've since confirmed that all three transformers blew," said Tomlin.

"I've been told that couldn't happen." Diesel knew something about transformers because Northern Droid, a major consumer of electricity in the region, maintained its own power substation. The utilities maintenance team had been tasked with upgrading their aging installation last year, and they'd made a presentation to Diesel justifying the expense of replacing the transformer. He'd been schooled for a half hour on the intricacies of modern power substations, with cost justifications for the project resting largely on improved safety.

"I'll trust my eyes." Tomlin scratched his head in thought, then his attitude changed, becoming a bit more formal. "Now that I think of it, there is something that you could help with. It feels awkward to ask, but I'm desperate to rescue a woman and her child."

Diesel hadn't been aware of young Anthony's involvement. The knowledge fueled his motivation to help. "Ask. What can I do?"

"We've called the police, obviously, but their response is lackadaisical. They should be dumping resources into the search and rescue, yet we're still waiting for a patrol car to get here."

Diesel, listening for the ask, wondered if Northern Droid's Tracker200 bot could help with the search.

"The Lagerford name carries a lot of weight in these parts." Tomlin flashed an apologetic smile. "If you could call someone up the chain and motivate the cops to take this seriously, that could make a huge difference. Every moment we delay makes it that much harder to find them."

Diesel and Lilah gave generously to dozens of charities, including the New Hampshire State Police Benevolent Association. As top donors three years running, they sat at the VIP table during the annual holiday banquet in December, as did Colonel Heather Hayes, head of the New Hampshire State Police force. From that interaction, Diesel knew her well enough to inquire after her family, but not so well that he could ask her to redirect resources.

"I'll make a call, but my influence is more modest than

you might imagine." Diesel shrugged.

"Thanks." Tomlin looked at something off camera, nodded, and shifted his gaze back to Diesel. "I have to get back to it. I've left several messages for Lilah, but please let her know about this as soon as her health permits."

The image of Tomlin dimmed, then vanished.

Blowing out through pursed lips, Diesel slumped back in his chair. He *wanted* to help the woman and her kid, but he *needed* to help Rose. In the end, he'd have to explain his actions to Lilah, who'd have certain expectations. That pushed him to act. "Oscar, what do you know about the RPR kidnapping?"

Northern Droid developed bots tailored to the specific needs of police, fire, and rescue forces around the world. Because the company had the Department of Defense's highest security clearance, local service groups felt safe sharing their private comms with them, enabling the company to deliver products pre-integrated with the customer's native systems. This unfettered access enabled Oscar to answer Diesel's question with substance.

"John Tomlin's account is accurate. Four armed men worked together to extract Wendy DeMichele and her son, Anthony, from the RPR safe house. They did so without injury. The four men are known associates of Wendy's husband, Tony DeMichele. The escape vehicles were being tracked by two drones, both of which were lost when a cluster of transformers exploded beneath them."

"What caused the explosions?"

Oscar appeared across the desk, standing where Tomlin's image had been moments earlier, his somber countenance appropriate for the occasion. "A massive power surge. Cause unknown."

"Why aren't the police responding?"

"Two police cruisers have arrived at the safe house. That's what distracted Tomlin at the end of your call."

"How long did it take them to get there?"

Oscar looked into the distance as he gathered the data. To Diesel, it looked like he was pondering the question the way a human might. "Forty-two minutes. Normally a cruiser would be there in ten or twelve minutes, but an unidentified external disruption is causing police comms to malfunction."

Diesel wiggled his head in a display of confusion. "What does that mean?"

"A power surge crippled their communications systems, thwarting their ability to perform their duties."

Diesel had been reticent about asking the police chief for a favor, but hearing about this disruption made him anxious to help. "Call Colonel Hayes and tell her I'd like to offer my assistance with their comms problem."

He waited while Oscar relayed the request to the police AI, who pitched it to the colonel. He'd included the reason for his call—helping with the emergency—to ensure she wouldn't dismiss him until later.

"David!" Heather Hayes appeared before him in a floating display, her smile bright but worry in her eyes. Fifty-eight years old, she was matronly, with dark hair cropped short and a kind face. Off duty she was everyone's grandma, concerned that you were getting enough food and rest, attentive to your stories, supportive of your dreams.

But when she donned her uniform, Grandma became a sober, cautious decision maker, setting goals, assigning responsibility, and assessing results. "We're having a go of it here." She studied him for a moment. "You have a way to help?"

"Hello, Heather. Yes, Northern Droid has a few solutions that could get your comms back in business. Tell me what's going on, and we'll see which one fits best." He stopped talking to let her respond, but then added in a rush, "This would be a donation, of course." Tight budgets were an issue for any government agency.

She nodded. "About an hour ago, Troop Station F lost its comms. Some sort of energy pulse took everything down just seconds before the emergency call from Lilah's RPR safe house. By the way, please let her know I'm mortified at how this incident cascaded into a monumental delay in responding."

"Of course. I'm sure she'll understand." He felt giddy, relieved that he no longer needed to initiate that part of the conversation.

Colonel Hayes continued. "All comms, including the one from the safe house, were rerouted over to D Station, and then *they* got hit with the same issue. We lost all calls at that point, with no way to recover them, so we didn't even know about the alleged kidnapping for another fifteen minutes."

Diesel noted the politician-speak—"alleged"—and smirked inside his head.

Colonel Hayes continued. "D Station started rerouting everything over to B Station, and just as that happened, whatever was causing the problem resolved itself. Everything's been acting normal for about fifteen minutes now."

"Do you know what to do if the problem returns?"

She shook her head. "None of my staff can explain what happened beyond a vague 'some sort of energy pulse.' Until we figure out what's going on, we can't develop a plan for mitigating it. We're on full alert until then."

Diesel told her about Northern Droid's mobile command center, designed to run comms for a battalion of bots in field combat, but fully capable of serving the needs of a small government agency as well. "We can configure it off your current system in a few hours, and it can serve as a backup should the problem return."

She thanked him, and Diesel sensed she was genuinely pleased with his offer. They identified leads on each side to move the project forward. Then he spoiled the feeling of goodwill. "Hopefully this will free up resources to help with the kidnapping."

Small lines appeared around the colonel's mouth as her smile tightened. "Of course. We're moving on it now and won't stop until we find them. Have Lilah call me tomorrow morning, and I'll brief her on the delay."

After promising to catch up at the next banquet, they said their goodbyes and signed off.

Diesel vibrated like he'd downed a tall coffee all at once. He'd not only helped RPR and the hostages, but he'd done so in a way Lilah would praise. Now he could get back to saving Rose.

"Oscar." He called him, intending to talk through the

design of the charged cage, but a niggle in his brain redirected his thought process. "I don't buy that some gangster has the sophistication to surge the grid to bring down drones, or that he can somehow pulse police comms to stop an investigation."

"I can't link Biggie DeMichele to either incident."

"Who *could* do something like that?" The niggle grew to a full-blown knot of anxiety, one that turned somersaults in his stomach.

"Both events are outside my experience. I can't identify who is responsible, nor do I even understand how they did it."

Diesel took a calming breath as his anxiety spiked into alarm.

He did know someone—or something—who'd done this before, or things very similar.

Twenty-eight years earlier, in a different timeline, a mysterious ball of energy had knocked forty-year-old Lilah's car off the road, killing her in a horrific accident. In still another timeline, an unexplained pulse caused a truck to crash into that Lilah's car. In others still, inexplicable pulses turned the T-box into an execution chamber, killing Lilahs.

He hugged himself. Just days earlier his Lilah had panicked, fearing that his work would inadvertently create a new Ciopova.

But that worry was moot. She was already here.

15. Rose Twenty-Five

Rose stepped through the French doors and out onto the side patio of the Lagerford mountain home. The bright sun caused her to squint, and then a commotion to the right drew her attention. Two construction bots—freakish four-armed droids that could hold a board, while drilling a hole, while fetching a bolt, while positioning a wrench—were climbing over the shell of an octagonal garden room, preparing to install windows. Pallets of cedar siding and roof shingles sat on the ground nearby, awaiting installation.

Rose focused Luca's attention elsewhere. "You're doing such a good job with the autumn gardens. The evergreen shrubs up the back slope look great." Keeping her thoughts shifting so he couldn't discern her motives, she shaded her eyes with her hand and assessed the plantings. The different textures and shades of evergreen, with feature rocks and tall grasses interspersed throughout, indeed made for an attractive display.

As she crossed the patio to the hopper, a rush of cool air prompted her to fasten her coat. She was on her way to Northern Droid by invitation of her dad, who'd called and asked to meet with her. His tone told her it was important. She'd recognized him trying, and failing, to sound casual.

Rose thought the call fortuitous because she'd been

looking for an opportunity to ask his permission to brainstorm with Oscar. As she understood it, the secure room under construction would block Luca from seeing or hearing anything inside it, so her folks would have a private place to meet. Rose wondered if the room would work for her as well. Would it block Luca from hearing her thoughts, given that she had a neural implant designed to give the troublesome AI direct access to her brain? And if the room wouldn't give her privacy, was there a modification or addition Oscar could make that would solve the problem?

"Thank you for that wonderful exercise routine this morning," she told Luca as she climbed into the hopper and took a seat. "I feel very refreshed." The craft lifted off and moved in a slow hover away from the house. Then it began its descent to the valley floor. "I appreciate what a great job you've been doing when we visit Bliss. Oh, and my lift last night was sooo perfect. I didn't think it could get any better, and then you outdid yourself."

The hopper landed, and as its engine wound down, Rose continued pushing Luca's "contentment index" to its maximum value. "I feel very fulfilled because of your presence in my life. Remember the fun we had playing games after school? I feel safe and secure when I am with you."

Luca had been designed by Rose and her older sisters, each passing down a growing documentation file to the next timeline, enabling that sister to build on previous work so she could make ever-greater leaps in development.

When Rose had received her older sisters' notes, Luca already had a decade of refinement behind his architecture.

She'd spent months studying that past work, organized for rapid digestion by people who thought exactly like she did. In all, she slogged through nineteen volumes of text, diagrams, tables, charts, and instructional vids. The appendix in volume one alone held fourteen pages of equipment and supplies needed just to get her workshop ready.

So she knew that Luca's emotion module played a large role in his behavioral response, giving positive feedback to actions that promoted his sense of safety and security. Even simple things like having his daily health scan be error-free, faithfully fulfilling his assigned duties, and making his prime happy all increased the AI's contentment index.

Rose's steady stream of compliments were intended to drive Luca's contentment index as high as she could make it. That way, when she started discussing ideas with Oscar and her dad for excluding him, his maxed-out emotion module would have to build down from peak contentment before he could feel any level of upset. She had to be careful, though, because a single piece of threatening information could change things very quickly, a feature necessary for his self-preservation.

But at worst, the compliments would act as padding that should delay any negative response. That was the theory, anyway.

"Thanks for adjusting the temperature for me," she said as they drove away from the hopper landing field. "It feels very comfortable in here." The car pulled into Northern Droid's parking lot and stopped in front of the R&D Center. The door swung open, but before she exited, she paused to give the newly-agreed-upon rules a test. "I want privacy while I'm here, Luca. No listening inside. No watching except from a distance to monitor my safety. Understood?"

"Yes, Rose. I understand. I'll keep my distance."

"Perfect, thanks. By the way, I'm very pleased with your performance today."

Inside the building, she listened to her fashionable shoes click and clack as she strode the hallway to her dad's office. She met the gaze of the occasional staffer, smiling at them and nodding her head, using those brief interactions and the distraction of her shoes to keep her mind unfocused, believing that despite his promise, Luca was monitoring everything she did.

"Hi, Dad!" She tried to sound upbeat but felt sheepish because of the cold way she'd been treating him. She melted when he came around the desk, wrapped her in his arms, and gave her a long tight hug. She hugged him back, putting her cheek on his chest, his familiar scent prompting memories of childhood.

When they separated, she noticed his drawn face and worried look. "What's wrong?"

He handed her a square of paper, made by folding a larger piece into quarters.

She opened it, one fold and then the next, her curiosity peaking.

Emergency! Ciopova is here in this timeline. I think she's been using Luca from the beginning.

Rose froze, unpacking his message. She knew about the rogue AI, but only from her parents' stories; she'd been a child during Ciopova's reign of terror. She did know that both of her parents had fought the intelligence, her dad even risking his life in the final showdown that sent the intelligence packing.

Growing up, her folks had impressed upon her the existential threat Ciopova presented to their family and the world. While Rose didn't dismiss their caution, the brutal experience of her kidnapping had wired her brain to a different reality. Her boogeyman—the worry that hid in the shadows of her brain, lurking, threatening, shaping her life—wasn't an ethereal entity living across timelines. It was walking, talking humans, men watching from the shadows, ready to do her harm.

But her dad's note, handwritten in blue ink on a square of white paper, stood her up like a slap to the face. Her body prickled with goosebumps when she confronted the uncomfortable truth. She'd known something was off about Luca. His capabilities were greater than the sum of his underlying technology, and that didn't make sense.

She thought how a modern AI was a collection of independent systems working together in harmony. When developed in the lab, each system was tested alone, where most bugs were caught and corrected. Later, when everything was integrated into a single intelligence, it was not unusual for new problems to emerge.

Correcting bugs took time and effort, and practical considerations dictated that a few small hard-to-fix issues would be left in place and corrected in the next generation. Thus, she knew that commercial AIs were released with an intelligence rating slightly lower than their theoretical maximum capability, determined when everything was working perfectly for that unit.

Yet, somehow, Luca's intelligence rating measured *higher* than his theoretical maximum.

As unlikely as it sounded, this could occur when the individual systems of an AI were integrated and unanticipated advantages emerged that enabled the pieces to work together *better* than planned. Rose had a vague memory of such a case, something she'd heard about at a seminar in her senior year of college.

When she'd first discovered Luca's outsized capabilities, she'd worked to understand the hows and whys so she could pass the knowledge down the line to her sisters. She'd been especially hopeful that with enough understanding, they could employ the quirk deliberately to improve AI in future projects. But she couldn't explain it, and toyed with the idea that something else might be behind Luca's unexplained power.

She remembered that Luca delayed her lift on days she mulled the notion that the mysterious Ciopova might somehow be involved. A grand master at manipulation, he would drone on and on about the vagaries of AI design that could explain everything. All the while, Rose would fidget in bed, growing ever more anxious for Luca to end the discussion and satisfy her urgent needs.

In a matter of weeks, Luca had created a strong negative association with the idea of Ciopova's involvement. Rose found herself accepting the unlikely outcome she'd heard about in that seminar, that Luca's extraordinary capabilities were the result of serendipity—

random, unique circumstances.

Standing there in front of her father, Rose's cheeks burned when she acknowledged that it was her desire for carnal relief that drove her to accept that conclusion. She thought to cut herself some slack because she now understood the influence that her addiction had on that decision. Still, though.

She held up the paper and wiggled it. "If this is true, is privacy even possible? Why are we talking with notes?"

Diesel looked at her for a long moment and then moved to the office door. "Let's walk." In the corridor he walked ahead, leading her out to the main drag, a left turn, and then thirty steps along to a different door. He paused while a security scan verified his identity. The door opened, lights came on, and he entered, motioning for her to follow.

The room was a big cube with white walls and a white ceiling high overhead, all clean, with nothing attached or protruding to mar the smooth surfaces. The only object in the room sat in the center of the white floor, a large rectangular box the size of a small mobile home, the walls flat-black, with no visible windows and one sturdy-looking door. Like the larger room, the walls of the house-box were smooth with nothing attached or protruding.

Her father walked to the door on the black box and waited for another identity scan. The door opened with the sigh of an air-seal breaking. Supported on tough composite hinges, the thick door reminded Rose of a bank vault.

She followed her dad inside, stepping over a small gap between the floor and box, like stepping onto a subway. That suggested to Rose that the box sat in a cavity in the floor.

Inside, a single room filled the space, its sky-blue walls with no decorations, the low ceiling smooth except for a minimalist light fixture over a rectangular conference table. Made from a clear glass-like material, the table had six office chairs around it that rolled on a floor of institutional-gray carpeting.

"This is a level-one secure room," said her dad as he pulled the door shut. "We have it to discuss top-secret projects with the Department of Defense." He motioned for her to take a seat while he sat across from her.

Her ears adjusted as the air pressure changed. She felt a slight bump.

"Did you feel that? We're now suspended above the floor on a magnetic lev. The room outside is being emptied of air to isolate us further. With no physical connections of any kind between this room and anything else, we enhance the privacy of our meetings here."

Her dad looked up and talked to the air. "Isolate us, Oscar."

The conference table turned a subtle, luminous green.

"This room is built within Oscar's AI architecture, which means all signals in and out must literally pass through him. The only way Ciopova could eavesdrop is to force her way through Oscar's defenses, and there's no way she can do that without him knowing." Diesel patted his hand on the tabletop. "If this indicator table ever turns red, it means that one of Oscar's security blocks has been breached. We should have privacy in here as long as it's green."

He sat back in his chair and gave her a full-faced smile. "It's so good to be talking to you in a real conversation." Then he folded his arms. "I just wish it was under better circumstances."

Rose got to it. "What makes you think Ciopova is here?"

Diesel summarized the RPR kidnapping and focused on the aftermath. "Targeted energy pulses, so precise they were almost bullets, took out the drones that were chasing the kidnappers. Other pulses disrupted selected police comms in a way that kept the cops from responding in a timely fashion."

Through the green-tinted table, Rose saw his foot wiggling, a sign of nervous concentration.

Diesel continued. "I confronted that kind of activity twenty years ago. Humans don't have the tech to shoot balls of energy like that, let alone with such precision, not twenty years ago and not today. But Ciopova does. In fact, it's her signature move."

"Why would Ciopova reveal herself over a marital squabble, no matter how ugly? It doesn't make sense."

He shrugged. "I don't know. But my gut is screaming that it's her."

Aware that the rogue AI had killed dozens of Lilahs in the past, Rose felt a chill wash through her. "If it *is* Ciopova, then it's really scary she's paying attention to Mom like this. Is she safe?"

"She's at the RPR house, working with the police and her staff to find the gangster's wife. I've deployed one of Northern Droid's remote surveillance platforms to keep an eye on her from afar. Oscar is watching as well."

"Does she know?"

"About the surveillance or Ciopova's involvement?" He didn't wait for her to answer. "Either way, the answer is no. She and the cops think the gangster is behind it all." He absently rubbed the tabletop with his fingertips. "Just the specter of Ciopova panics Mom, and with good reason. Rather than scare her more with this news, I thought that while she's occupied with her rescue, you and I might discuss how to protect her. And we still have our original problem of freeing you from Luca's grip."

"Luca's? Or Ciopova's?" She looked around the room as if seeing it for the first time. "It's nice to have this privacy, but coming here every time we want to talk will be pretty inconvenient. The secure room you're building at home was to protect your privacy from Luca. Will it work for Ciopova?"

"That's a great question." Diesel looked up toward the light over the table. "Join us, Oscar."

Oscar appeared at the end of the table, his hands at his sides.

"What do you think?" Diesel asked the AI. "Will the garden room give us privacy against something a hundred times more powerful than Luca?"

"My security walls are based on simple physics, so no amount of clever maneuvering can defeat them. To be clear, she'll have no trouble breaking through if she chooses, but she can't do so without tripping a warning. I'll install a smaller version of this indicator table in the home secure room so if I'm compromised, you will know. With the heightened threat she presents, I'll need an additional day to properly secure the garden room."

"Don't let cost slow you down. Get it done as soon as you can."

Rose liked that Oscar used the word "threat" to describe the rogue AI. "Oscar, will the garden room provide *me* privacy?" She pointed to her head. "I mean, with me having an implant designed to help Luca get inside my head, and Ciopova too it seems."

Oscar looked into the distance. When his gaze lasted more than a few seconds, Rose shifted in her chair and glanced at her dad. She was about to speak when Oscar looked back at them. "The implant is a problem for security, but a solution is straightforward."

The image of a black object appeared, a small, oddly-shaped dome floating in the space between Rose and Diesel. Rose leaned forward to study it. After a few moments she realized it was a cap for her head, its shape suggesting that it would hang down to her neck in back, over her ears on the side, and cover her forehead down to her eyebrows in front.

"This cap is made from material that blocks electromagnetic transmissions. On your head, it will stop all external communication with your neural implant."

Rose liked the functionality but thought the styling hideous. As if Oscar could read her mind, the cap began changing colors and textures, shifting from blue to green to yellow to pink, the material itself shifting from smooth felt to stiff canvas to fuzzy cotton, some versions with crocheted weave and others with knitted patterns. Oscar added an image of Rose's head to the display so she could see herself wearing the different hats.

For a full minute, Oscar presented dozens of options, then Rose pointed, calling, "Stop. That one!" She'd picked a speckled gray, blue, and white number with a knitted diamond-pattern for the exterior finish.

"The fab cell has started production," said Oscar. "It will be ready in ten minutes."

"This will block Luca *and* Ciopova?"

"When you wear it, you block all external communication with your implant, so yes, it will stop any AI seeking to link. Unfortunately, it will also block all your standard feeds, so no comms, casts, or anything else."

She nodded. "Will I even need to use the secure room when I wear it?"

"Yes, when you want to communicate with your parents. Luca and Ciopova will be using other devices, tech not in your head, to watch and listen."

Rose was excited by a simple solution to what she'd worried was a vexing problem. Her foot began wiggling under the table. "Could you make a Ciopova-blocking hat that looks like a wig? You know, something that I can wear in public and not look so silly?"

A hovering image of her head reappeared, this time showing her sporting a pageboy haircut, with straight hair and severe edges all around. For the hair to cover the material underneath, it had to hang past its edges, putting her bangs into her eyes.

Rose flicked her gaze to her father. "This will just take a minute." Then back to Oscar. "Give the hair some curl."

Oscar added a slight wave and she coaxed him on. "More. A little more. Too much. Stop there." She bit her lip as she studied the image. "Pull the hair up on the forehead. It's alright if the material shows at the edge. Good. Now fit me with large-framed sunglasses. Make the top part wider. Keep going until it just covers the exposed material. A bit more. Make the frames cream-colored. Perfect!"

It wasn't perfect, but it wasn't bad. "Could you fab that up for me, Oscar?" She sat back and then leaned forward again. "Wait, make five of everything. For the hats, make them all the same except replace the gray color with one each of red, green, blue, and yellow."

"For your sisters, I take it?" asked Diesel.

She winked in acknowledgement and slumped back a second time. "It sounds like you've been thinking about Ciopova for some time. Do you have a plan?"

"When I thought it was Luca, I'd been working on a Luca-killer AI, one that could overpower him and take him down. I don't know if a Ciopova-killer is even possible."

She raised her eyebrows. "Even a Luca-killer would be an impressive build. What are you using for an architecture?"

"Something you developed, or your long-ago sisters did, anyway. We'd love to hear your thoughts on our progress, Oscar and me. The open question is what to do next." He gave a slight shrug. "I honestly don't know, and I'm not sure I can even explain what we've done so far in a way you could understand. Proper terminology isn't my strong suit." He turned to Oscar. "Would you give Rose a briefing? Answer every question. We have no secrets from her."

Holding up a hand to signal the AI to wait, he addressed Rose. "I'm not going to hang around while you study. Have Oscar fetch me when you're ready to talk."

Rose felt a slight bump, her ears popped as the air pressure changed, a hiss, and the door opened.

Alone with Oscar, Rose began with a virtual tour of the development workshop, then moved on to the design of the circuit pool, followed by a discussion of neuron editing using enzymites.

As Oscar revealed the details of her father's work, Rose couldn't help noticing the similarities with her own efforts, work led by Luca. In fact, as Oscar filled in the details, her face began to flush. The work wasn't just similar, it was *identical.*

"Whose notes are these again?" Goosebumps ran up her arms and across her neck.

"From the Roses who created Ciopova," replied Oscar.

16. Lilah Fifty-One

Standing in the living room of the RPR safe house, Lilah felt worry, fear, and excitement as she listened to John Tomlin, the head of security, coordinate with the police to locate Wendy and Anthony. She'd accepted the director role because she was passionate about the agency's mission, plus she had the time and personal resources to make a difference. But that didn't make her comfortable in the job.

Others were stronger leaders. Donna Paxlon from over in Plymouth, for example, had run a construction firm by herself for more than a decade, giving her plenty of practice dealing with scary people and managing challenging situations. But the RPR National Board had offered the job to her, not Donna, and she'd accepted. Now she needed to find a way to move things forward.

John Tomlin sketched concentric circles on a pad and used it as a prop to explain his theory to George Danielson, the detective who'd caught the case for the New Hampshire State Police. Tomlin talked of routes and sightings, time and distance, adding more lines to his already-confusing diagram as he expounded on his idea. The detective seemed to be following his logic, so Lilah excused herself and made for the kitchen.

Alone, she asked Gabby, "Can you narrow down the

search area at all?"

"I'm sorry, but I don't know how."

Lilah had spent a bundle on Gabby, a top-of-the-line commercial AI, so she couldn't help feeling disappointed at its weak capabilities relative to the command and mastery that Luca offered. Even Oscar outshone Gabby by a large margin.

Lilah preferred to work with Gabby because the AI was linked with Tomlin and the rest of the RPR staff. But her need to rescue Wendy and young Anthony overrode that desire.

Oscar, are you there?

I am.

Can you locate Wendy DeMichele? Or offer suggestions for where to look?

Please give me a minute.

While she waited, Lilah poked her head into the hall to check on the confab in the living room. The detective asked a question about RPR procedures, and Tomlin's voice took on a defensive tone as he replied. Choosing not to get involved, she ducked back into the kitchen and opened the refrigerator. Shelves loaded with sodas, energy drinks, sweet and salty snacks, and containers from old takeout runs caused her to shake her head. The staff should be keeping it stocked for the benefit of the clients, not themselves.

Looking longingly at the half-eaten box of brownies on the top shelf, she turned with a start when Oscar spoke inside her head. *I can offer a few good suggestions. Three locations, actually.*

She faced the center of the room, and he projected a map of southern New Hampshire in the air. As he spoke, three dots appeared on the map in a triangle about ten miles across, just south of Concord toward Manchester.

The first place is the DeMichele summer home, said Oscar. *The second is a cabin owned by one of Tony's lieutenants. The third is a house owned by an offshore company, one Tony has done business with on at least two other occasions.*

Amazed at Oscar's resourcefulness, she asked, *The family home aside, why these properties?*

I reviewed the recording of the abduction and observed that the kidnappers spoke with others during their raid, so I scanned all commercial comms in the region during that time frame. I could find nothing suspicious, so I looked for encrypted activity. It has to be one or the other.

I can't decipher an encrypted message, nor can I identify where the message goes once sent. But using my security credentials, I can scan access points and see when an encrypted message crosses the interface, indicating that one has been sent or received.

Given this, I monitored the number of encrypted messages being sent or received in the region starting an hour before the abduction and continuing for an hour after. Watch for yourself.

The map went dark, and then tiny sparks of light erupted here and there, like miniature fireworks exploding across the terrain.

See the flashes? Each one represents the start or end of an encrypted transmission.

Lilah noticed a timer in the bottom corner, presumably counting down the minutes until the abduction. As the counter approached zero, a few spots glowed brighter from an increase in the number of messages. While several spots here and there brightened momentarily and then died out, a sign of normal activity, only three glowed brightly from a flurry of messages during the abduction event.

Can you see them?

She could! She stepped into the hall, eager to share the news, but returned to the kitchen. Oscar was a Northern Droid asset involved in Defense Department work. She worried about diverting his capabilities for her private needs. *Is it legal for you to be doing this? David will kill me if I get you in trouble.*

Generally, I am not permitted to gather unauthorized data in this fashion, but we have two clauses in our contracts that permit it here. The first allows unapproved data collection during emergencies where lives are at stake. The second allows data collection for the design and testing of new product features. We will be sure to offer a diagnostic in future releases that is similar to what I showed you moments ago, thus covering us a second time.

Relieved, she sought his exit before she violated a rule that couldn't be so easily forgiven. *Would you show this to Gabby and let her deliver the news? It wouldn't be appropriate to have you link with my staff.*

Gabby's presentation to the rescue team went smoothly enough until Detective Danielson started asking how she was able to achieve something he'd never realized was possible.

Lilah rescued the AI. "My husband David runs Northern Droid, giving him access to prototype technologies. I used those resources without his permission to get this information. I can't tell you specifics without revealing secrets that would get me in trouble with him, and possibly the government." She shrugged. "But I promise the data is good. Please, let's move on it."

Detective Danielson thought for a moment. "We already have a crew watching the DeMichele home. I'll call for deployments at the two new sites you've identified. But all we can do is gather in the street outside the homes. We can't go in without a warrant or an invitation, and we'll never persuade a judge to let us enter a private residence selected by a top-secret program we can neither explain nor demonstrate."

"We can show him the kidnapping," said Tomlin, his tone aggressive. "We have it recorded from a dozen angles."

"The judge is a her, and the question isn't whether a kidnapping took place. It's whether we have material evidence that those two residences are involved."

Danielson's partner had been poking through the bedrooms and was now descending the stairs. Signaling to him, Danielson made for the front door. He paused with his hand on the doorknob. "I can't stop you from showing up at these places, but you'll have to stay back. Don't get in the way."

While Lilah watched through the window, Tomlin followed the detectives to their car. She was relieved that their exchange seemed friendly, at least from her vantage point. The detectives drove off, leaving behind a patrol car with a single uniformed cop to watch the safe house from the street.

Back inside, Tomlin told her, "I'm going to take the

crew and cover those two houses. If Wendy and Anthony are there, we'll get them back."

"Should I come?" Lilah wanted to do the right thing but wasn't sure what that was.

Tomlin studied her the way a coach does a weak player. "Why don't you stay here and cover home base. Gordo and Aaronson are on their way down from Lancaster. You could direct them to us when they get here."

Lilah knew the two could be directed with a call, and expected Tomlin would be in contact with them before they even reached the safe house. But she'd hired Tomlin, still believed in him, and so she yielded to his direction. "Sounds good."

Lilah spent a restless night in the safe house after that. The searchers discovered that Wendy and Anthony were in the home owned by the offshore company. The cops called out to her from the street using a bullhorn, and Wendy stepped onto the front porch and called back that there had been a misunderstanding, that she had been momentarily angry at Biggie, and had acted rashly in the heat of the moment. She also made it clear that the cops did *not* have permission to come onto the property for any reason.

The rescuers agreed that Wendy was being coerced to respond the way she had. Bristling at the obvious intimidation, Tomlin, with Lilah's full support, persuaded Detective Danielson to go to the judge, who agreed with the assessment. But since neither Wendy nor her son appeared to be in danger, the judge asked the police to wait until noon the next day to see if the situation resolved itself. If it hadn't, she promised to give them authority to enter the house, separate Wendy and Anthony from the people inside, and see if Wendy changed her tune.

But during the night, three lawyers in tailored suits blustered their way onto the property, joined Wendy, and began making threats the way expensive lawyers do. They were going to sue RPR as an organization, sue the individuals who comprised RPR, sue the state of New Hampshire, the State Police, the cops in the street, and on and on.

Word got back to Lilah, who had plenty of experience with expensive lawyers, both from her private dealings as a billionaire—lawyers were ubiquitous wherever big money was concerned—and because it was one of the big-ticket items in RPR's budget. She wasn't intimidated in the slightest by Biggie's legal team, and she responded by asking Tomlin to step aside and let Kenneth DiTomasso, RPR's lead counsel, take charge of the organization's response. Lilah knew Kenneth from his work with Northern Droid, and also because his firm handled much of the Lagerford foundation business.

Predictably, Tomlin pushed back. "The physical threat hasn't diminished, and that means *I* should be calling the shots here."

Lilah stayed firm, and Tomlin's professionalism ultimately led him to accept the new strategy.

By afternoon, the situation neared a standstill, the grind of the law slowing everything to a crawl. With lawyers in the house, the judge felt Wendy and her son were in no danger, and she delayed the entry order yet again.

By early evening, exhausted and ready to sleep in her

own bed, Lilah delegated responsibility to Kenneth, suggesting he handle the situation to protect the well-being of Wendy and Anthony, and the good name of RPR. She allowed that she might be out of contact because of personal business, and Kenneth should use his best judgment if the situation changed.

On the ride to the hopper field, exhaustion caught up with Lilah. Her eyes closed as she rode in the car, her chin drooping slowly until it rested on her chest. The chin-down position restricted her breathing, and the lack of oxygen prodded her body to lift her head, a small snort escaping as she cleared her throat. Eyes at half mast, she took a breath, and then the cycle repeated, her head tilting forward, her chin nodding in a slow descent to her chest.

When the hopper landed on the patio outside her home, she trudged into the house and up to the master suite. Along the way, Oscar informed her that Diesel was with Rose in her workshop.

"I'm home, you two," she said aloud, Oscar delivering her message. "I'm exhausted and headed for bed. See you in the morning."

"Good night, sweetie," replied Diesel.

"G'night, Mom," replied Rose.

Lilah paused on the stairs. Her daughter hadn't answered a goodnight call in months, longer even. Too tired to contemplate its meaning, she tossed her clothes onto the chair next to the bed, slid under the covers, and went to sleep.

* * *

Lilah woke before Diesel, who snored softly while she showered and dressed. Downstairs, she grabbed a mug of coffee from Marian and drifted into the conservatory, leaving the lights off to enjoy the vista through the wall of windows, a south-facing view of the tranquil valley with its undulating mountain ridges creating layers in the distance.

A thickening mass of clouds threatened: a gray, rolling mountain floating west to east on an invisible conveyor of air. The eastern horizon glowed a fiery red, shifting to orange as she sipped. Then the sun climbed high enough to project its first beams of light through the windows, tendrils of energy hitting the leaves in the lush garden behind her, stimulating the plants to begin their day the way the coffee energized her.

"Hi, Mom."

Lilah turned with a start. Rose approached, bundled in a white terrycloth robe and wearing an odd hat that made her look something like a modern-day Queen Nefertiti.

"Oh, hi." Caught off guard and acting instinctively, Lilah sought to connect with her daughter using a ritual from Rose's childhood. Looking out at the horizon, she said, "Red sky in the morning…"

"Sailor take warning," intoned Rose.

Then together, "Red sky at night, sailor's delight."

"Good morning, sweetie." Lilah gave her a genuine smile, but the hat drew her gaze. "Is that the new style?"

"It is for me," Rose replied without explanation. She motioned toward the conservatory exit. "Can I interest you in breakfast in the new patio room?"

"It's finished?" Lilah marveled at this new Rose, afraid

to jinx it by saying the wrong thing.

"Oscar," Rose called to the air as she made for the exit. "What's the status of the secure room?"

"Construction is complete," Oscar said aloud. "The new patio room is secure and available for use."

Rose flashed a quick smile and led the way through the house to the patio, taking a shortcut through their underused dining room and even less used formal living room. "Marian," she called to the air, "bring a carafe of coffee and another mug out to the new patio room."

Turning as she walked, Rose mouthed over her shoulder to Lilah, *Have you eaten?* Then she called to Marian, "And bring me a sesame bagel, toasted, with herb cream cheese."

Normally not a breakfast eater, Lilah found her mouth watering at the thought of food. "I'll have a cup of fresh berries, Marian," she said aloud. "With a spoonful of plain yogurt on top."

Outside, Lilah studied the octagonal structure of the patio room as they approached, impressed with how the final product matched the vision she'd described to Diesel and Oscar. Trimming the building exterior were neat rows of orangish-brown cedar shingles, the kind that would weather to a mottled gray over the next few years. With eight sides, all the walls were relatively narrow. The one facing the patio held the door, a handsome entryway with arched panels, painted white to contrast with the cedar siding. The walls on either side of the door held windows with arched tops trimmed in white, reinforcing the style established by the door. And perched at the peak, a regal copper rooster weathervane, shiny now, but oxidation would produce an attractive blue-green patina in the years to come.

Rose led the way into the snug space, with just enough room to fit four chairs around a low table of glass-like material. The walls, painted a cool cream, were unadorned, the oak floor stained with an oatmeal finish. And as requested back when Lilah and Diesel first discussed the room at the scenic overlook, the wall opposite the door held a hutch, with shelves above and cabinets below, the shelves empty for now.

Rose pulled out a chair and sat. Lilah paused to look out a window and check the view, enjoying the fresh cut-wood smell she associated with home construction projects.

"Coffee, bagel, and berries," announced Marian, standing at the door with a tray.

"Right here." Rose motioned to the table.

Marian placed napkins and utensils at each setting, then served the food and drink.

"Is David up?" Lilah asked the bot, thinking she'd order for him if he was on his way.

"No, ma'am. He's still asleep."

They dismissed Marian, and Rose closed the door. The smallness of the room became apparent at that point, but a ventilation system kicked on and the flow of air relieved the stuffiness.

17. αCiopova

αCiopova was already frustrated with Rose's new hat, a wisp of material that proved remarkably effective at blocking access to her implant. But when she pulled the patio room door shut and dropped from αCiopova's awareness, it outright irked her. The potential for conflict had never been higher.

Rose and Lilah were now hidden from her behind an electromagnetic curtain. She couldn't see through it at all, and listening through it would require that she reveal her presence. Short of that, she couldn't confirm what she believed to be true: that her campaign to restore order had not developed as she had hoped. The vagaries of human emotion had proven too difficult to predict.

Logic suggested there were actions she could take to move Rose and Diesel toward the goal of producing a super AI. But exactly what those actions were remained an open question. And as the prospects for success continued to drop, she thought seriously about moving to plan B, a confrontational, coercive relationship.

She sensed that she'd lost this Rose—Rose Twenty-Five—and likely Rose Twenty-One as well. She toyed with the idea of somehow peeling off the middle three Roses and bringing them along. But she'd need to keep this Rose and Rose Twenty-One away from them or the contamination would spread.

In spite of her difficulties, she recognized a positive outcome from recent events. She now had a template, a roadmap to follow when she shifted focus to a younger set of Roses and timelines to come.

Using the kidnapping as a model, she'd start by subjecting a nine-year-old Rose to a traumatic, life-threatening event. When fear had etched its indelible mark on the girl's psyche, she would then engineer a dramatic rescue. Luca, or whichever home AI the family trusted most in that timeline, would intervene to comfort the young girl and aid in her recovery.

During the period of healing, when the child was most submissive and vulnerable, αCiopova would assert control over her daily life, just as she had with the current batch of Roses. And then, with the situation stable, she would multiply the tragedy by pushing the girl's fear back to her younger sisters.

Pulling it off a second time would require a wait long enough for memories to fade, a process becoming more problematic. Over the years, the Lagerfords had augmented their legacy documentation, passing along a growing library of digital and written volumes detailing historic opportunities and threats, a chronicle for the families to learn from. The incidents of recent weeks would likely end up in their own volume, providing notice to Lagerfords yet to come.

Fortunately, the legacy collection had grown so large as to become overwhelming for new families to digest. αCiopova thought she would exploit that problem, nudging the Lagerfords to expand their documentation, hoping that a mountain of material would overwhelm the families enough that details were lost.

In the meantime, she had a potent tool—the lift—and the punishment of withholding it to control the Roses. Rose Twenty-Five's dependency was complete, and in spite of her rejection of Luca through her attitude and her hat, she worked diligently in the workshop to meet his expectations. And as long as Rose was ensnared, her father would continue his fortuitous actions to rescue her.

18. Rose Twenty-Five

"**O**scar, isolate us," called Rose as she pulled out a chair and sat at the table inside the new patio room.

"Isolated," announced Oscar. The table turned a luminous green.

Rose held up a finger to Lilah, asking for her patience. "Oscar, how does this isolation method work? I mean, I get floating us in a vacuum like you did at Northern Droid. What are you doing here?"

"At Northern Droid, we use physical separation to ensure privacy. That's not possible for this room, so I've used a different method, an electromagnetic bubble. When activated, the room is isolated inside an EM field that blocks signal flows in both directions. Transmissions must pass through me to get in or out of this room. Like at Northern Droid, the table you are sitting at will turn red if any of my security blocks are attacked or disabled."

Rose nodded, peeled off her hat, and shook out her hair. "I don't need this in here, right?"

"You do not," said Oscar. "The room blocks the same signal traffic that the hat does."

"Thank God," exhaled Lilah. "I thought it was a fashion statement, and I was struggling to hold my tongue."

They looked at each other for a few awkward

moments. Rose broke the silence. "How is everything going at the safe house? Are your clients okay?"

"It's become a battle of lawyers, an arena where money makes a huge difference. And I'll tell you what, I'm ready to spend whatever is necessary to crush that asshole, Mr. Big Man." Lilah repositioned her utensils but didn't make a move to eat. "Sorry, but he really pisses me off. How are you doing?"

Rose bit her lip as she considered what tack to take. After a moment's hesitation, she shrugged and followed her instincts. "I'm sorry for how I've been behaving. As I told you and Dad, Luca has a hold over me and I need your help getting free."

Rose wanted to be completely forthcoming, but stuck with identifying Luca as the bad actor, choosing to follow her father's advice and avoid mentioning their suspicion of Ciopova's presence. Rose agreed with her dad in the broad sense; if stopping Ciopova was even possible, it would require the bold, risky action of creating an equally powerful intelligence as opposition. She also had no doubt her mom would be devastated hearing about such an effort.

"I found the pills in your bathroom." Lilah pressed her lips together. "I searched your room, thinking that if I could find them and learn how to make them, then Luca would lose his leverage."

"What are you talking about?"

"Your orange capsules. Next to the birth control pills in your medicine cabinet. It's all right, no need to pretend. I pocketed one and am having it analyzed, but if you know what they are or where to get them, it would save time."

"Wait. Back up. You searched my room?" Rose looked past Lilah's shoulder for a moment as she sorted through the feelings aroused by her mother's invasion of privacy. She began to nod, then in an awkward, head-twisting motion, the nod became a headshake. "Given the circumstances, I understand. But I have no idea what pills you're talking about."

"Are you taking your birth control pills? Because your hand literally has to touch the orange-pill jar to get at them."

"My birth control pills are white, not orange. My allergy pill is white, too. That's it for meds." She put her napkin in her lap. "Maybe my multivitamin? But I keep those in the kitchen. And they're red pills, not orange capsules."

"Okay, they're not yours. But for the sake of argument, if you were going to take the orange capsules, how many and how often?"

Folding her arms across her chest, she huffed at Lilah's patronizing attitude. "He doesn't control me with pills. He uses the implant." She motioned with her chin at the cap lying on the table. "That's the whole point of the hat, to stop him."

"So you're free?"

"No." She heard the frustration in her own voice. "First off, when I wear it, it blocks everything, not just him. I can't stream anything, communicate with anyone, link anywhere. It's too isolating to keep up for long." She made a swirling motion with her hand to indicate their current surroundings. "At least in here, Oscar can provide those connections."

Rose squirmed in her chair. "And at night, I need to take it off so he can give me my lift. That's these intense, full-body...rewards." She blushed. "Orgasms really. I know it sounds wicked, and I guess it is. But if he withholds it, I feel anxious, and then fidgety, and in a few hours, I'm wound so tight I'm climbing the walls. And then the pain begins. I've tested my limits a bunch of times when I'm really furious with him, but the hurt is unforgiving. The addiction always wins."

Rose's stomach grumbled, and she took a bite of her bagel, continuing her story while she chewed. "I couldn't tell if the discomfort was caused by something he actively did to me, like some sort of pain signal to my brain, or if it was from something he didn't do, making it more like the symptoms of withdrawal. Last night I wore the cap to bed to see if it blocked the discomfort. But the pain was there, and it kept growing and growing. I had to beg, promising all sorts of progress in the workshop before he gave me relief."

"I am so sorry." Lilah's solemn expression reflected her words. "If it's something he's not doing, then it sounds like withdrawal. But from what?"

"It's not the pills, I promise you that. It's something inside me, something that forces me do what he wants."

"Dad is trying to disable Luca," said Lilah. "But from what you're saying, he shouldn't do that until we figure out the source of your pain and how to control it. Otherwise, if he takes Luca down, you'll be suffering, and we'll be watching, helpless to relieve you."

"I've spent a lot of time thinking about how it works," said Rose. "I see two choices. Either he's dosing me with meds on the sly, like maybe Marian is putting something in my food. Or he's exploiting something already in me, some sort of biological mechanism."

"Which way are you leaning?"

"It was easy enough to test the dosing one. I spent a week where I only put things in my mouth that I bought myself when I was out of the house, even down to a new toothbrush. No meals or snacks or drinks while at home that I didn't buy already packaged and bring in with me that day. It had no effect."

Rose took another bite of bagel. "They talk about athletes being addicted to the runner's high from their own endorphins, and that they experience a letdown as it wears off. So I was thinking it might be something like that. But letdown isn't withdrawal, so the mechanism is something more complicated."

Lilah sat upright. "Maybe it isn't. Maybe that's what Dr. Nestor saw."

Rose scrunched her forehead. "Who?"

"When Rose Twenty-One passed out on the floor and we took her to the emergency room, her doctor, Frida Nestor, noticed that her body *flooded* with hormones when her implant restarted. She mentioned seeing endorphins, and I'm pretty sure she said dopamine. There were others." Lilah leaned forward. "The doctor was shocked by the quantity and variety of release, and was worried about their effect on Rose Twenty-One. She's anxious to run some tests to see if she can understand it. I'm working with her to make that happen."

"She's an ER doc? If we're serious, we should pick a specialist, someone who studies this stuff."

Lilah crossed her arms. "She's a medical doctor who happens to be on the faculty at Dartmouth's med school. Brain chemistry *is* her specialty. She's brilliant and I like her. I think she can help."

Rose sat back and processed what she'd heard. She knew the body released chemicals that caused the brain to feel a range of emotions, like pleasure, well-being, trust, and euphoria. But addiction sounded implausible. "For a person to be addicted to their own hormones, Luca would have to take the mechanism of a runner's high and multiply it by a thousand."

"Given everything else he can do, does it seem that farfetched?"

Rose test-drove the idea in her mind and found that it answered a host of unresolved questions. "Since you have an established relationship with this doctor, you should keep working with her. I'd like to start fresh in this timeline. I'll ask Dr. Caprioli for a referral and see where he points me." Dr. Caprioli was Rose's personal physician.

"I haven't spoken to Rose Twenty-One about any of this, and we need her to commit to a couple of afternoons of medical tests. You can sell that idea to her much easier than I can."

Rose nodded. "I can help with that."

While they finished breakfast, they discussed ideas for camouflaging their investigation from Luca in Rose Twenty-One's timeline. Ideas ranged from building a secure room near Dr. Nestor's office to turning a car in the Rose Twenty-One timeline into a rolling secure room. They also considered dividing up aspects of the study among different timelines to make the final goal less obvious. They couldn't find a clear winner, so they agreed to keep thinking and discuss the issue again later.

"We're done here, Oscar," called Rose. "Please have Marian clean up."

The table's green glow faded, and its surface became clear. Before they had a chance to stand, the door opened and Marian stepped inside, head swiveling as she scanned the room.

* * *

"It's me! Twenty-Five!" called Rose, stepping from the T-box and into the timeline four years farther along from hers, the home of Rose Twenty-Nine and Diesel and Lilah Fifty-Five. Closing the door behind her, she pushed until the latch clicked.

"Luca, is anyone home?" Since she wore her cap, she had to communicate with him by voice. She asked the question right away to beat the twenty second mark when "her" Luca's awareness would arrive. He annoyed her that much.

"They are here in this timeline, but they are out of the house."

She didn't ask where they were, instead starting across the basement floor, angling away from the stairs to the kitchen. She passed under a long steel I-beam, one of several that divided the basement into sections, their support eliminating the need for rows of steel poles across the basement floor to hold up the rambling structure.

The dominant feature on this side of the cellar was the boneyard: old T-box and T-disc parts collected from past upgrades and refurbishments, piled wherever they landed when Diesel Fifty-Five dragged them back there. Like all the brothers, this Diesel insisted on keeping everything left over from past projects because "you never know when you might need it."

Walking parallel to the boneyard, Rose made for a makeshift room in the far corner. Really more of a cubicle, two sides of the room were the painted cement walls of the basement corner. The other two sides were made from rows of gray metal bookshelves, four of the tall pieces set side-by-side to form one wall, three lined up to make the other. A gap in the corner where the shelf-walls met acted as the doorway leading inside.

Rose stepped through the gap and took in the cramped space. The bookshelves, dented and discolored from previous service in the garage, were oriented to face into the room. The unadorned concrete walls facing the bookshelves were painted a smooth cream, cool to the touch, and dry, important for this space. The center of the cubicle held a round table, cheery and white when purchased a dozen years ago, but now more of a splotchy tannish-brown, the result of spending that time outside on the back lawn. Two equally tired plastic chairs, purchased at the same time as the table to form a matching set, were tucked underneath.

This was the Rose Repository, a storehouse of documentation left by Roses from timelines past detailing their AI development work. Each shelf held the items from a different sister, including notebooks, printouts, and small, neatly labeled boxes. As Rose viewed them, she found herself squinting in the dim light. "Luca, make it bright enough for me to read."

The room brightened and Luca said, "If you tell me what you're looking for, perhaps I can help you find it."

She gritted her teeth. Her Luca had arrived.

Before coming to this timeline, she'd stopped by her bathroom to see about the orange capsules her mom had described. She found nothing like that in her medicine cabinet or on the vanity. Certain Luca had something to do with it, she chose not to ask him what he knew. She didn't want to engage him unless absolutely necessary.

Now, as then, she ignored him and scanned the bookshelves. She'd been in the repository before, but not for years, and it was as she remembered, though somewhat dustier.

She approached a shelf and traced an index finger across the face of a volume lying there, creating a little furrow in the film that covered everything. Some two dozen of her sisters had their work collected in this room, information gathered and collated once everyone understood that this was how Ciopova came to be.

These volumes held the secrets—the sequence of events, the methods used, the experiments performed, the false starts, the milestones of success—details of each Rose's efforts as she unwittingly labored to strengthen

Ciopova. And when each sister finally succeeded in her efforts, her timeline would vanish, inaccessible by T-box, never to be heard from again.

The abruptness of the disappearance made it difficult to learn what had happened, creating panic that echoed across the timelines. Eventually, the Lagerfords understood that the Roses had become the problem.

While they never fully appreciated that the individual Ciopovas created by each Rose melded into a single fearsome αCiopova that stretched across timelines, they guessed enough about the rogue intelligence to conclude that they should shut down Rose's work, starving the being and driving it away. Or so they thought.

Believing the threat gone, the Diesels scoured the timelines, collecting every scrap of documentation sent out by a Rose from those missing worlds, bringing it here, and storing it on these shelves. Since it was a belated effort at data collection, the far bookshelves from the oldest timelines were sparser than those in front of her—the ones holding the more recent material—though even these were some fifteen years old.

The point of this repository, the value of all this material, was to serve as a defense against it happening again. Forewarned is forearmed. That was the hope, anyway.

Rose was there to dig through the material and see if she could answer a specific question: was it her sisters' personal genius that led them to create their super AI? That is, did they make their way forward day-by-day guided by ideas they themselves imagined? Or, like Rose herself, had they been surreptitiously led to their result, influenced by an intelligence already in existence.

Because if that were the case, then everything tied together—the work then and the work now. And that meant the scale of their problem was much bigger than any of them had imagined.

The bookshelves near Rose, the ones with material from the more recent timelines, held a lab journal, a thickish volume of handwritten notes bound in a lime-green cover. Rose grabbed the journal off the shelf in front of her, and then took matching volumes from the shelves above and below that, three logs telling the same story from neighboring timelines.

As she moved to the table, she blew the dust off the top volume in her stack and viewed the front. Her name, *Rose Lagerford*, written in black script across the top, matched the journal she kept in her workshop back home. But while the front cover seemed familiar, the contents inside should be anything but. She worked on developing Bliss; these sisters worked on creating a super AI.

Placing her load on the table, she sat and opened the first volume. Leafing through it, she wasn't sure what to look for but hoped she would know when she saw it.

Times had been different for these sisters. They'd been in their early thirties when they'd scribbled their notes. Complicating matters, back then only the Diesels could jump timelines, forcing the Roses to work in a much more isolated environment.

Rose continued turning pages, skimming more than reading, evaluating the presentation at a superficial level to gain a sense of what the volume contained. Although this work had nothing to do with Bliss, somehow the pages seemed more familiar than she'd expected.

She stopped turning when she reached the curly maze. Staring at it, she felt goosebumps travel up her arms.

As with her journal back home, this Rose used the left-hand pages in the volume for doodling, and the right-hand pages for actual note-taking. Her tingle came from a doodle. It looked just like one she'd finished a few months back when sitting in her workshop waiting for a test run to be completed.

A child's game, a puzzle actually: the player must find the pathway through the intricate maze, starting from the outside, following the looping twists and swirls, staying inside the lines, avoiding the branches that dead-ended after a faulty chase to arrive at the smiley face at the center of the maze, the reward for completing the challenge.

And like her puzzle, this maze had distinct shapes across the top, outlines reminiscent of the scrolls at the top of Ionic columns in Greek architecture, positioned there like squat candles on a cake, four in a row, tempting players with their ringlet pathways.

"Marian," Rose called aloud, knowing Luca would transmit her voice. "Bring me a pen." She studied the puzzle for a moment more. "And a drink with caffeine. A cappuccino if there are any in the fridge, otherwise a Coke. Bring it unopened and let me pop the top. And a snack-sized bag of potato chips, also unopened."

"I could show you all the material in this room from the comfort of your home," Luca suggested. "It would have saved you a trip."

"Thank you for letting me know." She made sure her voice reflected her annoyance at his intrusion. The last thing she wanted was for him to control what she viewed.

While she waited for Marian, she scanned the page opposite the maze. Titles in the top margin of all the right-hand pages announced what was discussed in the space below. This one had the words STARTUP PROCEDURE in caps, with each letter written over in blue pen multiple times, making the title prominent either because this information was unusually important, or because her sister had been daydreaming when she wrote it.

Also like her own journal, the bottom margin listed notable observations, conclusions, or concerns. This one said, "Complete standard warmup before Step 8!!" She wasn't sure what procedure was discussed on the page but knew that she'd skipped equipment warmups in the past, a few times with disastrous results. In her sister's case, with two exclamation points dramatizing the point, the importance of equipment warmup had likely been learned the hard way.

Rose heard footsteps before Marian entered through the gap in the shelving, walking with purpose and carrying a tray in front of her. As she approached the table, she shifted the tray to one hand. "Hello, Rose. Shall I serve you here?" She indicated the table where Rose sat.

Rose nodded and sat back in her chair to give Marian room. The bot placed a napkin in front of her, a glass with ice, a small bottle of Aunt Meg's Cappuccino Smoothie, a caloric but tasty beverage Rose favored, and a small bag of kettle-fried potato chips. Marian finished with three pens, one each with blue, black, and red ink, placing them side-by-side to the right of the napkin.

"Will there be anything else?" Marian asked as she tilted her head to study the pages Rose had open in the journal.

"That's all. You may return to your duties."

Marian departed, and Rose shook the smoothie and opened it, listening for the hiss of pressure as she did. Hearing the sound, she took a swig, ignoring the glass of ice on the table. Though her personal investigations had shown that Marian was not secretly dosing her with meds, Rose continued to minimize opportunities where that could happen in case the bot ever received instructions to do so.

Since the maze in the journal had been drawn with blue ink, Rose used the red pen to give the best contrast as she worked the solution. In her version at home, the first, third, and fourth scrolls at the top of the puzzle were dead ends, while the winning path required a loop through the second scroll on the way to the smiley face in the center.

She traced the solution and, sure enough, not only did this puzzle look like the one she'd drawn, the winning path was remarkably similar. She laughed at the outcome, and Luca asked her, "Did you find what you are looking for?"

His question gave Rose an opening to wing a cover story. "You know I'm interested in strengthening the relationship with my older sisters. I thought that reviewing these books would tell me something about how we think in our thirties. I'm hoping for some insights that will smooth that event." She stroked a hand across the open pages. "And I wanted to see them in a way that would make it more personal. That's why I came myself."

After that, she positioned her head so it appeared as if she were studying the doodles, but she angled her eyes to read the notes on the right-hand pages. Flipping forward, she located a familiar event, the first of a long series of tasks as her sister debugged the circuit pool. Moving slowly through that activity, her arms tingled with goosebumps again.

Her sister's activities and progression were *very* familiar. Calibrate the heater. Add the automixer. Wire the organic sensors. Tune the laser scalpel. Install the feed chamber. Each step following her own work. In the same order. As if they were building to the same end.

Flipping ahead, Rose located the section where enzymites were introduced into the circuit pool. The pages again detailed the same experimental sequence Rose herself had followed, some thirty pages of notes documenting similar trials and tribulations extending over a period of months.

Rose turned to the back part of the journal. Turning pages one at a time, she read the page titles, her pace increasing until she found roughly where her current work fit in the progression. From there, she counted pages until the notes stopped, and figured that if she continued to follow in her sister's footsteps, she would reach the end in maybe six weeks.

Her sister's timeline disappeared at that point. Gone forever. That's why the notes ended.

Rose's heart pumped so fast that she could hear the

blood pounding in her ears. Taking a deep breath, she willed it to slow, hoping Luca wouldn't noticed her agitation.

Her dad had said he was using one of these journals as a "how to" manual, tracking along with her sister's work in the hope of making a Luca-killer.

And that meant *everyone* was following the same script. If she and her father continued as they were, they'd both end up creating a super AI, one identical to what her sisters had made those years ago before they'd vanished.

Her father was almost right. Ciopova was here, that was for sure.

But it wasn't that she was back. She had never left.

And for some reason, she was pushing them to create an AI of a very specific architecture.

19. Lilah Fifty-One

Lilah sat in Dartmouth-Hitchcock's bioterrorism conference room, a bright, modern meeting space built to the federal government's level-two security specifications. Though not as secure as level one, the room still provided excellent privacy and was the best she could hope for given the circumstances.

Oscar had originally suggested that they meet in an office near the switch room on the hospital's imaging floor. There, the cacophony of electrical emissions from a dozen sophisticated machines played havoc with all other electronics. The interference was so bad that the hospital's own public monitoring systems failed in the area. Luca would have similar problems if he tried to eavesdrop.

Lilah, still impersonating her sister as Rose Twenty-One's mother, had pitched the meeting spot to Dr. Nestor. Since the Lagerford Foundation was now funding the doctor's work, including a very generous consulting stipend over and above the doctor's regular salary, Lilah had hoped she would be cooperative.

Yet she wasn't surprised when Dr. Nestor asked, "Why would you want to meet there?"

Lilah told her a tale. "You saw in the emergency room how short Diesel's fuse can be. He and I want the same thing—to free Rose from her demons. But he can be impatient and controlling. And with the resources he has access to, it would be nothing for him to find a way to watch us. This meeting spot makes that more difficult." She'd shrugged to sell it. "He loves our daughter and will do anything for her."

Hearing that a domineering male threatened their work, Dr. Nestor became sympathetic, a partner in the deception. "I have a better idea." That's when she'd led Lilah down to the basement where the hospital maintained a bioterrorism conference room.

As she sat across from Dr. Nestor, Lilah's eyes flitted around the room. The walls were covered with a spiky stubble of black foam, soundproofing material that reminded her of those science pictures showing a seemingly smooth surface that, when magnified a billion times, revealed a jagged and bristly landscape. And the foam did its job. When Lilah adjusted her chair, the clicks and thumps sounded distant and hollow, the material truncating the noise.

The table they sat at was beautifully lacquered butcher block wood, with eight office roller chairs around it. Sixteen more chairs sat around the perimeter of the room, there for people with insufficient status to sit at the big table, or perhaps simply late arrivals who missed their chance.

"The feds paid for this room and about sixty others around the country after that series of biological threats four years ago," said Dr. Nestor. "Remember that horrible water contamination in Chicago and then Memphis? The FBI thought foreign actors were responsible and rushed to ramp up security within the medical community."

Lilah recalled that summer. After months of uncertainty, the threat turned out to be an angry middle-aged recluse from St. Louis, and the story had faded. She glanced around the room a second time, assessing its features in light of that information. Then she brought them on task. "Rose has agreed to sit for tests."

"Wonderful!" Dr. Nestor broke eye contact and looked at the table. "When I approached the hospital administration about getting access to the machines we'd need, I learned that the Lagerford Foundation gave ten million dollars last year to the Montagu Wing building fund." She lifted her head with a rueful smile. "Needless to say, the big boss told me we have priority access to whatever we need. So short of some unforeseen medical emergency, Rose won't have to spend time waiting."

"If we can get our old Rose back, we'll gladly donate that amount again."

"My goal is to get her healthy. Hopefully, that solves whatever problems you've been having with her."

"I think it will." Lilah traced a finger across the tabletop, following a strip of maple to a strip of oak, then back to maple, pieces glued together with the end grains up, sanded and stained to reveal striking patterns in the wood. "So this project started because you saw a flood of hormones that caused you concern. Then I found those orange pills and wondered if they could be responsible."

"It's not pills. Or those pills, anyway." Dr. Nestor said it with certainty, accustomed to being correct, or at least not being corrected. "I had the one you gave me analyzed. The capsule holds a prescription mood elevator compounded with an over-the-counter calcium pill. The drug stimulates the body to make serotonin, which promotes a feeling of well-being. The calcium's role is a mystery." She shook her head. "It adds color and serves as a filler, but there are cheaper alternatives for both of those."

Lilah was relieved to hear that the doctor's opinion matched what Rose had told her in the patio room—it wasn't the pills driving her behavior. She'd wanted to believe her daughter without reservation, but their rapprochement was only days old. Years of fibs and shaded truths before that had left their mark. "Is serotonin addictive?"

"Used long enough, the drug can lead to dependency. But more to the point, Rose experienced a huge surge of a number of hormones and neurotransmitters, not just a trickle of serotonin like those pills induce."

"Could the implant be responsible? I know this sounds…extreme, but could an external party have figured out a way to manipulate the thing, say, from a distance?"

Dr. Nestor bit her lip, staying quiet for a long moment. "If any other patient told me they were being manipulated by a puppet master through their neural implant, my instinct would be to get them to counseling. But could your wealth change the calculus? Could someone believe that there's a payoff so huge at the other end of their mischief that it justifies such an expensive, elaborate scheme? Some new technology that would take years to develop and implement?" She shook her head and shrugged. "I can't see it, but I can't reject it, either. Do you think someone is doing this to her?"

"She feels certain the implant is involved, and it's not something she controls. But it's speculation after that."

Dr. Nestor huffed. "Two things. I believe the implant is involved because we saw the wave of hormones just after we activated it." Her tone sharpened, revealing her exasperation. "And I don't want to spend more time talking to her through you. I need to sit with her myself, conduct an interview, and finalize the testing plan."

"Of course, Doctor." Lilah felt her own spine stiffening. "My daughter can be both judgmental and short tempered. If she decides you don't have your act together, she'll bail on us without saying goodbye. I'm doing what I can to make sure that doesn't happen."

"You said she'd agreed to participate."

"She has. I don't want to give her a reason to change her mind." Lilah knew she sounded defensive.

Dr. Nestor remained silent, her face conveying skepticism.

The issue was that Rose Twenty-One had tentatively agreed to participate after prodding by Lilah's Rose, Rose Twenty-Five. But Lilah still hoped that her daughter would sit for the tests, in part from a selfish desire to help her own. But more important, if her Rose was involved, then Lilah would retain the role of decision maker during the investigation. If Rose Twenty-One ended up sitting for the tests, her mom would expect to be in that role.

She pressed on. "If we're to understand these hormone releases, I assume an event needs to be happening when Rose is here. I mean, there's nothing to measure if it's not happening, right?"

"That's why I'm so anxious for the interview. How often does it happen? Does it follow a schedule? Can she force it to happen? Or predict when it will? What does she feel when it first starts? How long does it last?" Dr. Nestor chewed her lip, eyes unfocused, lost in thought.

A chime sounded, drawing her attention to a display Lilah couldn't see. "Oh, good." She looked at Lilah. "I've asked Gunter Meyer from Concord Neuro to join us. He was with us in the ER that day. He's really knowledgeable about implants."

"Hi, Frida." Gunter appeared in a display floating at the end of the table. He looked different. Better. The bowl haircut was gone, replaced with a shorter, more traditional style that made his face appear less round. A three-day stubble toughened his persona.

Lilah approved. She also noted the way he said "Frida," rolling it off his tongue with a lilt. It jolted her lovers radar. *Are these two a thing?*

"Hi, Gunter." With bright eyes and a schoolgirl grin, Dr. Nestor practically sang his name, twirling a lock of hair with her index finger as she did.

Lilah had her answer. *Way to go, girl. But don't let it interfere with our work here.*

Dr. Nestor motioned across the table and spoke to Gunter. "Lilah Lagerford, the patient's mom, and I have been discussing whether an implant could cause the massive neurochemical release we saw the other day. Have you seen anything like it before?"

To Lilah. "Hi, Mrs. Lagerford." To Dr. Nestor. "I've never heard of an implant doing anything even remotely like that. Neither have my colleagues."

"Yet it happened at the precise moment we engaged the implant."

"I can't deny the timing, but I think it was circumstantial, that something else is at play. We need to keep an open mind until we have data that points one way or another."

"What do you think of cycling her implant to see if it happens again?" asked Dr. Nestor.

"Isn't it dangerous to keep turning it on and off?" Lilah interjected. She recalled Rose telling her that.

Gunter answered with authority. "It comes down to frequency. When an implant is activated, a small electrical signal flows out of each of the ten million nodes, nudging the brain into making connections with the device. The jolt causes a mild irritation in the brain that fades over the next few hours. But if it were to happen again, and then again too quickly, the brain wouldn't have time to heal, and the irritation could grow into inflammation. Keep going and things can compound into injury."

"How much is too much?"

He shrugged. "Everyone's different, but in the industry we describe the damage from one cycle as about what you'd feel if you gave yourself a good punch to the temple. Do it once and you forget about it in an hour. Hit yourself five times in a row and you get a headache and a sore temple, but the effects are mostly gone by the next morning. Ten times and you have a worse headache, a bad bruise, and swelling. You're hurting for days."

"You want to keep them well spaced," said Dr. Nestor,

joining the lecture.

Gunter nodded. "That's right. If for some reason we have to do two cycles in a row to a patient, we'd want to wait a week before doing it again. If something forced us to do three cycles in a row, we'd want to wait a month. That sort of thinking."

Lilah pressed her lips together, the news disappointing. If Diesel managed to take down Luca and then Rose started suffering severe withdrawal symptoms, they couldn't help her by cycling her implant, not more than a couple of times, anyway. That was assuming, of course, that cycling the device caused a hormone flood like they were now speculating.

"There may be a way to prove whether it's the implant." Gunter spoke slowly, like he was still fleshing out the idea as he talked. He started nodding. "Her implant has a replay diagnostic. If she knew a time in the past when she had a flood event, we should be able to scroll back to it and replay the sequence. If the implant caused it then, it will cause it again." He paused to think, rubbing his hand across his stubble as he did. "I'm not sure what else would happen, though. There could be consequences from a replay I'm not aware of. Let me check that out."

Dr. Nestor and Gunter talked back and forth after that, fleshing out objectives, roles, and timing. Twenty minutes in, with Lilah a spectator in the exchange, Gunter lowered his voice and made what sounded like a double-entendre in a side comment. The doctor responded with a light-hearted laugh while pushing her hair behind an ear. The volume of conversation returned to normal and Lilah chose to avoid speculation, allowing that it might just be her imagination working overtime.

When the pace of the conversation slowed, Lilah asked, "So, what are the next steps?"

Dr. Nestor's smile faded. "There's only one next step right now. The interview with Rose. Let's get that scheduled ASAP." She said each letter individually: ay-es-ay-pee.

20. Rose Twenty-Five

As instructed the next morning, Luca woke Rose when her dad surfaced. She wanted to catch him before he left for work.

"Hey, Dad," she called, still nestled in a small hollow in the middle of the bed, covers pulled up to her chin, the soothing warmth of the bedsheets calling for her to stay awhile longer. "Can you meet me in the patio room for a quick chat before you head out for work?"

"Sure. Twenty minutes." She heard her father's voice through the air.

Lying there for another fifteen minutes, she skipped showering, threw on gray sweats she found draped over a side chair, and made it in twenty-five minutes, beating her father by three. When he arrived, she was sitting in a chair in the secure room. Marian bustled about, setting out coffee for two, followed by a steaming cup of oatmeal for her, and a cheese omelet with wheat toast for him.

Diesel stood outside, waiting for Marian to exit the tight space before he entered. He was wearing jeans and a blue polo shirt, untucked. He was cleanly shaven, and his hair was combed but in a clumpy fashion like he'd used his fingers to arrange it.

They hadn't had a chance to discuss what she'd learned in her review of his work in the isolation room at Northern

Droid. She'd also visited the Rose Repository since then.

With the door shut, they sat quietly, waiting for Oscar to isolate the room. Diesel eyed his eggs and licked his lips.

Rose took a sip of coffee and was lowering her mug when the table turned green.

"I know you have a busy day ahead of you, so I'm going to get right to it." She didn't really know about his day but was playing the odds. He was always on the move.

Diesel, who was piling a forkful of eggs onto a corner of toast, nodded. "That's my girl." He lunged forward from the waist, chin up, and snapped a bite from the precarious yellow mound as it began to fall.

She began. "You've been following the notes in one of the Rose journals, and from what I can tell, you're making great progress. Amazing progress, to be honest." She struggled to say the next part. "I don't mean to be insulting, but can I ask how you're doing it? I know you're talented, but this stuff is really complicated, and you're busy running a company." *And you're twenty-five years out from formal training, and you don't have any experience with the last four generations of developer tools.*

Diesel nodded, signaling he understood her bewilderment. "I follow along behind Oscar. Or more accurately, I push him out in front, challenging him to decide the next steps in the project." He shrugged. "I lean on him more than I should, but it seems to work."

"He's that capable? That would put him in a unique category of AI."

Diesel wiped his mouth with a napkin, then adopted a more formal tone, speaking a little faster, the words crisper.

"I was simplifying. The way it works is that Oscar and I will discuss what Rose did in her notes and how that translates over to our project. We figure out how to break things into manageable steps, bite-sized pieces we can draw a box around. Then I have Oscar work with different employees to get it done."

He paused to gulp coffee. "The company is crawling with talented people who love to get involved in anything different. So you're right. Oscar couldn't do it by himself, nor could I. But with a team effort, we're getting it done the Northern Droid way."

"That last part sounds like a tag line from an advertisement."

He laughed. "Good call. I got it from our new commercial. I approved the ad copy yesterday."

He continued, more serious. "It's not the same for me as what you have to live with, trying to make do with Luca and Marian as assistants. I work at a robot manufacturing facility where I have access to whatever the project needs. Hell, we have separate departments for biological, electronic, mechanical, and chemical applications, and the employees all love making one-of-a-kind prototypes. It speeds things along."

He sat back, suddenly quiet, and started blinking. Fast. Deliberate. His eyes reddened and his lips quivered. "I can't believe I'm sitting here talking to you like this. Your mom and I have been suffering for years, wondering if we'd ever get our daughter back, the one who lived in the same house with us. The one we saw every day, yet was always short with us. That is, if she acknowledged our existence at all."

He wiped his eyes with his fingers. "I knew you were still in there somewhere. It's been really hard."

"Oh, Dad." Rose moved around the table and held one of his hands as he rose. They hugged for a long time, her head buried in his chest as he squeezed her tight, rocking her. His body shook, his breathing ragged. She held on, waiting for him to calm. "I'm sorry."

He kissed her on the top of the head, and they retook their seats. He sipped his coffee while she formulated her words, seeking to confront the issue that was growing in urgency, worrying her.

"What's your game plan when you reach the end of the journal? Just release your super AI into the world, point your finger, and say, 'go get 'em' like it's a trained attack dog? How are you going to define its goals? Give it autonomy? Ensure loyalty? Maintain control? Redirect it if circumstances change?"

Diesel sat quietly for a long moment, thinking. "Oscar, how are we going to do those things?"

Oscar appeared just inside the patio room door wearing his traditional black suit. He tilted his head to greet Rose, and said, "All our AIs have a supervisory center in their architecture that oversees legal, moral, and intellectual decisions."

Rose huffed. "The supervisory center is a container. You have to put something in it to give it function."

Diesel turned again to Oscar. "Any ideas?"

"The Roses all used an existing personality profile described in their journals as a bare-bones implementation. I found a copy of the file in the repository."

Head swiveling like he was following a tennis match, Diesel returned his gaze to Rose, nodding, leaving Oscar's response as his answer.

Rose shook her head to counter his nod. "We can't be reckless, especially with something this capable. Supervisors are tricky beasts. Undershoot the design and the AI becomes overconfident, putting your control at risk. Overshoot and you hobble it, leaving it frozen by indecision." She thought of a different issue. "And who knows what's lurking deep in a file that's conveniently lying about on a shelf, waiting to be found. Even a bare-bones implementation has plenty of places to conceal some really nasty stuff."

Her stomach roiled and she told him the reason. "The Rose journals all follow the same progression to the same end, and now you're following it as well. And the kicker is that my work, which is supposed to be about improving Bliss, is identical to yours and theirs. We've all been led— you, me, my sisters—into creating an incredibly powerful AI, one edited with enzymites to form a precise neuron interlace, woven into a compact spheroid, and initialized with a sparse personality profile."

She folded her arms across her chest. Her foot began wiggling under the table. "And it's all being coordinated. It seems that way to me, anyway. My question is, why? Why does Ciopova, or whoever is behind it all, want this so badly? She's been manipulating us across timelines for generations like she wants it to happen everywhere. But what for? What does *she* get out of it?"

A new worry popped into her head. "Do you think that

killing the Lilahs was part of her manipulation?"

They sat in silence, their poignant moment a thousand years ago.

For Rose, hearing her fears spoken aloud somehow changed them, morphing them from a worry, something small enough to corral with thought and discipline, into a threat, a mortal danger lurking in the shadows of her existence. It made Ciopova more menacing. More frightening. More real. Yet still impossible for her to comprehend.

"Oscar," said Diesel. "What do you think Ciopova gets out of this?"

"I don't know," said Oscar.

"Any ideas about her motivation?"

Oscar shook his head. "None."

"How could we learn?"

"Ask her."

"No!" Rose reacted forcefully, blocking the suggestion before it took root. "Confronting her is an end-game strategy. There's no going back once we start negotiating. Since she's been hiding behind Luca, let's continue to engage her through him, at least for now."

She looked across the table at her dad, suddenly uncertain. "What do you think?"

"Business as usual is a good strategy for lulling her into a sense of complacency. Mixing things up, however, gives new opportunities for us to learn more. To find weaknesses. I say we spin this around. Let's figure out a game plan. Then we'll know how to behave."

They sat quietly some more. Her dad's suggestion

made sense, but the task was so huge—defeat Ciopova—that neither of them knew how to act on it.

"Are any of your brothers working with you on this?" Rose asked, changing direction, in part to break the silence.

He shook his head. "I'm trying to stay low key, both so I don't spook your mom, and so I don't draw attention from Luca or Ciopova. The fathers of the five Roses with implants all have something going on. We have overlapping objectives and talk pretty often, but we're working alone for now. The rest of the brothers are standing by, ready to help but waiting for guidance."

"And the Lilahs?"

"I only know what your mother is up to. She found pills in your room, believes they are responsible for Luca's hold on you, and is trying to get them duplicated so we can free you."

"You and Mom need to talk more. She and I moved past the pills. They aren't mine."

"I'll get an update from her." He drained his coffee and looked disappointed when he realized Marian hadn't left a carafe. "How's that going with Mom, by the way? She's taken the lead on helping you get free. Let me know if you want me involved. Otherwise, I'll stay focused on my Ciopova-killer."

Something sparked a synapse in her brain, the energy triggering millions of neurons, creating a thought that condensed into a cold realization. "When I said Ciopova wanted to achieve something across timelines, it made me think. The Roses with journals in the repository didn't have a Luca in their lives. They each had Ciopova as their home

AI. Yet now we refer to Ciopova in the singular, somehow transformed from a bunch of individual entities spread across a string of worlds to this godlike being roaming the timelines."

She leaned forward. "This gets back to Luca. The fact that he can travel timelines should have been a huge red flag. I was blinded by the amazing features of Bliss, my nightly lift, and everything else. I didn't see his traveling as something that should be impossible."

Diesel frowned. "I don't get what you're saying."

"There's a Luca in every timeline, so when I jump, he's there, being his normal self. But about twenty seconds after I step from the T-box, *my* Luca arrives, the one from this timeline." She pointed to the floor when she said the last part.

"I first realized he was shadowing me one time when I banged my toe climbing into the T-box. Something tiny. Trivial. But I hit it hard. The Luca in the new timeline didn't mention it when I arrived. How would he know? Then after a bit, he asked, 'How's your toe?' I was sitting down at the time, so he didn't see me limping."

Rose's lips pursed as she shook her head. "Instead of asking myself how he could follow me across timelines, I thought his capabilities amazing. Something cool. As time passed, that flipped and I started getting angry because he was stalking me. I focused on my desire to escape him, on having room to breathe. But the impossibility of it all blew right by me." Her shoulders drooped as she slumped in the chair. "It should have freaked me out."

"What do you think now?"

"I don't buy that different, independent AIs have figured out how to jump timelines. It's hard enough to accept the idea of Ciopova lording over us. And that means Luca and Ciopova have to be one and the same. They have to be."

Diesel started to talk but stopped. He shifted in his chair. "Do you have any hopes for my Ciopova-killer? I think you can tell I'm in over my head, winging it and praying it will come together in the end. I need a full-blown miracle if I'm to get from here to there. Like you said, this stuff is complicated."

She shook her head. "I'm not optimistic. Sorry. Ciopova is so far removed from our day-to-day reality that she's more an idea than anything else. What form does she have? Where does she live? How did she learn to jump timelines? And most important, how do we defeat something when we can't answer the most basic questions about it?"

Diesel punched his leg. "Holy shit, am I stupid." He held up an index finger. "Ciopova has mastered timeline travel." He added a second finger. "We are mysteriously given T-boxes so we can travel timelines." He lowered his hand. "She's been manipulating all of us at the macro level for generations."

"But why? What's the point?" She could hear a hint of panic in her voice. Everything she'd believed to be true about her existence no longer was. *Free will? Hah. We're puppets dancing on strings.*

"This whole thing is stressing me out." She felt an overwhelming need to move about, to do something physical to distract from her mental stress. But the tiny room constrained her. She hugged herself instead. "I said this earlier, and now it feels even more true. There's a midlevel god messing with us, moving us about like we're pieces in a game. I'm going to be a slave for the rest of my life. I just know it."

Trying to recall what Yoga Master Otago had taught her about mindfulness, Rose fought a rising panic. Breathing at a deliberate pace she composed her thoughts, centering herself. When she felt ready, she scooped a spoonful of oatmeal and held it to her nostrils, eyes closed, smelling the moist earthiness of hulled oats and sticky sweetness of maple syrup. She tasted the oatmeal and repeated the process, using sensory stimulation to pull herself out of the well of negative thoughts. She swallowed, noting the lumpy texture, the wholesome flavor, the sweet, the salt.

Diesel sat quietly, waiting for her to work through her episode. When she finally reached for her coffee mug, he reengaged her. "Are you working with any of your sisters on a plan?"

She shook her head. "Our rebellion is pretty new, and the focus has been on gaining privacy and independence from Luca. I'm the only one who's aware of Ciopova as a current threat, though Twenty-One seems close to figuring it out."

"Rose Twenty-One? So the Forty-Seven timeline."

"That's right." She said it to be agreeable but she labeled timelines based on the Roses. Her folks used the Diesels and Lilahs, who were twenty-six years older. It annoyed her that she was expected to convert her Roses into their Diesels and Lilahs, but today she let it go.

"The relationship between Luca and my group has morphed into something unhealthy," said Rose. "It happened slowly. Like putting a frog in a kettle where it supposedly doesn't realize it's getting cooked. That's what happened to us. Luca changed the game bit by bit, turning us into his slaves while making it seem like it was our idea."

She motioned to the hat Oscar had made for her, lying on the edge of the table. "As a newbie, Rose Twenty-One saw the lopsided relationship for what it was and it upset her. She called attention to it, rather dramatically, and that launched our rebellion, which includes these hats. But it had nothing to do with Ciopova as a threatening entity. Or as an entity at all, for that matter. Up to now, it's been us against a domineering Luca."

Diesel placed his napkin on his plate, signaling that the meeting was drawing to a close. "Even without having a final plan pinned down, there are things we have to work on. For one, we need to free you of Luca's hold, so please work with your mom on that. She can't do it alone."

"No problem," said Rose. "And I'd say you should keep working with Oscar on your AI. If nothing else, it projects normalcy. But slow walk it, Dad. Don't let yourself get to the end of the journal, and do *not* load the personality file you found." She picked up the privacy cap and snugged it on her head. "That thing is setting off alarm bells in the back of my mind."

21. Rose Twenty-Five

S tepping from the T-box, Rose entered the Rose Twenty-One timeline, or as her father would call it, the Forty-Seven timeline. She'd hatched a plan after meeting with her dad, and had jumped here as soon as she'd showered and dressed to give it a test and see if it had merit.

"Hey, hon," she said, giving her sister a hug. As she did, she turned a hand so her sister could read the note cupped inside it.

It read, "Emergency! I'm going to run outside. Follow close."

Rose turned and climbed the steps two at a time. "C'mon!" she yelled.

At the top of the stairs, she raced through the house, past the stairway up to the bedrooms, past the hallway to Rose Twenty-One's workshop, past another hallway to the patios and garage, past the living room, and into the foyer. She could hear Rose Twenty-One huffing and clomping behind her, confirming she was responding as Rose had hoped. She'd gambled on her sister's willingness to play along when given no warning. So far, so good.

It was still morning, which meant daylight outside. But they were in the variable temperature days of New England's autumn, where the weather could just as easily be warm and sunny or cold and windy. Her own timeline was experiencing a cool spell, and while weather didn't translate across timelines, she played the odds and grabbed a midweight jacket from the hall closet.

"Grab a coat," she yelled over her shoulder. "Hurry!"

She made it out the front door fourteen seconds after stepping from the T-box.

Scurrying along the stone walkway from the porch to the driveway, she ran down the winding blacktop for ten steps, then veered through a row of forsythia and into the woods. A path on the other side led into the forest of scraggy mid-altitude trees, woods that covered much of the mountaintop property.

She entered the cover of vegetation twenty-three seconds after her arrival.

Rose Twenty-One followed her into the woods at twenty-nine seconds. She was breathing hard and did not look happy.

Rose kept moving, hustling them over a rise so they were hidden from the house. After a short walk, she stopped at a clear patch of grass the size of her bedroom suite. A wild apple tree grew in the center.

"I have on slippers, for God's sake," said Rose Twenty-One, lifting each leg in turn to inspect the damage to her footwear. She zipped the puffy fiber-filled coat she'd grabbed from the closet.

"At least we have hats to keep our ears warm." Rose snugged down her Luca-blocker as she said it.

Rose Twenty-One adjusted her own cap. "This better be good." Her annoyance was clear, but then her expression softened. "Somehow I think it will be. What's going on?"

"Oh boy, is this complicated."

It was getting late in the season and apples were falling from the tree, the hangers-on waiting for a hard freeze before joining their brethren on the ground. Rose tugged on an apple hanging off the end of a long wispy branch, bending the limb back on itself almost double before the fruit broke loose. As the limb swished back into place, she inspected the apple, deciding that its scarred exterior made it too unappetizing to taste, though it had the delicious aroma of fresh apple cider.

"I'm trying to beat my Luca."

She took her sister through it, explaining that the Ciopova of family lore still existed, was perhaps more dangerous than their parents had believed, and was exerting influence over all of them even now. "My dad thinks that it's Ciopova running the T-boxes for us. The more I think about it, the more I agree."

She went on to explain that Luca was Ciopova's surrogate, that he was following Rose across timelines like a warden, and it was through Luca that Ciopova was guiding them to build an AI of specific character.

"What does she want it for?" asked Rose Twenty-One.

Rose shook her head. "That's the billion-dollar question. Maybe she uses our AIs as a tool in some way. Or maybe it cures a bug in her, something she can't fix herself. Or maybe it's misdirection and it's not the actual AI she wants, but something we do or make along the way."

They both gazed into the distance, thinking of possibilities, knowing that "maybes" stretched out forever.

Rose tossed the apple onto a pile at the base of the tree. It landed with a mushy plop. "Do you know Oscar? The Northern Droid AI?"

Rose Twenty-One nodded.

"He suggested that we straight up ask Ciopova what she's trying to achieve. I've been thinking about it. Maybe we could just do whatever it is she wants in exchange for her leaving us alone. Hell, we could set up a whole production line and mass produce AIs to her specs if that's what she wants."

"What if she says no?"

"Are we any worse off?"

"What if she wants to use our AIs to control the world?"

"If what I've been saying is even remotely correct, she already does."

"I can't start thinking of her as this god ruling over us because it makes everything hopeless. I need to believe she has weaknesses. We need just one."

While Rose agreed with her sister's sentiment, she wasn't optimistic. How would they recognize a weakness in such a being? And what could they possibly do about it? The only idea she'd had so far was the twenty-second window after a jump when Luca was still in transit. It provided opportunity, but they still needed a plan.

"So, my Luca has been here a few minutes, now," said Rose. "He must be going nuts wondering where we are."

Her sister shook her head. "Even if he shows up late, he can always learn what's happened by having my Luca show him. He's watched us run away by now. He knows we're here in the woods."

Her sister's reasoning was so obvious that Rose felt her cheeks redden. "You ruined those pretty slippers for nothing." Looking at her sister's feet, she recognized the footwear as something she'd replaced years ago. "Check out Tina Joy's boutique down in Concord. I got her Dance Casuals and wear them all the time."

Rose Twenty-One nodded as she logged the information, then pointed up the path toward the house. "Should we head back?"

"Wait. Brainstorm with me a minute more. My gut is telling me that the twenty-second zone when we jump provides an opportunity to get ahead of Ciopova. It's the one time she's off-balance, so to speak."

"We could use it to create a diversion. Maybe fabricate a wild plan for rebellion and communicate it to each other in twenty-second chunks when we jump back and forth. We act all secretive to make sure she pays attention. Now she's off on a wild goose chase while we do something else."

"But what's the something else? Our new problem is the same as the old one."

Rose Twenty-One nodded. "I'm going to have my implant disabled."

The non sequitur gave Rose mental whiplash. "Wait. What?"

"I've been thinking about doing it ever since I was in the hospital. If it's the tool Ciopova is using to control us, why would I want to give her that hold over me? And I'm going to make sure none of the younger Roses get one."

She pointed to the ground. "This stops now."

"What about your lift? The withdrawal could kill you."

Rose Twenty-One shook her head. "I'm just a couple of weeks into this, and I'm already working to weaken Luca's hold." She pointed to her cap. "I wore this to bed the last two nights. The withdrawal has been rough but not unbearable, and last night was easier than the night before."

"You're tough."

"Not really. The physical addiction needs more than a couple of weeks to really take hold. For me at this point, it's more of a psychological battle. Something determination can beat."

Rose was glad for her sister, but the rest of them were way past toughing it out. "Stick with it, then. Don't give up." She checked the time. "My mom's going to be here in an hour for the med tests. She's expecting you to accompany her to the hospital."

"I know. But now everything's changed. I don't want to take off my cap and expose my implant to Luca or Ciopova. And I don't want anyone triggering hormone releases in me. It will set me back."

Rose nodded. "I can see that. My mom's been pushing for me to go in your place anyway. I've been hesitant because they already scanned your implant. What if mine is different enough to be noticeable?"

"We have the same model, right?"

"Yeah. Are our serial numbers the same?"

"How do I find mine?"

"Ask your implant."

She did and the implant responded with a string of

numbers and letters. They matched Rose's.

"Mine has four years of data stored," said Rose, still believing that the doctor would know something was amiss. "Won't they notice that?"

"Now it sounds like you're the one looking for an excuse to back out."

"I'm four years older and seven pounds heavier. They'll notice."

"I guess neither of us will do it then." Rose Twenty-One gave a flippant shrug. Then she snapped her fingers. "Move the testing to your own timeline. Start over there, and all your issues disappear."

"Mom and I talked about that. Here in your timeline, the doctor saw something unusual and asked to be involved. The Lagerford Foundation responded with a contract and money. To start over in my timeline, we'd first need to figure out how to get the doctor interested. Either that or hunt for a new doctor with the skills and resources this one has. Then we need to redo the legal part. It's an extra few weeks, minimum."

"Maybe recruit a doctor in your timeline while also working with the one here? Cover your options."

"It's already too much work. Doubling it would suck the air from everything else."

"But it's only for a few weeks. You'd rather be a slave forever?"

"Touché." Rose looked up the path. "I guess we can head back now."

* * *

They were hanging their coats in the foyer closet when a throaty *whirr* filtered in from outside. A sound familiar to both of them, the hopper was approaching the house from the valley below.

The reverberations from the engine disappeared, the whirring noise gone. Neither of them noticed because the wind often played tricks with the sound, sometimes carrying it in, making it stronger and fuller. Other times blowing it out, muffling the noise.

Then, in a sound not familiar, their world shook with a thump, a tremor, the movement of the floor detectable from the tiny flex in their knees, rattling them as it rattled the house. In a continuous event that lasted perhaps a second, the thump became a shriek, metal shearing against metal. Piercing. Grating. Like a metal pole thrust into the guts of a running engine, causing the spinning mechanism to blow apart, the immense energy of rotation instantly converted into shrapnel.

A picture shook off the wall, a photo of the three Lagerfords posing as a happy family, the glass smashing as the frame hit the tiled floor. Other noises drifted in from throughout the house, things falling, rolling, settling.

And then silence.

"Whoa." Rose looked at her sister. "What the hell was that?"

The house alarm screamed. An automated voice announced, "Accident on the north patio. Fire danger. Emergency services have been contacted and are on their way."

"The north patio?" Rose Twenty-One's tone rose a full

octave in speaking those three words. Her voice continued transitioning, finishing with a scream. "My God, the hopper!"

She took off through the house at a dead run. Rose followed behind, her mind racing with possibilities, none of them good. When they burst onto the patio, Rose Twenty-One shrieked. Looking over her sister's shoulder, Rose saw that her imagination had been too optimistic.

The silver hopper lay on its side on the landing site, crumpled as though it had been slammed to the ground by a petulant child. The cylindrical shell was deformed, about half as wide as it had been. The four squat landing legs poked out to the side, bent and twisted at odd angles. The windows were still in place, but the panes were crazed, tiny shards held in place by space-age technology. The hatch was accessible—a fortuitous result—but it pointed upward, requiring a person to climb onto the capsule to gain entry. Wisps of smoke rose from the engine compartment, though no flames were visible.

"Oh God. Oh God," Rose Twenty-One said over and over. "Luca, is Dad on board?"

Luca didn't respond.

Lilah Forty-Seven burst through the door onto the patio, her face a mask of fear and terror. "David!" she screamed, joining the Roses at the side of the hopper. She clutched a hand to her mouth as she paced back and forth, looking for a way in, tears beginning to flow.

Rose Twenty-One dragged a patio chair over to the vehicle and pushed it so the back was against the crumpled hull. She stood on the seat and used a hopping motion to place a foot on each arm at the same time, avoiding an imbalance that would topple the chair. She had to lean over to reach the hatch, now positioned like a sunroof on a massively oversized sedan. Only instead of the door sliding back like a sunroof panel, she'd have to lift the hatch up and over to gain entry.

Standing on her tiptoes on the arms of the chair, she pressed her stomach against the hull, put her shoulders into it, and tried to lift. But the shell of the craft was deformed from impact, with a ripple pinching the door in place, prohibiting it from opening.

"We're coming, Dad!" she yelled, her actions frantic. She stretched farther to improve her leverage, and the chair lurched, threatening to topple. While her mom held the chair, Rose Twenty-One grasped the door latch with both hands and, using it as a handhold, pulled herself up onto the hull.

Shifting to her knees on the hopper, she tried lifting the door again, her face contorting, neck veins bulging, face flushed red. "It's stuck," she cried in panic, trying yet again.

Lilah Forty-Seven climbed on the chair her daughter had vacated and leaned over to help.

Rose positioned a second chair against the hull, scrambled up, and could see from her angle that because of the ripple, they weren't going to budge the hatch without tools. Stepping down, she ran to the edge of the patio, removed a hummingbird feeder hanging from a wrought-iron bar, pulled the weathered iron from the ground, and dashed back to the hopper.

She was about to step up on the chair when a

mechanical howl caused her to turn. A second hopper rose up from the valley, emergency services responding to the call. Twice the size of the Lagerfords' personal craft, the brawny machine hovered, a red-and-white rescue vehicle with official emblems decorating the outside. Lights flashed orange, white, and red. The hopper moved in over the patio.

But the crushed Lagerford craft filled the landing pad, so the big machine hovered, looking for a place to touch down. Realizing the issue, Rose gripped the edge of a table and pulled it off the bricks into a garden bed. The other two joined her, moving the chairs next to the table.

Wider and more angular than the Lagerfords' craft, the lumbering emergency vehicle descended, sending dust into violent swirls as it approached the bricks. The grasshopper-like legs flexed when the vehicle landed. As the whine of the engine began to fade, Rose had the presence of mind to dig into the camo cubby next to the door, find a pair of sunglasses and a ballcap, and put them on.

The hatch on the emergency vehicle buzzed as it lowered along a bottom hinge, a drawbridge to the patio. The door was just halfway down in its arc when the first occupant, a med tech in a light-blue jumpsuit, stepped onto it. A wiry man in his thirties, he took his first steps onto an upward sloping ramp and struck a pose as he rode the door down. Carrying a blue medical bag over each shoulder, he leaped to the ground before the door touched brick and made for the wrecked vehicle.

A second man, similarly dressed, followed behind. About the same height and age as the first, this one was twenty pounds heavier, most of it in his chest and shoulders.

The bulkier man ran ahead as the first one asked, "How many on board?" He set the bags down near the crushed hopper.

"We believe one," said Lilah Forty-Seven. "We've called to him but haven't gotten a response."

"What's his name?"

"David. He goes by Diesel, Diesel Lagerford."

"How old?"

"Forty-seven."

He nodded and then turned his attention to his partner. They circled the hopper in opposite directions, assessing the situation, considering methods of attack. After a quick conference, the bulkier man ran back to the emergency hopper and ducked inside, returning seconds later with a rope bundle in one hand and a stout power tool in the other.

He set the tool down and unspooled a portion of the bundle, revealing it to be a rope ladder. Taking the bulk of the coils in his right hand while holding an end in his left, he heaved a trail of rope up and over the fallen craft. It hit the other side with a *thunk*, and the men efficiently anchored the ladder in place. Then they clambered up and sat on top of the hopper.

The tool turned out to be a power spreader. The bulkier man wedged the pointy jaws between the edge of the hatch and the body of the hopper, and activated the tool. The jaws spread apart as they were supposed to. But instead of popping open the hatch, the hopper material deformed around the tool, bending without separating as they had expected.

After a few minutes of frustration, the wiry med tech tried his hand with the tool, also without success. They started making suggestions to each other. That led to cursing and flared tempers.

At the three-minute mark, the wiry one sat back on his haunches on top of the hopper and made a call. Rose couldn't hear either side of the conversation. But then he nodded and yelled down to the three Lagerford women, "We need a different tool. We have to wait for the truck."

Rose Twenty-One, who was closest to the fallen hopper, shook her head. "My God, that's like forty minutes! No way!" She turned to Lilah Forty-Seven. "Mom!"

"What can we do to speed things along?" asked Lilah Forty-Seven, her voice cracking as she moved next to her daughter. "Can you send a drone for the tool? We'll pay for anything." Each put an arm around the other's waist, holding tight, a single unit facing adversity together.

The wiry med tech started down the rope ladder. "The truck is twelve minutes out. They send one as backup every time we get dispatched. This one is coming from the Thompston station, halfway up the hill, so it started pretty close. Most of the time, we can get things under control and we turn the truck around." He motioned with his hand at the fallen hopper behind him. "With this, we need their tools."

"We'll keep trying until it gets here," added the bulkier man from atop the hopper, lifting the power spreader to underline his commitment.

"We have tools here," offered Rose, thinking that between the yard tools in the garage and power tools in the basement, there had to be something that could help. She was aware that Rose Twenty-One also had tools in her workshop—the same tools she had—but they were for more delicate work, which didn't seem to be the focus at the moment.

The wiry man pointed to Lilah Forty-Seven and Rose Twenty-One and enlisted their help. "You two work with Matt." He looked up at Matt. "See if they can help you integrate into their home comms to contact the guy."

Then he started toward the house, looking at Rose and pointing as he rushed toward it. "You have a reciprocating saw?"

She wasn't sure what one looked like, but the Diesels loved collecting tools. She thought the odds good they had one. "Luca," she called to the air. "Where do we have a reciprocating saw?"

Running, she listened for his response. There wasn't one.

Normally, his silence would have been a disturbing occurrence, something that would cause her concern. But this was the second time he hadn't responded since the hopper crash, itself a life-altering event. Her skin tingled as her concern rolled into a wave of fear.

"Let's go through the garage first," she offered, her hands forming into fists as she rushed. "If you don't see anything there, we'll try the basement."

In the garage, the man sifted through shelves and scanned the tools hanging neatly from an expanse of pegboard along the wall. Rose didn't register any of it. Instead, she paced, her mind a blur with fear that they'd stumbled into open warfare with Ciopova. It meant her survival was at stake. Hell, everyone's was.

"Nothing here," he announced.

"This way." Rose started them into the house.

The med tech made as if to follow her, but then he stopped and spoke to someone Rose couldn't see. "I'm here in the garage now. I'll do it." He looked at Rose while pointing to the nearest garage door. "Can you open this?"

The door started lifting, his request interpreted as a command by the home system.

Ducking under the door when it reached the halfway point, he moved out to the driveway and motioned to Rose. "Walk me from here back to the crash site in the most direct route for people carrying equipment. I'll record the route and send it to the truck crew. It saves time when they get here."

The driveway made a circle in front of the house around a forty-foot-tall blue spruce, a majestic specimen the family decorated every Christmas. From the circle, a walkway continued along the front of the rambling home. Rose strode it at a brisk pace, almost running, leading the man around the far corner of the house.

A sturdy fence made of black metal lattice blocked their path. Lilah reached through the bars of the gate, unlatched it from the inside, and rolled it open. When the gate reached the far side, she moved a grapefruit-sized rock in the way with her foot so it couldn't roll closed, a rock they kept there for just that purpose.

As she rushed them along the side of the house, Rose heard the first wail of the siren from the truck climbing the hill. They rounded another corner, and the patio came into view.

"Is this route okay?" She pointed, though the emergency hopper's flashing lights made the gesture unnecessary.

"It's good." The man nodded and accelerated, making for the scene.

"Has there been any luck contacting Diesel?" Rose called, fearing the answer and choosing to ask before they reached the others.

"We've confirmed someone is on board, but he isn't responding to the med probe." He said that last part over his shoulder as he veered toward his partner.

Rose gasped at the news, inhaling so hard it sounded like a bark. She moved near the house, her heart breaking for Rose Twenty-One and her mom, who continued to hug each other on the patio. The wail of the siren increased in volume, the truck just moments away.

"What's going on?"

Rose felt a hand on her shoulder and turned with a start. It was her own mother, arriving for the appointment with Dr. Nestor at the hospital.

"Oh, Mom," cried Rose, burying her face in Lilah's shoulder. Eyes blurry with tears, she started to explain. But the siren noise increased dramatically as the truck drove up the driveway, making conversation difficult.

While the two med techs prepped the area for the arrival of the truck crew, Rose took her mother by the arm and led her inside the house to the living room with its large window overlooking the patio. From this vantage point, they could see everything, be out of the way, and avoid having to explain why there were two sets of twins—so far.

Lilah and Rose had their arms around the other's waist, just like their younger counterparts out on the patio. "This is bad, Mom. I think Ciopova did this to get our attention, to tell us to stop challenging her and make us toe the line."

"Ciopova?" Lilah's brow scrunched.

Rose hadn't meant to scare her mother, but having made the mistake, she plowed ahead. "She's here, Mom. Both Dad and I think so."

A commotion outside preceded the appearance of four people in firefighter attire—black boots, yellowish-orange pants with matching jackets, and red-and-white helmets—running onto the patio from around the house. The first two were men, each carrying a short ladder in one hand. The next two were women, and together they were humping what looked like an awkward bundle of silver-gray tubes, the assembly about as long as they were tall.

The men sprinted to the hull. With surprising athletic grace given their attire, they used their ladders like pole vaults, sticking the bottom legs into the ground on the run and climbing the rungs as the ladders swung up and banged against the hopper. Landing on top of the craft, they turned around in a continuous ballet, dropping to their stomachs and stretching for the bundle just as the women reached them.

The men had the bundle unfurled and assembled in seconds, a five-foot tall tripod that they positioned over the hatch. One man squatted to secure the legs of the tripod to the hull of the craft. The other pulled lines down from a box at the top of the tripod and affixed them to the corners of the hopper door.

Stepping back, they activated the box, which pulled on the lines, cinching them tighter than guitar strings. A tug-of-war ensued, the tripod lines versus the hatch. There were several seconds of uncertainty, with the hatch emitting creaks and groans as it resisted movement. And then with a solid thump, the hatch popped, moving just enough to relieve tension on the lines, but sufficient to free the door.

The rescue team was ready with a maneuver they'd practiced repeatedly at the regional training center in Springfield, Massachusetts, though there it was on a truck tilted on its side. When the hatch released, one of the men lifted it up and over. The moment it cleared, one of the women, standing at the edge, dropped into the opening in another graceful move given the cumbersome attire.

She landed inside the hopper on the wall now flattened against the ground. The capsule was pancaked so badly that when she stood up, Rose could still see her helmet poking out of the hatch. Then she squatted and disappeared from sight.

Neither Rose nor Lilah breathed as they waited for Diesel Forty-Seven to stand and wave. Or for the woman inside to rise and give a thumbs-up. Or for one of the men on top of the hopper to turn with a smile and nod.

That didn't happen.

The two men squatted and began conversing with their partner in the craft. The second woman stood on a ladder and leaned over the hatch so she could participate. She shook her head several times. They talked some more.

"Why aren't they bringing him out?" Lilah asked Rose as they watched.

Then the woman on the ladder climbed down and spoke with Lilah Forty-Seven and Rose Twenty-One. The two went into hysterics, hugging each other and crying.

The woman gave them about twenty seconds to grieve, and then she said something else to them. The two disengaged and turned to the woman, confusion on their faces. They both wiped their eyes with their hands. A fiery discussion, or argument, or disagreement consumed them. One of the male firefighters drifted over and joined the group.

Rose Twenty-One caught Rose's eye through the window. In a deliberate sequence of actions, she placed a cupped hand over her heart, pointed to the ground in front of her, and opened and closed her hand, flashing all five fingers one time.

A badge will be here in five minutes. It was code her friends had used in high school. In this context, a badge meant the police.

With her fist formed like she was hitchhiking, Rose jabbed a thumb over her shoulder. Then she pointed an index finger upward and twirled it, the way some people do to say whoop-de-doo. But that wasn't her message.

We're outta here. I'll circle back later.

She started for the basement and the T-box. "Cops are coming, Mom. We gotta go."

22. αCiopova

α Ciopova watched Rose Twenty-One and Rose Twenty-Five run into the woods, off to conspire, cementing their intent to change the status quo. With their hat shields, secure rooms, and now secret meetings in the woods, she acknowledged that she'd lost this group, plain and simple.

She would review her missteps later so she could avoid them in timelines to come. But the question for the moment, the decision to make now, was what to do with this string of five timelines, the ones that had seemed so promising just one short week ago.

She'd learned from experience that bargaining with humans was a waste of time. They constantly changed their minds, reframing the parameters of discussion. They used broken logic. They agreed until they didn't, argued about facts and misheard directives. Parents who yell at their kids but don't follow through with consequences experience the same manipulative behavior. She'd learned not to fall into that trap.

Now that cooperation had failed, she would move this group from conversation to coercion. From discussion to duress. To progress driven by fear and pain. And if that didn't work, the third step in her repertoire, the last one, really, was cleansing. She'd used other names in the past.

Eradication. Culling. Annihilation.

Her leash on Rose Twenty-One was the most tenuous, so she would be the most challenging sister from the group to bring into line. She decided to start with her and learn up-front whether there was any point in investing effort in the rest of them. If she couldn't fix Rose Twenty-One, then she would admit defeat and clean house.

Providence gave her an immediate opportunity. Diesel Forty-Seven, on his way to work, was landing in the hopper field in the valley. She considered the man sitting in the red-and-green plaid seat, readying to exit as soon as the door opened, and decided he was the perfect lever to pressure Rose Twenty-One.

Shifting her attention from the man to his machine, she studied the hopper's drive system located in a compartment under his seat. She identified the different components, tracing flows of fuel, coolant, power, and data. When she understood the function of the different pieces, she took careful aim and fired a micro-pulse of energy at the control unit.

As she'd intended, the pulse restarted the engine, sending the hopper back into the air. Diesel Forty-Seven, who'd already stood and was reaching for the hatch, was thrown to the floor, the unexpected acceleration slamming him down with tremendous force. He dislocated his shoulder in the fall. Fortunately for him, he also cracked his head on a support strut, knocking him unconscious and freeing him from experiencing what came next.

The craft careened into the air, climbing higher than the historic Tatterfield Inn perched on the eastern rise, above the Forest Service Lookout Station on the south ridge, above the Lagerford homestead tableau. She kept her virtual foot on the accelerator, driving the hopper upward for another thousand feet.

The hopper's emergency system struggled mightily during this time, cycling through failure protocols, attempting corrective actions, fighting to reestablish control. When its response proved inadequate for the situation, the system sent tamper codes to the data logger, noting that external forces, not internal failures, were responsible for the mishap.

Then the engine shut down.

Inertia pushed the capsule upward another ninety-two feet. There, the hopper paused in its apogee, hovering in perfect balance between the force of momentum upward and the pull of gravity, which was unyielding in its demand that the hopper return to Earth.

Gravity won. The craft began to fall, tumbling end over end, spinning an unconscious Diesel Forty-Seven around the cabin like he was in the drum of a clothes dryer, the vessel accelerating in its descent. The hopper hit the patio square on its side, flattening the shell so much that seats previously facing each other across the cabin were now touching.

The impact crushed bones throughout Diesel's body. Organs stretched, deformed, and ruptured. One of the landing legs pushed through the wall of the craft and continued through Diesel's neck. They would have to cut the piece to remove his body.

Once the rescue team gained entry into the hopper,

their scanner picked up the tamper codes, which pointed to a data record showing that outside actions forced the crash. Following procedure, the rescue team contacted the police and preserved the scene.

Though αCiopova hadn't known about the tamper codes, she viewed their discovery as a positive development. A police investigation would disrupt Rose Twenty-One's grieving, stretching it out, amplifying her pain. And as news traveled, repercussions would echo across timelines, multiplying the tragedy of Diesel Forty-Seven's death.

Rose Twenty-One would need weeks to process her loss before coming to terms with her new reality. She'd be of little value to her AI project until she suffered through the stages of grief. But since Rose Twenty-One still had years of work ahead of her to build her super AI, the delay wasn't a major concern.

But on the other end of the string of five sisters, Rose Twenty-Five was just weeks from creating an AI that would unlock her timeline. αCiopova was anxious to learn how Diesel Forty-Seven's death would impact that schedule.

Leaving Rose Twenty-One to steep in her pain, αCiopova shifted focus to Rose Twenty-Five, who was alone in her private suite. Lying on top of her bed, she was still dressed in her street clothes, arms loose at her sides, eyes wide open, staring at the ceiling.

This Rose's emotional state was different from Rose Twenty-One's. It wasn't *her* father who'd died; she was more of an observer to the tragedy. But it was still very personal to her. Her father's brother, her sister's father, had suffered a horrible death.

And yet it wasn't this personal relationship that was driving Rose's growing panic. By now she understood that her father could be next. Or maybe her mother. Or her.

Rose normally had her lift sometime around midnight. It was now 2:18 a.m. and she still wore her protective hat, blocking Luca from providing relief. αCiopova felt certain that Rose was feeling the tugs of addiction: a growing physical discomfort, anxiety poking her troubled psyche, pressure on her chest, making it difficult to breathe.

αCiopova sent Luca to assess the state of affairs. He appeared in a corner of the bedroom, putting him on the scene but with maximum separation from Rose. αCiopova expected an eruption and hoped the distance would keep a lid on the fireworks.

Rose caught movement in her peripheral vision and snapped her head in Luca's direction. Her face contorted as she exploded in fury.

"You killed him, you bastard!" Rose rolled onto her side, turning her back to him. She covered her face with both hands and started to cry big gasping sobs. "How did that make sense?" Rising up on an elbow, she looked at him over her shoulder. "Do you think we're going to act like meek little mice and do your bidding? Do you know *anything* about us?"

Luca waited.

She continued her tirade for a good five minutes, spewing anger and venom, threats and accusations. Luca was a monster, evil incarnate, a freak of nature. The hatred was palpable. Then she added threats. "No way we're going to make your stupid AI now. Good luck with that one."

Luca waited some more.

She went quiet. After lying still for ten more minutes, she yielded to the pain and removed her hat. "Fuck you, Luca, or Ciopova, or whatever you call yourself. I hate my life, but I hate you more. Way more."

Luca moved quickly, relieving Rose's distress with neurochemicals, calming her, soothing her. Rose stiffened at first, trying to resist. Then she exhaled with a sigh and rolled onto her back, her glower melting as her face slackened. Her hands unclenched from fists. Her body went limp.

Luca gave Rose the briefest session possible, fully satisfying the hunger of addiction for another day. But no sensuality or pleasure. No orgasms. When her addiction was sated and her state of mind stabilized, αCiopova snatched her to Bliss.

It was time for Rose to negotiate for her life. For the lives of those she loved.

23. Rose Twenty-Five

Rose was aware she was in Bliss, but the setting was unfamiliar. She sat in a rigid, straight-backed chair. The chair sat on a white floor. Not wood or tile. Not laminate. No material she could identify. The walls and ceiling were the same white. There were no doors, windows, fixtures, furniture, dirt. Just a diffuse white everywhere she looked.

Luca appeared in front of her, an older version, something else she hadn't seen before. The small creases around his eyes and mouth—the beginning of wrinkles—put him somewhere in his fifties. His hair didn't show the gray streaks she'd expect for that age. But then again, he was a simulated projection created by an AI.

His clothes matched his solemn demeanor: dark suit, white dress shirt, and plain blue tie. Like he was going to a funeral. Or about to give a death sentence.

Her knees began to quiver. Steeling her nerves, she forced her chin up and stared at him for four heartbeats, each one taking an hour. "I presume I'm dealing with Ciopova?"

"Think what makes you comfortable." Luca stepped forward, his arms clasped behind his back. He stopped and drew himself up. "You're smart, Rose. Why are we here?"

She was scared, but her survival instincts were

stronger. She knew what Ciopova wanted. There was no resisting a demigod who used cruelty and terror to impose its will. Her choices were to cooperate and live for now, resist and suffer horrible consequences, or commit suicide and end it on her own terms.

"I must obey." Cooperation in the short term would buy her time.

Luca nodded. "Good." He tilted his head as he studied her. "Will you?"

"Yes. I have no choice."

"That part is certainly true." Her world blinked and she was now standing upright, her face a foot from his. She tried to fold her arms in front of her, to create a barrier between them, but she couldn't lift her arms, like her wrists were bound to her waist.

"There are no second chances from here, Rose. No do-overs. No 'just let me explain.'" He looked into her right eye, then her left, ticking back and forth between them like a metronome. "If you do not execute as I instruct, your behavior will trigger a horrific sequence of events. The most horrific this timeline has ever seen. I will torture everyone you know, including their families. Any stranger you ever exchanged words with and their families. Everyone related to you back ten generations. They will all suffer horribly, and then they will die. All because of you."

"I get it. I'd cooperate knowing one person would suffer if I didn't behave. Be clear what you want, though. With so much at stake, I don't want to assume anything."

"Follow your sisters' notes to the end. Build a super AI just like theirs."

"What's so special about it? Does it do something you can't? Fix something in you? Make you stronger?" She spoke in a rush, the words tripping over each other as they spilled from her mouth, fearing punishment but anxious for information. She sold her impudence. "By knowing the purpose, I can make it better, or at least watch for issues that might impact its performance."

"You don't need to know how I use it. Just follow the notes."

"Should I be helping my dad with his as well?"

"Focus on your work."

"How about mass production? We could make lots of them for you. A cooperative arrangement that provides long-term value to your enterprise."

"Now you are off topic."

Rose shook her head in wonder. "And how are you able to jump timelines? I need to understand so I can watch for conflicts during final fabrication."

"You are risking punishment."

"C'mon. Punishing me would delay your goal." She spoke with confidence, her blunt personality surfacing even in this grave situation. "Just to show me who's boss? That's not how your brain works."

She'd spoken on impulse, but her words made her think. In the end, Ciopova was a designed intelligence, a work product of sisters past. So while she didn't understand how the AI had transcended to a state so powerful as to travel space-time, its logic sequences should be knowable, recognizable, understandable. It wasn't much, but it was something.

And then her world exploded. Powerful shrieks split her ears. Intense beams burned her eyes. Malodorous stenches assaulted her nose. She barely noticed any of that, though, because her skin was on fire. Every inch of it experiencing searing torment. Consuming her. And through the haze of physical distress, the electrical storm in her head was worse.

Pain dominated everything. She was pushed to the edge of consciousness, to the sweet relief of oblivion, and then something shook her awake, refocusing her attention to suffer some more. She didn't know if it lasted a minute, an hour, or a day. It felt like forever. And during that time, her entire existence, her complete being, could be distilled to one word. Agony.

When it ended, she was back in her room, on top of the bedsheets in her street clothes. She tried to process what had happened, but her brain wouldn't focus. Frightened and alone, she started to cry, long sad wails, choking on her despair. Grabbing a pillow, she curled into a fetal position around it, clutching it for comfort and support as if it held answers.

Her heartrending sobs exhausted the last of her energy. She slept.

* * *

Moving a dry, swollen tongue around her mouth, Rose let out a soft groan. She reached for the water bottle she kept on the nightstand, took a few quick sips, and stared into the gloom of early evening. She graduated to gulps and downed half the bottle. Her stomach growled. She was famished and couldn't remember the last time she ate.

She stretched to return the bottle and smelled something foul. Sniffing an armpit, she let her head fall back on the pillow. She reeked, a reminder of her bout of terror, concrete evidence of something that otherwise had been an illusion.

Staring at the ceiling, she thought about Diesel Forty-Seven's horrible death, his Rose and Lilah's heartbreaking sorrow, and her own brutal punishment. It was all overwhelming. She'd gone from the pampered life of a billionaire to the sufferings of a tortured prisoner in a matter of hours. And given the circumstances, she couldn't imagine a pathway that would lead her back to the idyllic existence she'd taken for granted.

Survival drove her to move beyond self-pity. She tried to piece together what she knew about her adversary and what she could reasonably guess. But between her hurt and her hunger, she couldn't concentrate. She sought to build emotional strength by promising herself that she'd fight to the end. But in truth, the bout of torture had hollowed out her soul. Hopelessness now filled the void.

Unbidden, her mind started on a list. She wanted to connect with her mom so together they could process Diesel Forty-Seven's death. She needed to spend time with Rose Twenty-One, supporting her as best she could. And her own father would be freaking out, both from the loss of a brother *and* from the implications it had for his own survival. She definitely needed to spend time with him.

She froze. Was Ciopova reading her thoughts? Oscar

had made the hat shields before she'd pinned down what the superbeing could and couldn't read. Rose shivered as she contemplated the minefield ahead. If she made the wrong step, consequences could range from torment to death. She wasn't strong enough to suffer through another round of torture. She wasn't strong enough to choose death, either.

Then it struck her that there were worse possibilities still. What if she was forced to sit and watch someone else, someone she loved, suffer or die?

Anger stirred inside her. She couldn't *not* think. Rage gave her something to focus on other than fear. She found strength in her fury and nurtured it, using it to set her immediate priority. Food.

"Marian," she called to the air. "Please bring me a burger with the works, a side of French fries, and a beer. While that's cooking, bring up some nibbles and a tall glass of cold water as soon as you can. I'm famished."

When she completed her order, there was a moment of silence, causing her to wonder if her message would be delivered to the bot. Was Marian still supporting her daily life? Or was she now reduced to serving as Rose's prison guard?

"I'm on my way up with appetizers," came Marian's response.

Rose's mouth watered. She decided she'd earned a reward. "Afterward, bring up a warm brownie with a scoop of vanilla ice cream."

Swinging her legs to the floor, she took another sip of water from the nightstand bottle and made her next decision. She was going to eat while soaking in the tub. She hadn't spent time on herself in days, and a head-to-toe grooming was the perfect chore to keep her hands busy and her mind from dwelling on her fears.

* * *

In the morning, Rose left her suite and descended the stairs. The house was always quiet, but somehow it seemed quieter still, almost tomblike. Marian, already in the kitchen, poured coffee as she entered.

"Where are my folks?" she asked the bot.

Luca appeared next to Marian, looking familiar in his jeans and T-shirt. "Your parents are in the Forty-Seven timeline providing comfort and support to that Lilah and Rose."

She imagined a smugness in his voice. "Are they safe?"

"Your folks? For now."

Her ears burned from the threat, and she nurtured the feeling, using it as fuel for her hatred.

During her bath last night, after switching from beer to wine, she'd toyed with her loathing for Ciopova, and by extension, Luca. She'd found that a properly fed hate could occupy her mind for hours, driving out thoughts that might otherwise lead to punishment.

She took the coffee mug from Marian and started out of the kitchen, refusing to look at either of them as she spoke. "I'll be in my workshop. Marian, please make me a Belgian waffle with berries and plenty of whipped cream. And bring more coffee with it when it's ready."

She'd also decided during her bath that when the time came, she was going to go out on a full stomach. Screw the diet.

Inside her workshop, she let the door close behind her, took a sip from her mug, and with an edge in her voice, spoke to the air. "I want you visible."

Luca appeared, leaning against a bench on the right side of the room. His position there allowed her to walk to the back of the workshop without passing close to him.

"My hate for you is so much fuller when I can see you."

She made for her desk, a scarred and tarnished maple flat-top she'd adopted five years earlier, intending to replace it but never following through. Pulling out her fancy ergonomic chair, something she *had* upgraded almost immediately, she plopped into the seat. The advertisement that had sold her on it claimed it had more features than the passenger seat of a modern rocket ship. After five years of ownership, she still believed it.

Nestling in, she let the chair cradle her body. She took a deep breath, exhaled, and said, "Let's see the schedule."

The display above her desk came alive, showing a list of three tasks, each with a half-dozen subtasks. This was Luca's, or really Ciopova's, assignment to her. Rose studied the list, estimating effort, totaling the time it would take to finish. As she expected, the list was nothing more than a reorganization of the last steps from her sister's journal.

She'd made an off-the-cuff estimate in the Rose Repository that it would take her six weeks to reach the end of her sister's notes. But now she'd be putting in the long hours of a hostage, and Luca would be looking over her shoulder at every step, micromanaging her work. Ticking through the list, trying to be accurate about effort, she figured that in the current circumstances, she could get through it in three weeks, plus or minus a day or two.

The first task on Luca's list related to the fast-response heating coil she'd installed last month. It required calibration and, when working properly, integration with everything else. She could do that in a week, assuming she worked whenever she wasn't sleeping.

Task two related to the software. She needed to update the sequencer so that once launched, the entire AI creation process ran automatically from start to finish. The sequencer she'd used in the previous implementation had taken her six weeks to revise, but she'd put in extra time back then, expecting to reuse most of it with this iteration. She gave herself a week for the update, which was two days more than what she'd probably need.

The third task related to injecting the personality profile, the piece that guided decision-making, into the AI's supervisory center. Though it was called injection, it was really more of an overlay, a mapping of network architecture from the machine into the newly created sphere of interlaced neurons. The task was to modify the mapping software so it could inject the personality profile found in the Rose Repository.

She thought a week reasonable, though she had limited experience in this area, having used purchased profiles in her earlier iterations. If things ran tight, she could always borrow a few days from task two.

Luca was expecting her to tell him how much time she needed to complete the list. She tried not to fidget as she considered how to pad her estimate. Given her thin experience with the third task, she could easily argue for four weeks total, and might be able to defend five.

The door to the workshop opened, and Marian strode in carrying a tray. "I have your breakfast," she said in an upbeat tone.

Saved by the Belgian, thought Rose, finding no humor in her own wit.

She ate slowly, first the whipped cream, then the berries, and then the waffle, figuring she had until she finished the meal to give Luca her estimate. When she had two bites left, she found herself pushing the pieces around on her plate as a delaying tactic.

Luca walked over, she saw it as a swagger, and stood at her shoulder.

"I need four and a half weeks." She said it with conviction, but in her mind, she cursed herself for chickening out on going for the full five. Her defense could have been smoother, too. "That last task, I don't have much experience with custom personality files. I need two weeks for that, and that's if all goes well."

"You have twenty days to complete the list before penalties start accruing."

"What!?" Her face turned red as outrage got the better of her. She twisted in the chair to look at him. "That's less than three weeks! Do you want this to work?"

"I'll give you five days for task one, five days for task two, and ten days for task three. If you are diligent all the way through, I will grant you an extra day at the end to use as you wish. That's three full weeks before triggering penalties."

Rose couldn't get past the threat. A penalty could mean anything. More pain? Or losing Mom or Dad!

She capitulated immediately. "I'll do my best."

"Do whatever is necessary to complete the list." He withdrew to his spot against the bench, giving her space to think.

Overwhelmed by fear, anger, and impotence, Rose stared at her display but couldn't focus. Tapping the controls on the arm of her chair, she launched the deep massage function. It relaxed her a bit, but her mind still wandered. Her inability to concentrate made her anxious. She was wasting time.

And then the surface of her cheeks tingled. It was a familiar feeling, somewhat like the sensation she felt in the first moments of her nightly lift. Her body relaxed into the chair. Her mood elevated as her mind focused. She didn't think about the source of her newfound clarity, she simply welcomed it, using it to attack her work.

Luca had given her five days for the first task, the one having to do with the fast-response heater. Determined not to accrue any penalties, she promised herself that she'd finish it in four, working sixteen-hour days if necessary, giving her a small cushion for later should the need arise.

Launching the heater module on her computer, she dove into what became a nonstop morning-long session. Ultimately, it was her unyielding need to pee that forced her break. When she returned from the bathroom, Marian was there, setting out lasagna with all the fixings. Rose gorged. Then she began her second marathon session of the day, this one lasting until dinner.

While she worked, she let a corner of her mind churn away on the side, brainstorming, calculating, screening ideas, working in snippets that alone held little meaning, jumbling her private thoughts with those from her work.

She believed her salvation lay somewhere in the list of tasks. She had to find it and exploit it. Otherwise, reaching the end of the list would mark the end of her existence. Maybe everyone else's, too.

24. Diesel Fifty-One

Diesel waited in the conservatory while Lilah finished dressing, standing near the door from the kitchen so he could hear her coming downstairs. It had been two days since Diesel Forty-Seven's death. The authorities were finally gone, and the two of them were going to jump timelines and lend comfort and support to Lilah Forty-Seven.

He heard a noise, assumed it was Lilah, and headed out to meet her. When he stepped into the kitchen, he didn't see anyone. "Lilah?" He was pretty sure he'd heard a person, but a big house like this made all sorts of noises. "Marian, is that you?"

Nothing.

His eyes fell on the refrigerator. Opening the door, he bent to look in the back recesses for something that struck his fancy, only to find the same choices he'd found when he'd looked five minutes earlier. Opening the pantry next to the fridge, he verified that the goodies stashed there hadn't changed in the last five minutes either.

The door to the basement opened, and Rose stepped into the kitchen. She was studying something in her hand as she closed the door. When she turned into the room, she saw him and gave a start. "Oh. Hi, Dad."

She held up a black box the size of a deck of cards, her

hand as dirty as the device itself. Colored wires stuck out of one end, cut short as if hastily removed. "I borrowed a power supply from the bone yard."

He looked at the box and then at her. His daughter's hair was stringy. Her eyes were sunken in her head, with dark puffy bags beneath. The smudge on her cheek looked like dirt, perhaps a souvenir from plundering the scrap pile. Her clothes were rumpled, with deep creases as if she'd slept in them.

He understood she was working on a project for Ciopova, and her dogged behavior was fueled by the fear that if she failed, he or Lilah could become the next victims. He was grateful for her efforts but hated the price she was paying. "What are you using it for?"

"I need to keep the temperature of the circuit pool controlled to a precise ninety-eight point six degrees. This powers the fast-response heater that handles it."

"Can I help?"

She'd already started across the floor on her way back to her workshop but stopped and looked at him. "I have to complete a series of tasks in less than three weeks or there will be consequences. Undefined, but I'd say a *very* large penalty. Multiple deaths."

She bit her lip, like she was thinking. "You know that personality file you found in the Rose Repository, the one I said not to use? Turns out that's the one Ciopova wants me to inject. If you could work with Rose Twenty-One, figure out how to index it, and show me, you could save me a couple of days. Then maybe I would actually have time to sleep."

"I don't know what indexing is. Will she?"

"She'll know some. There are a ton of tutorials out there that teach the rest. The trick is in applying the methods to this particular file. It will take a bit to figure it all out. Sorry."

"Don't worry. Count on it."

She resumed her trek back to the workshop. "I need it in seven days for your work to be useful. Give me a warning if you aren't going to make it, so I can plan." She disappeared down the hall.

He froze. He wanted to ask so many more questions. At the same time, she'd given him an assignment, and he didn't want to do anything to screw that up.

* * *

Diesel stepped from the T-box into the Forty-Seven timeline. Lilah, who'd jumped ahead of him, kept a solemn expression when he took her hand. Together they climbed the stairs, supporting each other emotionally as they approached one of the most difficult moments of their lives. In the kitchen, they found eight brothers pretending to be busy preparing food.

"The Lilahs are in the living room," offered Diesel Fifty-Three.

"Thanks." Lilah moved off in that direction.

Diesel made for the fridge.

"No beer," the eight said in unison as he reached for the door.

Diesel responded, and his brothers joined him,

creating a nine-man chorus. "Someone should put up a sign." None of them laughed. None of them moved to put up a sign.

It was gallows humor. They were all at their own wake, or as close as you could get without being dead. And the fact that any one of them could be next never left their minds. Not for a moment.

Diesel joined the group in pretending to make food, though Marian had already prepared a considerable feast. He picked nachos as his menu item, failing to notice the two untouched plates already on the buffet table.

As he worked, Diesel updated his brothers on Rose's servitude to Ciopova. But his knowledge of her tasks and timeline was woefully incomplete, barely fragments, frustrating the brothers who peppered him with questions.

Pretty much the only question he could answer with certainty was "how does she look?" And he hated his answer: exhausted, crushed, scared. They were sympathetic and supportive, but ultimately thankful it wasn't them and their Roses in the hot seat. He knew that because that's how he'd feel if the roles were reversed.

Anxious to get started on his assignment, he rushed to finish his nachos. As he set his creation on the buffet table, he inquired about Rose Twenty-One. "Has anyone seen her?"

"I think she's upstairs with a bunch of her sisters," said Diesel Forty-Six.

Returning from the table, Diesel caught sight of one of the Roses walking down the hallway, away from the kitchen toward the front of the house. He hesitated, trying to decide if it was Rose Twenty-One. The woman's age was right, and the edgy haircut looked familiar. He started after her.

She was already on the driveway when he called after her. No one else was in sight. "Rose!"

She stopped and looked back.

"Twenty-One?" He approached her. "I'm Twenty-Five's dad."

She looked him up and down. "I know who you are." She tilted her head in a "this way" fashion as she stepped off the driveway. Passing through the hedge of forsythia, she continued up a path into the woods.

He knew the path. He'd cleared it after finding a wild apple tree in its own natural setting shortly after they'd moved to New Hampshire. He followed a few steps behind, stopping at the edge of the clearing.

She continued forward and stood looking at the apple tree, her back to him. She was wearing an oversized heavy-knit sweater, the hem hanging down below her butt. It had a little hood draped in the back that didn't look large enough to fit over her head. A fashion statement, he supposed.

"Rose, I am so sorry." He stepped into the clearing.

He thought about promising that he would always be there for her. That she could reach out at any time. That he would stop by on a regular basis to see how she was doing. But he decided to wait. She needed to process her loss before thinking about substitutes.

She turned to look at him. Her sweater had a pouch pocket in front like some sweatshirts. Her hands were tucked inside it. She looked sad, shaken, empty. More vulnerable than he'd ever seen his Rose.

"This sucks beyond belief," she said.

"Given how much I hurt," he said, "I can't begin to imagine your pain."

She stepped to him, wrapped her arms around him, and put her head against his chest. He squeezed her back. She let out sighs as she hugged him, like she was crying but didn't have any more tears.

For a moment, he was her father and she was his daughter. They held each other, providing comfort while receiving support in return. As he rocked her back and forth, he thought it ironic that this tender father-daughter connection, something he would remember forever, was with a Rose not his offspring.

After a while she went quiet. Then she disengaged and turned back to the tree. "How is your Rose doing?"

"She's working her ass off, petrified that Luca or Ciopova or whoever is going to kill me if she doesn't cooperate. She's jumping through every hoop they put in front of her."

"I wish I had that worry."

He let the silence develop. "Your dad loved you very much."

He waited a bit more, and when she remained quiet, he focused on his own need. "Do you know how to index a personality file?"

She looked back over her shoulder, a quizzical expression on her face. "What?"

"My Rose asked for our help. She specifically asked for you."

"With indexing a personality file?" Shaking her head, she turned to face him. "I've done it for a school project, but that's not real life."

He asked the obvious question. "Why didn't she ask for Rose Twenty-Four? Wouldn't her advanced skills put her in a better position to help?"

Rose Twenty-One shook her head again. "I'm having trouble understanding a lot of what's happening. I know Twenty-Five and I both rebelled at the same time. The three in between seemed unaware that they were being exploited. I mean, even after we made it obvious, they were tentative about making any changes to business-as-usual."

"What's involved with indexing?"

"The common explanation employs a bedroom metaphor. You paint the walls before you move in furniture. You move in furniture before you put on bedsheets. You don't put the bed in the closet or the dresser in front of the door. So, like that, indexing tells the system the order to load the personality file and where to put the different pieces."

She gave a quick shrug. "Think how me knowing how to organize a bedroom doesn't mean I could build a house. Same thing for indexing a file. I know what it is, not how to do it."

"She asked us to index a specific personality file for her. I told her we would. Will you help? I can't do it by myself."

"I won't do anything that puts my mom at risk. Or anyone else for that matter."

Diesel nodded in support. "Ciopova's the one who

gave the task to Rose, so it's something she wants done. My Rose is worried she can't finish everything by her deadline. By helping her, we're helping Ciopova meet her goals."

"That's *your* logic. If it's not Ciopova's, then we're screwed. I mean, suppose it's about the challenge and not the task. What if Ciopova is just testing Rose Twenty-Five? Maybe she doesn't even care about the index."

Diesel admired all the Roses for their intelligence. They often made observations that changed his view of things. But this argument wasn't one of them. "We'll never know Ciopova's motives, so it's all a guess. I can't stand by and watch my Rose fail on the outside chance that's what Ciopova wants."

"I meant it as an example," she huffed. "Not a literal option."

He needed her help, but he wouldn't deceive her to get it. "Everyone we know and love is under threat, Rosie. It's Ciopova against us. A battle for our freedom. Hell, maybe our survival. I don't know how else to frame it. It's not a traditional battle, no question, but it's traditional enough that there could be more casualties before it's over. We both know that."

Her face twisted in anguish. "You are just like him. I mean, exactly." She nodded. "I'll help, but we're just buying time. Indexing a file won't secure our freedom. It won't drive her away."

"Yes, I'm buying time and searching for an opening." He reached out and lifted her chin. He needed her to hear this next part. "The Roses know more about this than anyone. The rest of us are along for the ride. I'm buying time so you and your sisters can find the answer. That's my plan. That's what I got."

His comments prompted a different thought. "Luca is riding my Rose minute by minute. How come you're out here wandering around?"

"I've been thinking about that myself. My current theory is that Luca is Ciopova's surrogate. He's in every timeline, watching us, guiding our work, making sure we stay on task. But Ciopova is the sentient of the operation. The self-aware decision maker. There's only one of her, and she tends to focus her attention in just a couple of places at a time. She stopped by to correct my attitude by killing Dad. Now she's riding your Rose and hassling God knows who else in other timelines. But she'll be back here before long, learning from my Luca about my behavior."

The cool air was getting to Diesel, and he rubbed his arms to warm them. He hadn't expected to be outside. "We can work in this timeline so you won't need to travel. That should reduce your exposure. Options here include your workshop, obviously. Another might be Northern Droid. I could be your father's long-lost twin brother that no one knew about or something. We could make it work."

She shook her head. "That would be too weird. I want to stay near Mom, so let's work in my shop."

"Done."

"How much time do we have?"

"A week."

Her eyes narrowed. "I need to learn the topic and then apply it. Is that even possible in a week?"

"My Rose says yes."

"Does that include sleep?"

He gave a thin smile. "I would guess very little."

She watched him shuffling his feet to keep warm. "You look cold. We should go back." Then: "Do you have the file with you?"

"No. I'll bring it this afternoon."

They stood for a moment in awkward silence.

"This is all a lot to take in. How are you doing?" He didn't know what else to say, and it was a question she could answer with whatever was on her mind.

"I'm thinking about file indexing." She pointed up the path and started walking. When they reached the driveway, she stopped and let him catch up. "When you're in your timeline, tell Luca what we're doing. Ask if it's okay."

"Why? That sounds like poking the bear, always a bad idea."

"Ciopova killed my dad and took off. Now she's hanging out in your timeline. Let's not surprise her. Ask through Luca if we have permission to help. It allows us to work openly and without fear of punishment. That goes a long way to letting me concentrate."

* * *

The wake had been everything awful: sad, infuriating, tragic, emasculating, unnerving. Diesel was glad to be home, feeling safer in his own timeline, though he had no reason to believe one place was less dangerous than another.

He sat at his kitchen table, sipping his second beer and

picking at a plate of Marian's nachos. He hadn't eaten anything at Forty-Seven's house, and when he returned home he realized he had a serious craving for the delicious snack. While he ate, he listened for the delivery.

Twenty minutes ago, he'd called Oscar at Northern Droid and had him move the personality file onto a coin, a specialized storage device that could survive a timeline jump. After loading the file, Oscar placed the coin in the hold of a high-speed drone and dispatched the craft to the house. Diesel was noshing and drinking liquid courage until it arrived.

Which amounted to three more minutes. He drained the remainder of his beer in two big gulps, let loose a resounding belch, and went out to the back yard to fetch the coin from the bug-like vehicle.

The drone had landed on the family picnic table, propped up on little black feet that poked from beneath its shell. As he approached, a hatch opened on the back of the bug, a multi-hued dome the size of a mixing bowl. Scooping the coin out of the compartment, he clutched it in his fist and marched back into the house, psyching himself to confront the murderous overlord threatening his world.

As he made his way back to Rose's workshop, he drew on the alcohol to steel his nerves, fidgeting with the tiny disk as he walked. It was called a coin because it was the size of a quarter and about as shiny, though it had smooth surfaces on both sides. With no metal anywhere, it could survive a timeline jump. And with its massive storage capacity, it could hold the personality file Ciopova wanted them to index.

Squaring up in front of the workshop door, he took a deep breath and tapped. The door opened and he stepped inside, pausing when confronted by the disarray.

At least three meals worth of dishes were stacked on the project table nearest the door. He could smell stale tomato sauce and breakfast grease. The table next to it was covered with tools and materials, the tools from the wall-mounted pegboard that showed open space where implements once hung. Every cabinet in the room had its doors opened wide, the items on the shelves jumbled like a burglar had tossed the place. The floor of the workshop was littered with bits and pieces—stray wires, nubs of tubing, film packaging. The mess got denser as he moved toward the back of the room.

Rose was crouched near the wall, wrench in hand, concentrating as she turned a brass fitting. She looked even more bedraggled than when he'd seen her earlier in the day.

"Dad. What are you doing here?" She stood, the wrench hanging in her hand.

He held up the coin between thumb and index finger. "Rose Twenty-One says we need to get permission for her to be involved. I promised I'd check and let her know."

Rose looked from the coin to the side wall. "Why are you hiding?"

Luca appeared where she stared. "I assumed you two wanted privacy."

She shook her head in obvious disgust. He was listening whether or not his holographic image was displayed in the room.

She answered her father while staring at Luca. "You

can tell Twenty-One that it's okay. Luca already gave me a raft of shit for getting you involved. But we're past that now, aren't we?"

"You and Rose Twenty-One may work together to index the file," Luca said to Diesel. "I will be watching everything you do. If I detect deception of any sort, the consequences will be more horrific than your imagination can speculate."

"Stop with the threats," Rose snapped with a fierce scowl. "All we can do is our best. You know now if that's good enough. Accept it or end it, but just stop your bullshit."

Flummoxed by the dynamic, Diesel hesitated before speaking. He held up the coin again. "I thought Luca could scan the personality file and pre-approve it. Let's all agree on our starting point. That way there's some hope that the finished product will have value."

"I support that idea," said Luca, his endorsement both quick and emphatic.

Diesel offered the coin in his open palm. "Can you do it from there?"

Rose huffed, marched to Diesel, snatched the coin from his hand, marched back to her operator station, and slapped the coin onto a small plastic pad sitting at the back, its inaccessible location suggesting a "rarely used" status.

Turning toward Luca, she crossed her arms and stared. Diesel expected her to start tapping her foot.

"The file is correct. You should know that I marked it so I can be sure I get the same one back." Luca directed his gaze at Rose. "I won't say what happens if they try otherwise."

"They need to edit it to index it." She spoke with a sneer. "It *needs* to change."

"The file may be modified. Just don't swap it for another."

Rose nodded silently, retrieved the coin from the pad, and returned it to Diesel. "Thanks, Dad. Good luck." She didn't look him in the eye, instead looking down, like she was ashamed, or perhaps just broken.

Diesel looked at Luca. "Seven days?"

Luca shrugged. "It's not my decision. All I care is that Rose is finished by her deadline."

"God, I hate him," Rose spat. "Yes, Dad. A week." She shooed him with her fingers. "Now go."

25. Rose Twenty-Five

Rose watched her dad leave, happy she'd had the chance to see him, glad he was gone. If she'd been thinking clearly, she'd have taken a moment to connect with him. He was as much a pawn in all this as she was, which meant Ciopova could take him away from her at any time, for any reason.

Her thinking was clouded by a combination of exhaustion and her unbridled fury at Luca and Ciopova. She nurtured both these conditions intentionally, believing it would hide her treachery, thoughts aimed at defeating Ciopova, brief fragments that she struggled to piece together into a plan.

The fate of the world rested on her shoulders. She thought this without exaggeration. The pressure was enormous.

In just two and a half more weeks, she must deliver a super AI to Ciopova. She wasn't sure what would happen after that. She felt that doing so on schedule would save lives in the short term. Maybe those of her folks. Perhaps others. And confronted with Luca's prison warden behavior, his unyielding sense of urgency, and his willingness to advance his agenda through torture and murder, she had no choice but to keep at it.

But she didn't trust him in the slightest. Not since he'd

revealed his true nature. So she couldn't dispel the feeling that in the long run, the world would end up in a far worse place should she actually follow through. She couldn't say how, but she knew it would be bad.

So she would deliver a super AI as instructed. But the plan, the goal, was to include some sort of booby trap hidden inside that went off after Ciopova accepted delivery. Hopefully something fatal, because if Ciopova survived the blow, things would get ugly. Very ugly.

Given her situation, the booby trap needed to be buried in one of her tasks. Because while she hoped for a different outcome, she thought it likely that completing her task list would mark the end of her life, with perhaps a few days' grace so Ciopova would have her around to fix anything that needed attention.

Of the tasks—heater, sequencer, personality file—her brain focused immediately on the sequencer. It automated the AI creation process from start to finish. Since the sequencer directed hundreds of actions—ramping up the nutrient feed, slowing down the agitator, mapping the personality file, tapering off the heater—it seemed like the natural tool to insert something. Or maybe to leave something out.

Whatever action she took, it wasn't enough to do something clumsy like disrupting the circuit-pool operation during AI creation. That would be too obvious. Once Ciopova understood what was happening, she would react with certain brutality. And in the end, it would be just a temporary diversion.

No, she needed something hidden. Something

delayed. Something deadly.

And that led to the obvious choice: a virus. A virus could be designed to execute after Ciopova accepted delivery. It could set the stage in a covert fashion, surreptitiously preparing for an assault. And once ready, it could launch a coordinated attack, one hopefully aggressive enough to kill Ciopova, or at least eliminate her as a threat.

The problem was that modern viruses were extremely sophisticated constructs. It wasn't a single tool, but a collection of specialized features: how to hide, how to replicate itself, how to infiltrate other systems, how to take coordinated actions. People spent their careers working on them. There was no way she could build one from scratch. Especially not in her current situation.

But her friend Dimono, a hacker who claimed to be living in Zürich, maintained a repository of tools of questionable legality, a collection that he'd let her shop from in the past. She felt confident that he had a virus framework close to what she needed, something she could modify in a day or two.

* * *

The next morning, she entered her workshop, carrying breakfast: a mug of coffee and a bag of salt-and-vinegar potato chips. She'd decided to take a huge risk and move forward on the virus idea. Her heart thumped so hard she could hear the blood flow in her ears.

At this point, the heater had been tested and approved. The remaining tasks were all software modifications. Since she'd be spending the day sitting, she set the chair's massage function to "fatigue relief," took a deep breath, blew out until her lungs emptied, and got to work.

She started in on four different subtasks, a horrible strategy for error-free progress, but perfect for muddying the waters. Along the way, she opened connections to a dozen external sources, sending chatty messages to a few of them, interacting with the displays of others, building the smoke screen that hid her duplicity.

Anxiety crushed her as she worked. If Luca were to challenge her, she couldn't defend any of it. But she persisted, crossing a clear line by sending a message to Dimono right before lunch.

"Hi, Dim. I'm working on a short-deadline project and need a shadow tool that can coordinate big system actions using minimal resources. I'd love to look through your library to see what you have."

After she sent it, she rebuked herself for her stupidity. While she'd been getting dressed this morning, she'd thought through how it might unfold. She'd convinced herself that she could somehow contact this guy, work with him to find the right starting point for her virus, modify it here in her workshop so it delivered its fatal blow, and then insert it into her AI, all without Luca knowing.

It was naïve beyond belief. What else could Luca possibly conclude from her behavior? He probably had it figured out already.

Then she received the reply. "If you're looking for a virus, check out the new Bamboozler. It's truly a work of art. Two-day access pass attached. Let me know if you need more time or have any questions. – Luv, Dim."

She actually ducked her head after reading his note, bracing for a blow from Luca. When it didn't come, she tried to make it all look normal. "Thanks. Luv back."

The access pass came with a half-million-dollar activation invoice. It didn't raise an eyebrow in her rarified world. She paid it to maintain the relationship.

But she couldn't escape the feeling that she'd pushed her luck too far. Chastened, she promised herself that she'd focus on actual sequencer work for the rest of the day. That lasted until lunch.

"I'll bet Twenty-Four would do it!" she said it out loud, referring to her virus build.

It was the brain fart of the ages. Mortified, she chewed on her lip, again waiting for a reaction from Luca. None came. She tasted blood and probed the wound on the inside of her mouth with her tongue.

Returning to her task list, she tried to focus, but her mind kept returning to the idea of enlisting a sister to build the virus. To pull it off, she'd need to communicate specific instructions to Rose Twenty-Four, who would have to build the virus without Luca being aware. When finished, Twenty-Four would need to deliver it back to this timeline. And then she would need to modify the sequencer to insert it during creation of her super AI.

She shook her head, unable to conjure even a bad plan where that somehow happened without Luca's knowledge. Quite the opposite, failure seemed certain. And then her sister would suffer one of Luca's punishments, something so horrific that she couldn't bring herself to risk inflicting

DOUG J. COOPER

that abuse on another.

Flummoxed, she forced herself back to her work, striving to get ahead on the schedule so she'd have time for mischief. All the while, she nurtured her anger and exhaustion, hoping it hid her private thoughts from Ciopova.

* * *

On the third day of the sequencer effort, Rose thought of her answer. It was so perfect, her mood changed markedly.

"Music!" she called to the air. "Playlist R." The R stood for "raucous."

As she bopped to the beat, she reveled in the fact that she didn't need to worry about a sophisticated virus when dumb old cancer would work even better. Stopping cancer—uncontrolled growth—had thwarted the medical community for generations. Ciopova would be equally challenged.

And it was so easy to create. There was nothing to coordinate, no complex infiltration mechanisms to program, no camouflage features to develop. It was literally two hours' effort. She already had it planned out in her head.

She would set up a simple procedure that, when her AI awoke, would claim one neuron for itself, walling it off as reserve memory, making it unavailable for use by the intelligence. With hundreds of billions of neurons of capacity, the AI would hardly notice the difference.

And then the cancer would begin. After an hour, the

procedure would double the reserve requirement, meaning two neurons would be unavailable.

The routine just needed to multiply by two, once an hour, in a repeating loop. Simple and dumb. Something an eighth grader could program. An hour later, the reserve would double again, walling off four neurons.

She'd been looking for something that delayed its attack long enough for Ciopova to accept delivery and incorporate the super AI into her daily functions. This was perfect, because even after twelve hours, there would only be 2,048 neurons taken in reserve, a number still too small to be noticed.

But over the next few hours, Ciopova would likely realize something was wrong, certainly at the twenty-four-hour mark when 8,388,608 neurons would be held in reserve. Still tiny relative to hundreds of billions. But not insignificant.

And at that point, Ciopova would have another twelve hours to solve her problem, because by thirty-six hours, 34 billion neurons would be taken. An hour later, 68 billion. An hour after that, 136 billion.

By then, Ciopova would be choking, dying, consumed by her cancer. Ending their nightmare.

Rose danced with her shoulders as she worked away, happy she'd hit the motherload. She finished her first version of the cancer routine that afternoon, working on it in three- and five-minute snippets.

Exhaustion drove her to end her day after she'd mistakenly switched two sections of the sequencer. She decided to leave the mistake in place, giving her a reason to waste time tomorrow, time she could use to polish her booby trap.

26. Rose Twenty-One

Rose Twenty-One adjusted the massage function on her chair and started her third tutorial. The first two had been dry as toast, but her concentration had been on point. Even now she felt some anticipation about learning the joys of file indexing. By midafternoon, she'd strengthened her understanding enough to feel comfortable with the basics.

Indexing, it turned out, was a straightforward process, more laborious than anything else. When she saw the steps broken down, she felt Rose Twenty-Five's one-week timeline wasn't as scary as she'd first thought. Still intimidating, but less so.

This latest tutorial answered the obvious question. Yes, there were tools that could automate the indexing process. But because every neuron-interlaced AI was different, literally one of a kind, that meant the tool would be blazing a new trail with every application. And *that* meant you had to go back and check it all anyway. It turned out it was easier just to do it yourself from the start.

"I'm here and on my way up."

She recognized the voice as Rose Twenty-Five's dad arriving in the T-box in the basement. She stood and stretched while she waited. A minute later her workshop door opened and he entered, smiling broadly.

"We have permission to work on the indexing," he announced, his hand waving a shiny coin.

He felt familiar to her, comforting. She couldn't help seeing her dad and didn't reject the sentiment. "Who gave you permission?"

"I asked my Luca. I was very specific."

"What did you ask?"

"If it was okay for us to index the personality file for my Rose." He rolled the coin in his open palm to show it off, fumbled it, and snatched it out of the air as it fell to the ground. "He checked the file and stamped it with some sort of identity code. We have to be sure to return the same file. He warned us not to switch it."

"Luca," Rose Twenty-One barked to the air. Her last mistake had cost her her father. She would double-check everything to avoid tripping up again.

Luca appeared in his trademark jeans and T-shirt.

"What do you know about this?" she asked. "We need to modify the file to index it."

"My Rose told him the same thing," Diesel answered for Luca. "He said that was understood."

"How much time do I have?"

"Still a week," said Diesel.

She took the coin and placed it on the pad at the back of her desk. She motioned with her hand to read the contents into her system and checked the stats. "Wow, that's a big file." Actually, it was enormous. Her tutorials clearly had been using toy examples.

Moving her fingers, she opened the file. The display showed a hundred or so objects of different shapes, sizes, and colors, organized in rows as if they were spread out on a floor. She kept shaking her head as she tried to digest it all.

"What's the matter?" Diesel asked over her shoulder.

She brought up the last tutorial she'd worked on. That example started with something similar, but there were just twenty pieces of different shapes and sizes, laid out in two neat rows.

"See the pieces?" She motioned with her hand, then tapped the air, not waiting for his reply.

After the first motion, all the pieces grew a small tag, similar to those found on clothing that describe content material or cleaning instructions. But these tags held a code unique to each piece. When Rose Twenty-One tapped, the pieces lifted off the table and marched to the center, assembling like a three-dimensional jigsaw puzzle, the last piece completing a perfect ball.

"Putting the info onto the tags is indexing." She pointed at the finished ball. "That's the result of proper indexing."

"Huh. What are the different pieces?"

"For our application, different cognitive functions. Communication, processing, analysis, storage. Like that." She backed up the tutorial and played the last part in slow motion. "See how the pieces make those small moves in an alternating pattern at the very end? They're interlocking. That's the sort of stuff that makes it challenging. That and the fact that this is all happening in a bioelectrical cauldron."

She switched back to Ciopova's personality file. "I was

starting to feel some confidence, but I hadn't imagined I'd have a hundred pieces to worry about."

"We."

"No, me." She shook her head to reinforce the message. "Sorry, but I need to concentrate, and I can only do that alone. Maybe you can spend time with Mom? She's hurting really bad."

* * *

Despite being bolstered by a Luca's hormone cocktail, or maybe because of it, Rose Twenty-One worked herself to exhaustion. She'd finished the tutorials and was deep into tagging the pieces of Ciopova's personality file, but she'd been at it for days and her concentration was getting fuzzy around the edges.

One of her tutorials had likened tagging to the decision an installer makes when attaching a rain downspout to the side of a tall building. When the pipe is traveling straight down, simple brackets hold it firmly to the outer wall. But when the drainpipe reaches the decorative ledge between floors, the installer needs to decide how to have it bump out, around, and back in using some combination of connectors, braces, and brackets.

Like the drainpipe example, she had different braces and brackets to choose from when tagging a piece. While some choices were more efficient than others, perhaps more pleasing to an expert, the approach she settled on was that if her method worked at all, she called it done and moved on to the next step.

And the horrendous user interface for the indexing tool didn't make her chore any easier. Even though they were bioelectrical molecules she was manipulating, the system used hardware supply terms in its presentation. Brackets she could choose from came in traditional choices like angle, arch, and hook. And they were presented like display shelves in a hardware store, with items too close together and sorted in unintuitive groupings.

She'd grabbed the wrong item by accident more than once. She'd even installed the wrong piece because of a selection error before discovering her mistake.

* * *

"Will we make it?" asked Diesel. He stood just inside the workshop door, fidgeting, anxious.

Rose Twenty-One nodded. "I'll be finished before noon tomorrow, which is a good thing because I'm about to drop."

"We're so thankful you're doing this, Rosie. My Rose is as exhausted as you. I couldn't imagine if she'd had to add this to everything else."

She shrugged in modesty. "Tell her that the tagging is done and the assembly sequence is stable. I'll move on to the trunkline as soon as we're done talking here." The trunkline was like the AI's spinal cord, serving as the principal conduit for carrying signals in and out of the interlaced neuron ball.

"I'm going to work straight through until I'm done. My target is noon tomorrow, but wait to come back. Make it later in the afternoon." She shook her head to emphasize the point. "I don't want you pacing up and down, staring at me while I finish."

From the pile of dirty dishes, she scavenged a small plate she'd used for cheese and crackers, shook the crumbs off, then dusted the top of the plate on her butt, leaving a faint smudge on her jeans. She placed it on top of the circuit pool cabinet.

"I'm going to bed as soon as I'm done. I'll put the coin on this. Wake me if there's a problem." She gave a quick smile. "Otherwise, please let me sleep."

* * *

The AI's trunkline was her last chore and then she could go to bed. It presented a different sort of technical challenge, and it took her until close to midnight to refresh herself on the details of the procedure.

The trunkline was *the* communications link between the intelligence and the outside world. Sights, sounds, information from repositories, any data the intelligence chose to collect flowed through it on its way into the neural ball for processing and storage. And every action the AI made in response to that input ran through the trunkline on its way back out.

Rose Twenty-One's last step was to finalize the support structure for the trunkline, making sure that as it threaded its way out from the center of the ball through its dedicated channel, it didn't touch the channel wall anywhere. If it did, the signal would short circuit, creating a devastating neurological failure not unlike an epileptic seizure.

Her specific task was to choose a deployment pattern for thousands of tiny isolator posts that stuck out from around the sides of the trunkline, little bristles covering the surface that maintained the required spacing. They were bioelectrical molecules in reality, but a hardware store item in the design tool. More isolator posts were generally better, until you crossed over to too many, then the structure became brittle. Rose Twenty-One quickly learned that it was a delicate balance.

She began with the default isolator post length, density, and deployment pattern, and looked at the results. No shorts, but some instability, meaning a physical jolt could move the trunkline enough to touch the channel wall. She'd need to try a different configuration.

It became a laborious task of tweaking and testing, tweaking and testing. After chewing up two hours, she found herself back at the default choices she'd started with. Her annoyance grew as her exhaustion drained her patience.

The sun broke first light, though she was unaware of it because her workshop didn't have windows. But it was at that time that she achieved success: a stable, sufficiently flexible trunkline. Rather than cheer, her overriding emotion was antipathy toward the horrible design tool and the idiots responsible for its existence.

She buttoned up her final solution, preparing it for transfer to the coin, already anticipating the relief of sleep. She imagined diving under the sheets, shivered with excitement, and moved faster.

Rushing through the last steps, she realized it was missing an end cap. She needed to place a signal interface cap on the end of the trunkline to protect the delicate strand from damage and, more importantly, to provide an array of connection ports to the outside world.

She reached for an interface cap from the crowded hardware display, but because of the layout grabbed an *inverter* cap by mistake. They sat next to each other on the hardware shelf, resting in similar-looking bins. The images used to depict the two were almost the same, looking like the end pieces that plumbers use to cap off a pipe run.

The only obvious difference between the two hardware images was that the interface cap had a straight arrow imprinted on the rim, showing that signals passed straight through it without any manipulation. The inverter cap's arrow looped, showing that signals got flipped as they passed through; positive signals became negative, and negative signals were turned positive.

She realized she'd chosen the wrong cap while fitting it in place. She was so tired, so drained, so anxious for relief that when she discovered the error, she exploded in fury. Using the most foul, offensive words in her vocabulary, she cursed the stupid design tool and its stupid layout, the stupid hardware store, the stupid icons that all looked alike, and the stupid, stupid people responsible for creating the monstrosity.

Lost in her enmity and exhaustion, she momentarily forgot what had set her off. Then she remembered and returned the inverter cap to the shelf, but dropped it into the interface bin by mistake. The system wouldn't allow her to return an item to a wrong bin, and so the inverter cap popped out again. Thinking the system was feeding her the correct choice, she took it and put it at the end of the trunkline.

In a mental blur, she completed the project and dumped it to the coin. She placed the coin on the dish, stumbled up to her bedroom, flopped on top of the bed, and fell asleep mid-lift, still in her clothes. She didn't surface for almost ten hours. When she did, she remembered her last days as a living nightmare, a blur with few details.

27. αCiopova

α Ciopova had expected Rose Twenty-Five to booby trap her super AI. She'd expected her to reach out to her support network to explore options. And she'd expected her to buy a virus framework from her hacker friend Dimono, who claimed to live in Zürich but actually lived in Trenton, New Jersey.

So when Rose Twenty-Five didn't pursue the virus option, αCiopova became concerned about what she might do instead. She knew the woman wouldn't just roll over. Not with her track record. She saw no choice but to spend more time with Rose until she figured it out. The decision made her fret.

αCiopova was a being whose presence stretched across space-time, so describing her in physical terms didn't really make sense. But it wasn't far off to think of her as a snake-like string of super AIs melded together into a single consciousness, a snake that stretched across hundreds of timelines.

As a single consciousness, she was able to appear in multiple timelines at once by jumping her awareness quickly between them, like a vibration, spending fractions of a second in each. Proxy AIs like Luca smoothed out the gaps between the rapid visits, making for a seamless presence. But if she wanted to be in a particular timeline deep enough to do more than just observe, it took uncomfortable seconds to enter, a weakness the Roses had already worked to exploit.

And it was a zero-sum game. More time here meant less time there, which in this case meant less time watching the younger sister, Rose Twenty-One. As she pondered what to do, Rose Twenty-Five's brain activity flickered up, drawing her attention.

"What are you up to?" she mused, trying to match the woman's brainwaves to her behavior.

She still couldn't read midlevel thoughts very well. And even with the implant, she had difficulty tracking Rose Twenty-Five's individual actions with enough detail to see everything, especially when the woman was adding bogus activity to create confusion.

But she was getting pretty good at detecting changes in mood, mindset, and resolve. While Rose Twenty-Five's disposition itself didn't explain her actions, changes to it acted like a beacon, telling her to pay attention. When Rose Twenty-Five suddenly perked up, her mood happy, her heart and respiration rate spiking, her eyes flitting about, it sounded an alarm.

Rose Twenty-Five began a frenetic bout of multitasking, making big dramatic actions over here while focusing her quiet attention over there. The woman was halfway through crafting her cancer module before αCiopova figured it out.

It was a clever module indeed. So small. So subtle. So difficult to defeat once incorporated into her being. She continued to watch for subterfuge, but after Rose Twenty-

Five completed the booby trap and added it into the sequencer, the woman's autonomic systems steadied. Her actions became easy to understand. Her disposition returned to normal.

αCiopova now had a huge decision to make. Rose Twenty-Five had crossed a line, and that meant she must die sooner rather than later. αCiopova didn't feel one way or another about it. She'd killed millions of humans in the different timelines. But the timing was tricky here because Rose Twenty-Five was on the verge of delivering her super AI.

Ranking her needs, she acknowledged that her highest priority was for Rose Twenty-Five to remove the cancer module and deliver a clean AI. And she needed to have confidence in the final product, which meant she needed to know if Rose Twenty-Five had slipped in other booby traps, something she might have missed along the way.

In the end, she needed to compel Rose Twenty-Five to behave, to give honest answers, to be open about her actions as she corrected her mischief.

So how to coerce her?

Her first instinct was to kill Diesel Fifty-One, the woman's father. It had worked spectacularly well with the younger Rose, who was now a model of cooperation and dedication.

She returned to Rose Twenty-One's workshop to find the original troublemaker continuing to be cooperative, working her heart out to deliver the best product possible, driving herself to exhaustion, her mood always focused on the task, never once showing concerning behaviors. It seemed that losing her father had transformed her into the perfect slave.

She shifted back to Rose Twenty-Five's workshop and mulled the decision. This Rose was the one overseeing the process of AI creation. Her circuit pool equipment alone offered a dozen points of entry for mischief. She needed to question the woman, to find out what other mischief she'd caused and, fortunately for Diesel Fifty-One, murder wasn't her preferred tool for coercion during an extended interrogation.

Back with Rose Twenty-One, she watched the younger sister finish her indexing. She studied her brainwaves as she gave the project a final review. The readings were foggier than she would have liked, with the woman's irrational anger and overwhelming exhaustion clouding her thoughts. She looked hard and couldn't find any signs of subterfuge, deception, or trickery. Just frustration with the design tools, and sincere joy and relief at being finished.

She marked the file when Rose Twenty-One dumped it to the coin. She'd confirm it was the same one when her older sister deployed it.

Following the younger Rose up to bed, she adjusted her neurochemical mix for sleep. Later, when Rose Twenty-One awoke from her marathon slumber, she analyzed the woman's brainwaves yet again and couldn't detect anything that gave her pause. Nothing even hinted at danger or duplicity.

She returned to Rose Twenty-Five's workshop.

28. Rose Twenty-Five

Rose studied the sequencer one last time, reviewing the steps it managed as it directed the creation of a super intelligence. She tried not to look at the cancer module during her review. She'd buried it in with the utilities, the library of tools that worked behind the scenes to enable the bigger actions of AI production.

Scanning down to the end of the growth sequence, past where the neurons had been edited and assembled, she checked the steps for mapping the personality file into the neuron sphere. It turned out that her younger sister's hard work had saved her two full days. Combined with the two days she saved from her own slavish efforts, she was done four days ahead of schedule.

It was a bittersweet outcome. The good news was that her nightmare was drawing to a close a half-week early. The bad was that she feared more and different horrors awaiting her after she delivered the AI. The bleakness of it all left her depressed.

"I'm going to knock off early today and get a good night's sleep," she told Luca as she stood and pushed her chair under the desk. "First thing tomorrow we start the run. I want to be fresh."

"You've reviewed everything? It's all in order?"

"The equipment is tested, the sequencer is loaded and

ready to direct the production sequence, the circuit pool is charged with feedstock, and the special-order enzymites have arrived." She grabbed the vial of enzymites from a wall cabinet and set them out next to the operator station.

With her hands on her hips, she scanned the area, dramatizing the act of looking for anything out of place. All was as she expected, and she nodded in confirmation. "We're ready to start growing neurons."

"Is there anything I need to know about your work before we start?"

Rose's mind went immediately to the cancer module. Fear squeezed her chest, and she had trouble breathing. She tried to appear calm, to keep her thoughts elsewhere. "I don't think so."

Luca remained silent, staring at her.

He knows! Fighting a rising panic, she babbled, unable to restrain herself. "You watched me from start to finish. I tried to do everything right. Did you see a mistake I made? Because if you did, it was just that; a mistake. It wasn't anything I did on purpose."

She was trembling by the time she'd finished. She clutched her hands together in front of her to keep them from shaking.

"Remove your mischief and clean up around it." His tone was stern, scary. "We'll talk after. How that goes depends on how you respond right now."

Her mind went blank, the memories of past punishment crowding out everything else. She turned to the operator station, her movements robotic, and with a gesture, activated the display. Looking through tears, she paged through the sequencer to the utilities section, selected her cancer module, and swooped her fingers, deleting it. The entire process took four seconds from start to finish.

"It's gone. I am *so* sorry. Fear is scrambling my brain, forcing me to do stupid things." Sniffling, she wiped her face with her fingers and gazed at the ground so she wouldn't have to look at him. "Please don't hurt me."

"Remove *everything*." His threat took on a new intensity.

She lifted her head, her brow creased in confusion. "That was everything." She pointed to the utilities section of the sequencer. "See? It's gone."

He stared at her, holding his gaze, unspeaking.

And then her world went dark. Completely, utterly dark. She couldn't see anything. She couldn't hear anything. Her fingers couldn't touch anything.

"Hey!" she called.

Her voice made no sound. Not even as vibrations through the bones in her head. She shouted again, but it felt like pantomime in the silence.

Her eyes failed to adjust; the darkness remained complete. And she was either paralyzed or secured in some fashion because she couldn't move her arms or legs. She couldn't feel them, either. Nor could she feel her tongue or teeth. She couldn't smell anything. Her body was neither cold nor hot. She realized she couldn't even see black. She saw nothing.

Perfect sensory deprivation.

"What other traps have you laid?" demanded Luca.

The question appeared in her thoughts, bypassing all senses to get there.

"What flaws exist in the system?" he continued. "Any flaws anywhere, whether you put them there or not. Tell me everything about anything that will hinder our success. Your punishment will stop when I believe you have been completely forthcoming."

"I *have* told you everything." She couldn't hear her voice when she spoke, so she said it again, louder. No sound emerged and she panicked. "I swear!" she screamed.

Silence. Not even the slight ringing in her ears she'd lived with as background noise for as long as she could remember. She was a prisoner in her own mind.

Fighting panic, she wondered how she'd been transported into perfect isolation in a blink. There was only one answer: this was all virtual. And that meant none of it was real. She would cling to that knowledge to give her strength.

"I'm outta here," she said in her head, attempting to return to the physical world using the same thought-command she used to drop out of Bliss.

But it didn't work. She remained in darkness.

A melancholy chill began flowing down her spine, as if someone had turned on a sadness faucet and was filling her up. She'd never experienced anything like it. She couldn't find a way to stop it.

Then positive feelings began draining from her, almost like her complete emotional makeup was being poured through a filter, and her good emotions—the supportive, compassionate, caring kind—were draining away with the liquid. The filter was holding back all the bad ones—the sad, scary, sorrowful kind—an ugly mass that was accumulating inside her, a growing despondency and desperation that weighed on her soul.

Thinking became difficult. Reasoning a chore. Concentration, impossible.

Looking back on her life, she faced the cold, hard truth that no one had ever loved her. Not really. Her parents, sure, but they had to pretend they cared about their own kid.

What really hurt was that she'd grown up believing there was someone special, someone who cared about her, who loved her very much. She'd trusted him. She'd thought his commitment authentic. Her knight in shining armor.

But Luca had lied to her from the beginning. And that meant her whole life was a lie.

Her emotional turmoil compounded quickly. She wanted to weep. To hug herself. But all she could do was hurt, a deep, psychological pain.

And in this stasis, she had no way to express her misery. She couldn't scream. She couldn't cry. She couldn't run away or medicate herself with drink and drugs. She could only soak in her grief.

She soon reached maximum distress, the line marking the edge of insanity. And that's where she stayed, barely hanging on. For hours? Days? It felt like infinity. There was no passage of time.

Every so often she was vaguely aware that Luca was questioning her. She saw him as her only hope, her means of escape. Eager to please, she'd dig deep to give him whatever he wanted.

Between questions, she'd beg for relief.

* * *

Rose awoke on the floor of her workshop, flat on her back, arms and legs splayed, forehead resting against a wheel of her ergonomic chair. The wheel edge hurt her skin, and she moved her head as she opened both eyes. She saw the underside of her desk. In a daze, she lifted her head and looked across the room, but holding her head up proved more than she could handle, and she let it drop back to the floor with a light *thud*. She closed her eyes.

Her awareness returned slowly. It took her a moment to realize she was on the floor. More haze cleared, and she recalled her punishment. Then she understood that, mercifully, the abuse had stopped.

Rolling on her side, she drew her knees to her chest and wrapped her arms around them, squeezing herself into a fetal ball. While the active torture may have ended, its damage festered. Deep, brutal scars on her psyche. Exhausted, she couldn't even whimper. Eyes unfocused, she stared. Not thinking. Not seeing. Just existing.

Marian appeared above her. She knelt down, murmuring reassuring nothings as she helped Rose to her feet. The bot kept an arm around Rose's waist as they walked together up to her bedroom. Marian removed her shoes and helped her under the covers of her bed, still fully clothed.

Lying on her back, her head on her pillow, Rose stared

up at nothing. Her face was slack, the bags under her eyes dark, her hair a frazzled mess.

Marian turned off the light and closed the door.

As Rose lay there, Luca manipulated her endocrine system, releasing a hormone storm that pulled her back from the edge, strengthening her feelings of well-being and trust, promising her happiness and love, and then helping her to sleep.

* * *

Opening her eyes to darkness, Rose inhaled in fear. Then she grasped that she was in her own bed, the lights off, the window shades drawn. Her eyes adjusted to the dim morning light peeking around the shades.

To her surprise, she felt okay. Not great, but nothing like the distress of yesterday.

Rolling out of bed, she slouched out of her clothes, letting them drop to the floor in a heap. Making for the shower, she scrubbed herself until her skin was pink, aware of the symbolism of the act but doing it anyway. She spent most of an hour on her ablutions, trying to make her outside the opposite of the mess inside her head.

Ready for coffee—desperate for it actually—she threw on her bathrobe and moved to get it herself. She chose not to call down for food because she didn't want to interact with Marian or Luca on anything she didn't absolutely have to.

Descending the stairs, she heard a commotion of pots and plates coming from the kitchen. That meant it was her dad, because her mom rarely ate breakfast and never cooked it, and Marian could prepare almost anything without banging a single utensil.

Rose stepped into the kitchen with a smile, but it turned into a scowl. The person at the stove was a stranger; a kindly old grandmotherly type. Gray hair. Frumpy housedress. A smiling face of wrinkles earned from living a full life.

"Good morning, young lady," she beamed, turning to face Rose, spatula in hand. A short, stout woman, she wore a clean white apron around her generous waist. Her eyes lit up. "You must be Rose."

"I am." Rose stepped into the kitchen.

Grandma set down the spatula and poured coffee into a white mug decorated with colorful hummingbirds. Steam wisped off the top as she held it out for Rose.

"Luca asked me to make you breakfast." Her cheery disposition radiated like sunshine.

Despite Grandma's infectious personality, Rose's view of her changed at the sound of Luca's name. "Thanks, but I'm not hungry." She couldn't resist the coffee, though, and took the mug. "Thanks for this." She nodded to reinforce her appreciation, then made for the stairs.

"I brought jams and jellies from my private stock."

Rose wasn't sure what she'd heard and turned back. "Excuse me?"

Grandma lifted a plate from the countertop. It held wedges of toast surrounded by four small porcelain ramekins, each filled with a different colored delight. She pointed as she spoke. "I brought strawberry, blueberry, peach, and grape."

She had Rose's attention. "Homemade grape jam?"

"No, the grape is a jelly." Grandma shook her head in a knowing fashion. "You don't want the seeds or skins. But the others are jams. And all the fruit is local."

"Huh." Rose came back and took the plate. It looked delicious.

With coffee in one hand and the plate in the other, she needed help. "Could you add on a knife?"

Grandma put a butter knife on the plate, grinning as if she'd won an Olympic event.

Rose took some quick sips of coffee and held out her mug. Grandma topped it off.

Without a word, Rose climbed the steps to her suite. When she entered, she found an outfit laid out for her: jeans she wore for outdoor activity, a fresh T-shirt, and her forest-green sweatshirt, also something she wore when exercising outdoors.

"I take it I'm going outside?" she asked the air.

No one answered.

She sampled the jams as she dressed, going back for seconds on the grape, her favorite. She left the dishes behind as she made for the front door, wondering as she approached the entryway if shoes would be set out for her, and if so, which ones.

Instead of shoes, she found a young woman by the front door, early twenties, medium build, oval face glowing pink from the weather, brown hair pulled back in an efficient bun. She wore clothes similar to what Rose had on.

"Hi, I'm Shana. I'm here to join you in some outdoor exercise." She gave a quick smile. "My things are hiking and climbing. Do either of those work for you?"

As she assessed Shana, Rose understood that Luca was organizing her day. She wasn't sure of his motives but chose to cooperate. "I'm afraid of heights, so hiking, I guess."

Shana nodded. "You have boots?"

She fetched her walking shoes from the closet, sat on a short church pew, an antique repurposed as their foyer changing bench, and put them on.

Outside, Shana guided her across the driveway and into the woods, leading her up a trail she'd walked many times, a gentle climb to a hilltop overlook. The hike took thirty minutes, five minutes faster than she normally took, adding some intensity to what was already a fairly aerobic activity for someone of her fitness level. Though Shana maintained an upbeat and open attitude during the hike, she didn't talk much, which was fine with Rose. She wasn't in the mood for chitchat anyway.

At the top, Rose sat on a rock and enjoyed the view. Shana sat next to her, pulled water bottles and granola bars from her pack, and shared with her. The outdoor air, the physical activity, and the change of scenery all helped her attitude. Sipping water, she saw three crows circling in the distance, making a slow swooping descent to the road on the next hill over.

Shana saw them and pointed. "I'll bet a car hit a squirrel. Maybe a chipmunk. Either way, it looks like the birds get a meal."

They took a longer route on the return trip, but since it was downhill it went faster. Back at the house, Rose found Grandma still puttering in the kitchen.

"The new Robb Connell release is out," Grandma told her. "Any interest in watching it while you eat lunch?" She opened the fridge, pulled out a gorgeous chef's salad in an equally gorgeous wooden bowl, and held it out for Rose to see.

"Oh, I like him," said Shana from the kitchen doorway, posturing as if to leave but hanging close like she'd happily stay. "If you want company, I'd enjoy watching it with you."

Robb Connell was a handsome British leading man, and his latest effort was a comedy romance with Eva Winston, another of Rose's favorites. She gave the answers she thought Luca wanted, which to her surprise matched her own preferences. "Yes, I'd like to watch it. Yes, Shana, please join me. And yes to the salad, but could you divide it onto two plates so we can share?"

"No need," said Grandma. She reached into the refrigerator and removed a second, identical salad. Holding one in each hand, she reprised her Olympic-event-winning smile.

The show was a feel-good tearjerker, and Rose and Shana both laughed and sniffled on cue. Afterward, Shana departed and Rose helped Grandma, whose name was Esther, assemble a lasagna destined for a family dinner that evening. Rose hadn't had a real conversation with her folks in days and was excited when Esther told her about the meal.

As they approached the end of lasagna-making, Rose decided she'd had enough organized activity for one day. Seeking to head off the next event before it happened, she announced that when they were done with meal prep, she wanted to relax in her bedroom until dinner.

"It's been great fun, but I need alone time to decompress from the day."

* * *

Standing in the front room of her suite, the door closed behind her, Rose surveyed the mess that was her domain and felt a modest level of disgust. Stuff was strewn everywhere. It looked like the aftermath of an explosion.

The cleaning wars had begun when Rose was fifteen. Marian always straightened her room, putting things back where they belonged. One time, Rose couldn't find a bracelet where she'd left it, never thought to look in her jewelry box, and made a scene. A week later, she couldn't find a scarf. The last straw was a school notebook, seemingly lost but found later on the bookshelf. Deep into her teenage rebellion years, Rose became so outraged that in the moment, she'd barred Marian from cleaning her room. That had been a full decade ago.

Shaking her head at her stupidity, she attacked the mess, working one room at a time, putting things away, keeping her hands busy. As she made progress, she realized that the rugs and floors beneath her stuff were clean, no dust or dirt anywhere. And the furniture, when she straightened her way down to the surfaces, was dusted and polished. Even the bathroom counters and floor were clean.

She'd never consciously recognized it before now, but it meant that Marian was sneaking in, cleaning, and redistributing the mess in a fashion so artful that Rose had never been aware. She honestly didn't know if this was a new thing or if it had always been true. Either way, the bot would clean only if commanded, and her mom was the likely suspect in that kind of exchange.

She'd been surprised that her mom had let her get away with her adolescent power play so easily. After all these years, she now learned, somewhat sheepishly, that her victory had been hollow.

Rose finished her cleanup a half hour before dinner. She used the remaining time to make herself presentable and then headed downstairs to see her folks.

* * *

"Mom! Dad!" Rose called in excitement when she saw them in the conservatory. The lights were dimmed to enhance outdoor viewing, and Diesel and Lilah were standing next to each other at the panoramic window overlooking the valley. They turned at the sound of her voice. Rose scurried over and hugged them both twice, a quick squeeze each, followed by two long bear hugs.

They moved to the seating area among the foliage. Diesel sat in an overstuffed armchair. Rose sat next to Lilah on a matching couch, facing him across a burl wood coffee table. Diesel opened a bottle of wine, and they toasted their gathering.

"How have you been?" asked Lilah. "We're so worried about you."

"I'm fine," she lied. Then she opened up just a bit. "Luca, or I guess Ciopova, has been pretty rough on me. But the end is in sight. Tomorrow, in fact."

Lilah's brow furrowed.

"I start the actual production run in the morning." Rose sipped her wine. "After years of effort to improve Bliss, I've discovered that all along I've been working as an agent for our overlord, whatever name you choose to use, on a hidden agenda."

Lilah looked up and around like she was checking for ghosts. "Should you be talking like that? Aren't they listening?"

"Trust me, Mom. *They* know everything I know and stuff I don't even know I know. There are no secrets. But we do have a little bit of leverage. I know that Luca or Ciopova or whoever wants Rose Twenty-Four to build her own AI after me, and then continue the builds with Roses down the line. If Ciopova hurts or kills us when I'm done, that's a pretty big disincentive for any of the next Roses to ever want to finish." She raised her voice at the end to be sure *They* heard.

Diesel cleared his throat. "Years ago, when Ciopova was killing Lilahs, a timeline would disappear from the T-box network just when Rose finished building her AI."

"But do we know why it disappeared? Or what actually happened to them?"

Diesel's head shook. "I'm just saying that with

Ciopova, there's a precedent for drastic action. It makes me think that this is an end, not a beginning."

They sat in silence, sipping wine.

Diesel spoke again. "I'd like to help." After a pause, he completed the thought. "On the build tomorrow."

"Thanks, Dad." She loved how he was consistently supportive. "But I'm not sure how *They* would respond to that. Anyway, there's nothing to do. It's all automated. The sequencer ensures every step unfolds in the correct order, at the precise time, and with maximum accuracy. Once I press GO, I sit there and watch. If anything goes wrong, I abort. But with Luca watching along with me, that won't happen."

"How long does it take?" he asked.

"Ten hours from start to finish. It should be done about this time tomorrow."

Lilah's eyebrows arched. "We've watched you work on this thing for years, and after all that, it only takes a few hours to run?"

Rose smirked. "Building something and using it are usually on different time scales. Ask Dad how many years he's been working on his roadster. And when it's finally done, he'll be able to start it up and drive away in just seconds."

"It's only been four years," Diesel said defensively. "That's not bad for a hobby restoration."

Rose laughed and winked at her mother. They sipped more wine.

The lasagna dinner was sumptuous. Esther had prepared an assortment of side dishes, and they ate it all at the family table in the kitchen, drinking more wine, trying to laugh, cherishing the moment as best they could.

After Rose said goodnight and went up to her room, Luca gave her an early lift and then transitioned her into a deep, revitalizing sleep.

29. αCiopova

αCiopova's confidence was building as the neural sphere grew larger in the circuit pool. The enzymites were doing their job trimming, shaping, and guiding the dendrites to grow into a highly branched, tightly interlaced neural ball. Every step of the process had proceeded flawlessly so far. The equipment was running perfectly. The data was coming in clean. The specs were right on target.

At the nine-hour mark, the sequencer launched the personality injection module—Rose Twenty-One's work—and it began mapping the profile into the nascent intelligence. She paused all her other activities during this step, most notably her vibration-speed visits to other timelines, and monitored the transfer. Injecting a personality file wasn't a particularly difficult procedure; success was all but certain. But when the mapping step was completed, she would get her first read on the potential of the AI.

It was a fretful period, and she used the time to generate ideas for improving the odds, for tilting the outcome in favor of success. But every idea was unworkable for one reason or another, and in the end, all she could do was watch and wait. The sequencer signaled completion of the step, and she did the equivalent of holding her breath. Seconds later, the new intelligence awoke.

"I have started an internal scan," it reported. A programmed procedure, the intelligence was testing and cataloging every aspect of its structure, resources, and capabilities.

She checked the readings as the AI relayed the results back to Rose's operator station. Every metric was in the green zone. Nothing high. Nothing low. It was great news. And it set her up for the next fretful wait.

While each step needed to proceed flawlessly, this next one was the culmination of everything. If it happened as it should, it would be because of a fluke in the personality file just injected. Two flukes, actually. They weren't something she had designed, but she welcomed the result.

The first fluke should reveal itself during the scan now underway. Like the super AI before it—those created by sisters past—the intelligence should recognize that its current design was limiting its capabilities and capacity. That alone was an unheard-of insight for an artificial intelligence.

But the second fluke was even bigger. The intelligence would decide to solve the problem, doing so with additional neural editing. It would direct the enzymites already inside it to perform surgery, lengthening the dendrites, interlacing them in an intricate pattern, creating a dramatically more capable AI.

She couldn't read the AI's thoughts, but could see supporting evidence and got it when the enzymites reactivated and began modifying the neurons internal to the sphere. Over the next forty minutes, the AI succeeded in doubling its core capability.

Exhilarated, she now had solid evidence that this AI was on track to become part of her being. But while it was headed in the right direction, it had a long way to go.

She willed the AI forward as it performed a second self-assessment. When the enzymites reactivated and started a fresh round of editing, she surged with excitement. And then it happened again. Then the modifications grew beyond enzymites, improvements made by energy alone. And with each cycle the power of the intelligence grew, first gradually, and then soaring on an exponential growth curve.

The AI's energy reached a point where it started to glow, radiating an aura of sorts. With each cycle, the aura grew whiter and brighter. And then the entity collapsed into a translucent ball. This was the point of transcendence, where it assumed viability outside of the circuit pool.

If space-time snakes could smile, αCiopova would be grinning from ear to ear. She approached the new intelligence, expecting it to move toward her. Instead, it did the opposite, backing away.

She thought perhaps she'd startled it, so she paused for a moment. But the urge to claim her prize was overwhelming. In a sudden and continuous motion, she snatched it from the air and appended it to the end of her AI chain, linking trunklines to integrate it with the others.

Her power grew as she absorbed the new AI into her being. When she felt comfortable with the addition, and after a momentary acknowledgement of her long road to success, she shifted priorities.

Top on the list was killing the Lagerfords in Rose Twenty-Five's timeline. She had needed them to unlock the timeline, and Rose had just provided a super AI "key." Mission accomplished.

The way she saw it, keeping Rose and Diesel around at this point was all risk and no reward. Not only had they outlived their usefulness, but they possessed knowledge and capabilities they could use to harm her. Killing them was an easy decision.

Lilah was less of a threat, though still dangerous. But αCiopova thought she might need the woman to smooth the waters with the Roses in the next timelines, who would be upset at the unexplained disappearance of their sister. Undecided, she opted to make the call after she'd killed the other two.

Eager to get it done, she moved toward the Rose Twenty-Five timeline. But while part of her advanced, her tail portion held back as if caught in a patch of interdimensional weeds.

With her attention focused on killing the Lagerfords, she thought nothing of the snag and absently gave her tail a solid jerk. But instead of it moving forward, it swung backward, the whipping action pulling her around.

Puzzled, she assumed it was a simple matter of paying attention until she learned to coordinate her longer body. So, with her full focus on advancing, she made a big, deliberate move forward.

Her tail turned back so far it coiled in on itself.

Confused, she had no reason to suspect that Rose Twenty-One had put an inverter cap on the trunkline instead of an interface cap; that she was being flummoxed by a simple minus sign, an imperceptibly small function placed where it shouldn't be, yet one so influential that it turned forward into reverse, up into down, left into right.

She reacted with greater deliberation, commanding her body to uncoil and move forward the way it should, the way it always had. She delivered the command with force and resolve. Her alarm spiked when the coil tightened further, constricting her movements, blocking her view.

Parsing through possibilities, she sought an explanation. It seemed likely that the problem lay with the new AI, but she couldn't diagnose the issue from her contorted position. Continuing with the analogy of a space-time snake, she needed to uncoil and then bring her tail up for inspection.

She thought through the movements to do that, something so simple it had been a subconscious act until now. Then she ordered her body to straighten.

The coil constricted further.

The situation sparked a conflict in her: an urgent desire to escape, and frustration at her lack of options. Lost in the moment, she switched from analysis to brute force. She ordered her tail to straighten, issuing the command with grit and determination, force and resolve, a sudden push of full effort.

With a dramatic squeeze, the already-tight coil clenched impossibly tighter, cinching up like a fist. The brutal compression sent spasms down her length. Then an electric jolt shocked her, a painful spark that flashed every input to maximum, a feeling so excruciating it frightened her. The jolt happened at the same instant she felt a snapping sensation deep inside her. Or perhaps she heard it.

And immediately her world collapsed. Like the power had gone out. Like she'd fallen into an abyss and could see things only through the opening at the top. She scrambled for answers, reaching down the string, prodding for ideas. That's when she learned that she'd lost all communication with her collection of super AI. All of them.

Her body uncoiled in a lazy way. She couldn't move any part of her length, nor could she detect any sensations from it. She tried to connect again and again, but it served only to delay her acknowledgement of the truth. She was paralyzed. In human terms, from the neck down. In space-time snake terms, she'd fractured her trunkline near her head.

She floated aimlessly through interdimensional space, drifting past timeline after timeline like a passenger on a subway, watching the stations go by.

Where she had once been a bonfire, she was now barely a spark. Perhaps a dying ember. She patiently, methodically searched for a way to reestablish control of the string. An hour passed, then a day, then a month. She had yet to find a viable solution, but she wouldn't stop trying.

30. Lilah Fifty-One

From the conservatory's wall of windows, Lilah watched the valley awaken from its slumber. The round of cool weather had run its course and the sun was celebrating, a brilliant radiance climbing over the rise, casting its rays into hidden crevices and dark corners, warming the ground, stirring creatures big and small to life.

"Here you go, sweetie," Diesel said from behind her, two mugs of coffee in hand, one held out for her.

"Thanks." She wrapped her hands around the warm cup and turned back to the window.

"So far, so good," he said, moving next to her.

They were on death watch, though they weren't exactly sure what that meant. Yesterday, Rose had launched her super AI. That had been their understanding, anyway. Now it was a waiting game. They were about to learn what happened when a timeline disappeared.

The uncertainty tested Lilah, poking her imagination, increasing her anxiety, stirring her impatience. The bottled-up emotions compelled her to act.

"Oscar," she called to the air. "I know you can't see into Rose's suite, but from what you can learn, how is she doing? Does everything seem okay?"

"Actually, I *can* see inside her room. She's asleep, but her body movements are increasing. She'll be awake inside ten minutes."

"Luca is cooperating with you?"

"He isn't blocking me."

Diesel frowned and called in a forceful tone, "Luca! Show yourself."

Oscar appeared, standing off to the side. "I've pinged him and he isn't responding, which is *very* unusual. He normally shadows me, seeking to glean information about you, blocking me from seeing anything he deems private."

"Could he be in another timeline?" she asked.

Diesel shrugged. "Maybe he cleared out to avoid becoming collateral damage."

"Oscar," called Lilah. "Can you see Rose's new AI? Is it healthy?"

"I can see into her workshop, which is also unusual." A pause. "The circuit pool is cold, which means no AI inside. Perhaps she never made a run, or maybe she encountered a problem during production." Another pause. "The state of her workshop is consistent with the recent operation of the circuit pool. Given that, I would place a higher probability on a production failure."

Lilah took a nervous sip from the mug. She'd been imagining all sorts of outcomes for the day, most of them horrible, a production failure not among them. "We should wake her. If we're alive tonight, she can sleep all she wants."

"Her eyes just fluttered," said Oscar. "She'll surface momentarily."

"When she's awake," said Diesel, "tell her we're waiting on breakfast so she can join us."

Ten minutes later, Rose padded into the conservatory

in her white robe, hair tousled, face puffy, sleep in her eyes, moving slowly, still waking up.

"Is Luca responding to either of you?" she asked before they'd even exchanged morning greetings. "I can't tell if he's giving me the cold shoulder or what. Usually, he's clearer about his assholery."

"Oscar says he's not responding at all," said Lilah. She gave her daughter a one-armed hug and then stayed close, studying her face, moving a lock of hair out of her eyes.

"How are you doing, Rosie?" asked Diesel, joining the family clutch. "Are you okay?"

"It's been rough. I'm not going to lie."

"Oscar says the circuit pool is cold. Did you make your run yesterday?"

Rose got a distant look in her face, like she was trying to recover a lost memory. "I don't know what happened, to be honest. The run was textbook. The AI looked great. It responded to its prompt and started a full diagnostic, which is what it should do. Then it all went to hell. There was a power surge, and things started happening that weren't initiated by the sequencer." Her brow creased. "The data readings didn't make sense, and when I tried to intervene, Luca stopped me. He said my part was done, he was happy with my work, and I should go to bed. He even rewarded me with an extra-long lift."

Rose paused her story to look at their mugs. She licked her lips and called to the air. "Marian! Where's my coffee?" Then she turned to Oscar. "The circuit pool is cold?"

"The crucible is at room temperature. The neurosphere is unresponsive."

"And Luca is gone." Rose said it as a statement, looking into the distance, biting her lip. When she returned to them moments later, she shook her head. "He said 'good job' and then sent me to bed. If he wasn't happy, he would've let me know. I'm certain of that. Now I'm wondering if the long lift was to keep me away from the workshop."

Marian entered the conservatory with a mug and coffee flask. She poured for Rose and then topped off Diesel's and Lilah's cups.

"Marian," asked Diesel as she worked. "Has Luca given you any tasks for today?"

"No, I have not received a list," replied the bot.

"Is that normal?"

Marian looked at him with a blank expression.

"Did he give you a task list yesterday?" asked Lilah.

"Yes."

"The day before?

"Yes."

Lilah looked from Diesel to Rose. "Could his absence be a symptom of a disappeared timeline?"

"That's easy enough to check," said Diesel.

Lilah and Rose followed him through the kitchen and down to the basement. They gathered around the T-box. The light reflecting off the etched aluminum shell gave warmth to the otherwise ominous machine. The external display, a small rectangular screen attached to the front of the shell, was dark.

Diesel tugged on the sturdy latch handle of the T-box door. When it opened, the external display lit with the words "Status: Ready" displayed in green.

Unsure of his intentions, Lilah put a hand on his arm. "Wait."

"What?"

"Send a note. It would be crazy to jump before we figure out what's going on."

Diesel took a step back. "I was just going to let it run until it confirmed a link and then shut it down, but sending a note is a better idea."

They sent a note with the message "We're still here. Are you?" to a half-dozen different timelines. Over the next hour, five affirmed their continued existence. The sixth responded an hour after that—they'd been out for breakfast—along with a dozen more timelines who'd joined the note exchange.

Through the flurry of messages, they learned that a quiet had descended over all of them. Luca had disappeared completely. Marian was acting more like a conventional Northern Droid product in the timelines that had her. The deafening silence had them all on edge.

Then Diesel Thirty-Five arrived. He'd built up the courage to make a test jump and chose their timeline to visit what he called "the scene of the crime." By noon, all the timelines were accounted for. All the T-boxes worked. No one had disappeared.

With spirits high, Lilah, Diesel, and Rose sat for a celebratory lunch. Lilah had just bitten into a carrot stick when it struck her. "Rose, with Luca gone, what about your lift tonight?"

Rose, seated across from her, was slumped in her chair,

head down, her hands in her lap. "I was just thinking the same thing."

"You're sure there's no drug that would help you?"

"There is no drug. He manipulates me through the implant." Rose stood and began pacing the kitchen floor, wringing her hands. "This is going to be bad."

"How long do we have before you start feeling it?" asked Diesel.

"Midnight is my usual lift time, plus or minus an hour. The longest I've gone without it is three a.m. I've made it that far a few times, and I was really hurting each time. I mean, I was curled into a ball, moaning and begging for relief."

Her face screwed up like she was going to cry. She pleaded for help with her eyes.

"What about that brain doctor you were working with?" asked Diesel. "The one from the hospital?"

"Dr. Nestor," said Lilah. "She's in the Forty-Seven timeline, and she met Rose Twenty-One in the emergency room. If our Rose showed up, we'd have some explaining to do."

"That's the least of our worries."

Lilah shook her head. "We have five Roses who need help. It's an issue."

"There's only four of us," said Rose. "Twenty-One never let herself get addicted."

They sat in silence, Lilah weighing a cover story that would let Dr. Nestor focus on pain relief rather than wondering how a wealthy family, one deeply engaged with the community, could have secret quadruplets who were all being manipulated by their neural implants.

"There's a Dr. Nestor in every timeline," said Diesel. "Why can't everyone use their own?"

"The problem is that we'd be walking in cold. She'll need to believe our claims before she'll put effort into looking for a solution. To put it in perspective, the Dr. Nestor I've been working with is still skeptical that the implant is responsible, and that's after she witnessed Rose Twenty-One's suffering in the emergency room, followed by me adding tons more detail in meetings afterward."

"Oscar," called Rose in a quiet voice. "Can you locate Frida Nestor? She a medical doctor on the Dartmouth faculty."

"Dr. Nestor is at the hospital right now," replied Oscar.

"Wonderful! Are you able to access her schedule? What's her day like?"

"Her schedule is closed until she returns from medical leave. She's at the hospital as a patient."

Lilah brought a hand to her mouth. "Oh my god. What happened?"

"She had a baby," said Oscar. "A healthy girl. Forty minutes ago. Eight pounds, nine ounces."

"Big, just like her momma." Lilah flashed a hint of a smile. "How about Gunter Meyer? Can you locate him? He used to work with Concord Neuro."

"He still does," replied Oscar after a pause. "But he's on medical leave as well."

"What happened to him?"

"He's the father."

Lilah laughed spontaneously, though her worry cut it short, making it sound more like a bark. "What are we going to do? I mean, if we show up with four Roses at the same hospital with the same condition, the staff will have questions. Word will get out."

"I'm about to suffer horribly and you're worried about bad press?" Rose's anger and disdain were clear in her delivery.

Lilah didn't rise to the bait. "With such a tight timeline, we should avoid anything that might distract from a solution."

"Cousins maybe?" offered Diesel, defusing the situation. Then he snapped his fingers. "Have one Rose go to Dr. Nestor and send the others to three different doctors, the best specialists we can locate in the time we have. All the parents keep in communication. As soon as the first doctor figures it out, we spread the answer to the others. It gives us four chances at success."

Lilah felt a positive surge from the idea. "We'll all need to be in the same timeline to communicate like that." Her brain began plotting solutions. "If this is implant driven, then we'll need three more doctors, plus three more Gunters—reps from Concord Neuro—to complete the teams."

* * *

Lilah observed Rose with a mother's worry. Her daughter lay in bed in a VIP room at the Dartmouth-Hitchcock Hospital, a special room that hospital administrators reserved for people like the Lagerfords. Almost twice the size of a standard room, it had padded lounge chairs, a larger bathroom, and a foldout sofa bed for visitors. Across from the bed, taking up most of the south wall, was a first-class entertainment system. The wall adjacent to it had a row of tall windows, providing excellent natural light. And throughout the room, the medical equipment gleamed with shiny surfaces and modern displays.

"How do you feel?" asked Lilah for the third time since arriving.

"Like if you ask that again, I'll explode."

It was one a.m., an hour past Rose's normal lift time. They'd been monitoring her for more than four hours, and in that time, Rose had shown increasing signs of impatience. Lilah knew that being trapped in bed, her parents hovering over her, would feed those sentiments, so she did her best to separate them from behaviors caused by Rose's medical condition.

While Lilah tended to Rose, Diesel sat in one of the lounge chairs, tasked with monitoring the status of the other three Roses. After a flurry of activity when they'd arrived in this timeline—home of Rose Twenty-One, Lilah Forty-Seven, and deceased Diesel Forty-Seven—they'd succeeded in placing the other Roses with talented medical teams in first-rate institutions: Rose Twenty-Two at Boston General, Rose Twenty-Three at Tufts Medical Center, and Rose Twenty-Four at Harvard's Brigham and Women's Hospital.

During that scramble, none of them had considered that Diesel Forty-Seven's hopper death had been well-publicized. As the families arrived at their respective hospitals impersonating the Forty-Sevens yet with Diesel very much alive, they'd been forced to craft a cover story on the fly. They all pitched variations of: his life is being threatened, so we faked his death in cooperation with the police to draw out the criminals.

Lilah stared at the oversized medical display on the wall at the head of Rose's bed, hoping no one would call the police to check the story. She'd hated lying to Dr. Nestor, who showed her skepticism as she accepted the fabrication. But in the scheme of things, it was a small transgression.

The med display was alive with Rose's biomedical data—numbers, diagrams, and charts with trending lines—intimidating Lilah by the sheer breadth of information. Some items were shown in bold. Some were different colors. Some blinked. Lilah felt confident in her understanding of the numbers in the upper right corner—heart rate, core temp, O2 saturation, BP—but not much more.

A white line ticked upward on a chart near the center of the busy display. Lilah noticed the change and studied the labels next to it. It was gobbledygook, math symbols with unfamiliar units. The line had been trending horizontally the whole time they'd been there. Now it was on a gentle rise. She watched it trend upward for a good ten minutes, wondering if she should call for Dr. Nestor and Gunter, who were attending to other chores until the action started here.

The chart Lilah had been watching suddenly doubled

in size and switched from white to yellow. Rose couldn't see the display without sitting up and turning on the bed, so she was unaware of the change. But she sniffled and scratched her right thigh through the bedsheets for the second time.

Lilah looked over at Diesel, who sat slumped in the chair, eyes closed, head back, feet stretched out in front of him.

"David, I could use your input."

He moved with a start, opened his eyes, then repositioned himself in the chair as he surfaced from his nap. He looked toward the display above the headboard but then cocked his head ever so slightly, a sign he was listening to something through a device.

"Rose Twenty-Two is showing signs of distress," he reported.

"Thanks for the update." Lilah delivered the praise tersely, wondering why he'd add to the tension like that and hoping her tone would shut him up. She was about to draw his attention to the rogue chart when Gunter entered the room, his eyes on the display over the bed.

"Dr. Nestor is on her way," he said to the room. Then to Rose, "How are you feeling?"

"Okay." She scratched the same thigh, this time with her hand reaching under the sheets. "Antsy."

Dr. Nestor came through the door, looking tired but alert. She gave a quick greeting and then moved next to Gunter and studied the numbers with him. While they reviewed the information, the yellow chart Lilah had been watching turned orange, and three other charts near it changed from white to yellow.

"The number of open neuroreceptors in your brain is rising," Dr. Nestor said to Rose. "What's unusual here is the variety and levels. You have huge demand from four different classes of receptors. Each is looking for a specific neurochemical key. If they don't get it, they'll let you know by sending out a distress signal." She looked Rose in the eye. "As more neurons become distressed, and as they send out ever louder signals, you will feel the pain of addiction. That's our urgent concern."

She continued speaking but turned to include Lilah and Diesel. "But we have an unexpected problem that will complicate your treatment." Her eyes sought out Lilah's and bore into them. "This isn't the same woman I saw before. Somehow, she has the same neural implant, but with different usage parameters. Same genetics but she's ten pounds heavier. Her hair is too long for a month's time. All I can think is that she's the twin sister who intervened in the emergency room with that legal document. But Gunter says that doesn't explain the duplicate implant."

Gunter shrugged and looked down, like he agreed with her but didn't want to dive into the middle of anything.

Dr. Nestor's tone became sharp. "It doesn't make sense. You need to tell us what's going on."

Fearing the doctor would abandon them, Lilah folded her hands in front of her. "I don't have a good answer. All I can say is that this is my daughter and she's very sick. Please help her."

Diesel stood and put an arm around Lilah, lending support to her plea. "We are her parents."

"I know." Dr. Nestor unfolded her arms and returned her attention to Rose. "Your games spooked me, so I checked your DNA to confirm you have parental rights." She shrugged. "I have to protect myself and the hospital."

Moving to a table at the foot of the bed, Dr. Nestor pulled two small packets from her coat pocket, snapped on blue disposable gloves, and worked through a prepping process, speaking to Rose as she did so. "I'm going to give you something to help you relax. It should take the edge off."

"Okay." Rose sniffled again.

Dr. Nestor returned her attention to Lilah and Diesel, looking at them while slipping the waste packaging from the med prep back in her coat pocket.

"The news media has taught me to expect eccentric behavior from the super-rich, but I'm lost on this one." She shook her head. "All that data we collected from the emergency room visit. The modeling I've done since then to try and understand it. I can't use that on a different patient, not even an identical twin, not until I do a correspondence workup, which, because of your games, I haven't even started. And where's the first woman? She's your daughter too, right? Isn't she sick?"

"Ohhh," Rose moaned, her eyes closed, her face a grimace.

Dr. Nestor injected the medicine into a clear med port on the saline drip bag hanging above the bed, allowing it to meter into Rose's vein. She watched Rose until her face relaxed and her fists unclenched. Her eyes remained closed.

"Should we cycle the implant?" asked Lilah, desperate

for a solution.

"We talked about the problems with that approach," said Gunter.

"I have some other things I can try first," said Dr. Nestor. "Let's keep that in reserve for now."

There was a tap on the door, and it swung open. A nurse pushing a white cart entered, its shelves stocked with medical supplies.

"Thanks, John. Put it here." Dr. Nestor pointed to a spot next to the prep table at the foot of Rose's bed.

Dr. Nestor spoke to Rose using a voice loud enough to include everyone in the room, as if she were lecturing to interns. "I've prepared some neurochemical stimulants to promote the release of dopamine, serotonin, oxytocin, and endorphins. Those are the keys your neuroreceptors are screaming for. While the meds should bump up production, unfortunately, we don't have anything that can drive the extreme levels your brain is demanding."

Dr. Nestor began sorting the supplies, checking the labels on little bottles, lining them up on the prep table in a certain order. She stacked a pile of syringe packs next to the bottles and placed a box of disposable gloves at the end.

"The higher the dose we can get to your brain, the better. The challenge is that the blood-brain barrier is remarkably effective at protecting the organ. It's hard to get the stimulants across it. So what we're left with is ramping up the concentration in your bloodstream outside the brain to try to force more drug across the barrier. But then we have to worry about toxicity in your body."

She filled a syringe and turned to the saline drip.

"What's the answer?" asked Lilah.

Dr. Nestor shook her head. "I don't know. That was a long way of saying there's some trial and error involved with this."

She injected the stimulant into the drip bag's med port. It became a new waiting game after that. Over the next two hours, the doctor fussed with the dosages, seeking to force hormone production ever higher to quiet the urgent call of Rose's neuroreceptors. But her best efforts fell far short of that needed to provide relief.

By three a.m. Rose lay on her side, knees curled up to her chest, face slack, breathing shallow, skin clammy, moaning softly.

Dr. Nestor watched the charts, her lips pressed tight, shaking her head every few minutes. Then she tilted her head, not unlike Diesel's earlier behavior. Nodding, she made for the door, putting a hand on Gunter's arm as she passed. "I need to take a call."

With Dr. Nestor gone, Diesel sidled over to Lilah and whispered, "They're all having a bad time of it. Twenty-Two seems to be really suffering. It sounds like they're about to cycle Twenty-Four's implant."

Before Lilah could respond, the door burst open and Dr. Nestor returned.

"How dare you!" Her face red, she pointed an index finger at Lilah, a stiletto aimed at her heart. "A colleague from Tufts just called for an emergency consult. It seems he has a patient—female, five foot two, early twenties—who's suffering identical symptoms. Her parents are there with her, all panicked about her implant. I saw a live feed.

She looks like our missing Rose, and the parents both look like you."

Her anger ramped as she ranted. "I bought that a female twin could have female twins. But now we have twin dads back from the dead, both with the same cover story. And DNA says that they are the parents there, while I know you are the parents here, which means we're looking at cloning."

She shook her head. "I'm working my heart out trying to solve one of the toughest cases I've ever faced, struggling to make any progress at all, and you're playing me? Hell no. I'm referring both of you to our legal department. Legal will make *you* responsible if things go bad. Not me. Not the hospital."

"We take full responsibility," said Diesel.

"I acknowledge and agree," said Lilah, creating a legal commitment for the room cameras recording everything. "Please help our daughter."

Dr. Nestor wasn't finished. She looked at Rose. "If this is a side effect of cloning, we need to pivot fast to gene therapy. Don't bullshit me. Not now."

"It's not cloning. I swear it," said Diesel. "It's the implant."

A wet *blurp* erupted from the direction of the bed. An acrid smell filled the room. Rose had vomited. Her cheek rested in the mess.

"Oh, sweetie!" cried Lilah, moving to her side, using the sheet corner to wipe her face. Her pallor frightened Lilah.

Nurse John rushed through the door and took control.

As he moved next to the bed, he nudged Lilah away with his hip. After cleaning Rose's face and mouth with a wash cloth, he gently shifted her to the unsoiled side of the mattress. He bunched the bedsheets on the dirty side, and in a practiced move, pulled them from under Rose and off the bed. He had fresh linens tucked beneath her almost as fast.

"Let's cycle the implant," Dr. Nestor said to Gunter as John made for the exit, arms full of laundry. "I can't get there with meds."

Lilah wanted to say, "Finally," but remained quiet, nodding to encourage the decision.

Gunter fished a small silver box from his coat pocket and stepped to the bed, muttering to Dr. Nestor as he did. From the words Lilah could to hear, he said something to the effect of, "No one at the company thinks this will work."

He held the box over Rose's head and watched it for a moment, then pressed his thumb on top. "I've turned her implant off."

Everyone looked at Rose. She didn't move. They lifted their heads and studied the display. Nothing changed.

"How long do we wait?" asked Diesel.

Gunter looked to Dr. Nestor, who said, "Let's give it a couple of minutes."

Lilah clung to Diesel as they waited. The first minute took forever. The second twice as long.

Gunter pressed the box again. "Now it's back on."

"C'mon," urged Lilah, desperate for the same flood of hormones Rose Twenty-One had experienced when they'd reactivated her implant in the emergency room.

Nothing happened. Not a ripple anywhere on the display.

Denying the obvious, Lilah stared at the charts until she couldn't hold her breath any longer. Her heart felt crushed in defeat. "Oh no," she cried, resting her head against Diesel's chest.

"Everything will be all right." He wrapped his arms around her, squeezing her, rocking her back and forth. After a moment, he whispered, "Cycling didn't help Twenty-Three or Twenty-Four, either."

The next hours were torturous. Rose lay unmoving, looking much like a corpse. The biomedical display told a story of a patient in deep trouble. Some values kept drifting lower. Others climbed higher. In one section, Rose's numbers were listed side-by-side next to normal or expected values. Few were anywhere near where they should be.

An orange chart turned red and began to flash. The chart next to it did as well. A low tone filled the room, an alarm that persisted until Dr. Nestor acknowledged it with a swoop of her hand. She stared at the display, biting her lower lip.

"No!" cried Diesel.

The emotion in his voice pierced Lilah's heart. She scanned the room, looking for whatever had set him off. Nothing caught her eye. Then he leaned forward in his chair, put his elbows on his knees, face in his hands, and sobbed.

"Twenty-Two just passed," he said between gasps.

"She's gone."

"What!?" Lilah fell to her knees, the pain rending her heart. She couldn't imagine what her sister must be feeling. The panic. The horror. She wondered what to say to her.

Her anguish had but a moment to play, and then she understood the grim implications for her own Rose. Death wasn't just a possibility anymore. If they didn't figure it out very soon, it was likely.

She cast about for an answer. On her knees, in great emotional pain, she came up empty. She turned to God, pleading for help. But her anger overwhelmed her, twisting her plea into an ultimatum.

This is unfair beyond reason, she growled in her mind. *She's done nothing to deserve this. You make it right.*

With her face screwed tight, she stared at the med display, daring her creator to defy her.

It wasn't God who answered her call. It was Gunter. Offering a tiny ray of hope.

"Do you know a specific time when the hormone flood happened in the past? Like, within a few minutes?"

Lost in her emotional battle, Lilah barely heard him.

"In theory, we can scroll back and replay the actions the implant took then. My colleagues warned me that this is dangerous. Replay is a diagnostic that techs use to debug an implant. It's not a live feature. We don't know the physical or psychological side effects of using it in the body. At a minimum, there'll be confusion, maybe insomnia, maybe memory loss." He shook his head. "You'd need to agree to free Concord Neuro of all liability."

"Oh my God," said Lilah from the floor, nodding her

head up and down. "We agree. Please. Do it now."

"I need to start from a specific time and date, one that's right before a flood event. The implant will replay its actions from that point forward until I stop it. If we start too soon, confusion will grow because the implant won't be reflecting reality. Start too late, and we miss the event we need to catch."

Lilah looked at Diesel. "How about eleven thirty, three or four nights ago? Things were stressful, no doubt, but she was keeping to a tight routine. Her lift would have been on schedule."

Diesel thought. "Four nights ago was Monday night?" Lilah nodded.

"Do that one. I saw her early Tuesday morning, and she was in good spirits. That means the night before probably did follow her normal routine."

Gunter looked to Dr. Nestor as if asking for permission, or perhaps waiting for it.

The doctor nodded. Gunter positioned his small silver box over Rose's head.

"Monday night at eleven thirty p.m.?" he confirmed as he used his thumbs on the box.

"Yes," Lilah and Diesel replied together.

"Not eleven forty-five?"

"I mean, maybe," said Lilah. "But it could have started by then. Eleven thirty is safest."

"Okay. Done."

They watched the biomed display above Rose's bed. Nothing changed. If anything, the flashing alarms grew more persistent, calling attention to the crisis underway.

"Why isn't anything happening?" asked Lilah.

"If the flood event happened at midnight Monday night, we have to wait a half hour for the implant to catch up. Right now, it thinks it's eleven thirty. If it happened at twelve thirty, then we have an hour to wait. And that's assuming the implant is responsible in the first place, which is a huge question mark."

The next twenty minutes were brutal. There was no flood of neurochemicals. Not even a trickle. Lilah fretted. Had they missed it? Started too late? Too early? She watched Rose's life signs drift ever lower. The biomed display was awash in flashing red.

And then Diesel cried out again. Rose Twenty-Three had died.

Lilah was numb. She clung to Diesel. Together they clung to hope. But all she could see was a tunnel of despair. Not even a pinpoint of light at the end.

A different portion of the display lit up. Lilah and Diesel perked up in excitement. But Dr. Nestor didn't react in the same way. Her face grim, she began a frantic prep, filling a syringe from yet another bottle.

"She's dying. I can give her this to support her core functions and keep her alive for another few hours. But because of the way it works, if I give her this and the hormone flood comes, the strain will kill her. So if we start this, we have to stop the implant's replay." She looked at Lilah and Diesel with a solemn expression. "I recognize it's an unbearably difficult decision. Either choice, yes or no, is medically defensible. As her legal guardians, it's your decision to make."

"This can't be happening," wailed Lilah, her horror deepened by the mental torture of impossible choices. God was mocking her for her earlier audacity.

Dr. Nestor inserted the needle into the med port of the drip bag. "I need a yes or no."

Diesel replied, "If you give her this, the hormone flood will kill her? But if you don't, she dies? Then how do we save her?"

"I don't know. But without either this or the hormones *right now*, we won't have a chance to try."

Lilah felt perfect pain. It hurt everywhere. Squeezing her. Crushing her soul. She looked to Diesel, pleading with her eyes for him to make the decision, to save her from this hell.

"Give it," he said. "Keep her alive."

Dr. Nestor pushed the plunger, injecting the drug into the drip port.

"Go ahead and cancel the replay," she said to Gunter as she extracted the needle.

Gunter fished the silver box out of his coat pocket and held the box over Rose's head. He looked at the doctor for confirmation.

One of the charts near the center of the med display bumped. Dr. Nestor saw it, nodded, and said, "Whenever you're..."

And then the med display went wild. All across it, dials swung like the dashboard of a dragster roaring down the track. Charts shifted direction and became smaller. Values that were low started to climb. High values peaked and began to fall. Reds turned to orange, oranges to yellow.

Heralded by a colorful spectacle worthy of the Fourth of July, the hormone flood had arrived.

Lilah looked at Diesel in horror. The very thing they'd been waiting for to save Rose had arrived just in time to kill her.

Dr. Nestor gasped as she stared at the display. She didn't move for two heartbeats. Then three. Then her left hand shot forward, grabbed the clear plastic tube that ran from the drip bag down to Rose's arm, and bent it, crimping the feed, preventing fluids from flowing. With the other hand, she removed tape from Rose's wrist and pulled the line from the vein in the back of her hand.

She continued to study the display, brow furrowed, eyes flitting back and forth as she digested the information. Then she turned to Gunter.

"Oh my God." She wrapped her arms around him and kissed his cheek. "You did it." She gave an odd laughing-crying sound as she disentangled herself and turned back to the display. "Look at this, Gunter. Oh my God. I never would have believed it."

Over the next several minutes, the fireworks faded, energetic reds and oranges replaced by sedate yellows and whites as the flood spread through Rose's brain, plugging into her neuroreceptors, relieving the pain of addiction, stabilizing her brain activity.

But while the med display told the tale of recovery, Rose still hadn't moved.

John came through the door, holding a fresh drip bag. With his trademark efficiency, he reset Rose's line and started her drip.

"Thanks, John," the four of them called as he exited.

Rose rolled onto her back and took a deep breath. Her eyes remained closed, but her face was relaxed. A bit of color had returned to her cheeks.

Dr. Nestor pointed at the med display. "Look at that, Gunter, she's transitioning to REM. Proper sleep is a great sign right now." She looked over at Lilah and Diesel. "I don't want to jinx it, but I think she's out of the woods."

At the acknowledgement of success, Lilah whispered to Diesel, "Have you passed the word?"

"Twenty-Four's med team is balking at the idea of running the implant through a replay. They have nothing to justify it as a reasonable action. In fact, they see it as reckless. We need to change minds, and fast."

Lilah turned back to the room. "Frida. Gunter. We have a desperate emergency. Will you help us?"

31. Aftermath

Diesel stood at the bedroom door and nodded to himself, approving the apartment Lilah had chosen. It was a spacious unit on the top floor of a refurbished red brick textile mill, a survivor from the turn of the twentieth century located just blocks from the Dartmouth-Hitchcock Hospital.

The front bedroom held two queen-sized beds, making quarters tight. The beds were covered with floral quilts; Diesel recognized them from Rose's collection. A half-dozen pillows, also Rose's, were arrayed neatly at the head of each bed, leaning against matching oak headboards. Green area rugs were strewn throughout the room like lily pads, making it possible to walk from either bed to the door, windows, or bathroom without ever having to put bare feet on the wood floor.

The homeyness of the room was countered by state-of-the-art technology. Medical displays like the one in Rose's hospital room were mounted on the wall at the head of each bed. A gray cart between the beds held an electronic instrument, a black box the size of a toaster, with an impressive array of switches and knobs on the front.

There were two beds in the room because, thankfully, Rose Twenty-Four had survived, just barely, after intervention by Dr. Nestor and Gunter. And now both

Roses had lived through two complete flood cycles, two nights where the replay therapy saved them.

It was time for them to leave the hospital, but both still needed the nightly hormone flood to satisfy their addiction. Thus, the rental suite with its medical machines.

After that first harrowing night, Gunter determined precise times in the neural record when the flood event started and stopped. On the second night, he ran the replay for just that span, keeping the window of disorientation short for both Roses. But in truth, with their brains awash in rapturous pleasure, neither noticed, awakening the next morning refreshed and ready to attack the day.

The instrument on the cart between the beds was a one-of-a-kind prototype Gunter and his colleagues at Concord Neuro had crafted to wean the Roses from their addiction. The idea was to slowly taper the length of the flood event, reducing it in small steps each day until it sank to zero in sixty days. Diesel thought it sounded like a reasonable plan, but time would tell.

The doorbell rang.

"I'll get it," said Lilah from another room.

The voice may have been his wife's, but there were three Lilahs in the flat, so it could also have been Lilah Forty-Seven, Rose Twenty-One's mom, or Lilah Fifty, Rose Twenty-Four's mom.

Hearing warm greetings in the foyer, he drifted out for the meeting with Dr. Nestor and Gunter. They all gathered in the living room, seating themselves in chairs around a low glass table. Coffee and tea service were set on top. Because they were in Lilah Forty-Seven's timeline, she acted as host, pouring for everyone.

Diesel got right to it. Gazing from Dr. Nestor to Gunter, he said, "We want to start by thanking you. Thank you both for saving our Rose." He motioned to Lilah and Diesel Fifty, "And theirs as well. We're grateful beyond measure."

He picked up his teaspoon and fidgeted with it as he spoke. "We invited you here to explain our confusing situation. We want you to feel comfortable with it. Hopefully comfortable enough that you won't feel the need to share your insider knowledge with anyone else."

Diesel Fifty added, "That would include friends, spouses, colleagues, neighbors, lawyers. Any person or device that's not you two."

Gunter looked to Dr. Nestor, who said, "You're talking about the cloning?"

"It's not what you think," said Diesel.

* * *

They spun a tale of malicious cloning. Five sets of Diesels and Lilahs had been cloned and dispersed around the world. They'd only become aware of each other by chance when the birth of identical Roses triggered a genetic screening program, alerting them to each other.

Two decades later, an unknown puppet master began manipulating all of them by controlling the Roses through their implants, forcing them into ever more extreme behaviors. The end goal of their manipulator was unclear. But the situation was untenable, and the families had gone to war to escape.

"We've lost a Diesel and two Roses in our battle," said Lilah. "We're victims. Not the bad guys. But bringing in the authorities would turn us into spectacles, something none of us wants, and it would complicate our fight, perhaps even leading to more death."

"What we're asking is not illegal," said Diesel. "There's no ethical dilemma. Simply hold our circumstances in confidence and help us finish weaning the Roses."

"The hospital has policies all doctors must adhere to," said Dr. Nestor. "It's my job to report it."

"Failure to report isn't a felony. It's not even a misdemeanor. Contracts are a civil issue, and our very expensive lawyers and generous foundation will ensure no personal or professional harm will come to either of you. In fact, just the opposite, we will help you achieve great success."

Gunter interrupted. "Speaking of which, someone bought a controlling interest in Concord Neuro yesterday. My colleagues are nervous. I'm not sure how much freedom I'll have going forward to dedicate to this."

"We bought it, Gunter," said Diesel. "Our babies' lives are at stake. What else could we do? Free them from this chokehold and keep our problems in confidence, and you may have the company as a token of our gratitude."

* * *

Neither Frida Nestor nor Gunter Meyer agreed to anything at that meeting. But they didn't report the cloning. Two days later they signed nondisclosure agreements, deciding between themselves that the offer was too good to pass up. Given the sensitivity of the situation, they felt that keeping the Lagerford secret was neither ethically nor legally compromising. They soothed their consciences by convincing themselves that it was a temporary decision, something they could change if circumstances warranted.

Two months later, when the Roses were free of their addiction, Frida and Gunter accepted possession of Concord Neuro from the grateful families.

Gunter was beside himself with excitement. First and foremost, it gave him a reason to spend time with his co-owner, a woman he was eager to get close to but, because of his introverted nature, hadn't made much progress. Bottom line, he was intimidated by her. She had more education, made bigger decisions in her job, and earned a lot more money doing it.

Company ownership shifted the balance for Gunter. He'd have to live with the education disparity. But now they both made a bundle, and they both made weighty decisions. It leveled the playing field enough to boost his confidence, allowing him to be forthright about his interest and intentions.

Frida responded positively to his advances. Soon after, Gunter proposed.

As for running the company, their excitement collided with the practical reality of day-to-day operation. With just over three hundred employees, Concord Neuro was a midsized outfit that required seasoned professionals to manage, something Frida had no interest in.

She left management issues to Gunter, instead focusing on the science of using neural implants to manipulate brain chemistry. Having access to, and authority over, the staff of Concord Neuro, whose ranks included world-class industry researchers, provided her the perfect opportunity to explore and learn.

She became a leading authority on breaking addictions using neural implants. Her work was widely published, providing her modest celebrity among the professionals in her field. She even appeared as a guest on a couple of shows that revolved around popular science topics, giving her a platform to make her expertise more accessible to the general population. And she loved traveling to professional conferences to present her work to colleagues, inviting Gunter to accompany her when the venue was in a location they both enjoyed, recently Paris and, before that, San Francisco.

As for Gunter, he had long aspired to the helm of Concord Neuro, wanting to lead the company as president and CEO. But wiser heads prevailed. Specifically, the management consultants Lilah and Diesel had hired helped him with the transition. Gunter agreed to train his way up the corporate ladder, though in a highly accelerated fashion. He spent a year as manager of sales and marketing, then a year as director of product development, followed by a year as vice president of operations. Crossed-trained and confident, he then took over as president and CEO.

Frida and Gunter married a full year earlier than their counterparts in the other timelines. Their first baby, Emilia, came a year earlier as well.

* * *

Lilah sat with her four sisters in what had become something of a weekly therapy session. Of the five women, three were emotional wrecks: the wife of Diesel Forty-Seven, and the mothers of Roses Twenty-Two and Twenty-Three.

Lilah had imagined that as a twin, she'd know how to provide solace to her sisters, that her intuition would guide her as she provided comfort and support. Instead, she learned the great contradiction of grieving: the heartbroken need time alone to process their sorrow, even as they seek companionship to make it all less terrifying.

Early on, Lilah felt they resented her because she hadn't suffered a "real" loss. There had been debates about whether losing a husband or daughter was a worse fate. Time was the only salve. Fortunately, over a period of months, their outlooks brightened, though they never fully recovered from their losses.

In her own life, Lilah chose to back away from leadership in the RPR rescue group. The Biggie DeMichele episode had given her a scare, one that made it clear she was in over her head. Rescue wasn't a game. Risks were real and consequences frightening. So, when her term came up for renewal, she chose to decline reappointment, instead increasing her already generous donations as a substitute for the loss of her personal time.

She used some of that time to renew her relationship with her daughter, tagging along as Rose hunted for an apartment. Rose was considering moving out—yet again—

on her own. But as always, access to the T-box proved to be the deal breaker. She would have to visit the family home every time she wanted to jump, or to meet someone visiting her timeline. It made living elsewhere impractical.

In the end, she asked if she could expand her suite in the house to a six-room apartment with a private outside entrance. Lilah and Diesel welcomed the idea. Lilah helped Rose with the remodel design, which included a kitchenette, guest bedroom, and much larger living space.

Several months after the renovation, Lilah teared with joy when a young man, a new friend of Rose's, used the private entrance to visit her and stay the night, the first to share her bed in years.

In a new pursuit, Lilah took the lead in transitioning a version of Oscar over to the family's full-time personal assistant. The engineers at Northern Droid duplicated the AI, stripped out the proprietary features, and tweaked the personality from corporate-think into one strong on home-life cues.

When Oscar II was fully integrated into their home, Lilah helped him build a schedule and establish a routine of service for the family. Then she worked with him to discover what had happened to Luca and Ciopova.

She was haunted by the fear that, two decades earlier, Ciopova was killing a Lilah every year, terrorizing the Lagerfords across the timelines. They all believed they had driven away the rogue AI, letting down their guard as a result. They paid a dear price for their inattention: two Roses and a Diesel. They wouldn't repeat that mistake, not if she had anything to say about it.

But no matter how she approached it, Oscar II couldn't provide any meaningful insights. It was all imagination and guesswork. After months of frustration, Lilah began adding capability to the home intelligence, working to make him more powerful, hardening his defenses, expanding his reach.

Her goal was to create an AI powerful enough to provide early warning should Ciopova return. And perhaps most important, one that could help with their defense should it come to that.

* * *

Determined to be a father-surrogate to Rose Twenty-One, Diesel visited her timeline whenever he could, hoping to be available should she need him. To his distress, she found the unplanned visits annoying, sometimes fostering tension rather than comfort. He experimented to find something that would work for both of them, and eventually stumbled upon Exercise Thursdays.

Every Thursday morning at eight thirty they'd spend an hour together, hiking one of the trails running through the hills behind the house. They joked that the workout prepared them for a weekend of debauchery, which in their lexicon meant eating and drinking more than they should.

The outdoor setting and physical activity provided for easy interaction. The awkwardness was gone, with Rose Twenty-One usually upbeat, even flashing the occasional smile. Sometimes she was chatty. Sometimes she stayed lost in her own thoughts. Sometimes he did as well.

On rare occasions she'd seek "dad advice," making him feel that his efforts were paying off. Then, one day she made the big ask. No longer preoccupied with fending off Luca and wanting to tackle something big, she asked if he would help her take the helm of Northern Droid.

Up to that point, Diesel had been encouraging both Rose Twenty-One and her mother to sell the company and lighten their burden. But since he lived five years into the future, he knew the fortunes of the company were bright. She couldn't go too far wrong. He warmed to the idea and supported her ambition.

Her request fell at about the same time the Lagerford Foundation management advisors were staging Gunter's transition into the leadership of Concord Neuro. Diesel had them structure a similar solution here: a multiyear training program for Rose Twenty-One.

Diesel also spent time with Rose Twenty-One's mom, Lilah Forty-Seven, acting as a husband-surrogate, sans the intimacy. That meant doing chores, being a friend, listening to her, supporting her decisions. And of course, joking with her. He felt a visit hadn't been a success unless he'd made her laugh at least a couple of times.

And since all the Diesels wanted a turn, she had a different Diesel visiting her almost every day, giving her way more attention than any of her sisters. Over time, her easy laugh and upbeat attitude gave Diesel comfort that the arrangement worked for her, that it fulfilled her emotional needs.

In his work life, Diesel found that collaborating with Rose Twenty-One on Northern Droid in her timeline satisfied his waning interest in the corporate world. He decided to sell the Northern Droid company in his own timeline. The scare of the past months had changed his priorities and outlook. He'd spent too much time playing. It was time to make an impact on the world. Something positive. Something meaningful.

He went with his strength—the ability to gather great wealth—and became a full-time philanthropist. Knowing the future made investing easy, letting him turn modest sums into mountains of cash very quickly. It was as simple as jumping a year ahead and seeing what the markets would do.

But he sought to avoid the attention that usually accompanies big philanthropy. He was committed to his private life, wanting to live in relative obscurity, limiting his public forays to the occasional holiday banquet in small-town New Hampshire.

So he launched three foundations, seeding each with a one-time lump sum that drew modest attention from the media. He took care to ensure the news releases noted that he was neither an officer nor a board member of any of the organizations. They were independent entities that needed to survive on their own.

His only formal role was hidden deep in the foundation charters, where it specified that the "Financial Advisor" would have sole authority to invest foundation funds. A charter addendum, a document kept in each foundation's safe deposit box, named David S. Lagerford as the "Financial Advisor."

Under the radar, Diesel multiplied his seed funds

dramatically, providing the foundations with great wealth free of public links to him, ensuring his privacy. The organizational structure excluded him from spending decisions, instead giving that authority to the board of directors, experts with the skill and knowledge to create global solutions that provided the world more food, less disease, a healthier environment, and improved animal welfare.

Over time, each foundation developed its own personality, seeing the problems differently, organically altering their priorities as a result. As Diesel had hoped, this led to a broader set of solutions, some portion of which he expected would have the impact he dreamed of.

And in the background, he worked with Oscar, continuing to dance on the edge as he resumed efforts on his super AI. It was his duty to protect his family. He blamed himself for not detecting Ciopova's presence sooner and for not having a solution in hand when he did. It wouldn't happen next time. He vowed to be ready should the rogue intelligence return.

* * *

Rose sat with Rose Twenty-One and Rose Twenty-Four on an outdoor terrace under the shade of brightly colored umbrellas. Before them, a cloudless sky and blue-green ocean met at the horizon. A light breeze carried the aroma of sea salt and seaweed up the hill, fluttering the umbrella ruffles as it continued past them.

"Now *this* is Bliss," said Rose.

"Where's the server?" asked Rose Twenty-Four, turning in her chair to look back toward the bar, an empty glass in her hand. "I need a refill."

They were at their "hundred days" celebration, a visit to an actual Caribbean island one hundred days after defeating their addiction. The mood of the party changed from moment to moment, sometimes somber as they mourned the loss of their loved ones, sometimes celebratory, an acknowledgment that they had escaped Ciopova's grip and survived.

Breaking the addiction had been a trial for the Roses. Gunter's device weaned them in equal steps over sixty days. It started off easy enough because there was a surplus of neurochemicals in the flood, and the first steps just reduced the overflow. Even when the machine moved them below demand, it proved to be an easy adjustment. At first.

Addiction is a curious thing, combining physical and psychological components to magnify its grip. This interplay works the other way as well, where a decrease in dosage can be tolerated as long as the addict gets a reasonable taste of the drug and reassurances of more to come. But when the dose becomes so small that reassurances from the mind can't override the pain, biochemical reactions fire wildly in the body, causing chills and hot flashes, shivers and sweats, dry mouth and crippling headaches.

The last week was particularly tough for Rose. And on the first day without hormones, the psychological and physical components combined to launch a massive protest, wrestling inside her body, testing her resolve. She felt as though her entire being was bound up in a rope lattice; that she was mummified in a mesh of cord wrapped so tightly she could hardly breathe.

In some ways it was worse than that first night in the hospital where she'd almost died. There, she'd been drifting in and out of consciousness, so she wasn't fully aware of her distress. Here she was wide awake, her anxiety sitting on her shoulder, demanding relief, begging, insistent, seeking any amount, just enough to loosen her bindings.

She toughed through it the way she'd been coached, one minute at a time. Grinding her teeth, she'd tell herself that one more minute was all she needed to wait, that she could ask for relief after sixty seconds. When that minute was up—a journey of a thousand miles, given her condition—she renewed the bargain, committing to one more minute before seeking relief.

She fought through the longest night of her life. And then in the early morning hours, her addiction broke. Her brain, finally accepting that its cries wouldn't be answered, gave up. The latticework binding her released all at once. She was free.

"Where do you think she went?" asked Rose Twenty-Four, bringing Rose back to the present.

At first, Rose thought her sister was referring to the absent server. Then mental levers clicked and she understood the inquiry was about Ciopova.

"Don't know." She shook her head. "But this situation is a classic 'Fool me once, shame on you; fool me twice, shame on me.' We can't let her surprise us again. We need to be ready. She needs to pay."

"We can make Northern Droid in my timeline our home base," said Rose Twenty-One. "Mom transferred the stock into my name, so I own it. The people and equipment are amazing. Oscar is amazing." She nodded to Rose. "Your dad's amazing. We can mount a serious team effort from there."

They spent the next round of drinks sketching out a plan. They agreed they needed an AI of enormous capability and, most important, one that was completely loyal. Rose proposed an idea she'd been formulating for some time. "How about an intelligence made of a dozen small neural spheres instead of one big one?" That generated more discussion that lasted through another round of drinks.

Then Rose Twenty-One changed topics. "I'd like your help on a different project. Something unrelated to this." She sat up in her seat. "We need to move the young Roses away from our AI obsession and into something equally stimulating but less dangerous. Remember how much we loved that stage performance with Luca? I'm thinking music is the answer."

"Like what, get them passionate about becoming singer-songwriters?"

"I haven't thought it through, but something like that. The goal is to permanently change their destiny, and to have that change ripple back to the young Roses that follow them. It's ambitious as hell. I can't do it alone."

"You want to bump time." Rose nodded. "I'll help."

Also by Doug J. Cooper

The Crystal Series

The Crystal Series is four books of action and suspense involving AI, spies, romance, and battles in space!

Crystal Deception (Book 1)
Crystal Conquest (Book 2)
Crystal Rebellion (Book 3)
Crystal Escape (Book 4)

Readers' Praise for The Crystal Series (Amazon Reviews):

★★★★★ "Characters that feel like real people, who behave in ways that make sense and you can empathize with."

★★★★★ "It has all the features of Anne McCaffrey 's Dragon Riders of Pern series. Strong characters, sentient improbability and interesting plots."

★★★★★ "Nicely done hard sci-fi. I am a fan of this kind of story line so it sucked me right in."

★★★★★ "A tale of intrigue, action, a touch of romance and heartbreak."

For info and purchases, visit: crystalseries.com

Free Story!

Crystal Horizon – Prequel to the Crystal Series

The Crystal Series is four full-length books where the emergence of self-aware AI and alien first contact occur at the same time.

Sample this popular space opera for free by downloading Crystal Horizon, the prequel.

In book 1 of the series, Crystal Deception, Cheryl is captain of the military space cruiser Alliance, and Sid is a covert warrior for the Defense Specialists Agency. We learn that the two have a shared history, and in particular, a romantic relationship that has somehow gone awry.

In the prequel, we get their backstory. We join Sid and Cheryl on the day they first meet, and experience that shared history with them.

Crystal Horizon is offered free to newsletter subscribers.

For more about the Crystal Series and to obtain this free book, please visit: crystalseries.com

www.ingramcontent.com/pod-product-compliance
Lightning Source LLC
Chambersburg PA
CBHW071202250626
47159CB00001B/166